I'M GONNA GET YOU BACK

Also by Eva Des Lauriers

I Wish You Would

I'M GONNA GET YOU BACK

EVA DES LAURIERS

Henry Holt and Company
New York

Henry Holt and Company, *Publishers since 1866*
Henry Holt® is a registered trademark of Macmillan Publishing Group, LLC
120 Broadway, New York, NY 10271 • fiercereads.com

EU representative: Macmillan Publishers Ireland Ltd, 1st Floor, The Liffey Trust Centre, 117–126 Sheriff Street Upper, Dublin 1, D01 YC43

Our books may be purchased in bulk for specialty retail/wholesale, literacy, corporate/premium, educational, and subscription box use. Please contact MacmillanSpecialMarkets@macmillan.com.

Library of Congress Control Number: 2025029760

First edition, 2026
Book design by Abby Granata
Printed in the United States of America

ISBN 978-1-250-91057-8
10 9 8 7 6 5 4 3 2 1

For my mom, my guiding light in the dark

CHAPTER ONE

REID

THEN

THERE WAS THE VIEW, and then there was her.

Clara stared out at the lake below, a breathless, awestruck look on her face. Her green eyes wide and soft, color high on her cheeks from the hike.

Camera in hand, she panned the vista, entirely focused on getting the shot and not at all aware that I couldn't take my eyes off her. Nothing could pull her attention when she filmed.

Not that I didn't still try.

"Look at how the light bends over those pines," she said reverently. "Just there. Stunning, right?"

"Right."

The light *was* nice, but it wasn't enough to distract me from her.

But her turning the camera toward *me* was.

While it didn't bother me, being filmed made me self-conscious—too aware of my arms and hands and the fact that she saw so much through that lens.

"Can I help you?" I asked.

"Don't talk," she said, a smile in her voice. "Stay broody. You look perfect."

My entire body rushed with heat. As charged by her as the world around us that bounced with sunlight. I pulled off my beanie. "I'm not broody."

"Have you seen you?"

I pushed my hand through my unruly hair, sure it was sticking up all over the place with the way Clara's eyes bounced to it. "Meaning?"

"You're, like, the definition of broody. *Quintessentially* broody. If I were making a documentary about the broodiest guys in Woodhurst, the list would begin and end with you."

"Why would you make a documentary about that?"

She scoffed. "It's an example."

"An example of how you're obsessed with me," I teased, the corner of my mouth lifting.

That rosy flush I loved blossomed across her cheekbones.

When our eyes met over the camera, hers narrowed playfully. "You wish. As usual, just ignore me."

"*As usual,* that's impossible."

Her responsive laugh was airy as she circled me, capturing whatever shot she envisioned. There was a focused fluidity to her movement that reminded me of the hawks soaring above us. Free and attuned all at once. "How ready are you to get out of Woodhurst?"

The question confused me a moment. We still had a few months before graduation. Though my future was all but decided, I wasn't ready to think about it yet. The worn collar of my jacket rubbed against my neck as I shrugged. "I don't know if I am . . . I like it here."

Her eyes flicked to mine over the lens. "But you're meant for bigger things, Reid."

So everyone kept telling me.

"College is going to be amazing," she said, her tone reassuring. "*You're* amazing."

My pulse picked up, a spike of annoyance flaring, but at what, I wasn't sure. "Why? Because I run fast?"

"No." She lowered the camera, her expression pinched as she shook her head. "Because the fact that you run fast is the least interesting thing about you."

My chest swelled near to bursting.

The next moment a gust of wind shook the trees around us. I draped my jacket across her shoulders just as she pulled her hair down to take a photo of us—the first.

"You smell like a meadow," I said in place of all the other things I longed to tell her.

She laughed again and showed me the picture. It was the kind that somehow captured both the moment and the beating heart within it. The kind you frame.

I blinked in surprise when she wrapped her arms around my waist and let out a contented sigh, her warm breath skimming my throat. Confidence surged through me every time she allowed herself to soften to me.

"I do love it here," she said.

"Me too." But I wasn't talking about the overlook.

I held her tighter. Relishing the rare opportunity of having her to myself—suspended for a moment from the looming Legacy decision and all the overbearing rules and suffocating pressures that came with it.

All that we were up against.

My hand trailed the side of her rib cage down to the hem of her shirt. Her eyes fluttered closed when I slipped my fingertips under it, grazing the warm skin of her hip bone and drawing her close until she was a breath away.

Her tone was playfully scolding when she said, "Are you quite done?"

"*Done?*" I smiled against her lips. "Pretty sure we're just getting started."

CHAPTER TWO

CLARA

NOW

TEN DAYS UNTIL LEGACY BANQUET

FILMING HIM ALWAYS FELT as easy as breathing.

But watching this footage of Reid now cuts my air clean off.

In the clip, the late-afternoon sun streams through the trees as he looks out over the mountain from my favorite trail. Our trail. Only the soft ends of his dark hair peek out from under a beanie, curling at the nape of his neck. He's looking at me over the camera with a bright, unguarded light in his eyes.

Nothing like how he'd look at me now.

I should turn it off. If I don't want to cry, I should definitely turn off this clip I accidentally opened. But an overwhelming longing roots me to the spot. The memory flooding as I watch it play out in real time on the screen of the laptop that I've indefinitely borrowed from Woodhurst High despite having graduated five months prior.

This must have been last spring, just before it got warm.

"Can I help you?" Reid asks.

It's a shot straight through my solar plexus hearing his deep voice again. I thought I remembered it well. I fall asleep replaying our conversations in my mind often enough. But I forgot the subtle gruffness. The teasing nature that he reserved just for me. I make it through the next moments of it fine until I hear myself say off-screen, "As usual, just ignore me." My disembodied voice is lighter and happier than I've felt in months.

The corner of his mouth lifts. "*As usual,* that's impossible."

I can guess that off camera I'm rolling my eyes the way I always did when I tried to hide how he unraveled me. Because on camera he grins the way he always did when he knew that he had.

I want to reach for my phone to text him, call him—*anything* him. But I squeeze my eyes shut against the impulse. Against the familiar tidal wave of missing him. That was then.

As if ensuring I don't do something reckless, the wail of the smoke alarm sounds overhead. I whip around at the scent of burnt popcorn and see the smoke streaming from the stovetop.

Perfect.

I rush to turn it off and use a dish towel to fan the smoke out the open window, willing the alarm to shut up. I don't need any of our neighbors, who are mostly my family, popping over to check on me like they do when Mom's on overnights at the hospital. Ever since Dad left for good last year, they've been *hovering*. Within an hour, an exaggerated story about how my house almost burned down would be all over Woodhurst. This town is too small for its own good.

With a few more shakes of the towel, the alarm stops just as the front door opens.

"Clara?" Mitchell calls. "Whoa! What died in here?"

I slam the laptop shut and force my features into benign amusement by the time he reaches the kitchen. "Oh, just my dignity."

I dump the burnt popcorn into the trash.

Mitchell's blue eyes crinkle with his smile as he holds up a grease-stained bag. "This is why I bring the food and you choose the movie. We gotta stick to our strengths."

I force a laugh and pull two plates down from the cabinet.

The whole purpose of this night isn't to torture myself with old clips of when I used to be happy. It's to torture myself by finally showing someone the new documentary I've been working on all summer.

Mitchell isn't an expert, but he is my closest friend these days. It's been just the two of us since most of our group graduated and moved away in August. He stayed because he's a year younger and in his senior year.

I stayed because I lost my Legacy scholarship and couldn't afford California Film Academy without it. Because I had no choice after my life was upended.

When I asked about deferring, CAFA informed me that they don't allow it due to the number of applications they receive. I had missed the deadline for loans. I had no way to pay for college.

I simply had to give up my place at my dream school.

Now I have to start all over; either reapply to CAFA in a few weeks or find film festivals, competitions, and scholarship opportunities for the upcoming year. All the programs I'd ignored before since I had counted on Legacy.

Or I could just stop altogether, which honestly sounds the most appealing. But Mitchell basically demanded a screening of my new idea tonight, so I figured I might as well show him.

I trust that he'll tell me the truth about it. Like Reid, the guy is incapable of lying. Must be a brother thing.

After we open all the windows and finish the burgers, we plant ourselves on the couch.

My finger hovers over the space bar, but I can't bring myself to hit PLAY. I need to do my ritual to shake off these nerves. I press my hands into a prayer pose and hold them against my chin.

Mitchell groans, "Every time," just as I launch into my best David Attenborough impression.

"What you are about to witness is nothing short of extraordinary. After two failures, several months, and a near-death experience, *Throwing Shade,* a Clara Suarez original documentary short, is complete."

I look at Mitchell significantly, but he just stares back. I drop into my regular voice, shattering the illusion I so clearly drew. "Dude, you're supposed to clap."

Mischief flashes through his eyes as he launches himself up off the couch to clap furiously. "Wooooo! Go, Clara!"

His floppy brown curls fall in his eyes as he does this for a solid ten seconds.

I stare at him, unamused. "A sarcastic standing ovation is hardly supportive. This is art."

He closes one eye like he disagrees and holds up his fingers to make air quotes. "'Art.'"

When he plops back beside me, I elbow him *hard,* and he laughs.

"You're a bad friend."

"Pretty sure you mispronounced 'amazing,'" he retorts.

As I'm about to hit PLAY, both our phones vibrate on the cushions between us. That's weird. Who would be texting both of us anymore?

Mitchell gasps. "Oh my god. Oh my *GOD.*"

"What?"

"It's Kenji. In RUN FORREST RUN."

My heart drops. RUN FORREST RUN. The name of our group chat that withered and died a few months ago after everything went down.

My face feels weird, my head too hot. I mentally run through the list of everyone on the chat. Me, Mitchell, Kenji, Delaney.

Reid.

"'Guess who's coming home for Legacy Weekend, B-words!'" Mitchell reads aloud. "A full two months at college and Kenji still doesn't cuss."

Mitchell types back right away, and I pick up my phone when it vibrates again. HELL YEAH CAN'T WAIT!!!! When will you all be here?

I've been willfully ignoring the fact that it's Legacy Weekend next week. It's not like I can avoid the buzz around town—the banners strung across the town square and the signs in every shop window.

But that doesn't mean I'm ready for it.

Legacy Weekend is when all Woodhurst High alumni, most notably the five most recent Legacies, come back to Woodhurst for a three-day spectacle to celebrate them and the program. It's bigger than homecoming, bigger than Thanksgiving break if you ask a local, and everyone who left for college comes back home for it.

I've been dreading it all summer.

But why is Kenji resuscitating the group chat? Is he *trying* to be chaotic?

A selfie of him shirtless at the beach baring a wide, relaxed smile comes through then with no other context. Guess that answers that.

His black hair is longer, his olive skin sun-kissed. Formerly short and scrawny, he's like the poster child for a post–high school glow-up.

I sneak a glance at Mitchell. "How mad are you that he got cuter?"

Though most people don't know yet, I'm not the sole person Mitchell's out to. But I am *definitely* the only person who knows how he really feels about his best friend.

The flush that seems to appear only when he talks about Kenji dusts Mitchell's cheeks. He makes a dramatic gagging sound before he says, "So embarrassing."

Mitchell gives Kenji's photo a thumbs-down on the group chat, which is basically admitting to his crush then and there. Not that Kenji would ever notice.

When no one else responds right away, Mitchell shrugs and puts down his phone before unceremoniously slapping the space bar to start the doc.

"Hey!" I exclaim.

"*Shhhh*—it's *art*."

The establishing shot is of the trail Reid and I first hiked together—where we shared so many firsts—and my chest hurts the way it always does when I walk that path now.

I try to tell myself that seeing him again couldn't possibly make it hurt *worse*.

We watch the doc in silence. It's not very long, since I started it only this summer. As the final scene ends, I blink back to the present, having bitten my pinkie nail down to a painful nub. I sit up a little straighter and wait for Mitchell to say something. Anything. Well, not *anything*. I'm definitely waiting for him to say something along the lines of "Perfect, no notes. You're not a total fuckup."

It's the slight purse to his lips that tells me a second too late that I don't want to hear what he thinks after all.

"Okay . . . I was willing to let the Great Depression sweatpants go, but this"—he waves his hand over the laptop—"is a problem."

I search his face for the joke, only to realize he's being serious. Looking down at my legs, I ask, "What's wrong with my sweatpants?"

"They're symptomatic." Mitchell turns, jutting his knee into the back of the couch. Beside it, a small tear has formed in the green plaid cushion. "Your movies are obviously breathtaking, Clara. The look of them. But this is—a lot of thoughts at once. A lot of sad, miserable, depressing thoughts."

"It's not *that* bad—"

"You basically said the earth is on fire and it's all our fault and there's nothing we can do so we might as well give up. This whole thing just doesn't feel like . . . you."

I close the laptop quickly. As if shutting it down will stop the river of embarrassment now flowing through me. I started this doc because I thought this was what the film festivals would want. What CAFA would want. Something that they would take seriously.

But this is exactly what I was afraid of—that I have no idea what I'm doing anymore. Both as a filmmaker and in my life. There's no guarantee CAFA will accept me again, and if I don't make something undeniable, I'm stuck here all over again. Failure *can't* be my legacy.

"Seriously, are you okay?" he asks.

The earnestness of his question is unnerving. Is he actually worried about me? I know what that's like. I hate that I could be acting just like my mom does when her depression takes over. Still, it's impossible to lie to Mitchell. "Would you be?"

His face goes sympathetic, and he shakes his head.

Our phones vibrate again. This time with a text from Delaney. My heart thumps so hard I think Mitchell must hear it.

Delaney: I'll be home Thursday! Dance Legacy represent!!!!

She then sends a photo of herself doing an arabesque on a foggy San Francisco campus. I can imagine her propping her phone on some bench to get the shot. It's the first time I've heard from her in over a month, and I want to cry looking at her photo. Everything from her shorter hair to the third piercing in her ear is different. She looks older. Worldly.

"She looks . . ." But I finish the thought in my mind. *Thin.*

I wonder if Mitchell stalks them like I do. Kenji living in a beach town, Delaney in a big city. I've examined every snap, every post. Their cool new friends. Their cool new dorms. Their cool new lives that are so different from my own.

In my weaker moments I check up on Reid at Stanford, too. I know I shouldn't. I have no right to. But when the craving to see him overpowers me, I can't help myself. So far it hasn't made a difference, anyway, since he never posts anything. Sometimes he's tagged in things, but it's almost always race pictures where he's flushed and focused in a sea of other runners.

There's nothing about his new life. Nothing about how he's doing. Nothing about the real him.

Without leaving me any time to realize what's happening or to fix my hair or *murder* him, Mitchell snaps a selfie of us and sends it. To the chat. Straight to Reid.

"Mitchell," I say evenly. "What the actual fuck?"

"Everyone else sent one. Relax, you look perfect." Mitchell turns the phone toward me even though the photo pops up on my screen. Okay, despite the sweatpants, it could be worse. My dark hair is clean at least and full of volume, falling over one shoulder. The green of the couch brings out the green of my eyes, which are wide in surprise at Mitchell holding up the phone. The sunset light outside adds a glow to my fair skin.

I wonder what they'll think when they see me. What Reid will think.

Maybe I look a little older, too.

If I do, it's probably in the grizzled, weathered way old cowboys do. Not in the cool, college-campus way.

"You've been underground long enough. You're going to have to face everyone again next week anyway," Mitchell continues, "so we might as well start with your actual friends."

God, I hope not everyone. My stomach is only knots.

Will Reid respond? He always hated the group chats. He openly admitted to putting us on mute the majority of the time. But every now and then he'd chime in, so I know he checked it.

Every buzz creates a leap of anticipation. But his name doesn't appear once in all the back-and-forth.

Mitchell purses his lips, scrolling quickly. "Okay, obviously, all the Legacies are coming back. Josh just posted about it and so did Nicole."

We exchange a look, and I drag a hand down my face. Fantastic. The guy who ruined my life and the girl who got Legacy over me.

Mitchell continues. "Dramaaaaa. Now *this* would be a good doc." He goes still and lowers his phone. "Wait, weren't you already working on something like that?"

My stomach twists again because, yes, I dedicated my entire senior year to gathering footage of our class and following the experience of becoming a Legacy. I even submitted a short sample as part of my own Legacy application with the full intention of finishing it at the culminating event of Legacy Weekend.

This Legacy Weekend.

But that was before my future got completely derailed.

I pivoted to learning about nature docs this summer because I wanted to forget about how volatile and messy and awful humans can be. Trees only take care of one another. Plus, they communicate via fungal networks. *Fungal networks.*

"Okay, think about it. Everyone coming home is always a hot mess." Mitchell pinches the fabric of my sweatpants at the ankle. "The documentary competitions would eat that shit up," he presses.

He's not wrong. When people come home, drama follows.

"But—"

"If you say anything about fungal networks, I swear to god."

I glower at him. "You're so annoying."

"Clara, your video was amazing last year—"

"Uhh—"

"I mean, what I saw of it before the *scandal*—"

I use my Attenborough voice again, hoping a joke will cut this off. "We do not speak of the scandal."

But Mitchell doesn't bite. "Maybe we should."

He ignores my glare and keeps going.

"With everyone coming back, you could finish the doc like you always planned. You might even figure out what happened at the assembly last year. Find out who sabotaged you. Get some closure. It could be good for you."

I don't like this tiny spark of interest in my gut.

Even if I can see his point that the tree doc isn't great, I abandoned the Legacy idea for a good reason. It would be humiliating to face them all again. Torturous to revisit the most intense year of my life. To tear open everything I've tried to keep closed.

I can't—*won't*—do it.

"It'd give you an excuse to talk to Reid," Mitchell says casually.

I glare harder, and he grins wider.

My phone buzzes again, and the name that appears wraps a band around my ribs and squeezes.

Reid.

CHAPTER THREE

CLARA

THEN

REID WAS NEW TO our school but already known. Rumors like *gunning for state champion . . . the future of the sport . . .* got to Woodhurst long before he did. When I caught him with my lens for the first time, the thinking—about angles and lighting and shot lists—all stopped and instinct took over.

For as many people who were excited about someone of his caliber joining our team, I'd heard even more were stressed that he was a lock for a coveted Legacy spot, which would leave only four left for the rest of us. But I hadn't given it much thought. I'd been otherwise too consumed with all the ways my life was imploding.

Only, now, he had my attention.

Dirt crunched under my running shoes as I stepped to the side, locking on to his profile just as a break in the clouds streamed sunlight over his dark messy hair. He was wearing navy running shorts and a faded black shirt with the sleeves cut off, his tan, toned arms on full display. But I was more captivated with his stillness. His fixed concentration.

Something told me to go wide and capture the way the group responded to him.

The serious runners got quiet, focused as he approached. Several girls greeted him. But he adjusted his earbuds and kept his eyes on the trail. I'd only ever seen him talk to his stepbrother, Mitchell.

I was about to take another step toward him when a tug on my arm made my shot wobble.

"Clara? Hello?" Delaney had clearly been talking while I filmed, but only now were her words registering. "I get it, he's pretty, but can you pause your stalking for a second?"

My scoff was light, my response automatic. "I'm not stalking, I'm *documenting*."

Never stop shooting. Capture everything and the story will emerge. That's what all the great documentarians said, and I intended to do just that until I was among them someday.

But my focus didn't derail Delaney. "*Or* are you trying to act like you didn't just tell me you hooked up with *Josh* last night?"

Of course at that exact moment Kenji walked up to us. "I'm sorry, I think I just hallucinated—do you mean Josh West? As in captain of the team and chairman of the bros?"

Officially ripped from the moment, I looked at my two best friends. Delaney's Disney-princess-like features were screwed up into raging disbelief and Kenji was shaking his head.

I whispered, "Could you two not *yell*?"

We were near the trail lot, far out of earshot from the rest of the cross-country team, but you couldn't be too careful in Woodhurst, and

I needed no one else to *ever find out* this information. I was still not even sure how Delaney got it out of me.

Thankfully practice was about to start, and it gave me an excuse to busy myself by putting the camera away. I had never been a particularly good runner, but anything was better than being home. I walked fast toward the group, but they both kept easy pace, waiting for an explanation I didn't really have.

"We kissed. That's all." That wasn't all, but I didn't want to admit it.

"But . . . why *Josh*?" Delaney scrunched up her face. "Wow, sorry—that came out judgy."

I let out a humorless laugh. "Please judge me. I deserve it."

In the light of day, the whole thing was utterly humiliating. They knew I didn't date—that I had *zero* interest in a boyfriend. And Josh West wasn't someone I'd usually *ever* go for, anyway. But the previous night wasn't usual and he was . . . there. Cute enough in a generic, bro-y way. Distracting me from the real reason I went to that party in the first place. The crunch of pine needles under Dad's truck tires in the driveway. The slam of Mom's bedroom door in response. The revolving door of leaving and coming back.

It was a sloppy mistake.

Kenji's and Delaney's expressions made it clear they were desperate for more details, but I just wanted to forget about it and start senior year—Legacy year—right.

Woodhurst's Legacy Program offered a massive scholarship, and only five students were awarded one out of every graduating class. It was ultracompetitive, which meant I couldn't afford to make sloppy mistakes or to break any of the rules. I needed that scholarship if I had any chance of going to California Film Academy.

Every move I made would matter going forward.

I wrangled my hair into a ponytail, and when I secured my hair tie, I stopped walking to hold out my pinkie to them. "*Please* don't tell anyone."

Delaney scoffed. "I'm offended you think I would."

I arched an eyebrow at her. Woodhurst was small and Woodhurst High was even smaller. News traveled fast, but gossip? Gossip had its own speed. And that speed was Delaney Whitlock.

"Swear."

With a dramatic exhale she hooked my pinkie with her own and promised seriously, "I swear."

"Me too," Kenji agreed. "I've already forgotten what we were talking about because the hottest brothers on the planet are looking at me. Gotta go!"

Kenji took off to go talk to Mitchell, and the two of them fell into easy conversation.

At the trailhead, a few of the varsity try-hards like Nicole Kelly were gathered in a huddle, talking in hushed tones. They were all friendly with Delaney, who was also captain of the pom squad, thus more popular than any of us, but they more or less acted like I didn't exist.

"Amaya just needs to dump him for good already," Nicole said as we approached.

Amaya? As in Josh's ex-girlfriend? *Oh no.*

"What are we talking about?" Delaney asked. Her brown doe eyes went wide with concerned interest. I didn't "girl" very well, but the way she did was masterful.

"Josh. Heather saw him go into a room with someone last night."

My bag hit the dirt so hard a plume of dust kicked up around it.

Josh and Amaya had been off-and-on since freshman year. Josh told me that they were definitely *off*. If that wasn't true, the whole situation had rapidly morphed from dumb mistake to royal fuckup.

But I kept my expression as neutral as possible. Growing up in a family that created *talk*, I'd learned to keep my emotions off my face. My mom called it the swimming-duck effect; I'm cool on the outside, even as I'm absolutely losing it under the surface.

Delaney lowered her voice, betraying nothing when she asked, "Do you know who it was?"

"No," Heather admitted. "It was too dark, and they didn't come out before I left."

"So, then we have no idea what happened," Delaney said.

"It was probably some clueless freshman," Heather continued, barely listening. "Since I don't know how anyone else could do that to Amaya."

Shame spiraled through me faster. Thankfully, Delaney thought so quickly on her feet it was dizzying.

"If anything happened, which we don't know if it did"—Delaney threw Heather a side-eye—"why are you immediately blaming the girl? What if Josh lied about them breaking up or something?"

Nicole sighed and rolled her eyes. "True. We all know how he is. Besides, how could anyone keep track when Amaya and Josh break up and get back together every other day, anyway?"

I was a little surprised by her response, since she and Amaya were best friends. Then again, I didn't know if anyone was as lucky as I was to have a best friend who had their back the way Delaney had mine.

The other girls nodded like Nicole had a point, and Delaney and I exchanged a quick glance. Had that actually worked? If so, then Delaney hadn't just helped me dodge a social bullet—she'd sent it in the opposite direction. I basically owed her my firstborn.

Mercifully, Coach Rousseau, Reid's dad, started practice and arranged everyone into our timed groups, separating us into varsity and JV.

I managed to feel relieved for a whole minute before Josh jogged toward us from the parking lot.

"Nice of you to join us, West," Coach called out.

"Sorry, Coach," Josh responded. "Late night." He winked at me in front of everyone, and my entire body went cold. The stares on my back prickled. The low whispers started instantly.

Just like that, the bullet righted its course.

By the time we started running, I felt like a wire about to snap.

I launched myself onto the trail, the first mile passing faster than any ever had. I pushed hard trying to block out every side-eye. Only, it didn't work as well as usual, so I forced my legs to move faster. My lungs seared with the effort. But no matter how hard I tried to push it out of my mind, I couldn't outrun my thoughts.

If Josh and Amaya were still together, that made me no better than the woman Dad left Mom for this time. It was one thing to make a mistake; it was another to hurt someone else while doing it.

By the second mile, instead of *right, left, right, left,* it was like the rhythm of my footfalls slapping the dirt were mocking me with the message in my head: *Dad left. Dad left. Dad left.*

Again.

Not knowing when he was coming back this time. *If.* But knowing all too well that if he did, Mom would take him back as usual. He'd apologize, and she'd forgive him, and they'd call it love. Only I seemed to know that it was bullshit.

At the fourth mile, a stitch formed right under my ribs. But I couldn't stop. I was almost done. Rounding the corner of the path back toward the parking lot, the towering evergreens shuddered above me in the breeze. I stretched my rib cage with a lungful of the piney scent for the final leg.

Reid was waiting at the trailhead the way he always did after finishing first. He watched everyone return, hands on his hips, his stare intense and narrow. He leveled it on me. Not on my face, but on my body. My alignment.

For some reason it had an *effect*.

My spine straightened on instinct; my running posture snapped into place. I activated my kick, pumping my arms, sweat pouring down my temples. I gave it everything I had as I crossed the threshold with a final gasping burst of breath.

A wave of nausea rolled through me as I slowed. I hunched over, hands slipping a bit against my slick knees as I gasped for air, my face on fire. Tears sprang from the backs of my eyes, but it had to be from pushing so hard. I couldn't be sad. I didn't *do* sad.

"You can get lightheaded like that," a deep voice said.

Reid said.

He never talked to me. Or anyone, really. I didn't know if it was because he was stuck-up, shy, or socially anxious, but he'd been fully standoffish since he arrived.

I cast a glance at him, and his hair was darker with sweat, his skin flushed across his sharp cheekbones.

I forced myself upright and shot him a baleful glare, my chest still rising and falling rapidly.

"I know," I gasped out.

Not that I was even in the same stratosphere as him, but I had been running cross-country for four years, too. I didn't need him telling me what to do. Reid nodded and turned away.

After a few panting minutes and several chugs of water, my breath returned. But when I took a step forward, a sudden shock of pain shot through my calf muscle. Just as Coach and the rest of the team took off for the cooldown run, I sank to the rocky dirt, clutching my leg. I tried to straighten it to release the muscle, but it didn't work. I couldn't help the tears as they pushed through my lashes this time. *Damn it.*

Suddenly, I felt a presence at my side. "You have to keep it straight."

My eyes flew open, and I swiped a palm across them. "Where did you—" I couldn't finish my sentence because another bolt of pain ripped through my calf.

"It's going to keep cramping until you straighten it out."

"I *know,*" I said through clenched teeth. "But it hurts too much."

Reid let out an exasperated breath as he crouched down. "Can I?"

My gaze bounced between his hovering hands and my leg. I nodded.

His fingers were strong, his hands warm as he kneaded the exact spot. His touch was clinical, gentle. Like he'd done it a hundred times. He probably had. State champion and all that.

As he grabbed my dusty sneaker to slowly guide my leg straight with his other hand, I slammed my lips together to avoid an embarrassing sound slipping out of me and fixed my gaze on the small black gauges in his ears. They made him look way edgier than anyone else in Woodhurst.

I let my eyes sweep across his face. There was a line between his eyebrows, the corner of his full lips tugged down as he concentrated. He was stunning on camera, but the up-close version was . . . an experience.

He pressed harder until I hissed.

"Too much?" he asked. His grip began to loosen, and I shot my hand out, grabbing his forearm to stop him.

"No, it feels good." I breathed. My calf was finally beginning to relax. But it wasn't until our gazes collided that I realized how close we were.

How suggestive that sounded. I let go of him and scrambled to add, "Um, I mean, you're—it's helping."

He cleared his throat and nodded. I was grateful he was so concentrated on my leg that he didn't see the blush shoot across my cheeks.

When the muscle finally released, he looked up at me again.

"Better?"

"Yeah, thanks."

I smiled. He didn't. In the few weeks he'd been on the team, I'd noticed he almost never smiled. Which was good because I could imagine even his smirks were dangerous. One of those guys who was just too hot to be anything but trouble.

He studied my face in a way that forced me to swallow. Hard. I was sure mascara was smeared under my eyes, my hair frizzing. My usually fair complexion an unholy tomato red.

But the way he looked at me didn't make me feel like he thought I was all that disgusting.

I pulled my leg back, and Reid's hands dropped instantly.

Everywhere he had touched crackled with tiny fireworks, and I ran a palm across my bare skin to rid myself of the sensation.

"Ready?" he asked, jutting his chin toward the trail.

I eyed him like he must've been joking and hauled myself up to standing. "Nuh-uh. No more running. I'm cooling down the way god intended."

I gestured toward the lake, and his eyebrows shot up.

"Coach won't like that."

"Oh, but I will," I said dreamily.

The corner of his mouth twitched.

I don't know what came over me—maybe it was the electricity still coursing through my leg from where he touched me that urged me on—but I said, "You coming?"

He glanced over his shoulder as if looking to see if anyone was watching, then nodded.

When we arrived at the edge of the tree line, I couldn't get my shoes off fast enough. The lake was shaped like a crescent moon around the mountain. Only a wide shot would manage to capture the size and striking blue of the water from the shore.

But Reid eyed the water warily. "There aren't eels, are there?"

I froze. "*Eels?* In Crescent Lake?"

He just stared at me. Good god, he was serious. I wanted to laugh, but the guy looked terrified.

"No. There are no eels."

I shed my tank top down to my black sports bra and plunged deep into the cool water. When I emerged, I looked around for Reid in the lake, only to see him still hovering at the edge.

"Can you not swim or something?" I called out.

His expression flattened, a competitive edge to his voice. "Of course I can swim."

"Then c'mon."

He hesitated.

"Dare you."

His eyes locked on mine as the first hint of fun entered his voice. "I take dares seriously."

"So do I."

The silence hung as he considered.

I turned to swim around like I couldn't care less what he did. A moment later, I felt the splash when Reid hit the water behind me. I smiled to myself and ignored the hum of satisfaction I felt. After he rose out and shook his hair quickly, I said, "Besides, the eels only come out at night."

I ruined the prank by cracking up at his horrified expression.

Reid narrowed his eyes at me and threw a mellow splash my way. "Mean."

"But funny." I grinned.

We floated in silence a few minutes before he swam back to the bank and pulled himself out. Water sloshed down the valley of his strong back, and I didn't realize I was staring until he turned and caught me. I quickly flipped onto my own back, letting my eyes fall closed against the sunlight.

Reid's voice cut through the quiet when he asked, "What made you push like that today?"

The question caught me off guard, and I straightened until my toes grazed the surface of a smooth, mossy rock below. Why did he care? Even if I wanted to talk about it—which I didn't—it wasn't like I could just open up about my own drunken mistakes, or Josh being a cheating bastard, or my parents' crappy, confusing relationship to anyone, let alone some guy I had never exchanged so much as a glance with before that day.

"Do you even know my name?"

He blinked. "Clara Suarez. Senior. Racing PR twenty-four, twenty-seven."

"You know our stats?"

He pushed his wet hair off his forehead and propped his arms across his bent knees. "I know *your* stats."

"I can't tell if that's creepy or cool," I said honestly.

He didn't miss a beat when he said, "Definitely creepy."

I burst out laughing, and his lips twisted again like he was trying not to.

"Do you know *my* name?" he asked.

"Everyone knows your name." I swam backward, kicking my legs up again until my polished blue toenails popped out of the water.

When he didn't respond, I looked over at him. His brow was furrowed, so I was pretty sure that was the wrong thing to say. At least I had successfully rerouted the conversation away from myself.

"Nice dodge, by the way."

Or not. Most people didn't notice when I avoided questions on purpose. It made my stomach flip that he did.

He looked over my head at the water when he said, "You need to train more consistently, or you'll keep hurting yourself."

That was, like, the fifth time he had tried to tell me something as if I didn't already know.

"I don't remember asking for your advice," I huffed.

"Fair enough." A pause. "But I'm still right."

I pursed my lips, trying not to laugh again. "You know, you're a little infuriating."

What I really meant was "fascinating." I itched for my camera, wishing I could train it on him again.

"So are you." He finally smiled, and my god it was worse than I'd imagined. It was warm and a little self-conscious. *Shy*, I concluded immediately. He was confident but also *shy*.

Time to go.

My feet squelched in my shoes as we walked back to the trailhead near the parking lot. Most of the team had cleared out already, but Coach watched us pointedly as we approached.

He gave Reid a disappointed once-over then said, "Just because it's summer doesn't mean you can slack on your training."

"Dad, she—"

"We'll talk about it later. Go stretch. You too, Suarez."

When we were out of earshot from his dad, I said, "Sorry, I didn't mean to get you in trouble."

The anxiety slipped off Reid's face as he shrugged. "Worth it."

My skin went hot where our elbows brushed. Before I could start stretching, Josh approached.

"Rousseau!" he called. "Nice hustle today." He flashed Reid an easy grin that sharpened when it landed on me. "*You* disappeared."

I didn't respond, but Josh didn't get the hint and just hovered there, waiting.

"What do you want?" I asked, my voice bored.

"We need to talk."

My pulse spiked as I noticed the varsity girls whispering to one another behind him as they watched us. "No, we don't."

"C'mon, don't be like that, Clare-bear," Josh said.

"*Don't* call me that."

His jaw ticked. "You liked it last night."

My entire face flamed. I didn't want to be having this conversation at all, but definitely not in front of Reid. Josh pushed his damp, dirty-blond hair off his forehead and reached for me.

I backed away several steps. "Just leave me alone, okay?"

His face turned sour. "Fine. Whatever. Be a bitch."

"Hey." Reid didn't need to raise his voice to draw our attention.

"Bro, no offense, but this doesn't concern you," Josh said, rolling his eyes.

Reid lifted his chin ever so slightly. If I had been filming, I'd push in there for the close-up to capture the subtle movement. "I'm not your bro. Full offense."

Josh blinked, shocked that anyone would talk to him like that. He was used to the protection he got from his dad being the principal. His chest puffed in response. "Okay, now I get why you don't have any friends."

Reid smirked. "Now I get why Clara wants nothing to do with you. Look at us both learning."

Josh's cheeks went red all at once. "What's your problem—"

"You lost, Joshua?" Delaney asked, appearing at my side. She linked an arm with mine and faced Josh with that cold stare of hers. She was tiny, but her ballet physique made her rock-solid. Still, she looked too pale after that run, and I wondered if the fact that she'd eaten only a few french fries off my plate before practice was the reason.

Josh wandered off muttering to himself. Knowing him, this whole thing was far from over. I just didn't know *why*.

"Byeee," Delaney muttered. She unlinked our arms and faced me and Reid. Her eyes bounced between us. Our wet hair and clothes. A suggestive smile spread on her face. "You two have fun?"

I could've killed her.

"I did," Reid said, sliding me a small smile. Sweet Jesus.

"I still have to stretch," I responded, just to change the subject. And for something to do with my hands and attention and racing pulse. When I finished, I pulled out my camera from my bag and panned the scene. The more footage I got, the better.

When I caught Reid in frame, his eyebrows sprang up.

"For the yearbook video," I rushed to say. "Just ignore me."

He narrowed his eyes, teasing. "Pretty sure that's impossible."

My flush was instant.

"Are you going to Kenji's party this weekend?" Delaney asked Reid, I'm sure for my benefit.

Kenji was always having a party. Not that I was eager to attend another one anytime soon, but if Reid went . . . Our gazes clashed above my camera, and I darted mine back to the screen.

"Um, maybe." He flicked his gaze toward his dad. "I don't go out a lot. I'm on a pretty tight training schedule."

I lowered my voice into a conspiratorial whisper. "If it helps, Kenji's is a strictly eel-free environment."

He appraised me with something like amusement in his eyes. "I wouldn't be so sure. They're sneaky fuckers."

I laughed, and that smile took over his face again. The first I caught on camera.

The first time I caught a beginning.

CHAPTER FOUR

REID

NOW

TEN DAYS UNTIL LEGACY BANQUET

@haikuforyou
Betrayal is a
thorn that lives under skin, an
awareness that grows.

I HAVE A PARTICULARLY brutal training session the evening my phone explodes. Sweat is slick against the backs of my knees as I do the last set of hamstring curls my trainer, Jason, is subjecting me to. He's beefy and bald and demonic.

And my only hope.

It's taking everything in me to finish this set. To pretend like my knee doesn't *hate* this.

It doesn't help that my phone is buzzing incessantly on the ground beside the workout bench. I flick a gaze toward it, worried it's Delaney. Hoping like hell it's not.

On the next curl, my knee is hurting so much, a grunt almost slips out. I glance at Jason in the gym mirror and notice just how closely he's watching me. His face is serious. Like he knows something's up.

I clench my jaw and ignore the pain. Running is a mental sport, and I wouldn't be where I am if I wasn't able to push past the limits of my own mind. Despite my buzzing phone's best effort to distract me.

Jason adds more resistance to the final three like a proper dick, and I have to block out everything except for the quivering in my leg as I complete them.

"And that's it for the day," he says when I'm close to puking.

I let my head hang over the bench for a second, breathing hard, my knee screaming. When I finally sit up to towel off the sweat, he smacks me between my shoulder blades.

"Nice job, Reid. You're gaining your strength and flexibility back. You keep this up, I think you can start jogging in a week or two."

I whip to face him. "Really?"

He grins as he jots down a few notes. "Really."

It's the first time since tripping and tearing my MCL on that course last month that I feel even an iota of hope. I was so sure I was going to dominate that race. Instead, it ruined the start of my season.

For weeks I've been forced to watch everyone else on the team compete and improve their stats while I've done nothing but go to doctor's appointments, bracing for more bad news. At least I didn't need surgery and I've managed to keep my dad in the dark about how bad it is. He knows I fell, that I'm rehabbing, but I don't need him worrying about my future.

Or my scholarship.

Now that I'm *finally* off the crutches, I have to push myself harder than my trainers are willing to or else I'll never catch up.

"Are you going to tell Coach Carr that?" I ask.

Jason keeps scribbling, his eyebrow quirking up in amusement. "I know you're eager to get back out there, but you have to take injuries like this one step at a time."

I force myself to ask the question. "But I will get back out there, right? I'll run like I did?"

"We both know that bullshitting is not what we do here," he says, gesturing between us. "You got a long way to go."

"I can't lose any more time, Jason. Regionals are next month."

His eyes are hard when they look up from his tablet. "You're not losing time, you're *healing*. You risk making things a helluva lot worse if you push through something like this, Rousseau. I can't guarantee you'll be ready for regionals just yet."

I grind my teeth. He doesn't get it. Sitting out isn't an option when everyone expects you to be great. *Needs* you to be great.

Jason hands me a compression wrap. "Take this, ice it tonight. Keep wearing the brace and do an Epsom salt soak if you have any soreness."

A soak. I immediately think of the hot springs back home. My favorite place on the entire planet. Sometimes I can get through the whole day without thinking about Woodhurst. Other days, I crave everything about it down to the pine cones. But those thoughts inevitably lead me to Clara. And I try to avoid ever thinking about Clara.

I collect my water bottle and phone, still buzzing every few seconds.

"Someone's got a girlfriend," Jason taunts.

I shoot him a glare, and he chuckles. But as soon as I finally check my phone, the screen goes black. Dead. Of course.

"Reid, man, don't stress. Injuries have a way of teaching us something we need to learn. And someday, this is all going to be a blip."

It's hard to imagine anything that's happened in the past few months will feel like a "blip," but I want to believe him.

"Thanks," I say.

It's dark and drizzling as I walk back to my dorm. *Injuries have a way of teaching us something we need to learn.*

If that's true, I wonder what that could mean for me.

Sweat is tacky against my skin by the time I get to my room—this strange, beige space that even after two months still doesn't feel like mine. I plug my phone in so it can charge while I shower.

I gather my stuff and make my way down the hall, past a few open doors leading to groups laughing, watching movies, sneaking booze. Connor's door is open, too, and when we make eye contact, my teammate yells at me to join them. But I can tell it's half-hearted. Everyone gets quiet when I'm around now. I shake my head and hold up my shower caddy as my answer.

He calls out for me anyway. "You bringing that blond around again any time soon?"

A few of the guys holler and elbow one another. I just roll my eyes and keep walking. I'm never bringing Delaney around these cretins again. Or at all. The familiar guilt I've been carrying since that night weighs heavier at the reminder.

By the time I get out of the shower, I'm limping, my leg locking. *Fuck*, if anyone sees . . . I close my eyes and pull in deep breaths, riding it out. I manage to make it to my room unnoticed, dress quickly, and ice my knee with the compression wrap Jason gave me.

Collapsing onto my bed, I shove a shaky hand through my wet hair. My running clothes are still in a heap on the floor, discarded and pathetic. Just like me.

My phone buzzes to life against my nightstand. The constant pressure that sits heavy on my chest these days quadruples when I see Clara's face on my screen.

I blink. That can't be right. We don't so much as follow each other on social media anymore, let alone text each other. I wrench my phone to look at it closer.

Oh, it's the group chat. RUN FORREST RUN. We haven't used this in months. Not that I ever used it much back in high school, since Kenji abused the space with his incessant stream of consciousness and random shirtless selfies.

Ignoring all the texts, I scroll right to the photo of her. My heart hammers in my chest as I stare at it.

Dark, tumbling hair. Emerald-green eyes. Those *lips*. Slightly parted like she's about to say something snarky.

I grip my phone tight as I take in the other details. She and Mitchell are at her house. Together.

What the hell? She never lets anyone in her house. I barely went over there. And Mitchell hasn't talked about her once since I left. Not that I've asked, but you'd think my own stepbrother would mention in our daily texts that he's been hanging out with the girl who shattered me.

I zoom in. Their knees are touching. Mitch's head rests on her shoulder as he leans back to take the picture.

It could be platonic.

Or they could be hooking up.

I almost throw my phone across the room at the thought. No one ignites the competitive spark in me like he does. It may not be by blood, but we're still brothers. I take a deep breath. No, they wouldn't do that to me . . . Though I've had a feeling Mitchell has been holding something back from me for a while now.

I shouldn't, but it happens without thinking, really. I pull up the photos from last year. I scroll through them in a loop of self-pity.

Tons of photos from the season. One of me and Mitchell after the Woodhurst Invitational that I won. I'm in my red singlet, laughing because Mitchell is pretending to bite the medal around my neck as if checking if it's real gold.

And inevitably, I scroll to the one I've looked at . . . too often. The one picture I have of me and Clara after our first hike together. The sky is a heavy gray behind us, and she's wearing my jacket because the temperature dropped suddenly once we got to the peak. She rolled her eyes when I put it on her shoulders, but she didn't take it off, either.

"I bet you hate pictures," she said, as she pulled out her phone.

I shrugged. "Not if you're in them."

She'd gone pink. Which she did a lot around me. I fucking loved that. I remember she let her hair down from its ponytail then, and it tumbled between us as we got close to fit in the screen.

Just before she took the photo, I said, "You smell like a meadow."

She burst out laughing and called me corny.

That's when she snapped it. Her—pink and pretty and laughing; me—grinning like I know how lucky I am to have my arm around her. Like I have no clue the clock is already ticking.

It's the shittiest thing about a breakup. The only other person who actually understands it from the inside out is the one you can't ever see again.

"Psh, shut it down," I say, dragging a hand across my face.

I close the photo and scroll to the top of the chat to read through it quickly—trying to understand how this bomb landed on my phone at the end of an already shit day. And there it is.

Legacy Weekend.

That's next week already? The email invite my dad sent me flashes through my mind: LEGACY WEEKEND: WITH SPECIAL GUEST OF HONOR!

I tried to turn it down. So what that it's a town tradition? So what that I already agreed and told Principal West I'd be there? He's an asshole anyway. After the way the Legacy committee treated Clara, I'm not proud to be part of this program. I still don't know if she ever got the answers she deserved. Like if they ever found out who did it. Or why. It was all so unfair.

But my dad insisted I accept the guest of honor offer. A stipulation of keeping my Legacy scholarship is coming back for the weekend anyway, and I need it if I want to stay in school. With my knee and grades the way they are, I could lose my athletic scholarship any day. Changing course isn't what I do. It isn't what anyone expects me to do. People are counting on me. Even if I'm still not really sure for *what*. I finally gave in.

But what would they do if they all found out that I'm full of shit?

I've managed to keep my own trainer in the dark about the extent of my pain. If he doesn't tell Coach I'm fit to return soon, I'll lose any chance at the kind of season—the kind of future—they all want for me.

The kind of future I'm supposed to want, too.

My phone buzzes again. This time it's from Mitchell to me directly.

Are you alive?

I respond immediately, Why are you with Clara?

Even typing her name is hard. But I have to know.

Mitch: He lives! Because we're friends.

I clench my jaw and respond, . . . and?

I brace for his admission that they're hooking up. Mitch and I don't lie to each other. It's why he's the only one who knows the extent of my injury. We couldn't be more different, but in this we're exactly the same. Honest to a fault. The kind of guys who feel like picking "truth" in truth or dare is cheating.

Though, I'm obviously getting better at lying to everyone else. Maybe he is, too.

> **Mitch:** . . . aaaaaaand friends hang out together? It's chill.

It's chill? What the hell does that mean? I go back to the picture he sent. She hardly ever posts anything on her social media anymore, because despite not following her I can't help but check. Sometimes she includes videos of the forest or views from her hikes but never photos of her face.

How is it possible she's gotten even more beautiful?

I squeeze my eyes shut, trying to ride this pain out, too. This time it doesn't work.

> **Mitch:** You two can figure your shit out when you come home. You ARE coming right?

I want to say no.

If a photo of her wrecks me this much, how would I survive seeing her for real?

Mitchell texts again, If you don't your dad's gonna riot. He keeps asking me if something's going on with you.

I lean my head back against the headboard. *Shit.*

Ever since Mom left when I was little, Dad's been panicked about my life. My future. That something else might fuck me up even worse.

When I showed a talent for running, he poured himself into it and became my coach. Then my team's coach. He's done *everything* to ensure I have a path forward. The more he knows about my life here, the worse it'll be. He might try to take out another loan. After his heart thing last year and with Mitchell going to college next year, I can't let him do that. I have to prove to him that I'm fine.

It's only three days, I tell myself. I can avoid Clara for three days.

Yep, I type, I'll be there.

As soon as I hit SEND, a foreign feeling surges through me. It's something like anxiety, only not bad. *Excitement?* That's . . . weird. I move over to the most recent texts in RUN FORREST RUN, and my frown deepens as I catch up.

Kenji: Who do we think the guest of honor is this year?

DL: It's not me. I have a guess it MIGHT be the OLYMPIC HOPEFUL????

Oh god, who started *that* rumor?

I take a deep breath and send the lyric that's been stuck in my head ever since Delaney played me the album when she visited: It's me. Hi. I'm the problem, it's me.

CHAPTER FIVE

CLARA

NOW

TWO DAYS UNTIL LEGACY BANQUET

A TAYLOR SWIFT LYRIC.

It's been over a week, and I haven't stopped thinking about the way Reid dropped into the group chat, *hours* later, with a Taylor Swift lyric. It was his way of telling us that (1) *he's* the guest of honor for Legacy Weekend, (2) he's officially coming back, and (3) *he listens to Taylor Swift now*.

I guess college really does change people.

Like with Delaney, who hasn't responded to any of my direct texts in a month. She hasn't even responded to me about hanging out this weekend, when on the group chat she's using a dizzying amount of exclamation points about coming home and seeing everyone. I don't know if it's all in my head, but after the way she started drifting after the assembly last year, I can't help but take it personally.

I pull my phone out like I have every three minutes for the past week to see if the buzzing is from Reid again. It's not. It's Kenji reminding us of his annual Legacy party tonight along with a follow-up text, ALUMNI ONLY (except Mitchell obvs). The vultures are circling already.

He then sends a link to an account that I don't recognize. When I open it up, I notice the five Legacies are tagged in it—Reid, Delaney, Amaya, Josh, and Nicole—as well as several other students from our graduating class.

And me.

> **@LEGACY_LORE**: Legacies are returning to Woodhurst this weekend for their final victory lap before passing the crown to the next crop of seniors. But were you at that disastrous assembly last year? There's a lot more to this class of illustrious Legacies than meets the eye. It's time you learned the truth about the so-called Woodhurst elite. The *real* story . . . More soon ♥

As I click through the profile, an unease snakes through me. Why is it anonymous? And what do they mean by the "real story"?

Or am I just on edge because that "disastrous assembly" ruined my life?

"Clara, we're about to open!" my manager calls out to where I'm perched on a bench overlooking the water behind the Lodge. It's the restaurant and equipment rental site that sits at the base of the mountain. In winter, it's a busy, cozy spot with roaring fires in the stone hearths and hot chocolate with so much whipped cream you could ski on it. But at this time of year, the weather hovering between late summer and fall, it's quiet and serene with the best view of the sunset over Crescent Lake.

Before I tuck my phone away for good, I quickly switch over to my favorite poetry account and refresh the page, hoping they've updated with a new post. They haven't.

Mitchell's text comes through the group chat just as I'm tying my apron. Is that account real? ALSO I feel like we should all wear matching shirts tonight. Thoughts?

I laugh away my disquiet over the account, a part of me wishing I could go tonight.

But even though I want to see Kenji and finally talk to Delaney, I shouldn't.

That post, innocuous as it might be, is a reminder of all the drama I've fought to forget as the disgraced, disqualified Legacy.

All the mistakes I have no hope of mending.

It would be different if Reid were going to be there. If I had the chance to see him and know, once and for all, whether I handled things between us the right way or mishandled them as wildly as I've feared every day since.

But Reid said he won't be here until tomorrow. Which means he doesn't want to be here any longer than he has to. I can't blame him for that.

Staying away from everyone is the best option.

Not looking up from my notepad, I ask the new table, "What can I get you?"

"Ah, just the person I was looking for."

The familiar voice causes me to freeze. It's the person I loathe most: Principal West. A stout white man with a salt-and-pepper beard and giant teeth. I've seen him around town plenty of times since graduation, but I've done my best to dodge him.

His teeth are blinding as he grins. "Nice to see you, Clara!"

Doubtful.

I give him a small, half-hearted wave and take his order as quickly as possible, barely looking at him.

But before I can escape, he says, "Actually, do you have a moment? There's something I'd like to talk to you about."

That's . . . unexpected, but my curiosity gets the better of me.

"Okay?" I keep my tone civil, but just barely.

He clears his throat. "As I understand it, you are still in possession of Woodhurst equipment."

My face instantly flames. Since when does the principal notice stuff like that? But before I can respond he holds a hand up.

"It's all right. In fact, it's ideal."

I frown.

"Turns out I'm in need of a videographer this weekend for a 'hype' video. The board has decided to rebrand and refresh all of our content for Legacy's twentieth anniversary, including replacing the video we play at the annual banquet."

I get why.

They've played the same stale video since I was a kid. A bland highlight reel that's basically a Woodhurst High brochure in video form, complete with early 2000s fashion and soundtrack. Watching it at the banquet every year is as much of a traditional Legacy event as Kenji's ragers or the Shakespeare show or doing the Fun Run.

He continues. "Unfortunately, what the videographer sent was not what the board had in mind, and I'm in a bit of a bind. I thought of you immediately."

My frown deepens, but he keeps going.

"We have several new donors and potential benefactors coming into town this weekend, and this video needs to feature everything our program does best. We were hoping for interviews and footage from this batch of Legacies especially. I recall you having quite a bit of that based on that documentary sample you submitted last year. And even better, you could get updated footage this weekend from current Legacies and alumni alike to really make it shine. I'm sure you're the person to do it."

A disbelieving snort escapes me, and I cross my arms. "Me? The person with 'questionable moral character'?"

My voice wavers, but my eye contact doesn't. I'm proud of myself for that.

West clears his throat and looks around before lowering his voice. "I believe it would serve all of us to put that particular unpleasantness behind us."

All of us or his precious program? My blood is boiling that he would even ask this of me.

"That 'unpleasantness' is the reason I'm here serving you coffee instead of at film school like I should be. I'm not interested."

"I would suggest you reconsider if you want to keep the equipment."

"You can have it," I spit out.

Seething, I hoof it out to the back of the restaurant. I grip my hands tight across the wooden railing and take in a deep breath. But it doesn't help.

It probably wouldn't matter to someone else. Someone who hadn't devoted the past four years to becoming a Legacy. Who wasn't stalled waiting for the rest of their life to start.

But it matters to me.

All last year especially, I made decisions based solely on whether it would improve my chances of being chosen. And it worked. I *was* named a Legacy. For a brief moment, I saw a glimpse of who I could be. Someone who achieved what her own mom had deserved, who followed in her father's footsteps.

Who was good enough for someone like Reid.

In the next breath it was all stripped away by whoever sabotaged me—a person who hated me enough to humiliate me in front of the entire town. Now I'm scrambling to pick up the pieces of my life that shattered the day the committee decided I'm not important enough to protect.

No matter what Mitchell said about me taking this opportunity with everyone back home to figure out what happened at the assembly last year, I can't imagine immersing myself in Legacy events, or following people like Josh and Nicole around with a camera like some sort of fawning fangirl.

The clouds shift over the water, casting a lavender glow across the surface. It's too breathtaking to ignore, and I pull my phone out to capture the gentle hush that it creates, wishing I had the DSLR to really do the shot justice. A pang of regret hits me knowing I'll have to give it and the laptop back now that I've turned down West's offer.

But even with this inferior camera, for a moment I'm suspended. Transported somewhere else entirely, my breathing slows, my pulse quiets. The right light is magic like that. It can turn the ordinary into something wondrous.

Like with the poetry I've been reading all year, I wish I could send this photo to Reid. To let him know I'm thinking of him. That I'm *always* thinking of him. If I wasn't so sure he hated me, I would. I tap my thumb against the side of my phone.

I can at least send it to the group.

Before I talk myself out of it, I attach the photo to the group chat. I don't know if it's an olive branch, a question, or an answer, but I hit SEND and hope he knows it's for him.

I'm about to carry on with work and put West's order in with a different server when my phone buzzes. My pulse explodes in a furious rhythm as I sneak a quick look at the screen.

Reid hearted the photo I sent.

I stare so long at the pink icon, the screen goes dark. It's our first direct interaction in six long months. It's small and fragile, but that heart is enough to feel the trail of his fingers across my skin; hear his voice in my mind again.

Maybe he doesn't hate me. Maybe if I had a *reason* to be around this weekend, he'd even talk to me.

My resolve starts to crack.

If I make the video for West, I'll be doing something that will help the school and this program. Something I vowed to never go near again. Not after the way the school treated me. The way the *Wests* treated me.

But it's also a way back in with Reid. I can edit a "hype" video in my sleep at the end of the weekend, but in the meantime, I can see how he's doing. Apologize.

Try to repair what I broke.

In truth, my decision has nothing to do with Legacy and everything to do with Reid.

I guess I'm going to a party.

CHAPTER SIX

CLARA

THEN

"**THIS IS THE FIRST** night I've been out in, like, months," Delaney said. It was a warm evening in early October, but she was wearing a baggy sweatshirt and only her manicured fingertips poked out of the sleeves as she drove to Kenji's house.

"I seriously need to unleash tonight. This Legacy shit is kicking my ass," Amaya said, checking her lip gloss and smoothing her already immaculately straight black hair in the visor mirror.

I nodded along with everyone else.

Between school, homework, cross-country, filming, and work, I was *always* busy. And it wasn't just me. Nicole had tacked on extra runs to her training schedule, Amaya had been cast as the lead in the fall play, and it seemed like no matter when I texted Delaney, she was at the dance studio. Though Legacies wouldn't be chosen for months once we submitted our official applications, they made it very clear all our behavior and extracurriculars mattered. No rule breaking, no missteps.

How were we supposed to sustain this?

My phone buzzed with a text from my dad—his response to my question from *last* week asking if he was going to come back for Legacy Weekend.

> **Dad:** Not going to make it. Briana doesn't think it's a good idea. Tell your mom for me?

I read it three times looking for the apology or acknowledgment that he hadn't reached out once since he left that summer.

Of course, there was none. Because the opinion of the woman who he broke Mom's heart for was apparently more important than his relationship with his daughter. I was no better than Mom in hoping that the lure of his former glory days might be reason enough to bring him home even if I wasn't.

"Awwww," Amaya sighed. "Josh just texted telling me to hurry up and get to the party. He was so distant when I was in New York this summer, but ever since I've been home he's been, like, so in love with me."

Guilt and shame roiled through me all over again about what happened with Josh. I guess I was no better than Dad, either.

As we made our way up the side of the mountain where Kenji lived, Amaya went on and on about what an amazing boyfriend Josh was.

Nicole rolled her eyes and finally cut her off by saying, "I hope Reid's coming tonight." Her voice was almost pained as she said it.

Amaya's laugh carried from the front seat. "You're so obsessed."

Delaney shot me a look in the rearview that I pretended not to see since I was *obviously* busy studying the fascinating buttons on my camera.

"Have you and Reid been talking?" Delaney asked Nicole.

I suppressed a smile at her protective tone.

Nicole bit her lip and nodded. "Well, sort of. We've been running together. He pushed me at practice yesterday, but in a way that made me *want* to go as hard as possible. He's intense, but"—she paused, searching for the right word—"sweet," she concluded.

Exactly, I thought. But I wasn't about to say that out loud. Though Delaney had squashed the rumor about the party in its tracks, and Josh and Amaya were back together again, stories about the "mystery girl" had spread through the school like an oil spill.

Ridiculous lies that he and the mystery girl had sex, that there was more than one mystery girl in the room, that there was more than one *guy* in the room. I sometimes wondered if Josh was the person behind it, spreading rumors about himself for some sort of locker room clout.

Delaney and Kenji told me they'd heard my name come up once or twice after that practice, but Amaya didn't believe any of it. It seemed I was in the clear. But my brush with calamity was enough to keep my mouth shut and my mind focused the rest of Legacy year.

We arrived at Kenji's and piled into his house, where music boomed and people were already yelling and laughing. The three of them beelined for the kitchen to get drinks, but after that summer party, I'd steered clear of alcohol. No more messy mistakes. I hid behind my camera as I wandered around.

The scene was familiar; people playing a drinking game around a table, a few girls having a teary conversation, the guys ribbing one another as they tested who could lift the heaviest stuff around Kenji's house. I captured it all, as unobtrusively as possible.

But not everyone liked the spotlight.

Nicole put her hand up to cover my lens when I got close. "Please don't," she said, annoyed.

I nodded and backed away. It didn't always work when I tried to catch people off guard. And sometimes they surprised me, too.

Like when Logan Harper, a lacrosse player with sandy hair and light freckles across his nose, reached for Mitchell's hand under the table across the room.

Above the table, they pretended like nothing was happening. Like they weren't even paying attention to each other. They played the part well, their eyes only snagging on the other for a brief moment.

But when Logan's thumb brushed across the back of his hand, Mitchell beamed in response.

I whipped the camera away. As far as I knew, neither of them were out. Sometimes it was unclear what was okay to document versus what was straight-up intrusive. But I definitely drew the line at outing anyone.

I quickly darted into the adjoining room, and my footsteps faltered because tucked into a chair in the back corner sat the very person I didn't know I was looking for.

Reid.

A few people milled around talking. I ducked behind a towering bookshelf and watched him for a second. I'd rarely seen him outside of practice and never in anything but athletic clothes. That night he was wearing a toffee-colored T-shirt and jeans. It was simple, but the color was so flattering he managed to make it look stylish. His head was bent over a notebook, pen flying across the pages. It was the same notebook I'd noticed he pulled out on bus rides to races or after practice sometimes. He tugged on an earring absentmindedly while he wrote.

It was practically offensive how good he looked in the soft light.

"It's rude to stare." He hadn't even looked up.

I startled and turned off the camera, quickly grabbing a book from the bookshelf to pretend to read. My heart hammered against my rib cage as his footsteps approached on the honey-colored hardwood. I realized too late I could've just greeted him like a normal person, but I was nervous. It confused me that seeing him made me nervous. I refused to look up when his feet stopped close to me, pretending to be completely absorbed in—

"*How Not to Get Caught Spying*," he joked, making up a title. He grimaced. "Don't think that one's helping you out much."

I looked up slowly—with *dignity*—and met Reid's eyes. They were cackling. It was *actually* book one from my favorite fantasy series that I loaned Kenji months ago that he clearly hadn't even opened.

"Hilarious." I slammed the book against Reid's chest, and he grabbed it before it fell.

He grinned. "Thanks, but I'm actually on book three."

I glared at him, thrown by the way his deep voice thrummed through my body. "You read *Glass Swords*?"

"*You* read *Glass Swords*?" Reid asked, the teasing tone replaced by surprise.

"Most people have never even heard of it," I said, suspicious that he was still messing with me.

He gave me a leveling look and walked over to his backpack, which was tucked beside the chair. He pulled out the green hardcover I knew well and offered it to me as proof.

Instead of lingering on the adorable fact that he brought a book to a party, I opened to where he was in the story. Oh. He didn't know yet that Yesenia didn't survive. I'd cried so hard while reading it that tear tracks stained my copy. He was only a few chapters away.

"Whoa, spoiler alert," he said.

My eyes went wide as they met his. "I didn't say anything!"

"You didn't have to. Yesenia dies, doesn't she?"

Shit, did he really get that from my face?

He pushed a hand through his hair. "I knew it. She sacrifices herself in an epic battle, forcing her brother to take the throne so Una can live a simple life with Felix. Right?"

My mouth fell open. "Wha— How did— I didn't say—"

He let out a massive laugh then. Shoulders shaking, the corners of his eyes crinkling. He was very pleased with himself. "Your face. Priceless. I'm rereading it."

I should have been more annoyed, but I had never heard him laugh before. It was loud and throaty and . . . addictive.

Still, I scowled. "I thought I ruined it for you!"

"With a look?" he said, his laughter slowing. "You're not that easy to read. Trust me."

The mirth shifted to something new that flipped my stomach. I turned my attention back to the book, running my fingers down the spine. "I can't believe we have to wait another year for the next one. I wish I could just read this all night tonight."

"Not in the partying mood?" he asked.

"Not really."

"Then why'd you come?"

For some reason, I felt the impulse to be honest. To tell him that I did whatever I could to stay out of the house when Mom was in a dark place, which had been happening more and more. Dread encroached knowing it would get worse once I told her about Dad's text.

But I swallowed the urge to air my sad little story and held up my camera. "Yearbook duty. Team events always give good content. I want to be a documentary filmmaker, and I need all the practice I can get."

I don't know why I told him. Guys I was used to, guys like Josh, usually made fun of my love for documentaries. *You're too hot to be so boring, Clara.*

I rushed to say, "I know it's nerdy, but—"

Reid's warm smile cut me off. "That's really cool."

The thud made us both jump when the book hit the floor. We each scrambled for it. Crouched down low, our eyes caught.

"Besides," he continued, "*Glass Swords* is *way* nerdier."

A surprised laugh escaped me. "True."

His gaze moved all around my face. Delaney had done my eye makeup a little darker than usual, and I wondered if he noticed. What he thought.

"Your sweater matches your eyes," he said.

The hairs on my neck rose, and my response tumbled over a nervous laugh. "That is such a cheesy line."

He frowned. "It wasn't a line. You look beautiful."

No one had ever called me beautiful before. Cute maybe. Pretty sometimes. But never beautiful. It kicked my heart into a sprint. I was so unfamiliar with whatever feeling was bubbling up in me I panic-blurted, "Nicole's gonna be so excited you're here."

His dark eyebrows furrowed further as we both stood slowly. "Nicole?"

"She's been talking about you nonstop," I said. "I think she likes you."

Confusion shifted to genuine surprise. "Oh."

I winced. In my nervous haste, I was pretty sure I had broken girl code.

"So, yeah, tonight," I kept going, my tone light, my mouth incapable of shutting up, "you're here, and she's here. You can hang out."

A group of juniors walked by, squeezing past us to get to the next room. It forced me to take a step closer to Reid, and heat prickled my cheeks. At five foot nine I wasn't used to people towering over me. He did.

He scanned my face again. "So. You want me to hang out with *Nicole* tonight?"

"No. That's not what I said—"

"Then you don't want me to hang out with her?"

Was he enjoying watching me squirm? "I don't care what you do. Just, be nice to her. Please don't tell her I told you all that. And definitely don't do *this.*" I gestured up and down between us.

He looked down at himself, then back to me. "Do what?"

"You know, your whole annoying, hot-guy thing."

"'Hot-guy thing'?"

"You missed the 'annoying' part."

Amusement lit his eyes again, and he shook his head slowly. "I don't think I missed anything."

My hands felt so heavy I didn't know what to do with them. Just like I didn't know what to do with *that.*

Flustered, I pulled my hair off my neck. "I just meant—"

From the other room, Kenji yelled in a singsong voice, "Who wants to play truth or daaaaaaare?"

Delaney appeared at my elbow and pulled me toward the circle in the living room. "We do!"

"We do?" I huffed. "Because we're twelve?"

"Because it'll be *fun,*" she whispered back, the vodka on her breath explaining her enthusiasm.

"Us too!" Mitchell called, yanking Reid by the arm.

Delaney exchanged a look with Mitchell as he pushed Reid down so we were seated next to each other in the circle. The narrow space between my arm and his hummed.

The game started innocently enough. Truths about worst fears and first hookups and *Was that really only mud on your leg at the Mount Diablo Invitational*? Dares to eat a raw piece of garlic, and do fifty push-ups, and remove an item of clothing (Mitchell chose one sock).

But the more people loosened up and drank, the more fiery it got. Amaya was dared to give Hunter Bishop a thirty-second lap dance that got entirely too uncomfortable and put Josh in a terrible mood. Jensen Hughes admitted that he and Heather hooked up in the bathroom at the Woodhurst Invitational last month—a fact that she had clearly planned on taking to the grave as she stormed out crying. Then Josh stepped in with an agenda playing out just behind his eyes. They sharpened on Logan.

"Logan," he asked. "Truth or dare?"

Logan's gaze shifted around the group, then back to Josh, assessing which option would be less painful. Finally he said, "Truth, I guess."

I tried not to cringe. Josh was the least creative guy on the planet. He would've dared Logan to chug a glass of milk or something. But truth? Josh would go for something juicy.

"Who gave you that bracelet?" Josh asked.

All eyes fell to Logan's wrist. It was a thin, braided-leather band that I never would've noticed. It was only the way Logan's hand flew to it, his cheeks flaming pink, that gave away it was something special. Private.

"None of your business," Logan finally said, flicking the subtlest of gazes to Mitchell on the other side of the circle.

Josh shrugged. "It's truth or dare, man. You had a choice."

Logan rolled his eyes. "I'm not playing, then."

"Oh, c'mon, just tell us! Noah would make you if he was here."

Logan visibly bristled at the mention of his older brother, a lacrosse

Legacy and Woodhurst legend for winning a championship game against our rivals. Though word got around that he had gone to rehab last year.

"She can't be *that* hideous," Josh prodded.

A few of the guys laughed. Reid didn't.

"Josh, let it go," Kenji said, his tone light but laced with annoyance just the same. Kenji was one of the few openly queer people at school, and I had a feeling he knew what was going on with Mitchell and Logan. I wondered sometimes if he threw parties like this to constantly stay on the offense. For as many people in Woodhurst who were accepting and open, there were just as many who weren't.

Logan's cheeks flamed brighter, and Mitchell's voice sprang out, cutting off all conversation. "Okay, someone else go!" He eyed Delaney, who picked up on it right away.

She set down her cup, her eyes a little glassy. "Yeah, my turn!" The attention fell to her when she said, "Reid."

He went still beside me. "Yeah?"

"Truth or dare?"

His expression didn't change as he eyed her closely. I wished I could've warned him that I had a guess as to what she was up to. We had a long-standing party rule to have each other's backs, which might have been why I let Nicole's crush slip. A conflicted part of me trying to help. Like when Delaney liked Marcus Jones in seventh grade? I rigged it so that they went into the closet together.

Best seven minutes of my life, she'd sighed afterward.

But we weren't in seventh grade anymore. She wouldn't do something so middle school in front of the entire team . . . probably.

Reid's deep voice cut through my thoughts. "Dare."

Delaney pressed her lips together, trying and failing to conceal her excitement. I remembered then that I had told her what he'd said to me at the lake: *I take dares seriously.*

Oh no.

"I dare you"—she exchanged the most obvious glance with Mitchell—"to kiss Clara."

There was a thrilled murmur from the group. I kept my eyes locked on Delaney's face, hoping she could read the absolute fury in them. She ignored me.

I slowly turned to face Reid; his expression was stark, serious. "I'm not going to do that unless she says it's okay."

"It's okay," I said, without ever giving my mouth permission to do so. I couldn't keep my usual cool for even a second.

That's when I knew I liked him.

"But you don't have to," I said quickly.

His gaze collided with mine. "I know."

My attention narrowed to the thud of my heart and the full shape of his lips as he closed in, his woodsy scent crowding me. Was it shaving cream? Cologne? I didn't care, I wanted to curl myself around it. Needed to be closer to him.

Around us, people were whispering and laughing.

He shifted, and the angle of his broad shoulders acted as a shield blotting out everyone and everything else. Our noses grazed, his breath hot across my lips when he said just to me, "This really okay?"

"Yes," I breathed.

Then it was happening.

A dared kiss was supposed to be quick. Over in a second. Besides, he was shy. I figured it would be a fast peck.

There was nothing shy about the way Reid kissed.

He took quiet command, his soft lips grabbing for mine. Once.

Twice. Harder. Goose bumps flew across my skin as I inhaled him, shocked at the need fueling me. I opened my mouth to his, urging him on. Still, it wasn't enough. I wanted to grab his shirt, thread my fingers through his hair—

"Okay, *we get it*."

Josh's sharp voice shocked me back into the room. I pulled away, breathless. I was faintly aware of conversation happening around us, but in that moment I saw only Reid. Who the hell did he think he was, kissing me like that? I was *not* prepared.

But reality crashed into focus as I tore my gaze away and looked around the room, immediately locking eyes with Nicole. Though her entire face had gone red, her expression was unreadable.

"Why do you care?" Amaya asked Josh.

"I don't, it was just getting excessive," he scoffed.

"You sound jealous," Amaya said.

"Babe, c'mon."

Worst of all was Logan, who looked at the ground, his face blank. It occurred to me how unfair it was that he didn't feel comfortable talking about an innocent bracelet, and there I was, allowed to kiss Reid like my life depended on it in front of our entire team.

"Calm down, it was just a dare," I called out, trying to get everyone to chill.

But it didn't work. Amaya and Josh started bickering louder.

Reid frowned at me, and I kept my voice low so only he could hear me. "Right?"

His stare was so penetrating it added weight to my limbs. "Right."

I swallowed, a thousand different feelings cascading through me like a waterfall.

Nicole's raised voice cut into the moment. "Josh, truth or dare?"

That got everyone's attention.

"Um . . ." He looked at Amaya as if assessing which was the right choice. "Truth."

Nicole's smile curled like a Cheshire cat's. "Who did Heather see you go into that room with at the party when Amaya was in New York this summer?"

My stomach crashed to the floor.

"*Nicole,*" Amaya shot out. "He said nothing happened."

Nicole scoffed. "And you believe him?"

Everyone stared at Josh, but he was focused on Amaya.

"She's just looking for attention as usual," he said dismissively.

Amaya scowled. "Don't talk about her like that."

"But she's allowed to call me out with bullshit like this?"

"You could've chosen dare," Nicole interjected.

"I have nothing to hide."

Amaya kept her gaze steady on Josh. "You swear you didn't lie to me?"

Josh's expression went soft. "Do you really think I would cheat on you while you were at the biggest audition of your life?"

He made the lie sound so effortless, *I* almost believed it. Which seriously grossed me out.

When Nicole scoffed again, Josh turned a glare onto her. "Why are you always stirring up shit between us, Nic?"

Nicole went pinker with the accusation, but she glared right back. "Why are *you* always doing shit that hurts my best friend?"

"You don't know what you're talking about."

Amaya buried her face in her hands, sounding on the verge of tears. "Stop it. I'm *so* sick of you guys fighting."

The truth was on the tip of my tongue; I was sure that everyone would hate me, that Reid would be disgusted with me, but at least it would be out in the open and we could deal with it. I hadn't known that they were still together. It didn't need to cause such a problem.

Then Logan chimed in, as if grateful to pounce on something that would get him on Josh's good side. "Maybe it wasn't Josh's fault."

Everyone looked interested in that theory, especially Josh. Sweat sprang to my hairline. What was he doing?

Logan continued. "I mean, some girls would do *anything* to get a Legacy spot. Following the principal's son into a room at a party . . . probably telling him no one had to know . . . hoping he'd put in a good word . . ." He trailed off.

Was that sexist comment seriously what he thought? What they would all think?

The group went quiet as the suggestion settled in, their eyes flashing at the blood in the water.

Reid's expression shuttered. "You can't possibly believe that."

But it was too late.

They already did.

CHAPTER SEVEN

REID

NOW

TWO DAYS UNTIL LEGACY BANQUET

@haikuforyou
The rain falls in sheets
lands in droplets on my hand
together, alone.

KENJI'S ANNUAL LEGACY PARTY is already packed when Mitchell and I get there. I can't believe he convinced me to come. I shouldn't even be home yet. But this morning, I was standing outside my bio class fully intending to go in when that photo of the lake came through the group chat.

I didn't think. I just walked straight back to my dorm, threw my laundry in the truck, and drove the four hours to Woodhurst for the first time since I left. Now that I'm here, I'm not sure why I was in such a big hurry.

A lot of people from my old team are catching up, and I already feel like a fraud walking among them. I could've at least put on a nicer shirt.

With its high ceilings and wide windows showing stunning views of the mountain, Kenji's place is one of the nicest houses in Woodhurst. The Yoshinos used to run some sort of tech company before they moved here, when Woodhurst started to become this odd collection of families who have Bay Area runoff money and the rest of us who . . . don't.

I follow Mitch down the carpeted steps to the basement where we used to hang out for parties. I weave through everyone as quickly as I can, my head swiveling around the crowded room, waiting to catch a glimpse of dark hair or sharp green eyes. I don't.

But her car's outside. I know she's here, and it's twisting me into knots. Ever since she sent that picture, I don't know what to think. She hasn't said a word since I hit the heart icon. We're off to a great start.

Someone calls my name, and my gut clenches as I turn. It's Nicole Kelly, a pretty redhead with a monster kick from the girls varsity team. We were always friendly, but we haven't really spoken since graduation.

Her sunny smile as she approaches takes me right back to the training trails. How she'd yell at me between breaths, "C'mon, Rousseau, pick up your feet."

"If you can talk, you're not pushing hard enough," I'd shoot back.

Which is exactly the kind of memory I wanted to avoid tonight, but I guess I don't have a choice. She hugs me quickly.

"How's school?" I ask.

Her hands stay planted on my shoulders, holding me a little too close to her. "The best! I PR'd at the Glenview Invitational."

Jealousy ripples through me. "Nice."

Someone walks behind me, and I step out of their way, subtly shrugging Nicole's hands off in the process.

"Seriously, I still can't believe I get to go there every day. Like, I think about it sometimes—if I hadn't become a Legacy, I would've had to go to my, like, fifth-choice school. Instead, I'm training with the best. I can't help but feel like none of this should be happening to me."

Because it shouldn't, I think. Nicole's deserving in her own way, but it's such a confusing thing to be happy for a former teammate when I know what *not* getting the scholarship did to Clara. How unfair that still seems.

"How *is* Clara?" Nicole asks, her tone thoughtful.

I shake my head slowly. Hoping that's answer enough.

She brightens. "Got it. *Sore subject, Nicole.*" She laughs, but I can't even pretend to. "Well, you should know that my coach lost it when she found out I used to run with you. I mean, it's not every day you run with an Olympic hopeful!"

"Don't believe everything you hear," I say.

She rolls her eyes playfully. "Okay, keep your secrets to yourself for now. Delaney has all weekend to get it out of you."

"Delaney?"

She laughs again. "Remember how she always knew everything about everyone?"

"Oh, right." I force a laugh in an attempt to calm my spiked pulse.

When I can tell she's about to ask me more about *my* season, I excuse myself, saying I need a drink. But really, I need air.

I swivel my head around one more time looking for *her,* only to run into Kenji. He wraps me in a bear hug.

"Mitchell with you?" he asks, pinching the cuff of his white dress shirtsleeve to adjust it.

As if on cue, Mitchell walks up holding two red cups. I don't want to know what's in them, but if he's gunning for Legacy this year it better not be liquor.

Kenji doesn't pull Mitchell into a hug when he sees him. Instead, he hits him gently on the shoulder. "Hey."

Mitchell grins and hits him back. "Hey."

I frown as I look between them. Why are they being so weird?

In spite of myself, I scan the room again.

"Clara's not down here," Mitchell states as if he can read my every thought. It annoys me so much I'm tempted to punch him.

"I don't know what you're talking about," I grumble.

He starts laughing. "Sure, okay."

"How's she been?" Kenji asks Mitchell. I'm pretty sure he does it so I don't have to, and I shoot him a grateful look.

Mitchell sighs. "Kind of a mess, honestly."

I wish that made me feel better, but it doesn't. I don't like thinking of her in pain. Or of anyone else comforting her.

"Reid!" It's Nicole again, tugging on my arm. "My friends at school don't believe me that I'm hanging out with you."

She holds up her phone and rests her head on my shoulder as she takes a picture of us.

"They're going to freak out. They're always like, 'You're such a liar!' But boom—sent."

I force a smile, dying a little inside. "Uh, happy to help."

"We'll have to get one of all of us Legacies," she says.

In the next instant, Amaya approaches and Nicole pulls her into a squealing hug. I don't know how to extricate myself this time, so I stand with them awhile as they laugh and talk and reminisce about high school.

"Did you guys see that Legacy Lore account?" Amaya asks at one point, her expression worried.

She must mean that profile Kenji sent earlier. I nod. I barely looked at it, but I didn't like it. Not the vague threats about us or the way it referenced the assembly last year.

"It's wild the way people come for Legacies," Kenji says.

Nicole rolls her eyes. "It has, like, twelve followers." She puts one hand on Amaya's arm and the other one on mine. "I doubt it's anything to worry about."

Amaya nods, but she doesn't look particularly reassured. I don't blame her.

Holding on to the privileges of Legacy—the sizable scholarship money and opportunities and status it provides—requires agreeing to several stipulations. Most important: not doing anything (at least publicly) that could threaten the Legacy image.

At the time, the money was such a help it seemed like a no-brainer to agree to the terms. But the more I have to hide, the more the golden handcuffs chafe. The more an account like Legacy Lore could do real damage.

Once the group is fully absorbed in conversation again, I take the opportunity to dip. I'm almost in the clear as I round the corner toward the stairs, except Delaney is standing there in a black dress and dark red lipstick, her blond hair up in a high ponytail on top of her head. She's pale, her cheekbones sharper than when I saw her just a month ago.

She tracks me immediately. My heart starts pumping harder as she stands there staring at me, as if expecting me to know what to say in this awkward-as-hell situation.

I don't, but I go with "Hey."

Delaney narrows her eyes. "So you *are* alive."

"I've been busy," I say, shoving my hands in my pockets.

"It's been a month, Reid."

I let out a breath. It shakes.

"I'm sorry." I mean it.

She must sense that I do because the stark line between her eyebrows smooths out. Then she hits me in the shoulder, *hard.* Delaney is small, but she's strong from her years of dancing, and I splutter out a surprised cough. "I've been so worried about you. Texting you, calling you."

I can't let her worry in. I don't want anyone's concern or care. "I know."

Her hands ball into fists, and she lets out a small, aggravated noise. "I'm starting to believe all the Olympics rumors."

"That's not it."

"So you've been ignoring me becaaaauuuuse?"

Heat shoots up my neck. "I don't know."

Except that I do. We both do.

Delaney tightens her ponytail and looks me dead in the eyes. "I can't keep doing this. The guilt is eating me up. Clara's here. You have to let me tell her, Reid."

My lungs go tight. *Fuck.* There are some lines you just don't cross. Clara would never get over it.

"You can't. You know you can't."

Delaney exhales hard. "I *have* to."

I step toward her, keeping my voice so low I have to lean in closer than I want to. But I don't want to risk anyone overhearing. "Delaney, *please.* I need time."

There's conflict all over her face, but before she can answer, Kenji's voice booms through a microphone. "Who's ready for karaoke?!"

There's an excited burst of sound from the group in response. With so many former theater kids here, it'll last all night.

Kill me now.

Delaney gets pulled away by Nicole for a picture, and I turn to leave.

Just like after that first party last year, when I kissed Clara on a dare—a kiss that messed with my head for weeks afterward—I need to get out of here. But there's a small group of guys laughing near the door, blocking my smooth exit.

Among them is the last person I want to see: Josh West.

My chest puffs up on instinct. I've dealt with guys like Josh on every team I've ever been on. They're obnoxious at best and dangerous at worst. Everything about him puts me on edge. When he notices me, his top lip curls into a sneer.

"Rousseau," he says.

I toss him an acknowledging nod, hoping to keep it at that. But he continues.

"Heard about the fall."

My heart drops into my stomach.

Of course he did. We're not in the same division, but word gets around in a sport as small as ours. Still, I have to remind myself that not even my own trainer knows the extent of my pain. He's sniffing me out, trying to get me to own up to something by pretending he already knows.

At least I hope he's pretending.

"You in rehab or whatever?"

"Or whatever," I respond.

Annoyance flashes across his face. "Always such a tool," he mutters.

I smirk. It's nice to know some things never change.

He takes a pull of his drink, then wipes his mouth with the back of his hand. "So now that you're damaged goods, is Stanford gonna drop your ass?"

"Who says I'm damaged?"

It's Josh's turn to smirk. "Your team likes to talk."

Coach explained early on they couldn't pull my scholarship just because I got hurt, but if my grades stay as bad as they are, not even my coaches can save me from academic probation. I just hope it doesn't come to that.

Or that Coach hasn't lost interest in me already.

"There's no way that Olympic shit is real," Josh states.

This time he's right. No matter what the Olympic coach and I talked about in April, I'm out of that conversation if I can't even get my ass to regionals.

I shrug in response because I owe Josh nothing and it's the best nonanswer to life's most annoying people.

Josh's eyes flash. "Guess you won't have any problem at the 5K tomorrow, then?"

Shit. I forgot about the Legacy 5K Fun Run.

The entire town is invited, but nobody usually shows up outside of the cross-country team and their families. Still, it's a little over three miles, and I've just ensured that Josh will give it everything he's got. If I don't beat him, everyone will know something's up with me.

But if I run, I could fuck up my knee even worse and completely screw myself over for regionals. For the entire year.

"How's Amaya?" I ask, pointedly changing the subject, knowing full well she dumped his ass and was shooting him glares during our entire conversation earlier.

He narrows his eyes. "How's *Clara*?"

Though I've been wanting to sock him since the first time he talked down to Clara, I keep my stance casual and say nothing. I've noticed the longer I let a silence stretch with a guy like Josh, the more likely he'll either spin himself up or lose interest. I watch and wait to see which way this will go.

Josh leans closer and gestures with a lift of his chin toward something over my shoulder. "I've heard about more than just your season."

I turn around and see Delaney dancing and talking with a few of the other girls from the pom squad.

He doesn't mean . . . No. There's no way he knows. I didn't tell anyone about what happened. Unless . . .

Did *she* say something?

You have to let me tell her, Reid.

Everything I've been shoving down or turning against myself comes to attention. What happened was bad enough. But *Josh* hearing about it makes it a lot fucking worse.

"'The Golden Boy,'" he mocks, quoting what our local paper once called me. "What a joke." He pushes past me, clipping my shoulder.

I lean back against the wall as he starts walking, thinking he bested me.

"The real joke is that I was already better at fifteen than you'll ever be."

He stops.

"Not to mention your dad picked me as the guest of honor over his own son." I cock my head to the side and grin. "Hilarious."

His face goes red as he lunges toward me. I push off from the wall with one foot in response, but before I can get close enough to swing at him, Mitchell appears out of nowhere and shoves me back with a meaty slap to my chest. Mitch may be younger, but he's taller than both me and Josh and looks every inch the multi-hyphenate athlete he is.

"You got a problem?" Mitch asks, swiveling his attention on Josh.

"Several," I mutter.

A sheen of sweat coats Josh's forehead and upper lip. His eyes dart between us.

"Watch your back, Rousseau," he says.

I give him a mock salute. "Easy enough since you're always behind me."

Mitchell's shoulders release once Josh steps outside, and he rounds on me. "Do you *want* to get your ass kicked?"

I roll my eyes. "That's not what would've happened."

Mitchell crosses his arms, unconvinced. "Since when do you go looking for fights?"

"Since when did you start sounding like your mom?"

He narrows his eyes. "Low."

Another karaoke song starts, and I wince. I've always struggled with clashing noise, and with the pop song in one room, and Amaya belting a Broadway ballad in another, every nerve in my body starts to fray.

Mitchell notices and shoves me into the hallway where it's quieter. "Seriously, Reid. It's not like you to let someone like Josh get under your skin."

I clench my jaw. I don't like that he's right. But I can't explain it, either.

"People change" is all I say.

Without waiting for a response, I finally escape by bounding up the stairs and heading to the deck where I used to sneak away whenever parties got too overwhelming.

As soon as I slide the door open and step out into the clear night, my heart stops.

Clara is standing there.

CHAPTER EIGHT

CLARA

NOW

I LOWER THE CAMERA and turn, somehow knowing who will be standing there a second before our eyes lock.

Reid.

Reid is *here*. Home. A day early. Wearing a gray shirt and dark jeans and an expression that's just as stunned as I feel. I'm pretty sure "Holy shit" tumbles out of my mouth, but I might just think it.

"Yeah," he responds, a little breathless.

Okay, I definitely said it.

His gaze slowly traces my face, my body, like his fingertips used to. I'm wearing a short maroon skirt and black tee. A sliver of my stomach shows, and I tug on the hem of the shirt a bit to make sure my tattoo is covered.

I'm not ready for *that* conversation yet. With anyone.

He lingers on my bare legs a fraction longer than anywhere else, and heat flashes across my cheekbones.

I stare back. I can't even pretend like I'm not hungry to take him in and absorb every detail. Everything new (the shadows under his eyes), everything familiar (the way he taps the side of his leg when he's nervous). His longer hair falls in a slightly styled wave over his forehead. My fingers twitch to weave through it and tousle it a bit. I always preferred it a little messy.

The deck creaks under my boots as I step toward him. But his shoulders go rigid the closer I get, and I force myself to stop. I fiddle with the camera strap and try like hell to play it cool. I don't want him to know how untethered I feel.

"The guest of honor has arrived," I say, my smile slowly rising.

An unreadable expression flickers across his features. Though the scent of woodsmoke floats around us from a neighboring fireplace reminding us it's almost fall, his skin still carries the golden tan of summer.

When he doesn't say anything, I try again. "I thought you weren't supposed to get here until tomorrow."

He clears his throat and doesn't meet my eyes when he explains. "My class was canceled today. Figured I might as well beat the traffic."

"Smart," I say, nodding too hard. "It's bad on long weekends."

Traffic. Months of silence and we're talking about traffic.

"You look—" I want to say "good." And while he's still every bit as devastating, he also looks wrung out. "Collegiate," I finish instead.

"That's code for 'tired,' isn't it?"

Damn. I forgot how good he is at sifting through my words for the real meaning. When I smile, the corner of his mouth lifts. It unfurls the tension in my chest a bit.

Is he still upset about everything? Or worse, over it? Maybe that's why he hearted the picture. Instead of it being a chance, it's proof he's moved on. Why is that only occurring to me *now*?

His eyes drop to my hands, and I release my twisted fingers.

"So, how are you?" I ask, lightly smacking his arm with the back of my hand. Casual, breezy. As if he's someone I barely know instead of someone who's trailed kisses down my spine. As if I don't torture myself with wondering if he's done that with anyone else. "Mitchell tells me nothing."

His jaw—sharper than it used to be—jumps. "Yeah, you and Mitchell. That's . . . new."

There's something I don't understand simmering under his words. "We're the last two standing from the group." I shrug. "It's chill, you know?"

Every line on his face sharpens with annoyance. He opens his mouth like he's going to respond, then closes it again as if thinking better of it. Shaking his head, he says, "Clara, I . . . don't think we can do this."

I always loved it when he said my name. Not like our friends or anyone else at school, but the way he's heard *me* say it. *Clah*-ra instead of Clare-uh. Except now there's a bite to it that was never there before.

My chest is rising rapidly, embarrassment crawling up my neck. "Do what?"

He shoves his hands in his pockets and looks past me instead of responding.

Frustration leaches into my tone. "We can't exchange pleasantries? That's kind of the bare minimum of human interaction. I ask how you are, and you say, 'fine.' You ask how I am, and I say, 'fine—'"

"Clara."

"Then maybe we mention the weather, or the traffic. But you did *that* already—"

"Clara."

"Then we go our separate ways." I ignore how unhinged I sound and cross my arms tight.

His dark brown eyes finally lock on mine, intense and stormy and still so hurt. But I keep my expression passive. Unbothered. My vibrating hands tucked firmly against me.

"So, are you? Fine?"

He sighs. "Not really. You?"

I take in a shaky breath. "Not really."

A thousand aching questions swirl between us.

"There," I say, my voice close to breaking. "We did it."

When his eyes go a little softer, my throat threatens to close on a sob. I swallow hard, forcing down every word that wants to spill out of my mouth. Every memory that wants to come back. Every hurt that ripped open the second he said my name.

He's studying me closely now. "This is hard for me, too," he says gently.

Tears do spring to my eyes then. *Damn it.* He was always so disarmingly honest. I loved that about him. I think I still do.

I force out a shaky "Yeah. I'll just . . . go."

We can't even get through a conversation. Why did I think he'd want to see me this weekend? That he'd let me film him? Interview him? I was right before, I should've stayed home.

But as I walk by him, he reaches out and closes a hand around mine. "Wait." He squeezes his eyes tight and exhales. "Shit."

We hover. My hand in his.

The urge to fold myself into him and feel the press of his body against mine is so strong it's a physical pain in my chest.

He swipes his free hand across his forehead. "I didn't expect to see you—I didn't know you were . . ." He trails off, gesturing to me.

"What? Here? I still live here, Reid. Never left." My voice is piercing and defensive, bordering on bitter. We notice at the same time his hand is still wrapped around mine. He releases it and meets my eye again.

"Filming," he clarifies. "I didn't know you were filming."

A self-conscious flush burns my cheeks. "Oh. Well. I'm boring." I point to myself, trying to make a joke. "Remember? Hates parties. Loves trees. Films to avoid people. I haven't changed."

His eyebrows come together. "You would've had to."

My expression must convey that I don't get what he means because he goes on. "You were never boring. Tough. Fun. *Nerdy*." The corner of his mouth lifts again, the barest hint. "But definitely not boring."

The distance between us hurts, but this hint of sweetness from him is agonizing. Because now I'm clinging to those words and stuffing them into my mind to turn over later.

"Are you working on something for CAFA?" he asks.

"No." I shake my head quickly and can't quite meet his eye. "I'm taking a break from all that."

I rush to fill the awkward pause by telling him about my run-in with Principal West and the video for the banquet. My voice sounds nervy when I say, "I'm supposed to interview every Legacy."

Reid and I have drifted closer. So close I can see the scar under his chin from when he fell off the swings in kindergarten. So close I could reach out and grip his hair in the way that used to make him hum.

So close I can really see just how different and unsure he seems.

Reserved. Or dimmed in some way. He's always had too much weighing on him.

While I know Principal West could insist that Reid participate in the video and I originally thought filming together could be a good thing, I realize how unfair it is to not give him the choice. He deserves that.

"I know an interview is a lot to ask after—" I cut myself off, afraid to bring up anything that will make this harder than it already is. "I just mean you don't have to."

He opens his mouth to respond when the sliding glass door opens and Kenji bursts out onto the deck, his guitar strapped across his back and fluffy blankets spilling out of his arms.

"There you are!" His eyes bounce between us, a scheme plain on his face. "We've been looking for you two. C'mon, we're going to the field."

Reid and I exchange an awkward glance.

He clears his throat. "Actually, I think I'm gonna head out—"

"Absolutely not, we never get to hang." Kenji tosses a blanket at Reid and grabs a hold of each of our arms, yanking us along. "*C'mon.* Just the crew."

With a heavy sigh, Reid goes with him. I could stay up here, or leave before they notice I'm gone. But as Reid walks off, it leaves me with more questions than before.

Was he limping? Why does he look so tired? What's really going on with him?

What if I never know?

The thought of him never opening up to me again—of it truly never being like it was between us again—is a stunning realization.

Something I don't fully understand steels in me. I can't let that happen.

I *won't* let that happen.

I take off after them, bolting down the stairs to keep up. But a group is rushing up at the same time, and someone knocks into me, sending my camera tumbling off my shoulder.

"Shit!"

Reid turns at the clattering crash of my camera hitting the ground, but I barely register him doubling back. I scramble to pick it up, examining it closely, hunched on the floor.

There's no obvious damage, but plenty could still be wrong. I check the focus and the lens, panning around the party. But it's too dark. When I step into the closest room and flip on the lights, I instantly regret it.

Because Nicole and Logan are tangled on a bed, kissing with enthusiasm. Enthusiasm that dies the second they see me and my camera pointed at them.

"Oh my god!" Nicole springs back, her hair mussed, her black shirt twisted around her torso. She scrambles away from Logan. "Are you *filming*?"

"No!" I lower the camera, flustered all over again. "Well, yes, technically it's recording, but I didn't mean to—I'll delete it."

I back up, but my shoulder blades hit a strong chest. It's only then I realize Reid followed me. The lift of hope I feel at that is instantly muted by the strangeness of walking in on two people I've barely ever seen talk to each other, all over each other. That Legacy Lore post pops into my head.

@LEGACY_LORE: There's a lot more to this class of illustrious Legacies than meets the eye.

They're not wrong.

My back is still up against the heat of Reid's torso, and I step away quickly. Nicole watches the whole thing, pressing her lips together in a way that increases the furious look on her face.

I spare a glimpse at Logan, who is fixing his hair in the mirror. He seems completely unbothered by the whole thing as he says, "West mentioned you're working on the new video. I'm doing sound for the banquet, so let me know if you need anything."

I nod awkwardly. Logan and I worked together on yearbook, and since he's majoring in audio engineering, he's always who I went to for help with sound issues. He leans in close and says something quietly to Nicole that makes her flush.

As he walks past us, he claps Reid on the back. "Room's all yours."

"God." Nicole smooths her hands down her shirt after Logan leaves. "My boyfriend and I got into a fight and this is the first thing I do... When will I learn that tequila is *not* my friend?"

"Do you want some water?" I ask.

"Don't worry about it." She hops off the bed, and her expression grows irritated as she appraises me, then says to Reid, "That didn't take long."

I'm not sure what she means other than to assume it's still the tequila talking.

When she's gone, Reid's smiling a little. "Wow. Never a dull moment in Woodhurst."

Even that shred of a smile makes me crave more. I cock my head to the side. "How badly would they kill me if I put this in the banquet video?"

"Oh, I think we'd be talking a murder only podcasters could solve."

I laugh, and his smile widens. It's the cheeky one that winks with amusement. We seem to realize at the same time that this immediate back-and-forth is weirdly familiar. Like old times.

Reid blinks and clears his throat, breaking the spell.

"Is it okay?" He gestures to the camera.

I lift it, capturing him in frame. I hold my breath as I test it out, zooming in. Trying not to get caught up in the way the camera loves the light and shadows of his face, the warmth of his brown eyes. His close-up features send my pulse into a frenzy.

The lens is locking up a little, but nothing I can't fix. "Yeah, it's okay."

When I lower the camera, his gaze sweeps over it in my hand before meeting my eyes again. "Why would you want to go back to all this?"

I realize he means the drama of the Legacy Program. The video.

He has a point. I *didn't* want to. After I lost my spot, I had planned on leaving all of this in my past and letting the documentary I spent my entire senior year working on gather dust for the next few years. Maybe forever.

Now after seeing everyone, seeing Reid . . . I'm as intrigued by this program as I ever was. I can't stop thinking about the stress on their faces. All the weird choices they're making. About someone creating an account to expose truths. There's something to that. Something catching hold of me that I can't ignore.

What if this is my chance to show it?

All of it.

Reid is still waiting for my response.

"Because after the way everything went down, it just feels like . . ." I trail off, searching for the right words. Our eyes catch and linger long enough that I find them. "The story isn't over."

CHAPTER NINE

REID

NOW

@haikuforyou
Life crumbles and shakes
Weighing us down with wreckage
Still I think of you

I HEAD OUTSIDE, CATCHING up to Kenji, who barely realized we got diverted. Clara's not too far behind us, and my entire body is buzzing with that fact.

We pass the crowd gathered and talking around the pool and weave our way out into the woods behind his house, the laughter and lights fading with every step.

Soon it's just the glorious quiet of the mountain and I can breathe again.

Kenji leads us down a familiar path to an open field that was always perfect for stargazing. Mitchell and Delaney are out here already perched on blankets and staring at the sky, speaking in low, reverent tones. My heart rate picks up wondering what they're talking about.

What she's telling him. Why didn't I realize Delaney would be out here, too?

At the sound of our footsteps, their conversation grows quiet. Delaney pops up when she sees us and pulls Clara into an aggressive hug.

Her voice is too perky as she talks quickly. "Clara! Oh my god, hi! Where have you been hiding? I'm so sorry I forgot to text you back! With midterms and rehearsals I'm, like, barely on my phone these days."

I grimace. Delaney's shifted into her pom-squad thing. The kind of act she puts on for everyone else but never Clara. Especially not at a party like this when they used to be inseparable.

Clara frowns at her, nodding slowly. "Um, yeah—it's okay."

Mitchell scoots over to make space for me between him and Delaney, but instead I lay my blanket down as far as possible from them, a sickening guilt worming through my gut.

Even though Mitchell gives me a confused look, none of this seems to register with Kenji, who plunks down between them instead.

"Finally, we're all back together!" Kenji collapses into Mitchell. "God, I feel like a herding dog."

"You look like one, too," Mitchell jokes, and ruffles Kenji's shaggy hair.

"*Hey.*" Kenji elbows him, and they both laugh.

I slowly crouch to the ground, leaning all my weight on one hand so I can swoop my bad knee around without issue and find a position that's comfortable. The sudden scent of Clara's flowery shampoo hits me and I realize too late that I settled myself right next to her. I feel the moment our gazes collide, and I'm grateful for the armor of the night sky.

That we can both hide a little longer in the dark.

As the moment settles, the five of us sit without talking as Kenji plays a calming melody on his guitar. We stare at the pins of light that don't seem to exist anywhere else. It should be peaceful, but I'm distracted by the warmth radiating off her and the jump in my pulse whenever she so much as shifts.

"I missed this," Delaney murmurs.

Kenji and I hum in agreement. It's definitely been too long since I was swallowed by the silent dark like this.

"Is it weird? Being back?" Mitchell asks no one in particular.

Delaney answers first. "Yes and no. Like, everything is so familiar but still somehow feels really different. I don't know; it's hard to explain."

I squeeze my eyes shut. Of course it feels different.

"Is it weird having everyone back?" Kenji asks, his plucking fingers never faltering.

"I thought it would be. But what's weird is how normal it feels," Mitchell says. "At least for me."

We all wait for Clara to say something. Or maybe that's just what *I'm* waiting for. But she fidgets with her hair tie and stays silent through the conversation as it meanders to college and the differences in our dorms, our towns. I don't say much, either. College is nothing like I expected, and I don't know how to talk about that yet.

"But, like, how do you get with anyone if you're sharing a room?" Mitchell asks seriously.

I reach around Clara to smack him. "Jesus, Mitchell."

Kenji laughs. "There are work-arounds. My roommate and I have a system."

Mitchell's laugh sounds forced, his words halting. "Oh. Nice—that—yeah, that *totally* makes sense."

"My roommate and I do the same thing. Her girlfriend lives off-campus, so they stay over there a lot, too," Delaney says. "Definitely makes it easier to have people over."

I don't realize I'm tapping the side of my leg until Clara glances at the motion. I close my hand into a fist as my gut churns with anxiety.

"We sound so slutty." Kenji laughs again.

Another fake laugh explodes out of Mitchell, too loud.

"It's not, like, all the time or anything," Delaney says over a yawn. "I barely have time to sleep anymore. Keeping up with classes and all the rehearsals for the different shows I'm in. I mean, if Legacy taught us anything it's how to juggle. Even if the whole Legacy process was *rough*."

"Would you be willing to talk about that on camera?" Clara asks. It's the first thing she's said since we sat down. Her husky voice is even more enticing in the dark.

"Talk about what?" Delaney asks.

Clara shifts, and now that my eyes have fully adjusted, I can make out the faint lines of her face. "Your experience of Legacy. Your *real* experience."

Delaney adjusts so that she can look at Clara directly. "I thought you were making a video for the banquet?"

"That's true. *Officially*."

Delaney narrows her eyes. "*Un*officially?"

"What if that Legacy Lore account is onto something about telling the truth about the program?" Clara asks.

Delaney and I exchange a glance that Clara catches. My pulse spikes higher.

"You mean the account that's targeting us?" Delaney asks, her tone incredulous.

Clara spins the hair tie around her fingers faster. I can practically hear how quickly her mind is moving. "I just mean, wouldn't it be great to show what the program is *really* like? The way it's impacted all of us?"

Delaney studies her. "I don't think that's what the account is trying to do."

"Maybe not," Clara hedges. "But what if that's what *I* want to do? Obviously not in a way that would compromise your scholarships—"

Mitchell sits up ramrod straight. "Wait. Are you saying you want to make a *takedown* of the Legacy Program?"

"Why did you just say that like Nicolas Cage wanting to steal the Declaration of Independence?" Kenji asks.

He grins. "Because I, too, am a national treasure."

Kenji sways into Mitchell as he laughs.

"I had always planned on finishing the doc I started last year, but then . . ." Clara trails off because we all know why she stopped working on it. When she got unfairly disqualified in front of everyone at the assembly because of that video, she told me that she was done.

With everything.

Just as the silence extends past comfortable, Mitchell pipes up. "And theeeen your smart and good-looking friend Mitchell reminded you to finish it this weekend and you've realized what a genius he is?"

Friend. I take a deeper breath.

Clara rolls her eyes but laughs a little. "More or less. But technically, it was always my plan."

"Details. I deserve a producer credit at least."

Kenji nods. "Sounds reasonable."

The rest of us laugh. Except Delaney, who's studying the sky as she says, "I don't know . . . I've gotten a lot out of Legacy."

Clara tenses. "Okay . . . you could talk about that, too," she starts, "but that doesn't mean it hasn't also sucked for a lot of us. Or did you forget about last year the way you've *forgotten* to text me back?"

Kenji's playing falters at the same time Mitchell sucks a breath in through his teeth. This is my fault. All my fault. Though I see Mitch elbows Clara, she barely seems to notice as she stares at Delaney.

Delaney's voice shakes a little. "Of course I haven't forgotten about what happened to you. You know I hate that Legacy didn't work out for you, Clara—"

Her scoff is high-pitched, her tone sardonic. "Didn't 'work out'?"

I rip out a clump of grass, the fury from last year building all over again.

Delaney shakes her head, looking miserable. "No—I know. I hate whoever did that to you—it was so cruel. But doing an exposé for revenge—"

"I'm not holding some petty grudge, Delaney. Someone *sabotaged* me—compromised my future. And I still don't know who did it or why."

The silence that follows is filled with hurt.

I know it's taking every ounce of Mitchell's and Kenji's self-control not to say a smart-ass comment to break the tension the same way it's taking every ounce of mine not to rub a hand down Clara's back to comfort her.

After a moment, Delaney's voice cuts through the soft cricket song around us. "You're right. I'm sorry—I get it. It's a good idea."

"Yeah?" Clara meets my gaze for a brief moment. "It's not crazy?"

I'm not sure if it's a rhetorical question or if she's asking me.

Talking about last year on camera with Clara is probably the last thing I want to do. But I get why she wants to do this.

Needs to do this.

Though I'm not sure I can. I have too much I need to contain. Too much I don't want anyone—especially her—to see.

But what she said to me in the house runs through my head again.

The story isn't over.

My voice comes out quiet but clear. "After the way they treated you? It'd be crazy not to."

She smiles, holding my eyes a beat longer than I can stand.

"Hell yeah. I may not be a Legacy but you know I'm in," Kenji says.

"Me too." Mitchell grins.

With the moment officially smoothed, they both spring up.

"Okay!" Kenji exclaims. "I think I should probably make sure no one is breaking anything inside."

"I'll go with you. I'm cold," Delaney says. I would think she's escaping, but her teeth are starting to chatter. It isn't warm, but it's not freezing, either, and she's in a heavy sweatshirt over her dress besides. "I should go home anyway. The Fun Run starts so early."

"Do you want a ride?" Clara asks hopefully.

"Um." Delaney darts me the quickest glance.

I know she wants to talk to Clara, but I plead with her silently, *Not now. Not tonight.* I just need a little more time. "I actually came with Nicole."

"Oh."

"Let's catch up tomorrow after the run, okay?"

"Sure," Clara says, obviously disappointed.

"You coming?" Mitch asks me.

Clara doesn't move. I should, but I don't, either.

Kenji and Mitchell exchange a look, then the three of them walk back to the house, leaving me and Clara alone again.

Her breathing goes stilted beside me, like she's trying not to cry. "Sorry—I didn't mean to make that so awkward. I just miss her."

Fuck. I rub my dry, tired eyes knowing with certainty I've fucked up beyond repair. Regretting that night with Delaney all over again. "You don't have to apologize." It's all I can manage to say as I try to summon the bravery I need to fess up.

Clara hugs her knees closer to her chest, staring up at the stars again. "You didn't say much before. Do you at least like it there?"

She means Stanford. College. The whole experience she doesn't get to have.

"It's all right," I hedge.

"Any favorite classes?"

I shrug since I barely manage to make it to them. "No, nothing in particular."

"Have you found your favorite run yet?"

I hesitate, rubbing my knee. I know what she's doing. It's her interview tactic. She starts with easy, mellow questions before going for the harder stuff. Trying to open me up like she used to.

"An eight-miler off campus through the trees. Reminds me of—"

I stop.

Reminds me of our *trail.*

Her curiosity clings to the words I didn't say, but I can't even approach the edges of this with her.

"Any new friends?"

She knows how hard it is for me to meet new people. How they confuse and exhaust me. Guilt churns my stomach more thinking of Delaney dragging me out that night.

You need to make some friends, Reid. C'mon, let's go to the party!

I clear my throat. "A few."

"That's good," Clara says, but she doesn't hide the thread of jealousy in her voice as well as she thinks she does. "Do you and your roommate also have a system?"

"I'm not with anyone," I blurt.

Her voice is tight when she says, "I wasn't going to ask that."

"But you were wondering."

She scoffs lightly. "How do you know?"

"Because I've been wondering the same thing about you."

I don't think she and Mitch are hooking up anymore. Their silly back-and-forth made it clear that whatever he's hiding isn't about her. But in what universe is someone like Clara single forever?

After a long silence she turns to look at me. "No," she says, her voice soft. "No one since you."

That last ounce of my courage fades. It should make me feel relieved to know she didn't find someone else immediately. But it only makes what happened with Delaney worse.

The air grows charged as she waits for me to say the same thing. No one since her.

In the past I always told her the truth. Sharing pieces of myself that I never had with anyone. And she never stopped pushing me away. Shutting me out. Almost like the more devoted I was to her, the more she couldn't bear it.

Now I'm the one who can't.

I don't want to lie, so I don't say anything. As I shift my weight, my small notebook in my pocket digs against my hip. When I take it out and set it down on the blanket between us, it lands heavy with everything I could never tell her.

She eyes it and a smile—sweet and sad—takes over her face. "You're still writing."

Dark irony laces my tone. "Nothing fuels poetry like heartbreak."

I was trying to be funny, but it cracks like lightning between us.

She's too good at evading my defenses. Always has been. And being alone with her under the stars, I need those defenses right now. It's the only way I know how to get through this weekend. To protect both of us.

"Reid, can we—"

"Stop." The word escapes me. Because now I know that too much has changed. *I've* changed.

Only, she's exactly the same. Overwhelmingly beautiful and compelling and . . . out of my reach. My voice softens. "Please, Clara. Just—stop."

A grunt escapes as I stand.

She doesn't follow. Only looks up at me, every feature limned in moonlight.

"I can't finish the doc without you."

I sigh. I was afraid she was going to say something like that.

"I don't expect—" She stops herself. Swallows. "It just feels like my chance to make it right. I really want to make it right."

My pulse ratchets up again.

Make *what* right, exactly?

Pushing a hand through my hair, I ask, "It wouldn't be personal? Just Legacy stuff?"

"Reid." She holds my gaze. "Legacy *is* personal."

I get her meaning. We all went through hell last year because of this program.

But her most of all.

Despite my goal of staying away from her this weekend, despite knowing what a bad idea it is to spend time with her again, I know my answer already. I owe her this.

"Okay."

I can't handle her grateful smile, so I start walking through the soft grass. I'm almost to the house when my phone buzzes in my pocket.

Desperate for a distraction from the chaos of my mind, I pull it out, blinking rapidly. The brightness of the screen is almost searing in the dark.

It's a text from Delaney with a screenshot of a new post and the message, Ummm???

> **@LEGACY_LORE**: Our 5 Legacies are all officially home. But they better get some sleep soon. Tomorrow's a BIG day for them. After all, betrayal doesn't come from your enemies . . . More soon. ♥

The hairs on the back of my neck stand up. Not just because of the words. But because of the picture—a photo of the crowd at *this* party.

I don't know what this person is trying to do, but I now know it's someone among us doing it.

Someone watching.

CHAPTER TEN

CLARA

THEN

IN AN EFFORT TO fly as deeply under the radar as possible after the truth-or-dare party, I tried to get out of homecoming. Especially because my mom had missed a few shifts at the hospital ever since I told her about Dad not coming home, and I needed to work every free night I could to help out.

But Delaney and Kenji convinced me to take a night off, saying we could go to the dance as a friend group with Mitchell and Reid.

Which worked for me since I wasn't particularly interested in seeing Reid with another girl after the way he kissed me. Though we'd barely talked since.

Delaney wasted no time as she went into full pom-squad mode, and bounded to the dance floor, moving her body with full confidence. It wasn't sexual, exactly, but there was something undeniably hypnotic about the swirl of her hips, the toss of her hair. A lot of people watched her, and she drank in the attention, as usual.

Amaya and Nicole joined her from another part of the dance floor, the three of them squealing and singing along to the music. It seemed like the two of them had started to ice me out ever since the party, but Delaney told me I was being paranoid. Delaney called out to our group, beckoning us to the dance floor with a curl of her finger.

Most of them followed. I would've bet a large sum of money that Reid wouldn't be one of them.

I would've lost.

Because he walked to the group and started moving with her easily. Confidently. Heat crept up my neck at the way his hands traveled the length of her torso before spinning her around.

My mouth fell open. "He can *dance*?" I spluttered aloud.

Mitchell, who was standing next to me, chuckled. "Oh yeah. He took hip-hop dance classes all through middle school."

I closed my eyes and put a hand over my heart. "It would be cruel to lie to me."

"Oh, trust me. Bop til You Drop," he said, laughing harder.

"*No!*" I gripped Mitchell's arm to steady myself on my heels while I cracked up.

"He's going to kill me for telling you that," he said.

"I'm sure he won't care," I said.

Mitchell scoffed. "C'mon, Clara. He has such a thing for you."

My stomach swooped. Obviously I wasn't oblivious to the vibe between me and Reid, but there's a difference between chemistry and someone having a *thing*. A thing implied . . . feelings. Mitchell must have been misreading the signs.

I mean, with the intense way he was looking at Delaney on the dance floor, anyone would think he had a thing for *her*.

Beside them, Logan had his arms around Nicole, but he kept looking over at Mitchell.

"Are you and Logan okay?" I asked.

On a recent long bus ride to a meet, Mitchell and I sat next to each other and talked the entire time. He ended up telling me about his relationship with Logan. How desperate he was for it to be public, but that Logan refused—worried it would affect his chances of being selected for Legacy, especially as the mayor's son. I'd noticed earlier that he wasn't wearing the bracelet anymore.

Mitchell shrugged, but his voice wobbled. "We broke up."

"Do you want to talk—"

"Not really."

I squeezed his arm.

The dancing went on awhile, and I took the opportunity to film. Which gave me something to busy myself with when Josh approached. He was in a hideous patterned dress shirt, his pale complexion red from dancing.

"You ever going to talk to me again?" he asked.

I could smell the booze on his breath. "We have nothing to talk about, Josh."

"You know you liked me before *Golden Boy* got here."

I stared because he couldn't have been more wrong. I didn't like him. I didn't think about him. What happened over the summer was something to get lost in on a really shitty night. To help me forget how alone I was. How easy I was to leave.

Besides, it had been months. The only reason Josh wouldn't let it go was because I *wasn't* interested in him and he wasn't used to that.

When I didn't respond right away, he narrowed his eyes to a sharp squint. "Unless you *were* just using me to try to get a Legacy spot."

My pulse spiked as I looked around, making sure no one was listening. "That's bullshit and you know it."

"Is it?"

Before I could say anything else, Reid appeared at my elbow just as the music shifted to a slow song. His jacket was off, his cheeks pink with exertion, and there was an attractive gleam of sweat at his temples.

"Want to dance?" he asked.

"We were talking," Josh said, stepping into Reid's space.

"And now we're done," I said pointedly.

"Hey, look at that." Reid clapped Josh hard on the shoulder to move him out of the way.

But Josh didn't budge.

"Back off, West," Reid said more forcefully.

Josh put his hands up in surrender, but the smirk never left his face. "Just trying to warn you, man." He leaned close and stage-whispered loud enough for everyone around us to hear, "She's a biter."

Reid's expression didn't change, but a familiar shame crawled over my skin.

Josh twirled on his heel and walked off as Reid led me to the dance floor.

Several people stared at us. Stared at me. Including Amaya and Nicole, who had clearly watched the whole interaction from across the gym. At least they hadn't heard what he said, but Amaya's eyes were red, and she glared at me like her crumbling relationship was all my fault.

Maybe it was.

Seeing firsthand what that kind of betrayal had done to my mom, I hated myself even more for that.

But I couldn't help but wish my mom never knew what my dad did. To spare her that pain and the ways she'd plummeted since. Even more than the rumors about using Josh for a Legacy spot, it was not wanting to hurt Amaya that kept my mouth shut.

Reid wove his arms around me, and the uneasiness melted away as my attention narrowed just to him. We began to sway.

"What's his problem?" he asked, glaring at Josh over my shoulder.

I took a deep breath, trying to quell the heat rising to my skin. "Haven't you heard the rumors about me and him?"

Reid shrugged. "Yeah. But I don't believe rumors."

"What if this one's true?" I challenged.

He was quiet for a beat, studying me. "Is it?"

I swallowed, my pulse racing so hard I was sure he could feel it under his hands. I didn't want it to be true. It shouldn't matter that it was true. And I wanted him—needed him—to keep looking at me like *that.*

"No," I lied.

Though he tried to hide it, his expression softened with relief. "Which is exactly why I don't believe rumors."

Desperate to change the subject, I infused my voice with as casual a tone as possible. "What about the Bop til You Drop rumor?"

His eyes flew wide, and a little color drained from his face. Oh, it was too good seeing the unflappable Reid Rousseau . . . flapped.

"I'm going to murder him," he growled.

I shook my head slowly. "You already look like . . . *that* and are freakishly athletic. Give the people some hope that there's a part of you that's dorky as hell."

The corners of his eyes crinkled as his chest shook with laughter against me. "I still have the T-shirt," he admitted.

My laugh exploded out of me. "Oh, please wear it sometime. I beg of you."

The shy roll of his eyes was totally disarming.

"You're blushing," I teased, trying to make him laugh again.

Instead, he swallowed and looked unnerved. "I know."

He pulled me a little closer, and I concluded then the woodsy smell was cologne. He used just a hint of it at his throat, and I hoped it would linger on me when we broke apart. When his warm brown eyes fell closed for a moment, I realized I'd been absently stroking my fingertips through the hair at the nape of his neck. I stopped and he took a deep breath.

My camera bumped against our hips as he turned me.

"Is everything you're recording really for the yearbook?" he asked.

I shrugged. "Mostly. But I'm also applying for this really exclusive film school, and I need to submit a sample. I was thinking of doing something on the Legacy Program." Feeling all too exposed I quickly added, "But you never know what might end up in a sweeping doc about my life someday. Or, more likely, yours."

He frowned a little. "What do you mean?"

"I heard you were talking to college recruiters, *state champion*."

He nodded.

"That is . . . *so* cool. You're like the poster child for a Legacy. I can see it now, you coming back as the guest of honor next year, having broken some record. We'll say we knew you when, and I'll have all the footage to prove it when they make a docuseries about you."

Reid laughed, but it sounded uncomfortable. "God, I hope not."

I frowned. "Why not?"

"I mean, my dad would love it. It's been his plan all along. But isn't it a little weird? All of this?"

I followed his gaze around the gym. "All of what?"

"The whole Legacy thing. That the entire town expects us to have our lives figured out already. What if we don't?"

Our dancing slowed to a barely there sway as we studied each other. "You don't?"

"Does anyone?"

And then I saw it. A flash of uncertainty behind his eyes like it lived there. Maybe his life wasn't golden. The more time I spent with him, the more fascinating he became.

We swayed in silence another minute. Electricity shot from his hands to my waist as he squeezed me a little tighter.

I had to concentrate to keep my voice light when I said, "You and Delaney looked like you were having fun."

"I'm a mere student of the art form. DL is a good teacher."

I threw him an arched brow. "What's with the nickname?"

That slow-rising smile of his should've been illegal. "You're jealous."

"Pff." I shrugged one shoulder up. "I'm . . . a concerned citizen at best."

He burst out laughing. "Do you want a nickname?"

"Don't patronize me."

"You do."

I huffed. "You can't make a nickname out of my name that isn't annoying as hell."

Clare-bear.

He nodded slowly, still terribly amused with himself. "You can't make a nickname out of Reid, either."

"You could go the Rihanna route. RiRi?"

"Yeah, no."

"I tried."

"Very hard," he deadpanned.

"It just seems like with Delaney—"

All at once we stopped moving. We were standing in the middle of the dance floor as he studied me. "It's not. I like someone else."

My stomach somersaulted. I knew I was going pink when the smirk on his face transformed into a lethal grin.

Something was happening here. Something I'd seen fall apart too many times. I didn't date for the same reason I didn't count on Dad. If I got too used to someone being there, it would be that much harder when they inevitably left.

"I don't want a boyfriend," I blurted. "I mean, that's always been my rule. Dating complicates things, and I don't . . . like complicated. And I just—I can't afford to get distracted. Especially not this year."

His face betrayed nothing as he took that in. But I felt relieved having said it. Better to ensure there was no confusion about what was most important to me. Legacy. Film school. Living the life my mom couldn't because she fell for the wrong guy.

Nothing holding me back.

"Okay," he said like he understood.

Or like he wasn't convinced.

Trepidation tugged at me, but his unwavering gaze was sweet. Open. The harder his eyes dug into mine, the harder it was to remember my own name, let alone why I should back away from him.

"But I'm not going to lie, Clara. Truth or dare kinda fucked me up."

I laughed a little. Me too.

He leaned in close, his lips brushing my ear. "When you kiss me again, I want you to mean it."

When.

CHAPTER ELEVEN

CLARA

THEN

IN THE MONTH AFTER homecoming, Reid and I texted every day, all day long. But despite getting closer, we hadn't actually seen each other much outside of school since the cross-country season was over. He was either training for track, having meetings with coaches, visiting college campuses, or catching up on homework he'd gotten behind on because of all the other stuff.

But he was finally coming over.

I kept checking my texts while I frenzy-cleaned my room. He'd been on the East Coast for nearly a week. I couldn't even keep track of which schools he visited—there were so many that wanted him.

Mom knocked on my door and leaned against the doorframe. "You've been working hard on that application. Going to bed soon?" she asked.

I had a pile of clothes in my arms. "Yeah. Soon."

She heard the lie in my voice and leveled her gaze at me. "What is it?"

I dropped the pile into my closet and closed the door. "Reid is coming over to help me with my CAFA sample."

It was almost ready, but despite hours of editing and combing through footage, I still didn't feel like I had nailed it yet. Which was why I needed someone to watch it before I submitted it to CAFA or the Legacy Program.

I had never let him see any of my footage. Like he had never told me what he was always writing in his notebooks. They were the sides of ourselves we hadn't yet revealed to each other. But for the first time I actually wanted to show someone what I had done. I wanted to show *him*.

Mom's eyebrows sprang up. "Does this mean the Golden Boy is your *boyfriend*?"

"*No*. And don't call him that."

Her eyes narrowed at the protectiveness in my tone. "Remember that you have your whole life for boys, mija. You need to stay focused on your own goals right now."

I looked up at the ceiling. "I am. He's *helping* me."

Mom was quiet a moment as she studied me closely. "I'm just asking you to be careful. I know his parents, and they have big plans for him. I wouldn't want you to get swallowed up in a relationship—changing your direction for him. Men force you to bend yourself for them until *you* break."

A frustrated scream lodged in my throat. She'd been telling me this my entire life, but still taking my dad back every chance she got.

I squared my shoulders, jutting my chin up defiantly. "He's different."

"I'm sure you think he is." The soft sympathy in her voice made my face flame. She held up her hands. "I'm not trying to upset you, I just want you to be smart. Find your *own* feet. Don't follow his."

Headlights streamed through my window as a truck pulled into our driveway, mercifully cutting off this conversation.

Mom sighed. "Keep your door open; he's gone by eleven. Got it?"

"Got it."

I waited for her to go into her bedroom, then I ran. I flung open the front door, cold seeping into my socked feet as I jogged across the frosty driveway. Reid was barely out of his truck before I threw my arms around him and sighed against his skin.

He laughed in my hair as he held me tight. "Hi."

"Hi." I breathed him in, a deep calm coming over me in his embrace. That was new.

A violent shiver passed through me that was definitely from the brisk night air and not at all from the sensation that just coursed between us. It was early winter, and in my excitement, I hadn't even bothered to throw on a jacket. Reid drew back to rub my arms, trying to warm me up.

When we got inside, he shed his jacket and boots in the entry and followed me to my room. Glancing across the hall to ensure my mom's door was closed, I closed my own behind us. Despite what she thought, and all the ways we'd gotten closer, Reid and I hadn't kissed since the truth-or-dare party. Maybe because we'd been so busy, or maybe because of what he'd said.

When you kiss me again, I want you to mean it.

I watched Reid as he took in my room. The pictures, my camera equipment—my tripod and the big round light reflectors in the corner I borrowed from school—and the messy, open story-map notebooks that covered my small desk.

We talked about his trip, what he'd missed around the mountain and at school while he was gone—most notably that Anderson Beck had been expelled after getting caught selling the answers to Mr. Garcia's notoriously impossible AP Calculus final.

"Kenji said everyone in that class has to retake the final," I said.

"*That's* why he sent that text about not playing Magic: The Gathering for a while."

I nodded, trying not to laugh. "Yeah, all recreational math is canceled for the foreseeable future."

He plopped in my desk chair and emptied his pockets, setting his keys and notebook in a small pile. It felt strangely right to have him in my space. Cozy.

"What are you always writing in there?" I asked, gesturing with my chin toward the notebook. The black cover was worn, the edges looked soft from constant thumbing.

He hesitated. Drew his eyes slowly to me. "Poetry, mostly."

"Okay," I said, my tone borderline acerbic at how unexpectedly hot that was. "I'm going to need a minute to process that."

He chuckled. "It's not good, but it does help me."

"How?"

His eyebrows came together. "My thoughts move really fast. Sometimes too fast and I can't sleep. For, like, days. It was worse when I was a kid. After my mom left. Poetry makes me slow down, considering each word."

He shot me a self-conscious look, worried he'd revealed too much. Watching him unfold himself even in small ways felt like a gift. I sank onto my bed directly across from where he was seated. "It always messes me up when my dad leaves, too."

He pointed to a photo on my desk that I usually put in a drawer before anyone came over.

"Your parents?" he asked.

I nodded.

It was their high school prom picture. It was so embarrassing. My dad had a dyed jet-black shaggy emo haircut that made his white skin paler, and my mom wore a truly alarming amount of eyeliner. But they looked happy. Which I'd rarely seen.

"Yep. They've been on and off since then. Classic nerd-jock situation. My mom won some science award and my dad was a football Legacy. But my mom had to drop out of college and move back here when she had me. My dad couldn't be bothered to do the same, even though he sat on the bench most of the time. 'Woodhurst remarkable is real-world mediocre'—that's what my mom always says. Not that it matters if Legacy actually gets you out of here."

I smoothed the comforter of my bed for something to do with my hands. Reid was quiet. So quiet it made me nervous. He turned toward me then, his brown eyes piercing in the small space.

"Why do you want to leave so badly?" he asked.

It was my turn to hesitate. Normally, I'd dodge the question with a joke or change the subject altogether. But as his brow furrowed with intent interest, I realized he had somehow made me feel safe enough to talk about the one thing that made me feel impossibly small.

"My mom gets depressed." It felt almost like a betrayal saying it aloud, my heart beating at a rapid rate. But I kept going. "And not, like, low-key depressed. Like . . . bad. She can get stuck in it for weeks—months. Sometimes she doesn't go to work, and then it's on me to take care of everything—" I exhaled, squeezed my eyes shut. "It's hard to explain."

I wasn't ashamed of my mom or the home she painstakingly built for me. I just hated feeling helpless. Hated that I related to my dad being so . . . restless. Hated that I was either caught in the explosion of them being together, or the implosion of my mom being alone.

Reid's deep voice went so soft when he said, "You don't have to."

Like instead of judging, he *understood.*

My traitorous eyeballs began to sting, and he crossed the room to sit next to me.

He didn't fill the silence or try to fix it. It was the first time in my life I didn't feel alone with it.

"I feel guilty sometimes for wanting to leave so badly, but it's what she wants for me, too. And it's not only about her. I spend all my time imagining other lives once I'm out of here."

"Other lives?"

Heat worked its way up my face. "Yeah. Okay, like, in one, I live at the beach and surf every day—like, it becomes my entire personality. I'm one with the waves."

"If you're in a bathing suit that's the one I vote for," he said.

I smacked him playfully and kept going. "In another, I live in Italy or France. I obviously become multilingual and buy pastries and flowers at outdoor markets and film the countryside while riding bikes through fields."

His smile widened as he listened.

"In another, I don't live anywhere—I live *everywhere*. After I go to CAFA, I make documentaries that let me travel the world, learning new things, meeting new people. Answering every question I could possibly think of. Making films that matter." I sighed. "The dream."

Reid studied me like he was really seeing me for the first time. I pulled on a loose thread of the comforter and asked, "What about you? Any other lives?"

That adorable line of concentration formed between his eyebrows as he considered the question. Finally, he said, "You know how sometimes in movies everything stops for a second?"

"Like a freeze-frame?"

He brightened. "Exactly. Everything's moving at a normal speed until suddenly the music, the action, the talking—it all just *stops*." He held up a hand, suspended in the air between us in a pause. "And you realize just how fast normal had gotten."

Our eyes met, and he slowly lowered his arm.

"That pause? That moment of complete stillness . . . I wouldn't mind living in that sometimes."

I rested my head against the headboard, taking in just how sweet he looked in the golden light. "You really are a poet."

His expression grew self-conscious and he joked, "Nah, that didn't even rhyme."

As our laughter faded, his eyes drifted back to the picture.

"Do you talk to him a lot? Your dad?"

"We try." I shrugged. "But since he doesn't ever stick around long, I don't see the point. He even forgot my birthday last year."

Reid frowned. "That's . . . *really* shitty."

My laugh was humorless. "I'm used to it. It's just another day, anyway. Except this year, when I can finally get a tattoo from my Aunt Lisette."

He arched a brow. "Of what?"

"I'm not sure yet. I have lots of ideas."

None of which really stuck for long, though. It needed to mean something real. To be something that would always matter.

"Well, I won't forget it," Reid said with a grin. "I already saved your birthday in my calendar."

My heart sped up in my chest. How did he do that? Stitch up a wound I didn't even know was bleeding.

I got up and fiddled with the track pad on the laptop to wake it up, avoiding his gaze and the fizziness coursing through me. "Ready?"

He nodded and settled deeper into the bed. "My first Clara Suarez original. I wish I had popcorn."

In my Attenborough voice, I said, "Please reserve your opinion until the end."

He gave me a small salute, and I gnawed on my thumbnail the entire time the doc played.

In the video, I featured those gunning for Legacy other than myself. First was Amaya, who had already secured a spot at NYU early admissions but who still seemed stressed about becoming a theater Legacy and securing the scholarship to pay for it. Focusing all her time on the fall and spring shows, as if moving on to the next level of such an incredible college didn't matter as much as proving she was someone to Woodhurst.

I included footage of Delaney's dance rehearsals and strict diet and the workout regimen she put herself through. She came across as strong but anxious. Too focused on her failings, so hard on herself. Like the way she weighed herself after every workout seemed too revealing. As her best friend, it was hard to watch, even though it was true.

There was no avoiding featuring Josh. His attitude and arrogance were a good balance to the other personalities, from a storytelling perspective. He was in the running for valedictorian and was sure to be named a Legacy for that alone. That and the heaping of nepotism. In all his interview footage he talked about expectations and the importance of the program—sounding a lot like his dad.

Then there was Reid.

Clearly the main character. I had spent countless hours ensuring the footage was balanced and the story was equally proportioned among them. But there was no denying that Reid shone brightest. His shyness was endearing on-screen, his dedication to his sport and team, inspiring. He came across as compelling and charming. Self-deprecating and relatable.

The perfect hero.

Like after a particularly brutal meet, where even he struggled due to the rainy conditions, I captured him as he went up to every single runner on the team, offering them water and an encouraging word.

There was something special, too, about the way his thoughtful silences translated to the viewer, reaching somewhere deep.

I was hesitant to include the scenes of the toll it took on his body and time. The few complaints he ever made about the pressure he felt. The grueling hours. Making his dad proud and the entirety of Woodhurst happy.

With Josh's jealous attention on Reid in all the cross-country footage, it inadvertently made him the villain to Reid's hero. I didn't have my camera out when he tripped Reid at state, but I caught the aftermath. The blood on Reid's arm, the bandage that was slick with sweat when he crossed the finish line, securing the championship. I also caught plenty of other times Josh would jeer or make jokes at Reid's expense. I felt uneasy about including them, but at the same time, it was the truth. Josh made *himself* look that way.

The entire time we watched it, I tried to see it through Reid's eyes.

But I was most disarmed by him seeing himself through *my* eyes. How close I would catch him in frame. The beads of sweat that dripped from his hair, the grimaces of pain when he pushed too hard, and the moments of total solitude I had invaded through my lens, even as I tried to capture them as unobtrusively as possible.

Someone watching might think I had feelings for him. Deep feelings.

God, did I?

When the doc ended, my stomach was in knots. It was honest. Raw. Exposing.

Reid sat up slowly, and my mouth went dry waiting for him to say something.

"Wow," he breathed.

I closed the laptop. "I know it's melodramatic. That's why I needed someone to watch it—"

His brow furrowed. "What? No. It's— Holy shit, it's amazing, Clara. You're so talented."

"You liked it?"

He nodded, and my stomach fluttered as he grabbed my hands. "Loved it. The way you captured everyone? I had no idea that when you were filming, you were focusing on all those different things."

He must've meant the way I zoomed in on fidgeting hands and lip biting and other body language that conveyed what words didn't. Or on what was happening in the background while someone was talking and how it either emphasized or contradicted their point. "It's . . . *honest.* Thank you."

I shifted uncomfortably. "For what?"

"For showing me. For tonight . . . I feel like I know you better."

I didn't know what to say to that, so I barreled on as my thoughts spiraled. "It doesn't seem incomplete to you? I dunno, there's something about it that doesn't feel ready or something."

But Reid shook his head. "It's perfect. You're a beast, Suarez," he said, nudging me with his shoulder.

I wanted to believe him.

"You're not so bad yourself, RiRi," I said, trying to force my discomfort away with a joke.

His face went deathly serious. "How many times do I have to tell you that is *not* the nickname?"

"Who's to say?"

He chuckled. But the mirth didn't last long the further into my own head I retreated.

He noticed. He always did.

"What's bugging you?" he asked seriously.

I'd never before shown anyone something so personal. And I'd just told him about my parents, my dreams—things I'd never even told Delaney. Nothing about any of that was casual.

"It's . . . a lot. Sharing all this with someone," I said.

He nodded, and his eyes fell to his notebook on my desk. "I get it. I'd probably feel the same way if I ever let anyone read my poems."

I looked down at our intertwined hands. The way I was now desperate to read his words forced me to ask, "Would you ever let me?"

His expression grew thoughtful, his thumb brushing across the back of my hand. "I think I would." He looked at me again and swallowed. "Though, you'd definitely know what I think about a lot."

The words were barely audible when I asked, "What are you thinking now?"

Without hesitating he said, "That I really want to kiss you."

His gaze dropped to my mouth. When it dragged up to meet my eyes again, his eyebrows came together to form a question.

There was only one answer.

I closed the remaining distance between us and pressed my lips to his. He responded instantly, pushing his large hands into my hair. He pulled me closer in a way that was both gentle and commanding. Just like him.

Every part of me responded. My lips moved with his like they were made to, every other sense on overdrive, aware of everything from the slight scratch of stubble on his chin to the steadiness I felt in his arms. I wrenched him closer, drawing his strong body as close as we could get. It felt like jumping off the tallest rock into Crescent Lake. Like soaring and falling all at once.

Reid moaned against my mouth when I sank my fingertips into his hair. I gave a little tug, and he chuckled like he liked it. It sent a wild shiver through me.

When we broke apart—just an inch—we looked at each other. His eyes were heavy-lidded, his voice deep and gravelly when he said, "You really like poetry, huh?"

I laughed against his lips and pulled back to look at him. "I think . . ." My heart was beating so hard I could hear its pounding roar in my ears. "I think I really like you," I whispered.

He snaked a strong arm around my waist again, his lips a breath from mine. "I know I really like you."

This time the kiss was slower. Sweeter.

Like we meant it.

CHAPTER TWELVE

REID

NOW

ONE DAY UNTIL LEGACY BANQUET

@haikuforyou
She is like a breeze
I can feel her but I can't
hold her close to me

I DON'T SLEEP. ALL night. Again.

I had the same problem when I was a kid. Right after Mom left. It's why my dad signed me up for every sport he could think of—to run me ragged until I collapsed into sleep. To help with the way I would have these mental dips that would last for weeks. Sometimes months.

Over time, it worked. Things settled, Dad started seeing Julianne, I got a brother out of the deal, and I forgot that falling asleep used to be the hardest part of the day.

Then everything with Clara imploded, and I moved away to school and it was nothing like I expected. After my injury, the insomnia returned full force. No matter how much I long for just a few hours of oblivion—a break from my endless thoughts—I rarely get it.

I roll onto my back and stare up at my bedroom ceiling. Watch as it slowly shifts from the darkest, dimmest blue to a bright, perky white as the sun rises. It's going to be a gorgeous day on the mountain. You can always tell by the light.

Clara taught me that.

Jesus, my mind swarms with her. I can still feel the warm weight of her wrist in my palm. The way her pulse flew against my fingertips out on the deck. A complicated surge of hope rushes through me, but for what, I have no idea.

Could it mean something that she isn't seeing anyone? Am I even allowed to care?

Why do I still care?

I push my hands in my hair, letting out an aggravated groan. I have to see her again today and pretend like it doesn't shred me.

I have to pretend like I can run today.

A knock at my door. My dad's familiar rap. "Reid? You up? We have to be at the starting line in an hour."

"Yeah, okay." My voice is gravelly. Hopefully I can play it off as groggy instead of so fucking tired my hair hurts.

At least with the chill in the air I can wear my knee brace underneath my running pants. I make it extra tight, and other than tweaking the hair on my leg, it feels good. Secure.

I meet my family out in the kitchen. It's a familiar scene. Mitchell hunched over the table, still half asleep; Julianne at the stove making something that smells incredible; and Dad running in and out as he loads the car with race-day extras. Giant crates of water bottles, tape, granola bars, and Band-Aids.

He's wearing running gear himself and sweating like he's just worked out. It's likely from having already ridden and measured the course with a Jones Counter on his bike. He always did that before my races when he could get away with it to ensure the distance was accurate and the course was fair. He could prepare me for anything and help me visualize every turn and bump that way.

If only he'd been there the day I fell to warn me how sharp the final turn was, how slick the course had gotten from the rain the night before. Then maybe I would still be okay. At least physically.

But I wish he'd take it easy. He's pushing too hard.

I noticed a pile of mail on the counter last night when I came home. The color of the envelopes varying shades of pink and red. The bills changing colors the longer they're past due.

Dad's mentioned this a few times recently. How stretched thin we are after his heart procedure last year. Though he has to be careful about stress, he's fully recovered, thankfully. But our finances aren't. "*It's not for you to worry about*," he told me the last time I asked.

As if that would work.

"There he is," Julianne says when she notices me hovering. She pulls me into a tight hug. She's a lot shorter than me, but the hug is almost more comforting because of that.

"Hungry?" she asks as she assesses me. "Made your favorite."

Julianne never pries. It's one of the things I like best about her. But she must be able to tell I'm not doing great because she got up early after working late to make me French toast with black cherries and a pile of thick-sliced bacon.

Tightness constricts my throat. I didn't realize how homesick I'd been.

"Starving. Thanks."

She squeezes my shoulder, a Band-Aid across her freckled hand, likely from a random burn she barely noticed but that Dad fussed over, and sends me with a heaping plate to the worn wooden table next to Mitchell.

"Where's mine?" Mitch asks.

She puts a hand to her ear. "What was that? 'Oh, Mother dearest, thank you for making this gourmet meal for me when I, a strong lad of seventeen, am perfectly capable of feeding and serving myself'?"

Syrup catches on my chin as I let out a creaky laugh, rusty from disuse. Mitchell grumbles to standing and fills his own plate, but he swings an appreciative arm around her on his walk back. "Thanks, Mom."

"Mm-hmm." She pats his arm fondly.

I blink down at my plate. I know she loves me, too. But it's different.

As we're wolfing down our food, Dad taps his watch at us. "Guys, let's go."

"Peter, relax. It's a *fun* run," Julianne reminds him. "Less stress, remember?"

Dad's shoulders release a little, but I can tell it's for her benefit alone. "Reid, I hear it's going to be a solid crowd today. You'll give them a show?"

My chewing slows, but I nod. "Of course."

Mitchell kicks me under the table. I kick him back.

"Good. West drummed up a lot of potential donors this weekend, and I think some of them may be interested in investing in your Olympic journey."

My stomach plummets. "What?"

His expression turns apologetic at my tone. "I *might* have let it out of the bag that we met with Coach Andrews back in April. His roster fills up fast, and it's not cheap. Until you get a brand deal, all we'd need is a sponsor, and seems like as good a time as any to do some networking."

I'm not even cleared for regionals and Dad thinks I'm ready for the

Olympics? I look up, and Julianne is watching me closely, a furrow of concern between her eyes. This is not good. Maybe it's time to tell them.

"'Today I will do . . . ,'" Dad prompts.

"'What others won't,'" I recite automatically.

"'So tomorrow I can do . . .'"

"'What others can't.'"

Dad grins. "Mentality of a champion!"

I can't remember when we started reciting this quote. I'm not even sure where it came from. But as a former runner himself, Dad knows training my mind has been as crucial as my body.

But now it's adding to the pressure instead of relieving it.

"Okay." Dad claps his hands together. "Let's get moving. Legacy traffic is a nightmare, and I want to be sure you're warm. Oh, and do something with your hair. Principal West wants you there for some pre-run interview."

Interview.

"What's wrong with my hair?"

But Dad's already out the door.

"You know you shouldn't run today," Mitchell says quietly.

Despite the rising panic in my chest, I remind myself that Jason said I was close to being able to jog anyway. I have a brace on. Could one run be so bad?

When I notice the date on my phone, I realize I forgot to turn in a humanities assignment. I log in to my student portal to send a quick message to my professor. That's when I see the notice at the top. I tap on it, and I lose the last of my appetite.

Academic probation.

Fuck. Now? Already? This isn't my first notice or warning, but I could've sworn I had more time to salvage things. To turn that one bio assignment in that was a quarter of my grade, and to retake the art history midterm I slept through. Didn't the first notice say by . . . I check the date again. Oh, it *is* today.

Even though they said I couldn't lose my scholarship for getting hurt, I could absolutely lose it for this. The Legacy scholarship has the same stipulations. You *have* to stay in good academic standing.

I could lose everything.

How am I going to keep this from Dad? The stress alone is more than he should face right now. If I lose my scholarships, it would then be up to my parents to pay for two college tuitions along with the medical bills next year.

It would sink us.

I can't focus on this now. So I distract myself by clearing the plates, and then we all hustle to the car. I say low to Mitch, "Do you know if this interview is with Clara?"

"Ask her yourself. This is me"—he takes a large, exaggerated step ahead of me—"officially out of the middle."

I roll my eyes and spend the short drive finger-combing my hair, but I don't think it makes much of a difference. When we arrive fifteen minutes later, there is a crowd of people at the starting line.

"What the hell?"

The Fun Run is usually the least-attended Legacy event. Shakespeare in the Vines and the banquet are the two big draws of the weekend. Not the *Fun Run*. But the group is massive. From the bookstore to the Lodge, they've completely taken over the town square.

"They're here to see you, kid," Dad says proudly. He's fully beaming as he scans the rows and rows of cars. "Our future Olympian."

My stomach sours further.

We park, and I walk through the town square, the energy electric in the air. People start waving at me, taking my picture.

Two kids, about eight years old, hover near the starting line. They're wearing shirts that read, *Future Legacy*, and they keep shoving each other excitedly. They remind me of when Mitch and I first became friends. Then one turns, and I see it: The name *Rousseau* is on the back of his shirt.

What?

"Principal West had them made as a fundraiser for the school," Dad says, following my line of sight. "Apparently they're selling well."

I close my eyes and inhale through my nose, releasing the breath from my mouth as if through a straw.

When I open them again, I see her. Clara's in black leggings and an oversize sage-green sweatshirt. Her long hair is up in a ponytail, and her cheeks are pink with morning cold. She has her camera bag slung across her body and her camera with the mic attached to the top in her hands. She's talking with someone on the Channel Nine news crew who has set up a camera as well.

Jesus. It's a circus.

When she notices me, she quickly walks over, keeping her lens trained on me. The rush of pleasure I feel at seeing her again so soon is concerning. She's flushed, and her eyes are bright and excited. She's in filmmaker mode.

"Are we starting?" I ask, gesturing to her camera.

"I was hoping to," she says, bending her head toward the crew a few feet away. "But Channel Nine pulled rank."

"But you're filming?"

She nods. "Getting footage. I'll be hovering around you and everyone all weekend pretty much. Asking questions occasionally. Is that okay?"

I nod. I told her I was in. I'm determined to see this through if it helps with what she went through last year. But I need to get my shit together first. There's nothing she doesn't see through that lens.

"We'll set up the formal interview whenever you have a break," she says.

Clara usually tries hard to *play* it cool. But with a camera in her hand, she *is* cool. More present. Like she forgets to be self-conscious and is the person few people get to know.

The person I got to know.

Her eyes travel over my face, and it reminds me of how she used to look at me. The way she drank me in. I had no idea attention could feel good until it was hers. She cocks her head to the side, her expression turning concerned. "You look tired."

I pull in another deep breath and look around. When I exhale, it comes out in a visible puff against the cool air. "I was so looking forward to this run, I had trouble sleeping."

Her expression is pinched, like she knows it's a canned answer. The kind I'll give Channel Nine in a minute.

"Insomnia," I admit.

Only her green eyes flick up, quick and sharp over the camera. I almost wonder if she can hear the slam of my heartbeat. I shouldn't have told her that.

"The guest of honor has arrived!" Principal West runs over. "Over here, sport, we have the crew all ready for you!"

"I should . . ."

Clara nods stiffly.

Relieved to be away from her watchful gaze, I get through my interview fine. Then they inform me they want B-roll of me warming up before "the big race."

After stretching and jogging around the square, testing my knee, I feel a little better. My knee doesn't feel great, but it's definitely been worse. I can do this. Probably.

But before I can make my way to the starting line, Kenji and Mitchell appear, looking stressed. Clara hovers off to the side, recording us talking.

"So, don't freak out," Mitchell says to me, pushing a hand through his curls.

"Always a good start," I say slowly.

Kenji rounds on Mitchell. "We shouldn't show him *now*."

"Is there an optimum time for something like this?"

"Probably not when he's surrounded by the entire town?" Kenji suggests.

"He's *always* surrounded by the entire town—"

"Show me what?" I interject.

They remember I'm standing right there, and Kenji gestures toward me like, *Might as well.*

Mitchell exhales. "Legacy Lore just posted."

I frown at the anxiety all over his face. "Okay?"

"About you."

Mitchell hands me his phone, and my pulse takes off as I read the post open on it:

> **@LEGACY_LORE:** Let's introduce you to our five distinguished Legacies. The *real* introductions. Starting with our guest of honor, shall we?
>
> Meet Reid Rousseau: State cross-country champion, our first Olympic hopeful if Coach Andrews has anything to say about it—we all know him as the pride and joy of Woodhurst. But given his mysterious

absence from the course this season and earning more than a few failing grades, is the Golden Boy starting to tarnish outside of his small pond? More soon. ♥

What? What the *fuck* is this? Last night this whole thing seemed like it could be a game. Someone letting us know they were watching to see what we were going to do this weekend. But this . . . I read it again. How could they know about my grades? I've told no one. It's impossible.

But true.

And this is a public account. Anyone can see this. My dad could see this.

More soon. Does that also mean whoever wrote this *actually* knows more?

There are a few comments already:

If this is true, he shouldn't be a Legacy!

This isn't all he's hiding. DMing you.

I don't recognize the second account, and it's private when I click on it.

I think of the other things it should be impossible for anyone else to know but are also *definitely* true. My eyes dart around the square, looking for an exit. A way out. I can't catch my breath.

"These are obviously lies to get a reaction out of you," Kenji tries.

I click on the profile, and though it's anonymous, it's not like I don't know who it is.

Your team likes to talk.

"It's Josh," I say.

Kenji and Mitchell exchange a look. "There's stuff about him," Kenji says, unconvinced.

I scroll to the second post:

@LEGACY_LORE: Meet Joshua West: Principal West's son, valedictorian, with a strong athletic record. An obvious choice for Legacy. But with the way he treated his girlfriend and nepotism on his side, what else is he willing to do to get what he wants? As the saying goes: Once a cheater always a cheater. More soon. ♥

"Everyone knows he cheated on Amaya. It would look too suspicious if he wasn't included," I say. "It's him. He's always had it out for me."

Watch your back, Rousseau.

"*Ow,*" Mitchell exclaims as I thrust the phone into his chest.

"Where is he?"

I find Josh across the square. I was hoping he'd be too hungover today to come, but he's here warming up with Nicole and the current cross-country team. He's talking and laughing with one of the JV runners from this year. She can't be more than fifteen.

Kenji grabs a hold of my shoulders before I can charge over there. "Nope. Principal protection, remember?"

I exhale slowly. He's right. Josh is untouchable because he's a *West*. It's why he did this—he knew he could get away with making an account like this in the first place to stir up shit and mess with me. But he's playing with fire.

"Don't stress," Kenji says. "It only has . . . a few . . . hundred followers. I doubt anyone will even see it or believe it."

I scoff. We all know that's a long shot.

Mitchell steps closer to me and asks in a low voice, "Are you really failing?"

Case in point.

But I don't respond because Clara is close and—*fuck*—getting all of this on camera. She looks concerned and I *hate* it.

I never wanted her, of all people, to know any of this.

"Can you turn that off?" My voice is sharp. It's not a command, but it sounds like one.

She frowns. "You said I could—"

"And now I'm saying you can't," I snap. My gaze is hard on hers. Dread and furious anxiety clawing at my stomach.

Her face reddens. I don't know if I've ever spoken to her like that, and I immediately wish I could yank the words back. But at least she lowers the camera and walks toward the course without looking back.

When Josh sees me, his gaze narrows. It's clear from his expression that he has one objective today: to beat me.

Yeah, like I'd let *that* happen.

Ready or not, I can't just get by today. I have to run like I haven't in weeks if I don't want these rumors to spread more. The last thing I need is my dad finding out and asking questions about my grades or pushing harder about my *mysterious absence from the course.* He's accepted my excuses for now, but I can feel the clock ticking.

Rumors become facts here. Nobody knows that better than me and Clara.

I need to put this to rest, today, on this trail—before things get out of control.

"You limping there, Rousseau?" Josh asks, loud enough that several heads swivel to watch me.

I concentrate on keeping my gait fluid as I approach the starting line.

"You still obsessed with me, West?" I ask.

He scoffs, but at least he shuts up.

"Just ignore him," Nicole says on my other side, rolling her eyes at Josh.

I shoot her a grateful smile. It takes a minute as we wait for Mayor

Harper, Logan's mom, to get in position with the starting gun. I should be talking to all the people around me who are giving me excited looks. Who came to see me. But I don't have a fake smile in me right now.

I put my earbuds in and scroll through my phone for my favorite running playlist. Amaya is on Nicole's other side, and though she speaks quietly, I hear when she asks, "Did you see those posts?"

I turn down my music.

Nicole nods, her eyes wide. "I've heard some of the same stuff about . . ." She trails off, and I see her bending her neck toward me. It's about as subtle as a shove. But I'm not worried. She told me herself that she's heard the Olympics rumors.

There's a note of panic in Amaya's voice. "*Really*? So they're true? What if they actually post about us next, then? I *can't* lose my scholarship."

I realize Josh could know real personal stuff about both Amaya and, by extension, Nicole. If he actually follows through on these threats, and anyone official sees these posts and decides to look into them, we could *all* be screwed.

What the hell is he thinking?

Nicole chews on her bottom lip. "Me either. But at least it's obvious who it is."

I nod to myself approvingly. She's never liked Josh either and probably knows him even better than I do since she had to hang out with him so much with Amaya.

But when Amaya raises a questioning eyebrow, Nicole continues, her voice dropping significantly. "Who has the biggest grudge against Legacies? Who follows everyone around all the time recording everything we do?"

"Oh my god," Amaya gasps. "*That's* why she's always filming!"

Wait—

Nicole nods, her expression turning sympathetic. "I mean, can you blame her for wanting some justice, though? I'd be bitter, too, after what happened at the assembly."

There's no possible way. Clara might be bitter—which she has every right to be—but she would never do something so cruel.

"You're being way too nice. She did that to *herself*," Amaya bites out. "She's so fake."

"*Hey*," I say, incapable of staying silent a second longer. They both startle as they turn to me. "Don't stir shit up about Clara. She wouldn't do this."

Amaya frowns. "Didn't she dump you?"

I suck in a sharp breath.

"*Amaya*," Nicole hisses.

"I'm just saying, why defend her?"

Nicole glares at her. "Sorry—Amaya's just a little cranky about seeing her own ex, *isn't she*?"

Amaya shoots Josh a sneering look. "Fair."

Nicole turns back to me, grabbing my arm. "I'm sorry. I shouldn't have said that. I'm just stressed about this account. It feels like we all have targets on our backs all of a sudden, doesn't it?"

I try to let my agitation from this conversation slip away because I get what she means.

I'm about to say as much when a hand slaps against my shoulder. It's Mitchell.

Low in my ear he says, "You don't have to do this, you know. We can tell them right this second about your knee."

I glare at him and side-eye Nicole, checking if she overheard, but she's already absorbed back into her conversation with Amaya. Thankfully, no one else seems to have heard, either, as Josh sets his watch, smirking, and my dad, who's in the group of runners behind us, shoots me a thumbs-up.

I shake my head. "No way."

Anyone following that account will know just how fine I am by the end of this race. All these people—the kids and my parents and the *news* and Clara—they're here for the show. I intend to give them one.

As soon as Mayor Harper releases the starting gun, Josh explodes ahead.

The guy never learns. I follow in a steady rhythm down the trail that leads to the lake. These paths I've pounded over and over. My knee doesn't even feel too bad. With every strike against the ground there's a sharp, short *zing* behind my kneecap, but it's tolerable.

I lead the rest of the pack slowly—for me—until the trail opens into the forest. With each step, each breath, I feel more like myself than I have in weeks. I follow the path through the trees, pulling in lungful after lungful of earthy air that smells like home.

When my watch beeps at the first mile split, I realize I still haven't caught Josh. Grimacing, I pick up my pace. The *zings* become sharper, the pain stretching further. After another half mile, I see him—his stride narrower, his shoulders hunched like he can't get enough breath. He burns most of his energy by the halfway mark every *single* time.

"You're flagging," I goad.

"You're favoring," he pants out.

Shit, am I? It's not too much of a strain to pass him.

But I don't shake Josh the way I expect to. He's still on my heels, his labored breaths as loud as my own. The posts and the comments swarm through my mind as if Josh is yelling them at the back of my head.

"If this is true, he shouldn't be a Legacy!"

"This isn't all he's hiding."

"More soon."

I lengthen my stride. Because being easy on my injury means I'm not moving fast enough. A sharp, burning current of pain radiates from behind my kneecap and up my thigh. Still I push.

I push until sweat pours off me. Until my lungs get sticky. Until the thoughts of what I'm up against are shoved back, back, back.

Until I'm nothing but breath and pain and regret.

As soon as I cross the finish line, I collapse.

CHAPTER THIRTEEN

CLARA

NOW

REID CROSSES THE FINISH line to a cacophony of applause. Only I seem to know he's going to fall a second before he crashes to the ground.

The gasps from the crowd are drowned by the roaring in my ears. I sprint toward him, but I can't get through the bodies that have surrounded him.

"Is he okay?"

"Oh my god, did he faint?"

His voice, ragged and winded, breaks through. "I'm fine."

"*Reid?* Excuse me!" It's Coach Rousseau, and he's shoving his sweaty arms through the crowd now that he's finished the race, too.

I can't see anything over their shoulders, but I can hear Reid. I lift my camera high, hoping to capture the scene to check if he's really okay.

"Dad, I'm fine. I tripped."

After a moment, Coach pulls him to standing and Reid waves to the crowd, who applaud in response. His palm and elbow are scraped from the fall. He pushes his noninjured hand through his hair as he walks slowly—really slowly—toward his dad, who's holding out a water bottle for him.

Reid takes a long pull, then hunches over again. He scolded me whenever I did that, telling me that position restricts breathing. He knows better. I zoom in more to catch his hand squeezing his left knee.

He's not winded. He's hurt.

He's gripping his knee so hard his entire hand is bright white. His dad is right by his side, saying something into his ear. Reid shakes his head and straightens to standing. I get closer and watch his lips move through the viewfinder.

I swear I'm fine, Reid mouths. *It's just sore.*

Whatever is going on, I think it might be serious. And Reid is pretending it isn't. What did that Legacy Lore post about him say?

"But given his mysterious absence from the course this season . . ."

It hits me then, the grimaces and the stiff way he sat down on the ground last night. He didn't injure it by falling, he fell *because* he's injured.

And he ran anyway.

Because he doesn't want anyone to know. I wanted to believe that Legacy Lore was right to expose the truth of this program. But at the cost of the people in it? If Reid is actually injured, that means whoever it is has real intel. Is airing *real* secrets.

Furious heat shoots through me.

I've been through enough of that. I can't let the same thing happen to him.

As soon as the crowd breaks up, Reid's face falls and he squeezes his eyes shut as if mentally preparing himself before he starts walking.

He's always been competitive. Too competitive. Even with himself. At the hot springs last year, he opened up to me about the mental tricks he plays on himself to stay motivated. I get that he couldn't get where he is without that fire, but I always thought that he pushed himself too hard.

I pause. *The hot springs.* He told me once nothing ever helped his thrashed body like the hot springs did. He needs to get there. Today.

Josh steps right into my frame then, breaking my concentration and ruining my shot. I lower my camera, and he's staring at me, a smirk on his face. He's beet red and smells like alcohol is leaching out of his pores.

"You catch me crossing the finish line?" he asks, gesturing to my camera.

"Yeah, I got everyone," I say, eager to rush over to see if Reid's okay.

"Making sure you're not just focusing on Golden Boy over there. You saw Delaney's posts, right? He shouldn't even be the guest of honor."

I frown. "What do you mean 'Delaney's'?"

Josh shrugs. "It's obvious she's the one making them. She always knows everything about everyone."

I open my mouth to defend her but pause as my thoughts collide.

She's been weirdly distant for a while now, avoiding me every time I try to talk to her, like something is going on or she's carrying a secret. She *does* love to gossip . . .

I shake my head quickly.

No. There's *no* way. I could see it if the posts were only about Josh, but she would never compromise her scholarship to start rumors about Reid. Not unless she had a reason I don't know about. Josh is trying to get in my head.

Probably because Reid's right and *he's* the one behind the posts. After the way he treated Reid last year, it's not hard to imagine that Josh would make an account like Legacy Lore just to take Reid down.

When I don't respond, he goes on. "I'm just saying, if my dad wants anyone featured, it's me—"

"I said I got everyone," I snap.

"Damn, chill." He pulls up his T-shirt to wipe the sweat off his forehead.

Principal West hasn't said one word about making sure I feature Josh. He's cared only about Reid.

"Joshua!" Principal West barks.

I inch closer and catch a snippet of their conversation on camera.

"I was ahead of him the entire first half of the race," Josh complains.

"But you didn't *finish* ahead, did you? You never do," West shoots out, his stern expression morphing into a smile as he greets someone else and walks off toward Reid at the finish line.

I manage to capture the hurt in Josh's eyes before he shuts it away when the older alumni surround him and the other runners. They make jokes and slap Josh's back, and though he's laughing, I don't miss the glare he shoots at Reid and his dad.

I cross the square and get close enough to hear what West says. "Nothing to worry about, I take it?"

Reid shakes his head. "Of course not."

"Excellent. Let's walk around—I have several new donors I'd like to introduce you to."

There's a spark of panic in Reid's eye, and I put my camera away and square my shoulders. I got interviews with older alumni and a solid one with Nicole earlier. I can step away for now. Though I should give him the distance he clearly wants, I know him. I *still* know him. Between running with an injury and his insomnia coming back, it's clear he's not taking care of himself the way he needs to.

"Reid!"

They both turn to look at me. Reid's eyes are guarded.

"We're still going to the hot springs, right?" I give Principal West a wide smile. "Team tradition that I'd love to get on camera for the video."

I shoot Reid a significant look, and he nods quickly.

"Uh, yeah."

West smiles. "Ah, well, I suppose there will be time to meet everyone at the Shakespeare event tonight. You're making headway on the project, then, Clara?"

I nod. "Oh, yes. Lots of really interesting footage."

"Excellent! All right, well, see you tonight."

With West still watching us, I start walking toward my car, giving Reid no choice but to follow me. I keep my pace purposely slow for him.

"Thanks for the out, but you don't actually have to take me to the hot springs—"

"Yes, I do."

Even if I don't quite understand why.

But we have to stop by my house first to grab a swimsuit. It's on the way on this side of the mountain. We pull into my driveway, and there are a few cars parked in it that weren't there this morning.

"The Suarezes have descended," Reid observes.

I laugh, but it fizzles out awkwardly when our eyes catch.

"You should probably stay here," I say.

He nods.

We both know the grilling he'd get from my Uncle Marco alone would take the entire day. Besides, he's holding on to his knee for dear life.

I open the front door, and our small house is bursting with chatter and sizzling pans and my cousins running back and forth. Aunt

Lisette is playing the piano, her tattooed arms moving rapidly, while her labradoodle, Moxie, lies at her feet.

It's pure, precious chaos, and I relax instantly. Especially when I hear Mom laugh.

Maybe the Legacy Weekend descent I've been anticipating isn't inevitable. If they're here and she's laughing, we've avoided the worst of it this time. At least I hope so.

"Clara! Do you have a dress for the banquet tomorrow?" Aunt Xi calls to me.

I'm in the kitchen hunting for a Ziploc bag to fill with ice. I find one in the cabinet and call back, "I have no idea!"

"Well, I finally cleaned out my closets this week and brought a giant box of clothes for you," she says. "They're in your room."

That's promising. Aunt Xi has the best style. And it's a relief, because even if I didn't have a dress for the banquet, we can't afford to go shopping right now.

I start to fill the bag with ice from the dispenser when my ten-year-old cousin, Sonia, grabs me by the arm to tell me I got home *just in time* because they're putting on an original play soon. I laugh and tell her I have other plans.

Sonia pops her hip impatiently, looking entirely too much like my Aunt Lisette. "With who? Delaney is almost done with Reina's makeup!"

Ice cubes crash across the linoleum as I accidentally let the bag overflow. "Delaney's here?"

Even through all the noise, all I hear then is Delaney's high-pitched "*Hi!*" when she calls from the hallway bathroom.

She must've come straight from the Fun Run. That's what she would've done a year ago—hell, a month ago—but we haven't spoken one-on-one in so long; she's just going to pretend her showing up at my house is totally normal?

I tuck the ice pack in my bag and head to the bathroom. Delaney is still in her running clothes, her hair frizzing a bit around the hairline. She's applying a shocking amount of blush to the cheeks of my eight-year-old cousin, Reina.

I grab my bathing suit and a towel from the rack behind the door and ball it up in my hands while I greet her. "What are you doing here?"

"Reina's makeup, obviously," Delaney says over Reina's shiny dark hair.

"I'm a fairy!" Reina announces.

"That's awesome," I say. "Um, why don't you go show everyone?"

She springs off the closed toilet where she was perched and runs out to the living room. I close the bathroom door, and Delaney leans against the sink, gripping the lip of it behind her.

I exhale, my heart pounding *hard*. "What is this?" I ask.

She frowns. "What do you mean?"

"You haven't sent me one text in weeks, you barely talked to me last night or at the Fun Run, and now you just show up at my house?"

She tucks her hair behind her ear. The new piercing winks in the light and aggravates me even more. "I know. I'm sorry. I know we need to talk . . . How's it going with Reid?" she asks, searching my face.

I frown. "I don't know. I'm not sure what I expected, but it's harder than I thought. He's actually outside—we're going to the hot springs."

Her eyebrows float up. "Oh."

"Do you want to come?"

She shakes her head immediately, and I'm sure there's something I'm missing here.

"What happened? Are you just busy?" I ask. "Did I do something?"

She swallows hard, her eyes going glassy. "No."

"Delaney—"

"I'm sorry. I didn't know you had plans. I should go."

She reaches for the knob behind me and pulls at the door until I step out of the way.

"Are you serious?" I call after her into the noise of the household.

She doesn't respond, instead grabbing her jacket from the hall table and rushing outside.

I follow her where the outdoor chill feels better against the sting of her distance.

"Delaney, what's going on?"

"Nothing, you're busy, and I have to get to the *Romeo and Juliet* rehearsal, anyway. They need extras, and all the performing arts alumni got roped in. Let's just talk later?"

"But—"

She turns. "Go easy on him. He's had a rough start to the year."

I fold my arms, my stomach going tight. How does she know that?

She doesn't even wait for me to respond before sliding into her car, which was hidden by my uncle's truck. I watch her back up and drive off, in disbelief. I don't understand her. I don't understand any of this.

What have I done to make her act so weird and avoid me like this? Was it my doc from last year?

I stayed up half the night watching old footage to prepare my interview questions. Delaney was central in all of it, and it reminded me how much she struggled last year. Is that what's going on? Is she upset that I included her in it? She never said anything, but maybe she's been mad at me since the assembly.

When I get back in my car and toss my bathing suit into the back seat, Reid shoves his phone in his pocket. "What was Delaney doing here?"

I let out an exasperated sigh. "I don't know. She's being so weird, I'm kinda worried about her."

"Why? What did she say?" he asks.

My eyebrows come together at his tone. "She said you've had a rough start to the year."

I watch Reid examine the scrapes on his arms, his mouth set like it does when he's being backed into a corner. He exhales and grips his legs, bracing.

"Oh, here." I reach into my bag and hand him the makeshift ice pack. "Looks like you need it."

He blinks down at the bag crinkling softly in his hands.

I don't know if I'm imagining it, but something new and heavy crowds the air between us. Did I overstep with the ice?

"Thanks," he says quietly.

I want to ask him what's going on. Why he seems so stressed—why he isn't sleeping. But he can barely look me in the eye. I remind myself it's none of my business and accept that at least I can do this for him. I'll have my chance to ask him questions during his interview.

"Hot springs?" I ask, trying to pull him out of his head. Trying to hold on to this fragile tether between us.

He nods. "Hot springs."

CHAPTER FOURTEEN

CLARA

THEN

TUCKED AWAY IN A part of the mountain only locals know about, the hot springs were sacred, and going there with Reid for the first time felt . . . significant. Despite our agreement to keep it casual, in the months after that night in my room, things had definitely escalated between us.

When we got there, I started to walk toward the springs I knew well. But Reid reached for my hand, weaving our fingers together, knowing by then how easily they fit.

"C'mon, I want to show you something."

He pulled me past even the most secluded springs. Fifteen minutes, a winding path, and a sharp incline later, I was panting and wondering where the hell he was taking me when there was finally a slight break in the trees I never would've noticed. Reid pulled me through it and down a small slope.

There, overlooking the pines jutting out the side of the mountain, sat a wide, natural spring that I'd never seen in my life.

The secret springs.

"How—*what?*" I spluttered. "I thought this was a Woodhurst myth."

He grinned. "All the varsity teams are sworn to secrecy. It's the perfect temp for muscle soreness."

"On the one hand, I've never been more annoyed about athletic privileges. But on the other . . ." I trailed off and gestured toward the view. The wide sky behind the towering trees.

"I know."

He released my hand to reach for the fabric of his navy Woodhurst High sweatshirt between his shoulder blades. He pulled it and his T-shirt off in one fluid motion. Mercifully, Reid pretended like he didn't notice my low gasp in response to his bare back, but the self-satisfied look on his face told me he hadn't missed it. Like he never missed anything.

I shed my clothes quickly and sank into the spring. The water felt *so* good. Hot as a bath, but not as uncomfortable as a Jacuzzi. Against the cold air it was especially heavenly, and every bit of tension in my body melted away as I slid in deeper.

A sharp breeze rustled through the surrounding trees. I found a small rock to perch on, and I laid my head back a moment, surveying the cold sky. The loamy scent of the forest meant it was definitely going to rain soon.

"I love it here," I said reverently.

"You showed me your favorite place," he said, referring to the overlook I'd taken him to on a hike the week before. "I wanted to do the same."

I bent my knees, settling deeper into the water until it was up to my collarbone. "This is your favorite place?"

He nodded. "But I don't let myself come here often. I have to earn it."

That caught me off guard. "What do you mean?"

"It's my ultimate motivation. When I'm training, when I race. I don't get to come here unless I win or PR or otherwise hit a new goal I've set."

I considered him. "That's kind of intense."

"You don't get to where I want to be without mental tricks." He pulled his elbows out of the water, leaned them back against the rock edge. Steam curled off his wet biceps. "There's this quote from Steve Prefontaine—you know, the god of distance runners? It goes, 'To give anything less than your best is to sacrifice the gift.' I don't know why I'm good at running when I'd rather be better at something that doesn't have an expiration date . . . like writing, maybe. But I am. It's the only way I even have a chance at college. So . . ." He trailed off.

"You're unwilling to sacrifice the gift," I finished his sentence.

He stared at me. "Exactly."

When he looked at me like that, I was all too aware how alone we were. How much closer I wanted him. As if reading my mind, he crossed through the water toward me, the look on his face searching and curious. My eyes followed the beads of water trailing down his throat as our fingers locked together.

Another gust of wind rushed around us, kicking my hair up as our lips met. The kiss was slow. Deep. But the more tender he was with me, the more anxious I felt.

The less certain that I'd be okay when this all inevitably stopped. When we stopped.

I was way out of my depth with him. The feelings coming up, too big. But I reminded myself that we *both* had grand plans. There was no way he'd want whatever this was between us to spiral much more, either.

I curled my arms around his neck and deepened the kiss with a ferocity I didn't know I had. Gripping my hips in response, he guided me to the edge of the spring, his mouth never leaving mine. As his hands wandered and explored my drenched skin, I coiled my body tighter against his. His stomach rippled into goose bumps against my own.

When the next blast of wind shook the trees, it carried voices. Were they just from the springs below?

We both pulled back, panting a bit.

"Reid," I tried weakly.

"Yeah?"

He wrapped a strong, wet arm around me, kissing me again, and I forgot what I was going to say. I'm not sure if I jumped up or he hiked me up or some combination of the two, but somehow my legs wrapped around his waist and he held me just above the water, his hands hooked under me.

And we were in that position, his mouth on my neck, when the varsity cross-country team came bursting through the trees.

"Oh my god! My eyes, my eyes!" Mitchell exclaimed, throwing a hand over his face and his other arm out in an attempt to block the guys behind him. As if that would do anything. They all saw us and started laughing and hollering.

"Fuck," Reid rasped as he slowly lowered me back into the water. I could feel that I was bright red.

A few of the guys looked at me like I had just gotten a lot more interesting. Well, this was going to do wonders for the rumors about me.

Kenji exclaimed, "Dude! We have one rule for the springs—no hooking up!"

I was a mess inside. Embarrassed and delirious and simultaneously grateful and furious with them for interrupting whatever *that* was turning into. But I shoved it all down and put my best skill to use as I swung around, my face placid.

"Relax. We stopped, didn't we?" I muttered, sinking low into the water.

"She's not even varsity," Nicole exclaimed from behind the guys as the girls' team brought up the rear. Because of course they were there, too. She had barely acknowledged me since the truth-or-dare party, but at that moment she was looking straight at me, disgust all over her face.

"It's a fucked-up rule. We're a team," Reid said.

"It's fine," I said just to him.

He frowned. "No, it isn't."

The rest of the girls followed Nicole's lead as they shot me judgy glances, further determined to ostracize me from the team, no doubt.

I had to admit that it stung.

Everyone else seemed to get over their shock by stripping down and getting in the spring themselves. Nicole and the rest of the girls were very obviously talking shit about me on the other side of the water, whispering among themselves, then looking at me and laughing.

I wanted nothing more than to leave, but I didn't want to give anyone the satisfaction of driving me out.

"Where's your camera?" Logan asked me once he got in the water. "She never goes anywhere without it," he told Hank, a junior he was training to take over the AV stuff for yearbook.

"She probably has it hidden back there to make a sex tape," Heather said.

Everyone exploded into laughter. Reid and I exchanged a glance, and he rolled his eyes in a way that told me to ignore them. Easier said than done.

"Please don't put that image in my head," Mitchell said, shuddering again.

Logan laughed, which made Mitchell turn bright pink. Turning toward Reid, Logan asked, "Ready for track this year?"

"Sure." Reid shrugged.

"This guy," Logan said to the same junior he'd been talking to before. "I can never fucking catch him in the fifteen hundred." Logan chuckled and slapped a congenial hand on Reid's shoulder.

I wasn't the only one who caught the flare of jealousy in Mitchell's eye. Kenji pulled Mitchell by the elbow away from the conversation and said something low that made him laugh. Logan pretended not to notice, but I saw his jaw jump in response.

"You got close a few times," Reid said, being generous. Logan was nowhere near Reid's level, but Reid was sensitive to Logan living in the shadow of his older brother, Noah. He never wanted Mitchell to feel that way. "How's your preseason going?"

Logan laughed again. "You mean you don't follow my stats?"

Reid's nostrils flared, but his tone was more playfully annoyed than angry. "I don't follow what isn't relevant to me winning."

Hank laughed along with Mitchell and Kenji, and my chest sparked with pride. I'm not sure what it said about me that I found the competitive part of Reid incredibly hot.

Josh, who had been silently watching us, rolled his eyes. "The guy's going to Stanford, so he suddenly thinks he's better than everyone."

I blinked. *Stanford?* He'd decided?

Reid's voice was sharp. "How did you know about that?"

Josh sneered, his lip curling up. "I haven't heard the fucking end of it since your dad told mine."

"I feel like Reid's dad would've really liked *Gossip Girl*," Mitchell chuckled, trying to clear the anger that had taken over Reid's expression.

Reid didn't laugh. He wouldn't meet my eyes, either.

Stanford. Holy shit. I knew it was an option, but . . . I didn't know it was the *choice*. Why wouldn't he tell me something like that?

Not long after, the sky darkened as the threatening clouds finally moved overhead. A plunking rain picked up to a steady, heavy rhythm. Everyone shrieked and scattered as we pulled ourselves out of the springs and gathered our clothes and shoes.

I wasn't as familiar with the narrow path back down the mountain. The rest of the team passed us as I descended slowly, Reid right in front, guiding me down the muddy trail.

Just as we got to level ground, the sky fully opened into a downpour.

"C'mon!" He grabbed my hand, and we ran, laughing, to the near-empty parking lot.

We landed inside the cab of his truck just in time. In a matter of seconds, it turned into a full deluge. The wind howled through the trees, blowing the rain sideways and rocking the truck a little.

"We should stay here until it calms down," Reid said, watching the swaying branches through the windshield. He had a point; the drive back to town was windy and steep, with a sharp cliff drop on one side.

We were completely soaked. His dark eyelashes spiked with water, his hair a wet mess across his forehead. We were still in our swimsuits, and he grabbed a dry towel from behind his seat. We dried off as best we could, and he wrapped the towel around my shoulders.

The truck was already warm, but Reid still cranked the knob on the dashboard, turning the heat up higher. He brought my hands to his lips, and his breath grazed my knuckles when he said, "I should've told you about Stanford."

I shook my head quickly. "It's fine." The needle of hurt I felt wasn't fair. We weren't serious. He didn't owe me anything.

"I wasn't keeping it from you, it's just not a done deal. But I do think I want to stay in California." He flicked a glance at me, then back down at our hands. "To be close."

California Film Academy was in the Bay Area—not far from Stanford. Did he mean . . . ?

"Close to what?"

"Here. Home. You know how my dad had surgery before summer training started? I know he's fine now," he rushed to say. "But . . . I want to be closer than the East Coast, which was my other option."

I nodded slowly. "That makes sense. It's actually the same reason I want CAFA over some of the bigger film schools. To stay close to my mom . . . in case."

Still, I hated myself a little for needing to leave, terrified of what it might do to her.

But Reid understood that. Understood me. My heart jumped as he drew small circles across the skin of my knee with his fingertips. "It doesn't hurt that Stanford will be close to you, too."

Fear spread fast from the center of my chest. I couldn't deny that I had the same thought, knowing it clashed with what my mom said to me.

Find your own *feet. Don't follow his.*

"*If* I get in," I reminded him. Reminded myself. "*If* I get a scholarship—"

"I know," he said, calmly cutting me off. I hoped that he really did know. That we shouldn't get our hopes up.

"But I wish you believed in yourself more, Clara."

Out of nowhere my eyes got hot. My own parents forgot about me most of the time. I'd learned long ago not to expect too much from anyone. Only, Reid kept showing up being exactly who I needed. I didn't understand it. I kept trying to resist it.

Because what if our lives went in opposite directions? What if it was never like this again?

When had that started to matter to me?

I held his gaze, trying to convey the torturous thoughts going through my head.

"Hey." His voice softened so much I wanted to cry. "What's that face?"

"You're really going to leave," I whispered, my voice almost breaking. It was the closest I could get to telling him how I felt. To describe the rush of longing and desperation coursing through my veins, thudding my heart so hard it ached.

He drew me closer, his fingers squeezing the soft flesh of my waist. "So will you," he promised.

In that moment, as the pounding rain shielded us from everything else, I needed to be close to him in a way I understood better.

The towel slipped off me as I pulled my hair out of its ponytail; the wet strands slapped against my shoulders. His grip on my leg tightened as the lilac scent of my shampoo filled the space.

Lifting my knee, I slowly hooked it around him. My hair fell across my face and neck as I moved, and his eyes widened when he realized what I was doing. I studied the near-invisible freckles across his cheekbones as I hovered above him, my legs on either side of his lap, my back bumping against the steering wheel.

He gripped my hip with one hand, while his featherlight touch brushed my hair behind my shoulder with the other. "Maybe we shouldn't."

"Why not?" I skimmed my nose down the line of his, dragging my nails along the back of his neck.

"I—I can't think when you do that," he said, laughing a little.

"Good," I teased.

He smiled against my lips before pulling back slightly. "I just mean . . . Do we really want to do it *here*?"

"We don't have to," I breathed. "But it's just us."

Us. A small word that meant so much. That broke so often.

In that searching look, we both knew what we wanted.

Our lips met in a gasp. He usually slowed me down, but we were as frenzied as the wind that shook the world outside. My hands went everywhere—into his hair, grasping down his bare back. I traced my fingertips along either side of his rib cage and felt the moan from his chest in my own.

All the while we barely broke apart. He kissed me harder, his skin hot against mine, and rasped my name across my mouth—my neck. It felt like a plea. I couldn't understand why tears sprang to my eyes. Why the closer we got, why the more we followed this feeling down each other's bodies, the harder my heart hurt.

"You're shaking," he whispered.

"I know."

But it wasn't from the cold. The rumors were wrong. I'd never done this with anyone.

I drew his lips back to mine, clung to him as hard as I dared. Enclosed in that moment, trying to seal it, knowing it was only a matter of time before it shattered. His mouth slid down my throat, and my head fell back, goose bumps rippling down my skin from Reid's reverent touch.

I let myself get lost in all the sensations jolting through me. Until his hands slowed, light fingertips across my jaw, down my neck, my sternum. My eyes flickered open, and I caught his gaze roaming the same path—my face, my hair, my body above him.

A newfound warmth overtook his expression that dropped my

stomach like a stone. Our panting chests rose and fell in tandem as we looked at each other.

"Clara." He swallowed. The corner of his mouth hiked up. "I—"

I pressed a panicked hand to his mouth. "Don't."

He blinked. Once. Twice.

I didn't know what I was doing, just that I needed to do it. That I didn't want to hear what he was going to say. There was no part of me that could hear it and still let him go.

I *had* to be able to let him go.

He frowned, and I lowered my hand.

"Don't?" he repeated, his tone disbelieving.

A heavy silence filled the space as he watched me, waiting for an explanation I didn't have. All I knew was that look told me we were headed for something I couldn't possibly handle. Sex was one thing. But this . . . this was something else. Something that almost overtook me.

I shook my head and slid off his lap, reaching through the pile of clothes for my shirt.

"You were right. We shouldn't" was all I said.

I snuck a glance at him—his hair mussed, his strong, bare chest glowing in the dim light—and he looked bewildered. Crushed.

"It's just better if we keep things—"

"Casual," he finished. "I know."

He didn't sound angry, but he wouldn't look at me. His brow was low, his posture tight just like it had been when I first met him. Everything he had opened to me the past several months had slammed shut the moment I wouldn't let him finish that sentence.

Wordlessly, I slipped my damp shirt on. He did the same, the muscle in his jaw jumping over and over. The storm outside had calmed, too. Enough to drive, at least. But he didn't start the truck.

"I'm sorry," I whispered.

He finally met my eyes again. They were yearning and sad, and I wanted nothing more than to fix it.

But I didn't know if I could.

Because making promises to him meant breaking promises to myself.

CHAPTER FIFTEEN

REID

NOW

ONE DAY UNTIL LEGACY BANQUET

@haikuforyou
The sky over the
mountain is still not enough
to hold what we lost

WE DON'T GO TO the secret springs. I wouldn't make it with my knee like this anyway. I nearly ruined everything when it gave out at the finish line. It was almost a relief until my dad came rushing over to me. The panic on his face was enough to make me play it cool.

I just tripped on a rock. No big deal.

"I'll be right back," Clara says as she heads to the one-stall bathroom at the nearby trailhead to change.

Being up here together has my traitorous brain flashing back to last winter. Muddy crushed leaves on the ground, Clara's limbs around me in the hot water just before the storm broke. Just us. Heat shoots up the back of my neck at the memory.

Still, as soon as she mentioned the springs when she rescued me from West, my body ached to be here.

The ice in the car helped, and I'm able to walk without limping to the hot springs closest to the turnout. A family I recognize is there. The mom works at the Haven bookstore, and she helped me find books from time to time. They all send me excited, knowing waves.

I have my part to play—the Golden Boy—and wave back.

There are a few logs to the side of the springs, smoothed over from time and touch. I kick off my shoes and set the towel down on the one with initials and curse words etched into the bark. I can feel the family's attention at my back, and I linger, checking my phone.

There's nothing new from Legacy Lore, but panic flares when I see the follower count on the profile rapidly climbing. Like walls closing in. Made more intense by Delaney showing up at Clara's earlier, making it clear my time is running out.

A combination of guilt and dread churn my stomach knowing I have to tell her.

Clara's approaching footsteps snap me to attention. I quickly tuck my phone into the rest of my stuff, covering it with my shirt.

When I look up, her hair is in a messy bun on top of her head, a navy-colored towel wrapped around her. The strings of a black bikini tied behind her neck peeking out of it. It's been hard enough to see her fully clothed. But glimpsing her smooth skin again, every moment between us floods my system, and my body doesn't know the difference between then and now.

I don't know why I let this happen—we shouldn't be here together. Especially not if she brought me here out of guilt. Not when I'm the guilty one now.

The towel slips a little as she kicks off her shoes at the edge of the spring. That's when I see it. A flash of black ink on the side of her rib cage.

A tattoo.

I know Clara planned to get one after her eighteenth birthday from her Aunt Lisette, who's a tattoo artist. But last we spoke about it, she hadn't decided what she wanted.

I'm burning to know what she chose to permanently etch onto her body. I can tell it's a small plant of some kind wrapped around words, but I can't make them out from this distance.

Clara catches me staring. Her cheekbones bloom pink, and I have to blink away from her gaze.

At least we're not alone here, I remind myself.

Of course, in the next moment, the family gets out of the water and starts toweling off to leave.

"I just have to say, we are so thrilled for you," the mom says to me. "Is Stanford as amazing as it seems?"

My chest gets tight. "Yeah. It's—incredible."

I don't miss the way Clara's eyes narrow.

A slight late-morning chill still clings to the air, along with the heavy pine scent of the surrounding trees. I wait for the family to drive off before I strip down. I don't have a suit, but my running shorts under my joggers are fine. I'm more embarrassed taking off the knee brace. Fully aware that Clara is watching my every move as I do.

I used to love the way she watched me. Especially here. But now, she's eyeing my knee with concern, and I fucking hate it.

Clara yelps as she quickly tiptoes across the cold ground. I keep my gaze off her, but at the edge of the hot springs, she drops the towel, and I catch a glimpse of her strong legs as she eases herself in.

I quickly follow. The second I slip into the springs, a sound escapes me from low in my chest. *Holy shit* it feels good. My sore muscles release one by one, and the jumping pain in my knee downshifts to a slow, tolerable throb. This is exactly what I needed.

And she knew it.

I appraise her across the water and am struck all over again by all the exposed skin. The flush high on her cheeks from the heat. So damn pretty.

"A tattoo?" I ask.

The silence stretches so taut it just may snap.

"A tattoo," she finally says.

I wait, but she doesn't elaborate and keeps her torso submerged so I can't see it.

"I guess that means you regret it?" There's no way I'm going to drop it like I know she wants me to.

She wades around, looking everywhere but at me. "Of course not . . . it's just . . . personal."

"Got it." My voice is hard even to my own ears.

I decide to ask her what I've been wondering since I saw her with that camera in her hand last night. She's doing this video for the banquet, to clear the past. But what about her future?

"What's going on with CAFA?" I ask.

She smiles a little. "Like, as an institution? They're still up and running as far as I know."

"Funny," I deadpan.

"I was planning to reapply, but I don't know." She shrugs as if to dismiss it. "There are a lot of film festivals I could enter instead. I could upload my videos online and try to gain traction that way. Why do I even need film school?"

"Because it's your dream," I say plainly.

She pauses, surprised. But no matter the strain between us, it feels wrong to act like we don't still know each other as well as we do.

"I've been working on a new doc all summer, but I don't think it's any good. Mitchell couldn't even follow it."

I scoff. "Mitch can't follow a straight line without getting confused."

A laugh bubbles out of her. I feel it everywhere.

"It's probably better than you think."

She shoots me one of her small smiles that I covet. "Maybe."

The longer we sit here, the more relaxed I get. But it's not only the healing quality of the springs. I realize it's . . . nice. Being here. Being with her. Which is exactly what I was afraid of.

I open my eyes, unsure when I closed them, and she's looking at me, her jaw set in that determined way before she starts asking questions.

"Why does it seem like no one else knows how much pain you're in?" she asks.

I blink, and the lie comes out automatically. "I'm not in pain."

She shoots me a leveling gaze. "Remember when Josh tripped you before state?"

The unpleasant memory forces me to frown. He was lucky all I did was rip my arm open. Hell, I was lucky that's all that happened before the biggest race of the year. Not that it made a difference, since I came in first over his forty-seventh-place finish. By pissing me off, he all but ensured my championship win.

"There was gravel in your hand, your whole arm covered in blood, and I don't think you even *winced*." She shakes her head in exasperation before she keeps going. "You get . . . eerily calm when you're hurt. Like you're unwilling to acknowledge the pain. You had the same look on your face when you crossed the finish line today."

I'm used to people watching me—but I'm not used to them *seeing* me. But she always did. It ignites a longing I've fought to subdue all year.

"*Shit.* This is why—" I stop myself, my voice coming out too loud. A breeze jolts through the trees again, ruffling my hair and raising goose bumps across my arms.

"Why, what?" she prods.

Injuries have a way of teaching us something we need to learn.

If that's really true, then this injury between me and Clara proved to me that I wouldn't survive losing her again. I'm barely making it through as it is.

I have to cut this all the way off.

My chest puffs with my inhale. "This is why I didn't want to do this with you. You bring me here—*here*—and act like that wouldn't hurt worse than my fucking knee."

"I was just trying to help—"

"I don't need your help, Clara. I can take care of myself."

"But you *don't*."

We become locked in a mutual glare.

"How long have you been injured?" she challenges.

I squeeze my hands into tight fists under the water. "Why does it matter to you? I'm recovering. It's no big deal."

"It's a huge fucking deal!" she snaps. "You're an elite runner, it's who you are—"

"No, it's *not*." My voice comes out like a thunderclap, and she goes still.

I push a hand through my hair. It's too much. The posts online, Olympic rumors—a *tattoo*. The heat in my chest with nowhere to go. I jump out of the water, toweling off quickly before I wrench my shirt back on. The water sloshes behind as she follows slowly. But I can't look at her. Not while she dresses.

Not until she says, "I didn't mean it like that." There's a catch in her voice.

"I know," I manage.

But everyone else does, and the frustration at all the limits it puts on me is getting harder and harder to push away. Worse that she gets that. Gets *me*. And I forgot how fucking good that feels.

After the way things ended, I expected her to be nothing but cold to me this weekend. But she's been the opposite. Warm and funny and . . . open.

I don't deserve it.

She steps closer, and all at once her arms are around me. Clara always preferred touching to talking. It was the way she softened to me. But the shock of her body against mine after all this time shuts my brain off for a second.

She nestles her face into the crook of my neck, where she always fit best. Confusing me more. Muddling everything. It feels so familiar, so right—so *deeply* unfair.

We weren't supposed to get personal this weekend. But the lines are already blurring. Embraced like this, I'm too aware that I still miss her. That I'm still angry.

That I'm still so in love with her it hurts to breathe.

But I remind myself she wouldn't even let me tell her how I feel. She never said one thing about the card I gave her on her birthday. Nothing's changed. And I fucked up any chance of it changing the second I let Delaney stay over, anyway.

My heart is banging around my rib cage as I gently draw back so I can get the space I need.

"I'm sorry," I say.

For so much.

"It's okay. I get it." She glides soft fingertips across my forehead to push my wet hair back. It's such a girlfriend move, and I wish I could understand why she does it.

We pull on our shoes in silence. As I pick up the towels to head for the car, I realize I don't know if I'll get the chance to be alone with her again. It's now or never.

"Look, I need to tell you something." I turn when I don't hear her following.

She's crouched down, frozen as she stares at my phone in the dirt.

My stomach plummets at the look on her face. At the way her features slowly, purposefully smooth out. The only way to know that she's upset is that her hands tremble as she gives me the phone.

"Is this why she's been weird?" she says.

I look at the screen, my heart in my fucking throat as I read the text. It's a screenshot from Kenji of the newest Legacy Lore post—Delaney's intro post. My chest goes concave as I read it:

> **@LEGACY_LORE**: Meet Delaney Whitlock. Prima ballerina and Woodhurst's own pom-squad princess, it's no wonder she's beloved by all . . . even her best friend's ex-boyfriend? More soon. ♥

Oh, *fuck* you, Josh.

Below it is a photo of me and Delaney from Kenji's the night before. When we were talking by the stairs and I begged her not to tell Clara anything. I'm leaning in, my lips close to her ear. The conversation looks heated, intense.

The first comment below the post makes everything worse.

Yeah I heard they hooked up in Reid's dorm.

I might throw up. Delaney was right. We should've told Clara everything last night before the story started getting twisted. But I won't let this bullshit threat of "more soon" make things worse.

"It's not what you think."

Clara's gone completely blank. That tough front is back—her jaw set, her eyes hard. Her voice is cold and emotionless when she says, "It's none of my business."

I rear back like I've been slapped. "Yes, it is."

She tries to walk away but seems to think better of it as she turns around to face me. "Why would I believe anything you say? You've been lying since you got home."

"You're right."

Her sharp green eyes pierce mine and I know I have one shot to get this right.

"I've lied about a lot. About school, about my knee. I kept this from you, but I would never lie to you about what happened." My gaze is pleading. "I promise."

She sucks in a breath and gestures to my phone. "Then start talking."

"I don't know who this is or what they think they know . . ." I swipe a hand across my forehead. "But Delaney did visit and stay over last month. She was on my campus for some dance thing."

Clara's nostrils flare but she nods. "Okay . . ."

"My teammates were having a party. I didn't want to go, but . . . she thought it'd be fun. She's still not eating much and she drank a *lot*—" I cut myself off, trying to shake the memory away. It was hard seeing Delaney like that. "We both did."

I think back, try to remember. I know we stumbled back to my dorm and started reminiscing. About high school and the team and Clara.

We talked about Legacy and how we both wanted to go back to what we'd been so excited to escape. At least Woodhurst was familiar when everything else was so new.

"I wasn't handling the changes or the pressure well. My injury was fresh, my head a mess. The guys on the team are hardcore, and Coach is relentless . . . It was all so intense."

Delaney tried calling Clara over and over. I tried calling Mitchell, too. Neither of them picked up, and that made it worse somehow. Like we were the ones who were left behind, even though we weren't the ones home.

Then Delaney lay back on my bed and started crying. Told me how lonely she was at school. I told her I was, too. The rest I mostly remember in flashes. None of them good.

"There was no way she could drive, so she stayed over. We talked awhile. And . . . I know we kissed."

Clara's eyes drill into mine, barely containing her anger. "*And?*"

"I don't remember much else."

Her eyes narrow like she doesn't believe me.

"I *know* I fucked up—" Shame cuts my breath short because the details are fuzzy. But there is one thing I know for sure. "We didn't have sex like this post is suggesting."

"Did you want to?"

"*No*. The whole thing was kind of awful, actually—"

"Oh, was it?" she snaps, her biting tone dripping with sarcasm. "Was hooking up with my best friend *awful for you*?"

"Yes."

My voice is strangled. She goes still, some of the anger draining as it's replaced with hurt.

"I can't believe this."

"It was nothing—"

"Then why keep it from me? Why didn't you text me or call me or *something*?"

Because I couldn't hear her voice knowing she didn't want me. I couldn't text with her like we were just friends. I couldn't believe what I had done.

But all I can manage to say is, "I couldn't."

I scrub my hands down my face, fatigue compressing my skull from the inside out. "It was a drunken mistake. I don't like her like that and never have, but I knew that—"

I stop myself as our gazes collide again.

"What?" she urges.

The air between us vibrates the longer we stare at each other. The longer she waits for me to finish that sentence.

"I know it's over. It's *been* over. But—" I sigh, push a hand through my hair again. "I knew the second you found out, I'd lose you for good."

It's an admission that she tracks instantly. That I had hope before that, despite the way things ended, we might stand another chance someday.

She shakes her head. "Wow. What a convenient excuse. Blame *me* for what you two did."

"That's not—"

But she's walking away, furious. Which is exactly what I knew would happen. Exactly what I deserve.

Fracturing all over again.

CHAPTER SIXTEEN

REID

THEN

THE EARLY HOUR OF the sunrise hike could have accounted for the reason Clara and I were both silent as we walked, but not for the tension hanging between us. That had been there ever since the hot springs, when I realized I couldn't keep things casual anymore.

Knowing that if I told her that, I could lose her.

"You're . . ." Clara trailed off, cocking her head to the side as she examined me. "Different today."

"Different?"

"Yeah . . . Everything okay?" she asked seriously.

I wasn't sure it would be once I gave her the card.

"Of course." I forced away my nerves with a cocky smile, just like I did before a race. "It's your birthday."

We were on a part of the trail that had narrowed to a single-file footpath. When the scrape of her boots stopped in the dirt, I turned. She was fighting a smile when she said, "You remembered."

I let out an exaggerated scoff. "You think I arranged a sunrise hike to your favorite overlook because I like getting up before dawn?"

"You athletes are weird like that."

I brushed the ponytail off her neck, placing a soft kiss below her ear. "Happy birthday."

She sighed. "You're trying to distract me. But something could still be up with you despite the global sensation that is my eighteenth birthday."

That pulled a laugh out of me. "If only we'd planned a parade."

"You mean you didn't?" Her mouth fell open in dramatic shock.

"Missed opportunity," I agreed wistfully.

She tapped the tip of my nose and grinned. "You'll do better next year." Our gazes caught, and she looked away quickly. "I mean, not that we'll still—" She squeezed her eyes shut. "You know what I mean."

Sometimes being with Clara felt like walking a tightrope of uncertainty. One minute we'd be joking or kissing or talking, and the next, something would happen that made everything shake.

As if trying to get us back to solid ground, she pulled out her camera and asked, "Message for the birthday girl?"

Instead of smoothing the moment, the silence extended as I held her eyes with mine, so ready to tell this girl how I felt. The words had formed on my tongue, only she stepped back and changed the subject with a joke the way she always did when she was uncomfortable.

"You forgot to get me a birthday present, didn't you? *That's* why you're being weird."

It was my turn to flush. I didn't forget.

That was why I had her card with me. I'd spent the previous week writing it, throwing it out, rewriting it. I brushed my fingers across the edge of the envelope in my back pocket, my heart hammering.

"Actually—"

Both of our phones buzzed with a text from Delaney in the group chat.

We read it quickly: I have it on good authority Legacy spots have been chosen!!! Can't believe we have to wait until tomorrow!!

"Doomsday approaches," I joked.

But Clara didn't laugh.

Birds chirped in the surrounding trees, their calls faintly echoing across the canyon.

"I have a bad feeling," Clara said quietly. "What if I don't get it?"

If I had learned anything from my years running, it was how competition *really* worked. Who was serious and who would fall away when the course tested them. Clara was as serious as they get. Determined to see her dream through. She'd already done the hard part by actually getting into California Film Academy. The day she found out was probably the happiest I'd ever seen another person.

"In that *highly* unlikely scenario, it wouldn't stop you. Nothing can stop you."

"Do you really believe that?" she asked, her eyes round with a mix of fear and hope.

"Yes," I soothed, grabbing her hands. "You're going to be chosen as a Legacy, get the scholarship you deserve for film school, and make amazing films that change the world." I trailed my finger under her jaw and lifted slightly. "So chin up, Suarez."

"What am I going to do without you next year?"

That stung, but for reasons I couldn't quite articulate. Why did she keep saying stuff like that? "CAFA is only a few miles from Stanford," I reminded her.

She pressed her forehead into my chest. "I know."

I tried to decipher that torn look on her face as she looked up at me again. To figure out what she was thinking.

To know if I was alone out there or if those two words meant she'd finally changed her mind about the future of us.

If she hadn't, I'd respect her choice like I had all year. It'd tear me apart, but I'd respect it. And I'd keep the card to myself.

But if she had . . .

I leaned down, losing myself in the softness of her mouth and that gasp across my lips when my palms found the bare skin of her waist under her shirt. Though I tried to slow us down and savor it, she threaded her hands through my hair and tugged. Was she trying to kill me? I let out a gruff, urgent sound, and she smiled. Yep. She was.

Holding her jaw, I deepened the kiss. She gripped me to her, kissing me back hard and hungry. As if trying to convey something new. Something that we were both chasing as we clung to each other.

It wasn't until the footsteps from nearby hikers approached that we broke apart. Her gorgeous eyes were half-lidded, her breaths heavy. It pulled a smug smirk out of me. I wasn't the only one dying here.

As we started moving again, those two soft words clanged around in my head.

"I know."

She could act tough all she wanted. But the way she kissed me—the yearning in her voice a mirror to my own—told me she felt the same way.

The next day at the assembly everything would change. She'd become a Legacy, we'd get out of Woodhurst and away from all this pressure, and she'd see that we could do this for real.

With a quick glance to make sure she wasn't looking, before I could quadruple-guess myself again, I pulled the card out of my pocket and slipped it into her backpack.

CHAPTER SEVENTEEN

CLARA

THEN

AT THE LEGACY ASSEMBLY, I was a wreck. Reid put a reassuring hand on my bobbing knee and squeezed. Things had become strange between us since the hot springs. He'd been distant—which I thought I wanted. We spent my birthday together the day before, and while I didn't mind that he hadn't given me a gift, it was unexpected. I didn't know how to act around him, either.

Especially not in this moment that my entire life hinged on.

The lights lowered as the assembly was about to start. The nerves weren't just about the decision, though. As part of my Legacy submission, I used the same documentary sample as my CAFA application. It was a short glimpse into the longer doc I was making about the Legacy Program and Woodhurst.

I had received a message the night before that they wanted to use the video to hype everyone up. That felt like a really good sign, but it would be the first time my work outside of yearbook videos would be seen by so many people.

The assembly began like it had every year prior, with a full-out dance performance by the pom squad. Delaney was front and center, sparkly and dazzling as always. When it was over and the crowd calmed down, the projection screen descended behind Principal West onstage.

It was time to announce the Legacies. My mom was in the crowd, still in scrubs, having rushed from work. But she was there, and that's what mattered to me.

Principal West propped his reading glasses on and, after a short speech about the importance of Legacy, he began to read out four names I expected to hear. Reid Rousseau. Amaya Masters. Joshua West. Delaney Whitlock.

The fifth and final name was one I'd only dared to hope for.

Mine.

Reid wrenched me into a hug. My mom waved to me from her spot in the crowd, eyes shining. Everything slotted into place. My dreams. My future. I was going to film school, and I was getting out of Woodhurst. It was a joyous, riotous blur. Maybe the best moment of my life.

"To celebrate, we have something very special to share with you. Clara, who is planning to attend California Film Academy this fall to study documentary filmmaking, has made a video about our esteemed Legacy Program. You'll see exactly why she was chosen as a Legacy."

The lights went out, and the screen flickered on, but the image remained black as we heard only the sound of heavy breathing and the *clack-swish, clack-swish* of what I knew were toe shoes hitting the studio floor over and over.

Everyone cheered as Delaney filled the screen doing pirouette after pirouette after pirouette. I'd cut her four-hour rehearsal down to a handful of seconds. She tried to get a new move exactly right but kept wobbling. After every slip she'd study herself in the dance mirror—drawing her hands across her collarbones or her hips, or squeezing her thighs then trying again. Especially when her dance teacher yelled at her in a clipped accent that she kept landing "heavy—too *heavy*."

It was a similar grueling opening for everyone featured. Amaya on the stage warming up her voice when she had pneumonia, Josh typing an essay on the bus after one of our races, Reid running sprints over and over on the school track.

I caught a close-up of Reid, sweat slipping down his nose as he caught his breath. He stood, dropped his water bottle onto the grass and went back to the track.

My voice filtered from off camera, asking him an off-the-cuff question, "You're going again? Aren't you tired?"

He shot me a devilish grin over his shoulder. I remembered being so proud I had the camera trained on him as he panted out, "It's about what you do when you're tired."

Everyone cheered again as the rock music I'd put over that moment swelled.

But then in an instant it cut out.

The screen went black on a part that I knew was supposed to cut to a close-up of the blood seeping through Reid's sweaty, dirty arm bandage at state that he refused to let Coach look at. It was the beginning of the real story of Legacy. How hard everyone pushed to achieve it.

But that's not what played. People clearly thought the cutout was intentional at first, but the longer the screen was dark, the confusion started to rise. Both in the room and in me.

Did something happen to the computer? The file?

It finally started up again. Only, it wasn't my doc. It was a blurry, bobbing image of a chaotic party. Of a girl wrapped around a guy. His back was to the camera. The room was dark and the video grainy, but the only thing that was absolutely clear was her face—*my* face—when I pulled back for a second.

Next to me Reid breathed, "What the fuck?"

Because it wasn't just a video of me.

It was a video of me making out with Josh at that party last summer.

The voices around us rose with laughter and shock, and Principal West stormed onto the stage, waving his arms frantically at the projection booth. Just in time for the image of me pulling his son's shirt off to be displayed across his chest. I had been so drunk, I didn't even remember doing that. I hadn't even realized someone else had come into the room.

Eons passed before the screen cut to black.

My ears rang, my body heavy and weightless all at once as I stood. Everyone staring. Low murmurs and shocked whispers.

Except from Reid, who looked like he wanted to set the gym on fire.

It was supposed to be a triumphant moment. Showing my work to the school. Becoming a Legacy. Securing my future out of Woodhurst.

My future with Reid.

I was in such shock, I wasn't sure how I got out of there. But my churning stomach forced me to my feet.

I burst through the auditorium doors and managed to make it to the hallway trash can before I threw up. Hands wrapped around my hair to keep it out of my face. Delaney's hands.

I cleaned up in the bathroom, rinsing my mouth and splashing water on my face over and over. Trying to convince myself I would be okay. Somehow I would be okay. But nothing worked. Delaney handed me some gum and rubbed my back. When we emerged, Reid, Principal

West, and my mom—more furious than I'd ever seen her—were all waiting in the hallway with somber expressions.

"Come with me," Principal West said.

I shook the entire way to his office. Embarrassed and terrified and so confused. Why would anyone record that? Play it?

Who could hate me so much they'd do that?

As soon as the door closed, my mom rounded on him.

West's expression flattened like he knew what was coming. "Dani—"

"What just happened to my daughter is *unconscionable,* Ryan!"

Hearing them call each other by their first names was always the creepiest reminder they went to high school together.

"This is simply not the kind of behavior the program can condone—"

The rest of Principal West's speech was exactly what I expected the second I saw my face on the video. All about the rules and expectations of a Legacy. His first concern was not about how this happened or who was behind it. Or how humiliating it was. Or protecting me, his student.

It was about the way a potential Legacy made the program look.

Made him look. Made his son look.

It took me a moment to fully understand what he was saying. Which was that I was no longer eligible for the scholarship.

"That's *ridiculous,*" my mom spat.

I tried to defend myself, my entire face burning. "Kissing isn't against the rules."

"What about the person who recorded it?" Reid asked.

"And just played it in front of the entire school?" Delaney continued. "Are *they* going to be punished?"

Principal West shook his head, holding his hands up. "Everyone needs to calm down. I appreciate you're upset for your friend, but this really doesn't concern either of you. I think it would be best if you left."

My throat constricted when neither Delaney nor Reid moved.

West sighed. "Clara, what just happened was . . . unfortunate. I enjoyed your documentary very much and appreciate all your contributions to Woodhurst. We'll of course do our best to get to the bottom of what transpired here today, but . . . I can't make any promises."

Reid's face went furious. "That's it?"

My pulse flew, but I met Principal West's eyes when I asked, "Is Josh disqualified?"

"Why would he be?"

The silence was cacophonous.

"Because he was in the video, too!" Delaney's arms flew to either side as she stated the obvious.

West cleared his throat. "Though less than wholesome, it isn't only what transpired in the video that is of concern."

"Then what's the problem?" Mom asked.

The leather chair West sat in creaked as he leaned back and rubbed his brow bone with his thumb and forefinger. "It's that word has gotten around suggesting some students with connections to the program have been used in exchange for putting in a good word for those seeking to use them."

"And you believe that?" I asked, my shaky voice almost lilting to a laugh at my utter disbelief.

He leveled his gaze on me. "It's not about what I believe. It is now too difficult to refute. Joshua *did* put in a good word for you, and it is now impossible to know whether that was done in good faith."

The fight in me started to wane. Maybe I *had* done nothing to earn it other than throw myself at the principal's son.

"Furthermore, Legacies are role models. We cannot choose someone who clearly has no regard for the rules." He sniffed. "Or their own reputation for that matter."

"This is *so* unfair. We all break the rules all the time—" Delaney started.

I reached out and gripped her wrist, telling her to stop for her own sake.

West shot her a disapproving look. "Be that as it may, *your* actions weren't just on display for the entire community, including half the board. I'm afraid my hands are tied."

There was no winning, though that didn't stop Mom from trying. She ushered me out after giving my arm a reassuring squeeze and closed the door firmly behind her. She and West argued in his office for what seemed like hours. Despite it all, he wouldn't budge. She went home, fuming. My friends went home.

Reid didn't.

We wandered outside. The assembly crowd had long since dispersed. We slowly walked along the road outside school when it finally hit me. It was over.

"I'm never—" I pressed a hand to my mouth because I couldn't bring myself to say it.

I'm never leaving Woodhurst.

In a few steps, Reid closed the distance I always tried to keep and swept me up. Pressed into the warmth of his neck, the tears came. He gently rocked me there on the side of the quiet mountain road as everything I thought I had been building turned to rubble and dust at my feet.

"It's a detour," he breathed. "Not a dead end."

I was terrified that the minute I let go of him, I would plummet into a level of low I had only seen from the outside. Into a hole so deep, no one could ever pull me back out. So I stood there and let myself need him the way I never let myself need anyone. Held him while I still had him.

After I calmed down, I pulled away, my thoughts careening in a thousand directions.

"What can I do?" Reid asked.

"Nothing. It's over. It's all over." I wanted to cry more, but no tears would come. A strange, welcome numbing spreading all over my body.

Reid shook his head. "We can fight this. This is *profoundly* fucked up. These are impossible standards, Clara. It's not your fault."

"Impossible or not, those are the rules," I said with a shrug.

He swallowed, pushed a hand through his hair. "The rules don't make sense. This whole program doesn't make sense! You can't let them win—"

"I just lost my one chance at college, Reid. Whoever hates me enough to do that—whoever wanted to humiliate me in there, did. They already won."

His expression flattened until he looked just like Coach. "When you're on top, people are always going to try to take you down. You can't just give up."

My laugh was sharp and empty. "Oh, I'm sorry I don't have the *championship* mentality right now."

"That's not what I meant."

"Why are you even here?" I pushed.

His eyes pierced into me, an edge of warning to his voice when he said, "Don't do that."

"You just saw me kissing another guy."

He balled his hands into fists and shoved them into his pockets.

"Do you want me to care about something that happened before we got together?"

Of course I didn't. But Reid was competitive. And he hated Josh. Why wasn't he yelling? Why wasn't he walking away? That's what everyone else did.

"You don't care that I hooked up with *Josh*?" I pushed again. "Or that everyone is saying I whored myself out so I could secure my Legacy?"

Reid inhaled through his nose, squeezing his eyes shut. His calm starting to crack. "I care that they're spreading lies about you."

"I lied to you, too," I said, my voice pitching higher with the urge to drive him as far away from me as possible. "Remember? I told you nothing ever happened."

He stayed quiet a beat too long.

"You can go, Reid. It's okay. We've always said this isn't serious."

"Clara—"

"Just because we were hooking up doesn't mean you owe me anything."

Reid's entire body went still as if I'd slapped him. A chilling, humorless breath escaping him. "Wow. Okay."

But he needed to understand that my door had closed, while his was as open and golden as ever. I didn't want him to tether himself further to my sinking ship.

He started pacing, visibly upset.

"I just meant I wouldn't blame you," I clarified. "Not that you're only a hookup to me. You have to know that."

He stopped, his scoff hitting me in the solar plexus. But he was eerily calm. It was much worse than if he had yelled. "How would I know that? You do nothing but mess with my head."

I reared back. "What?"

"The *second* you let me in, you shove me out again."

"I do not," I shot back.

"No? Then what just happened? It's the same thing that happened in my truck."

My cheeks blazed thinking of that moment in his truck when he looked at me with so much tenderness I thought I might combust.

When I didn't say anything, he stepped closer to me, thick gravel crunching under his boots. "You want me close,"—his voice went hoarse—"but you won't even let me tell *you* how I feel about you."

"Because I don't want to know!"

My pulse jackhammered through me when his dark eyes flashed with that same determined look he got before a race. He closed the last of the space between us until we were a breath apart, his voice dropping low and rough when he said, "You already do."

Fresh tears pushed through my lashes. I swatted them away, trying to think—trying to *breathe.*

His chest rose and fell, but he put a steady fingertip under my chin and lifted it, not letting me look away.

We stared at each other for a long time. He was never going to give up. The champion in him would go to any lengths. If I let this go on, he'd give us everything he had. Half stuck in Woodhurst with me.

But he deserved so much better; a clean slate. A real escape from the limits of this town and these terrible people. I couldn't be the person who held him back.

The ends of his hair were starting to curl in the damp air, and the hollows of his cheeks were flushed. He pressed his forehead to mine. "Why won't you let me in?"

I could've said, *Because I don't deserve you.* Or *Because you're destined for things so far beyond my reach.*

Or *Because it's not enough that I love you, too.*

I cleared my throat and backed away. "I can't do this anymore."

His eyes closed slowly. I went instantly cold when he dropped his hand. "So you're done? Just like that?"

My chest felt splintered when I said, "We were never going to work anyway."

"Clara . . . This is *something*."

I let my gaze trace every line of his face. To absorb what it felt like when he looked at me like that one last time. "I know it is," I admitted, voice shaking. I had to keep myself from throwing my arms around him and instead try to help him understand. "But it isn't everything."

My heart was screaming at me that I was making a huge mistake as I watched him walk in a daze to the driver's side door of his truck. The old metal creaked as he opened it, but he hesitated before climbing in.

Our eyes caught, and the corner of his mouth hiked up a little. "It was everything to me."

All breath left my body.

I watched him drive off, too stunned to cry again. When it was clear he was gone, that I had really ended the best thing that had ever happened to me, I slowly sank to the ground, wishing I was better. Wishing I was stronger. Wishing love hadn't found us.

Because it ruined everything.

Or maybe I did.

CHAPTER EIGHTEEN

CLARA

NOW

ONE DAY UNTIL LEGACY BANQUET

MY HANDS ARE VIBRATING against the steering wheel, tears streaming down my face as I drive home from the hot springs. When Reid told me at Kenji's last night that he's not with anyone, I assumed that meant he hadn't been with anyone since me. That it meant something significant.

Now I know just how wrong I was.

At least I managed to keep it together until I dropped Reid off at home. Until I was no longer confined in the same small space with him. But now that I'm alone, everything I've kept inside for months pours out of me.

How could they have done this?

My body feels cold all over, the shock and betrayal hitting me in waves. Delaney spent a night with Reid in a room I've never seen. Met his teammates and talked to him about his injury. Supported him. *Kissed* him. And who knows what else happened between them?

Even though he claims he doesn't remember, they were alone and drunk, and he's become too good at lying. How can I believe he would be honest with me about this when I wasn't honest with him about Josh? Maybe this was his way of hurting me back.

Hurting me *worse*.

Because even though we weren't together, and even if there have been others, this is *Delaney*.

I take a sharp turn too fast, memories from last year rushing through my mind as quickly as the trees blur down the road. Of her telling me how cute she thought he was, pushing me to go for it with him, her daring him to kiss me, her dancing with him at homecoming. The way she told me I was making a mistake after I broke things off. It was all so high school . . . but also stunningly present now.

I don't want to believe it's because she wanted him for herself.

But maybe that's exactly what it means.

Maybe Josh, of all people, was right that she's behind Legacy Lore. That she spilled this to let me know. To hurt Reid.

I realize I'm driving faster than I mean to when the approaching stoplight turns red and I have to slam on my brakes to avoid careening into the intersection. People are milling around the town square, talking, laughing—acting like the world didn't just shatter.

Waiting here, I pull in a shaky breath and remind myself that *I* was the one who broke things off with him. I was the one who wanted him to move on. Now that I know he has, I can finally shut down the ridiculous, pathetic hope that there's anything left between us. I can finally stop wondering if I did the right thing.

It's really over.

My spine bows as I hunch against the steering wheel, my shoulders shaking with heavy, fresh sobs. The pain acute from losing him all over again.

A quick honk behind me alerts me that the light's changed. I swipe my sleeve across my eyes and keep driving.

By the time I pull into my driveway back home, all the Suarezes' cars are gone, the house dark and silent. Matching my mood perfectly.

Sadness is contagious here. Sometimes it gets so big it becomes the center of everything—this immovable, choking force driving everyone away from us.

"Mom?" I call out, kicking off my shoes.

She doesn't respond, but I see a glow under her bedroom door. I take in a bracing breath as I pad down the short hallway to check on her, flipping on light switches as I go. The old wood door creaks as I open it, and the television lights her room. Mom is lying in her bed, covered by a rose-colored quilt up to her waist, eyes puffy and nose red as she watches.

I guess I was wrong about this dip not being that bad. Legacy stuff is always triggering for her. Once I lost my Legacy spot, she was despondent, and I wondered if my failure felt like her loss all over again. How she had to give up her own scholarship and dreams to have me because Dad wasn't willing to do the same.

I hate that I couldn't do right by her by winning my own shot at becoming *someone*.

And it was all made worse by Dad not coming home this weekend like she *still* hoped he would. A part of me wishes I could just scream, *He's never coming back!*

But I never would because I now understand what wishing for another chance does to a person.

I keep my grip tight on the brass doorknob, half in, half out.

"Mama?"

She blinks, startling a little. "Clara? Aren't you supposed to be out with your friends today?" She sits up, smoothing her mussed bedhead.

"I was, and I'll have to leave again in a bit for the play," I say, my nose stuffy from crying.

"All that Legacy nonsense." Her voice is imbued with bitterness. "What are you doing running around filming all the events? You shouldn't give them your talents after what they did. Doesn't it enrage you still?"

My gaze falls to my feet. She knows it does.

"Does it still make you mad you lost it, too?" I counter.

Mom's eyebrows spring up in surprise at the question, and she pauses her show. I gnaw on my bottom lip, desperate for her to share some sort of wisdom that might help me understand what I've been feeling all weekend. All year.

She seems to decide something when she waves a hand in the air and sighs. "Oh, hon, it was a long time ago." She unpauses the show.

My exhale shakes a little, but I hide my disappointment in another question. "Don't you have to work tonight?"

She smooths a hand down her shirt, only just noticing a tea stain. Her fingertips worry over the spot, trying to hide it from me. "Called in sick."

I roll my lips in so I don't say, *Again?*

I try to be patient and understand. To remind myself that depression doesn't have a rhythm or a reason. That the gravity of it becomes so strong, it's like nothing else exists to her. Not eating or showering or . . . me. That it just is.

But it also just sucks.

I tap my thumb against the doorknob several times before finally asking, "You've been taking your meds, right?"

Mom arches an eyebrow. "Yes, mija. Need I remind you who the mother is here?"

I really don't want to answer that.

The silence grows, so I say, "I was just going to make some food. Want anything?" If I don't make her something, she won't eat the rest of the night.

She nods, her eyes going heavy. Like that conversation took all her energy. I watch her a moment, trying to tamp down the terror I feel whenever she's this low. Trying to trust that this one will pass like all the others have.

Armed with a task and somewhere for all this agitated energy to go, I head to the kitchen, trying not to get swallowed by my own creeping anxiety.

Earlier, I was feeling excited about filming again, about making this documentary. I got a lot of interesting interviews this morning before and during the Fun Run, and the story map is coming together in my mind faster than ever.

But what if it's all bullshit? One setback and my mom abandoned it all. I always thought I'd be different, but what if I'm not?

What if *this* is my life—watching everyone else succeed while I . . . don't?

I'm so lost in thought while I pull the chicken mole leftovers, tortillas, and Spanish rice out of the fridge, I startle when my phone buzzes in my pocket.

Reid: You'll never know how sorry I am.

Pulse thundering, I stare at the words. Stare at Reid's name and the contact photo I never had the heart to delete. The picture is of the back of him as he lies across my lap—his sharp profile, my hand in his hair, and his fingers curled against my leg where he was absently rubbing it.

It was such a simple, soft moment that I never wanted to forget.

Because even though he claimed that I didn't let him in, he was the first person I ever really had. The *only* person who made me feel less alone.

Something lurches in me.

I could let what happened between Reid and Delaney go and forgive him. Or I could ask Reid for every excruciating detail all over again so the pain serves as the armor I need against him. I could tell him all the ways I miss him.

But then a different image flashes through my mind, the one Legacy Lore posted of Reid leaning in close to Delaney. Of her looking up at him like they were sharing a secret.

Given how good we are at hurting each other, I know what I need to do.

A hollow feeling takes over as I do it.

CHAPTER NINETEEN

REID

NOW

@haikuforyou
Pushing past the break
The sea floor too far to reach
Without us sinking

***FUCK.* AT HOME IN** the shower, I slump against the cold tile as the reality pushes in of how irreparably I've fucked up. I should've tried harder to explain. To tell her how much I regret it. That I've wanted her and only her since I met her.

But in the moment, my brain overrode my heart. Because telling her that would've freaked her out in a different way. While I know she cared about me, she never felt for me the way I did for her. Never *wanted* to know how I felt. If she did, she wouldn't have pretended like that card I gave her didn't even exist.

Though I send her a text now trying to convey the depth of my remorse, I don't expect her to respond.

I pull on a plain black T-shirt, gym shorts, and my knee brace, then make my way to the kitchen to hunt down something to eat.

On the table, I find a note for me and Mitchell from Julianne saying she and Dad will meet us at the Shakespeare play later tonight but that our picnic is packed and ready to go in the fridge. She could've just texted us. But she always does these small mom things, even for me. It used to annoy me. Like she was trying too hard to be my mom.

But now I understand that it's because my mom didn't try to be one at all. I rub my finger down the note, grateful for her all over again.

I grab an ice pack, and the leftover lasagna from the fridge, and eat it straight out of the dish. Mitchell's door busts open down the hall, and he saunters into the kitchen wearing a bulky Woodhurst High Wrestling sweatshirt. But his smile falls when his gaze locks on my leg propped up. The ice pack.

He quirks an eyebrow up, then grabs the casserole dish and fork right out of my hands.

"Hey—"

He shoves a massive bite into his mouth. "Is it bad?" he asks, gesturing to my leg.

"Just sore. I'm fine."

Better than it was before the hot springs, at least.

He settles in the chair across from me, his eyes glued on me while he chews.

"I saw that post about you and DL."

Fucking fantastic.

I pull the fork right out of his mouth. He grunts a protest while I say through gritted teeth, "Get your own." I stab a piece of congealed cheese even though I've lost my appetite.

Mitchell shakes his head slowly. "So it *is* true," he mutters. "How did Clara take it?"

A scornful half laugh escapes me, and I drop the fork on the worn wooden table where we've shared meals and games of chess and heated debates since we were kids. I bury my face in my hands, unable to meet his eyes.

After a beat he sighs. "Yeah, I figured as much."

It takes me a minute to steady my breathing. To work up the courage to ask Mitchell something so pitiful. "Did she ever talk to you about me? About what happened?"

"No."

It's like taking a bullet.

But after a thoughtful silence he continues. "You know Clara. She doesn't talk about anything that hurts."

I hate that he's right because it means he gets her. They really are close.

When I don't respond, he quickly changes the subject. "I really thought these posts were a joke, but this Legacy Lore account is out for blood."

My voice comes out muffled through my palms. "Tell me about it."

"Have you seen the new ones?"

Through the slats of my fingers, I watch him pull out his phone. He shows me the account, and I straighten to read them.

> **@LEGACY_LORE**: Meet Nicole Kelly: This scholar and athlete is determined to win at all costs. That cutthroat ambition will get you far . . . or get you caught. More soon ♥

Caught? That can't be good . . .

And the next one.

@LEGACY_LORE: Meet Amaya Masters: This leading lady with a powerhouse voice just may be Woodhurst's very first Broadway star someday! But a spotlight is unforgiving—just like this drama queen when she doesn't get her way. More soon ♥

How does this person know half this stuff—whatever it is?

She always knows everything about everyone.

Is it possible Delaney's doing this? She wanted to tell Clara, and I asked her not to . . . Maybe this was her way of forcing the issue.

I scroll back to the post about me.

But given his mysterious absence from the course this season and earning more than a few failing grades, is the Golden Boy starting to tarnish outside of his small pond?

Would she really say that about me?

There are comments now, too. Mitchell snatches the phone out of my hand before I can read them.

"You're grumpy enough," he says.

I was already freaked out by the posts this morning. But it's worse than I thought because by including that photo of me and Delaney, this person clearly has no problem twisting the truth. With their follower count rapidly rising, they're starting to have influence, too. More power than any of us anticipated.

And for some reason, they're trying to wreak havoc.

Mitchell clears his throat. "Since they were right about you and DL, are they right about the other stuff?"

He tries to keep his tone light, but I catch him staring at my knee again. He's worried. I ball my hands into tight fists. This is exactly what I need to prevent. I don't want him stressing about me when he has his own plans, his own future to think about.

I shake my head. "I've got it under control."

"Swear?" he asks, as he takes the fork back and gathers a large bite in the pan.

I nod, feeling a bit sick to my stomach when I say, "You know we don't lie to each other."

Something passes over his face, but it's gone so fast I must've imagined it.

I don't want to linger on the subject, so I move on, anger clipping my words when I return to the topic of Legacy Lore. "Who thinks like this?"

Mitchell pushes the empty lasagna dish away from himself and leans back. "Someone spiteful with a lot of time on their hands."

I let out a small laugh. But it does little to dispel the apprehension that arises when I think about all I'm still hiding. All I have to *keep* hidden.

"They're obviously hovering around. Maybe we can figure out who it is at *Romeo and Juliet* tonight. Actually . . ." He trails off and wipes his hands quickly before pulling out his phone. He starts tapping furiously, a scheme on his face.

"What are you doing?"

The answer comes a moment later when my phone buzzes with a text from him on RUN FORREST RUN: I have doth decreed another reunion! Tonight! Of Runneth Forrest Runneth at doth Shakespeare show.

Kenji responds instantly, as if in on it. Hear, hear! Shall we be fancy tonight and arrive as one?

Mitchell: Indeed! We are fancy now and thus must only speaketh as the fancy would. Thy chariots shall arrive post haste-ish.

I've always been baffled by their antics, and this time is no different.

"What is this?" I demand.

Popping into the group chat like everything's good is dangerously chaotic, even for him.

He grins at me over his phone. "Insurance. Kenji and I aren't about to let the crew fall apart because of this mess. If we don't let you all avoid each other, then you have to get your shit together."

My pulse picks up as I wait to see how Clara responds to whatever . . . this is.

Kenji: Too bad, Lady Clara! We shall pickest thou up at the hour of six!

Mitchell: Culture thyselves!

"*Yeesh*, she *is* pissed," Mitchell says.

I scroll up and down, confused. It seems like Kenji was replying to something Clara said, too, but I don't see a text from her on the chat. Is it a glitch?

"What? Did she text you?" I ask.

He frowns. "Yeah—you can see it."

"No, I can't—"

A cold realization hits me.

She didn't . . .

I stand and grab his phone out of his hand and read through it, comparing.

Clara: I don't need a ride.

Her texts are on his thread, but not mine.

She *did*.

"She blocked me," I say, my breath shuddering.

We hadn't spoken in months, we'd unfollowed each other online, but this—we never went so far as to cut off contact like *this*. I probably deserve it . . . Still, I'm shocked at how much it hurts. A crushing, twisting ache right through the center of me at the finality of it.

She's really never going to forgive me.

Mitchell grimaces. "Damn. Well . . ." He pushes a hand through his hair, uncomfortable but unpersuaded. "You can talk to her tonight."

"She *clearly* doesn't want to see me."

He chuckles, which annoys the fuck out of me. "She thinks she doesn't. But it's not *that* complicated to fix this. Well, wait—a few vital questions first. Are you into Delaney?"

"Not even a little."

Kissing her felt only like searching for Clara. Which made it all the worse.

He squints and whispers, "Did you give your flower to Delaney?"

I flit my eyes to the ceiling trying to keep my patience in check. "The way I want to punch you right now . . ."

"Then it's simple. Apologize."

Frustration flattens my expression, my tone dripping with sarcasm. "Wow, why didn't I think of that?"

He rolls his eyes.

"As much as I will deny I ever said this to you if Clara asks, this doesn't have to blow up your lives like this. You weren't together. Yes, obviously, if you were going to rebound it really should've been with literally anyone besides her best friend, but also *I'm* her best friend now, so it's actually insulting to me that she seems to be forgetting that—"

"Mitchell. Focus."

His spine straightens, and he takes the empty casserole dish to the sink to wash it. "Just apologize *again.* This is one of those situations where groveling is welcome. Nay, required."

Clearly, the Shakespeare speak continues.

"*How?* She's going to avoid me the rest of the weekend."

"You haven't done your interview yet, have you?"

I go still. I haven't.

She said she couldn't make the doc without me. Knowing how dedicated she is, there's no way she's going to abandon the project. Which means I still have a window to talk to her. Even if it's small.

I study him a moment, wondering when the hell he got so smart.

"As her best friend, shouldn't you be pissed at me?"

He snorts. "I *am* pissed at you. But as your brother?" He shoots me a look over his shoulder, wrist-deep in sudsy water. "I know what you've been through this year." We almost have a moment until he keeps going. "*But* I need you to stop bringing disgrace on the family and make this right."

I throw a dish towel at his head and he laughs.

"If you want to fix this, show her how sorry you are—however you can."

Show her. An idea strikes me, and I stand up as quickly as I dare given my knee is still aching. As I pass behind him at the sink, I ruffle his hair in gratitude before bounding off to the garage to look for the right box.

I hear the smile in his voice when he calls out behind me, "You're welcome."

CHAPTER TWENTY

CLARA

NOW

MY MIND REELS WHILE I dress for Shakespeare in the Vines, guilt pulling at the edges of my choice to block him. But I can't see his name on my phone or his photo on my screen. I can't breathe when I do.

Anxiety grips my stomach as I check the Legacy Lore profile again and see more people have been commenting.

> Dude **@reidrousseau** making the rounds after hooking up with that sluuuut all last year.
>
> The one who was disqualified??? WOW.
>
> This behavior is hardly acceptable for a Legacy **@reidrousseau**. My kids looked up to you!

There are at least a dozen more comments like that. All equally hurtful and judgmental. I'm used to the scorn of Woodhurst. But Reid isn't. He'll be gutted when he sees that last one. Which I shouldn't care about . . . but I can't pretend like I don't.

I know firsthand how damaging gossip can be. How hard it is when people believe the worst about you without allowing space for context or an explanation.

My phone buzzes with a string of texts on the group chat about carpooling tonight. *Really, Mitchell?* I should just leave this group chat and block Delaney while I'm at it.

But something stops me. Now that the initial shock has worn off, I realize I don't have to take Reid's word for what happened.

I check the clock. We still have a few hours before Shakespeare in the Vines. Without another thought, I snatch my keys off the hook and run to my car.

Delaney answers the door dressed all in black. Her makeup looks half-finished, but it's thick and theatrical for the play. She tucks her sleek blond hair behind her ear. "Hey, what are you doing here?"

"Can I come in?" I ask. My voice is too loud, my pulse wild.

"Uh—sure, I was just finishing getting ready."

I follow her through her house and into her bedroom. Agitated fury radiates from every single cell of my body.

I settle on her familiar purple bedspread, where her two chunky tabby cats, Tater and Tot, are snoozing away. I haven't seen them in months, and an ache forms in my throat at the sight of them. All the sleepovers where they would curl around our legs as Delaney and I talked for hours.

So much has changed.

Tater purrs in his sleep as I start to pet him, and Delaney settles back on the carpet in front of her full-length mirror, her makeup kit strewn around her on the floor in a cascade of tubes and jars of various sizes and colors.

Her eyeshadow brush never stops moving against her eyelid as she asks, "So, what's up?" All casual. Like this is totally normal.

"Did you see the post?" I ask.

She gets more shadow on the brush and starts on the next eye. "Oh god, is there another one? I've been avoiding it. What did it say?"

"Oh, it basically implied you and Reid had sex in his dorm room."

The brush freezes. We stare at each other in the mirror, and I watch the color drain from her face.

"What?"

Her shock seems genuine—it's almost enough to convince me she didn't make the post after all, but I can't be sure if she was so willing to lie to me about Reid. So willing to betray our friendship.

"Nothing stays a secret in Woodhurst. In case you forgot."

She spins around. "That's *not* what happened."

My pulse is thundering so loud my voice shakes when I ask, "Then what did?"

Eyes wide and lip trembling, she comes to sit beside me on the bed. But still she hesitates. The makeup brush twirls fast in her fingertips, and I want to snatch it out of her hands. The longer the silence stretches, the more freaked out I get filling in the blanks myself. "I swear if you don't start talking—"

"Okay." She takes in a steadying breath. "I reached out to him because I'd heard he'd fallen at a race or something, and I know if I got injured my first week at school I'd be freaking out. So I texted him and made plans to hang out when I went to his campus."

Was I the only person who didn't know about his fall?

"Why didn't you tell me that you were doing that?"

Delaney shakes her head. "I tried. I was calling you a lot then, but you never answered."

I don't meet her eyes. That's true. Which was why Mitchell kept giving me shit for avoiding everyone.

"When we met up, Reid just wanted to get pizza, but I was on one about going out. I just wanted to have some fun. He also seemed lonely, and he has a hard time making friends, you know? I wanted to help."

I swallowed.

"Anyway . . ." Tears are in her voice when she says, "I ended up drinking too much and had to sleep over. I don't even remember how it happened, just that one second we were talking, the next we were kissing."

Even though I was braced for impact, it's like getting sucker punched all over again.

Before Delaney, I didn't have girlfriends. I had Kenji to hang out with and otherwise was okay being a loner who didn't know how to do things like makeup and adhere to girl code. I broke it with Nicole and Amaya last year without meaning to. I know I'm not a perfect friend. But even I know that hooking up in any way with your best friend's ex-boyfriend is at the top of the list of *don'ts*.

"He stopped it before anything else happened. I'm pretty sure I initiated it because of how upset he got."

I don't know how to feel about that. Better? Worse? Each possibility makes the whole of my chest hurt.

"It was so shitty of me." Her voice breaks, and the tears spill over, streaking through her stage makeup. "I'm sorry, Clara. I'm *so* sorry."

I need to ask her what I'm most scared to ask. I'm surprised when my voice comes out as calm and even as it does. "Do you have feelings for him?"

She looks appalled. "*No,* it wasn't like that. It had nothing to do with him. Which is even worse, isn't it?" She wipes her nose, regret plain on her face. "I was . . . lonely and drunk and he was familiar and *there*. I'm pretty sure it was the same thing for him."

That stops my thoughts cold. That, above anything else, I get. Because it's exactly what I did with Josh last year. I bury my face in my hands.

"But it didn't mean anything," Delaney insists. "Reid was really mad about it, actually—especially knowing how hurt *you* would be. He cried, Clara."

My throat is dry and too tight.

Delaney goes on. "He slept on the floor and talked about you the whole night. Well, except for when he called me out for not eating anything and getting so drunk. Ever since, I couldn't get the intro of your video from the assembly out of my head."

The endless pirouettes and the full plates of food she never ate.

"After that night, I actually started seeing a therapist for my . . . body stuff. School has been a lot harder than I thought it was going to be. I'm *not* trying to make excuses—I've just been struggling for a long time, you know?"

Fresh tears are pooling in her eyes, and I can't help but feel her pain, too. Because I have known that. Instead of documenting it, I should have *talked* to her about it.

"It's only been a few weeks, but my therapist is super smart and doesn't let me get away with anything." She grimaces. "Honestly, it's really annoying."

I want to laugh because I've missed Delaney and her snarky humor. But my eyes heat instead.

"But seriously, Clara, it was a wake-up call. I think we were both just trying not to feel miserable for a minute. Obviously in a super-messed-up way that ended up making me feel worse than I ever have. I get it if you never want to speak to me again."

Silence fills the room. Her and Reid's stories are the same. Deep down, I know they're being honest. Both about what happened and how they felt about it.

I slump a little, my fingers curling through Tater's fur. "I'm really proud of you for getting help."

Her eyes go softer. "Thanks."

"I just . . . wish you had told me all this instead of ignoring me for a month," I say.

Delaney bites on her bottom lip, swiping at her eyes again as she considers her words. "You're right. I should have. I really wanted to. But after everything you went through last year, I was the last person who ever wanted to hurt you. I can't *stand* that I have."

The part of me that is afraid to need both of them wants to back away and act like I'm only angry. But the strange thing is, I'm not. Because I actually get it. I made the worst decisions when I was at my lowest last year and Delaney was so good to me through it, never judging me for any of it.

"I've already lost so much," I start.

Her face crumples, and she looks down. "I know, I'm so sorry—"

"I can't lose you, too."

Her head whips up, and she stares at me in disbelief before throwing her arms around me. I hug her back, feeling bruised and shaken but also lighter. I've missed her. This is awful, and I'm still hurt, but it's not bad enough to erase our friendship.

Or, I realize, how I feel about Reid.

The guilt from blocking him gnaws at me even more.

We talk awhile longer—catching up on everything from the past month. She redoes her makeup while we talk about her school, my doc, my mom. The shows she's in. The therapy she's doing. I apologize for sinking into my own self-loathing this summer and avoiding her calls.

She confides how disconnected she's felt from home and me and herself by moving away.

"But it hasn't been all bad," she assures me. "I love the freedom. I *love* living in the city. But ballet isn't an easy environment for me right now. If Legacy didn't prohibit it, I might even change majors. I just wish . . . I didn't feel like I was one mistake away from letting everyone down."

It reminds me of what Reid's been saying. The pressure they're both feeling to constantly perform well. That their entire hometown is invested in a trajectory they're not even sure about. Based on some of my interviews, it seems to be a similar struggle for all Legacies, even the older alumni.

Which leads me to ask, "Do you think that's why there's always drama when people come home? Everyone is so terrified to make a mistake they hunt out everyone else's?"

Delaney raises an arched eyebrow. "That's giving whoever did this"—she waves her phone—"way too much credit. It's such a dick move."

"I'm just trying to figure out why Josh would do this."

Her eyes bug. "You think this is Josh? No, this is way too sophisticated for him."

"Well, I thought it was you for a minute there," I admit.

Her expression is full of playful offense. "I could never be anonymous. You know I like to see people's reactions when I talk shit."

That pulls a laugh out of me. "You sound like a serial killer. Anyway, Josh seems most likely again. Who else would care so much to post all this stuff?"

"Who cared so much to sabotage you last year, too?" she asks.

Good question.

And one I still haven't answered considering how preoccupied I've been with Reid.

But we have to figure this out. No matter that I'm still upset with him and am not close with the other Legacies—I know what it's like to have your reputation ruined. For the entire town to look at you sideways. No one should have to go through that.

I have to do whatever I can to help.

Delaney already has her phone open, scrolling to the post about her. "Reid's team was there at the party that night I stayed over—so any of them could've spread this around. Look! The one who left this comment—'Yeah I heard they hooked up in Reid's dorm'—thanks a lot, asshole," she mutters under her breath. "That's Connor, one of Reid's teammates. Damn, his account is private."

"Why would a Stanford runner be following a gossip account about Woodhurst?" I ask.

Delaney narrows her eyes, thinking. "I don't know, but I'm going to ask him how he found it."

She grows quiet as she starts tapping on the comments and profiles, then sending DMs to Reid's teammates.

"You don't have to do this," I say quietly.

Her phone lowers. "Yes, I do."

We share a small smile.

"Okay! What was all the best gossip last year?" She holds up her fingers, rattling rumors off. "There was the one that flew around that Reid was on steroids."

I frown. "Wasn't that Josh?"

She squints, trying to remember. "Riiiiight. Okay, then there was the one about Amaya sabotaging her understudy's audition by telling her the wrong time. That Kenji was addicted to Adderall."

"When he literally just takes it for his ADHD," I interject.

Delaney rolls her eyes. "Exactly. Ummmm, that Nicole was the one who gave Logan the bracelet. Oh! And that you and Reid had a sex tape that you were blackmailing him with to get a Legacy spot."

I have to laugh. "*How* would that work?"

Delaney laughs, too. "I don't know, but that one captured the hearts and minds. Debunked, obviously, when your actual sex tape with Josh was released."

I give her a flat look.

"Too soon?"

I shake my head and laugh a little, feeling more hopeful than I have in months. "What does all this have to do with the posts?"

"I'm trying to figure out what Legacy Lore might reveal next. Depending on what they post, we might be able to trace it back to who knew what and figure out who's behind it—like this one about Amaya." Delaney raises a conspiratorial eyebrow. "Not a ton of people know about this, but I bet it's about her manifesto during *Mean Girls* rehearsals and the great unfollowing."

"The what?"

Delaney sits up straighter. "Oh my god, let me show you."

She hands me her phone to read through several screenshots of a text thread between the cast of *Mean Girls,* the show our theater department did for the spring musical.

> **Amaya Masters:** A leading lady is more than a role, it's a responsibility and today's rehearsal was some real bullshit. Like what are y'all doing? Do you seriously think the effort you're putting in is remotely good enough????? WE OPEN IN 2 DAYS.

Showing up late to rehearsals? Missing cues and lines when we all should've been off book TWO WEEKS AGO?????

This is UNACCEPTABLE.

Tech week is about drilling down and I've seen people laughing, goofing off, acting as if it's kindergarten recess. You wanna play go to a fucking amusement park.

This is THEATRE.

Once again, we open in 2 DAYS!!! I'm not talking about a zero-mistakes show. We need to transcend!!!! Legacy is on the line. This show is my last chance to lock it in and I will not lose NYU bc of your lazy asses. If any of you fuck it up for me I will end you.

END. YOU.

Alvin Guzman: Wut

Heather Madison: Hear you. Love you.

Lily Kim: I think Regina George has gone to your head Amaya lol

Jax Mills: Yeah this isn't the move you think it is

Logan Harper: How'd I get on this thread? I'm just running sound . . .

Logan Harper has left the chat.

Marcus Jones: I have my physics final tomorrow. I don't need this shit.

Marcus Jones has left the chat.

Alvin Guzman has left the chat.

Jax Mills has left the chat.

Lily Kim has left the chat.

"Heather sent these to me when it was all going down. The entire cast unfollowed her—apparently she was like this the entire run of the show, but she never wanted anyone to know. It's why none of them came home this weekend and the rest of us performing arts alumni have to help with *Romeo and Juliet* tonight. They want literally nothing to do with Amaya and were so mad when she became a Legacy."

"Do you think the account could be one of them?" I ask.

Delaney considers it for a moment, then shakes her head. "Eh, I think their issues were Amaya specific. Why go for all of us?"

I read the texts again, pretty shocked at Amaya's messages. She's always so kind—almost soft-spoken. I had no idea she was capable of this kind of ire.

Wait.

I gasp. "Do you think *Amaya* could be making the posts?"

Delaney's eyes go wide.

"Think about it—she hates me because of what happened with Josh . . . maybe by extension Reid?" I stand up, feeling the need to pace. "She could be trying to get me back for the assembly video by posting about what happened with you guys? And she's obviously still mad at Josh."

The idea picks up steam in my mind, some of the pieces falling into place. "Releasing this text thread would be embarrassing for her—it'd make her look like a diva. But it isn't actually risking too much.

Especially knowing a lot of other people were on the thread and could share these screenshots. It's not nearly the same as what's come out about you and Reid. It's, like, a juicy-enough tidbit to make it seem like she's threatened but not bad enough it would risk her scholarship."

Delaney exhales in a *whoosh*. "Damn."

"Right?"

"I mean, I'd be devastated because I have to destroy whoever is doing this, and I love the girl, but . . . yeah, this makes sense. We're going to figure this out."

I grin. "You think?"

She raises an eyebrow and sounds like a reality show villain when she says, "I *know*. Because whoever's doing this is playing checkers, but we're playing chess."

We share another smile, and I lunge for my bag. "Please say that again on camera."

After we finish filming her interview, I head home to switch out my camera battery and get the rest of my gear for the play. I go over my notes and take stock of who I still need one-on-one interviews with by tomorrow, more determined than ever to figure out who is trying to ruin my friends' lives and how to stop them before they do.

I have three interviews left, with Amaya now at the top of that list. If she really is behind Legacy Lore, I'll see it through my lens. But she'll be onstage tonight. Which leaves Josh . . . and Reid.

Even though Delaney and I talked it out, I'm not sure I'm ready to face him yet.

Now that I'm calmer, his words from the hot springs echo through my head again in a way that I can't shake.

I knew the second you found out, I'd lose you for good.

If that's true, he does still care about me—and rightly predicted that

I would back away instead of hear him out. Push him away instead of let him in. It's not that I can forgive Delaney and not him.

It's that he's the only person who manages to make me feel as wildly out of control as I did today. The person I want to be the best for but somehow always manage to show my worst.

Once I'm ready, I'm about to load up my car with my film gear when Mitchell pulls into my driveway. Despite telling them I didn't want a ride, he and Kenji showed up anyway.

With Reid.

CHAPTER TWENTY-ONE

REID

NOW

@haikuforyou
A light, searching knock
Soft eyes at the open door
Breaths become tumbling.

MITCHELL AND KENJI ARE determined to be the two most annoying people on the fucking planet. We're supposed to pick up Clara for the play, which was *their* idea, but they're so caught up in their warped version of Shakespearean English that we haven't even left yet. I forgot what they're like when they get together; they eclipse everyone else for each other. But I can't really be mad because Clara and I used to be like that, too.

I wonder all over again if Kenji has a thing for Mitchell. Mitch has always had girlfriends, that I know of, so I don't know if he even notices.

I catch one last glimpse of myself in the hall mirror before we go, and I almost laugh because I spent thirty minutes nervously messing with my hair only to get it to look how it did before I even touched it at all.

And I can't believe I'm wearing this shirt.

As soon as I walk into the living room, Mitch throws something at me.

"A notice for thee from the outside world!" he announces. The sharp corner of the letter hits me square in the forehead before landing on the floor. I glare at him while I rub the spot.

"'Thou art a boil, a plague sore,'" I mutter.

"Dude, you can't *actually* quote Shakespeare; that ruins it," Kenji complains.

But their voices fade to the background as my focus narrows to the envelope on the floor with the Stanford logo. The one holding a letter that probably says the same thing the email did this morning. Heart racing, I tear it open.

Fuck.

That's exactly what it is. The official notice about my academic probation. There isn't enough air in this room. This ridiculous shirt, too tight.

What's my dad going to say when he sees this? What's he going to *do*? The memory of his recovery flashes through my mind. How he had only been in the hospital a few days but had looked like he'd aged a year. How Julianne pled with the insurance company with panic in her voice.

I promised myself then that I'd do everything I could to help our family. And I'm *failing*.

If I don't figure out what to do, I'm going to lose everything we've worked for.

Everything my dad wanted for me.

Hopefully buying myself a little more time, I crush the paper and toss it in the kitchen trash. "We're late." My sharp tone cuts through their jovial one.

"You okay?" Mitchell asks me as we walk to the car.

"Fine. Let's just get this over with."

At least my knee is feeling better after the hot springs. If I can manage to stay off it the rest of the weekend, the rumors should die down and no one will be the wiser.

Well, except Clara.

We arrive at her house ten minutes later, and I'm a sweaty, nervous wreck. Still stressing about the letter sitting in the trash can, and the fact that Mitchell's warped perception of things probably gassed me up too much. Gave me too much hope that she'll talk to me. Her front door opens before Mitchell even comes to a complete stop, and she stares at the car with a furious look on her face.

"*Damn,*" Kenji says appreciatively as he watches her slowly walk toward us.

Both of us smack him simultaneously.

"What? I'm just saying what we're all thinking."

He's not wrong.

She's wearing dark jeans and a black long-sleeve shirt that clings to her. Her hair is tumbling across her shoulders, free from its usual ponytail, and her eye makeup is dark. She looks . . . problematically good.

Kenji rolls down his window. "Looking hot, milady."

"What are you doing here?"

"Reducing carbon emissions," Kenji says.

She twists her lips, trying not to smile. Thank god Kenji has that effect. Mitchell leans well across him to yell out his window at her. "Be the change, Clara. Get in."

Still she hesitates.

"You know parking sucks at the amphitheater," Mitchell goads.

She looks as though she may be considering it when her eyes dart to me in the back seat.

Get in. Please get in.

"Fine," she huffs. She gathers her gear and marches over to the other side of the car and slides into the back seat next to me. Her flowery scent has me gripping my hands tighter. She doesn't look at me, instead turning away to stare out her window. Not great. But she got in when she didn't have to, knowing she'd be sitting beside me.

It's a start.

Kenji continues the Shakespeare talk the rest of the ride to the amphitheater just outside of downtown, but I notice Mitchell is significantly less enthusiastic about the game.

God, I wish I could just reach for her. Grab her hand and pull her close and *fix* this. But neither of us speak the entire drive, and the air becomes so taut between us by the time we arrive, Kenji and Mitchell practically leap out of the car. They busy themselves with getting the stuff from the trunk.

Clara reaches for the door handle.

"Wait," I say. "Please."

She freezes. She doesn't look at me, but she doesn't get out, either. Something heavy hangs in the silence. That fortress of hers I can't ever seem to break through. "I just—I know you blocked me, but I wanted you to know that—just that I'm still in for the doc if—if, um, you need me." My words are halting. Stumbling. Because something about this moment feels like we could really be broaching an ending. I hold my breath waiting for her response.

"I talked to Delaney."

My eyebrows rise.

"I'm sorry for not hearing you out." She finally looks at me. "I should've—" She stops, her gaze landing on my shirt. The mix of bewilderment and delight in her expression makes the hour in my dusty garage worth it. "You are *not* wearing that."

"I'm not?" I ask, looking down at my neon pink BOP TIL YOU DROP shirt that barely fits. I loop a finger into the collar and tug, trying to stretch the cotton away from my throat. "Pretty sure I am. And in public."

Her laugh is wild. Radiant. *"Why?"*

Our eyes meet briefly, and her eyebrows come together in question. But she's flushed, which is all the encouragement I need to be as honest as I can. "You asked me to."

She blinks at me, disbelieving. "I can't believe you remember that."

"Hard to forget the way you laughed at homecoming when we talked about it. Your hair was down just like this." My gaze roves over the dark waves that I used to clutch in my fist when we kissed. "And I knew then that I'd do anything you asked—even wear this ridiculous shirt—if it made you laugh like that."

Her eyes dig into mine, green and fierce.

A quick rap on the window startles us both.

Kenji leans down to peer in at us, his voice muffled. "Hellooo? Have you kissed and made up yet? Because we need to go find a spot."

I glare at him, and he backs away slowly. But with the moment officially broken, we both climb out. Kenji's and Mitchell's arms are full with supplies for the picnic, and they both offload a few of them to me.

Clara clears her throat and turns to me as we walk. "What you said about helping with the doc—can I ask you for a favor tonight?"

"Anything."

"I think it might be Amaya making the posts."

I tip my head to the side. "Really?"

She fills me in on her reasoning, and while it does sound possible and also dispels the last of my worry it could be Delaney, the whole thing still mostly reeks of Josh to me. Maybe he and Amaya are in it together. I say as much.

Clara nods. "Good point. With Amaya onstage, it makes the most sense to interview him tonight. I doubt Josh will admit anything outright, but if I can get him talking about last year and their relationship, maybe he'll let something slip."

"What do you want me to do?"

The setting sun streaks through the trees behind her, haloing her in a soft glow. "Try to get under his skin. He's more talkative when he's mad."

The corner of my mouth lifts. "Easy enough."

Her eyes fall to my shirt and flit back up to meet mine, full of amusement. We exchange a quick, nervy smile. Both aware that something's shifted again. Something that has my heart punching me from the inside out.

She takes out her camera to capture everyone walking through the stone arched entrance. All holding some combination of blankets and lawn chairs and bags of food.

"I'm going to get as much footage as I can before we lose the light." With that she takes off, weaving through the crowd.

Mitch and Kenji flank me, and I don't realize I'm still staring at her until a hand waves in front of my face. I blink and swat it away.

"You've still got it so bad," Kenji mutters, then pulls Mitchell with him to scout a spot to sit.

I glare after him even though he's right.

I survey all the familiar people laughing and talking. A lot of the adults have full picnic setups on the grass, pouring wine from the vineyard next door. If they don't have students who go to Woodhurst High, they're likely alumni themselves. Everyone seems genuinely excited to watch a high school rendition of *Romeo and Juliet*. Something about their enthusiasm chips away at the loneliness I've felt since going to school.

As weird and warped as this town is, I guess it's kind of nice being back in Woodhurst.

"Reid!" It's my dad. He's got his usual coach apparel on: running clothes and a baseball hat. His face is lined with concern that stops my thoughts short.

Did he somehow see the letter from Stanford? Maybe that was the second notice I threw away. Sweat forms at my hairline, my entire body too hot.

"I noticed you came in with Clara," he says.

Oh god, this again.

"Dad, don't—"

He folds his arms and cuts me off. "It took weeks to get your training back on track after that assembly last year. Remember how you almost lost the fifteen hundred—to that slime *Harper*?" he whispers his name, knowing it's not a great look to be talking about the kids he used to coach. But Peter Rousseau is as much of a gossip as the rest of them. And that *was* my worst race in years.

When I don't respond, he goes on, lowering his voice even more. "She's a nice girl, but that video—"

"You mean the one that cost her everything and was a huge violation of her privacy? *That* video?" I glare at him, daring him to say more. We had this fight over and over last year.

Dad pinches the bridge of his nose and nods. "Let's not get into that here. I just don't want you to lose your focus all over again. This is your future."

Then why don't I get any say in it? I think.

It almost comes out of my mouth, but Principal West bursts into the conversation. "There you are, my boy!"

Josh shoots me the dirtiest look as he approaches behind him.

Oh goody, he's already in a bad mood.

But I notice he's not the only one looking at me sideways. Several people are glancing my way. Unlike the enthusiastic, smiling expressions at the Fun Run this morning, these are alight with intrigue or suspicion. The kind of looks that mean people are talking about you—and not in a good way.

I straighten my spine and wave at the family whose kid wore the *Rousseau* shirt this morning. The mom quickly averts her gaze and maneuvers the kid by his shoulders, ushering him in the opposite direction. I swipe at the sweat on my forehead, trying to calm down while West and Dad talk.

Josh appraises me with mock sympathy. "Tough day?"

Get under his skin.

My eyes go flinty, and I lower my voice so only he can hear me. "You can stop with the fucking posts, okay? You got me. I have nothing else to hide."

Though my knee twinges as if to disagree.

A humorless laugh escapes him. "You think that's *me*? As much as I enjoy watching your downfall, I have better things to worry about than contributing to it."

I scoff, not believing that for a second.

His eyes narrow, and he steps to me, speaking low. "If you think I'm about to risk my scholarship or my dad's program to talk about *you*, then you're even more of a jackass than I thought."

Before I can respond, Principal West wraps a gruff hand around my bicep and grins. "New couple just moved here from San Francisco. They're eager to meet our guest of honor!"

"I'm a Legacy; I could've talked to them," Josh says.

"Are you the state champion?" West asks coolly before leading me away.

Embarrassment prickles up my neck. I can't stand Josh, but that was cold even for West.

Dad shoots me a thumbs-up and heads back to his blanket with Julianne. I hoped I'd have tonight off from Legacy duty since this is the theater kids' night, but I plaster on a polite smile and follow Principal West. He introduces me to the couple, then takes me on a round of Legacy Weekend sponsors, benefactors, and other people whose names and faces all blend together.

I spend the conversations imagining how they'd react if I said, *I'll probably be getting kicked out of college soon, now would you like to invest?*

Maybe they'd finally leave me alone if I told them the truth.

When West finally releases me, I find Kenji and Mitchell, who have managed to nab a spot on the grassy knoll close to the stage. Mitchell tears into the bag Julianne prepped for us and pulls out sandwiches on thick deli rolls, cheese, and grapes. While we unwrap everything, Kenji slyly pulls out a reusable water bottle that I would bet good money doesn't have water in it.

He takes a long swig and his eyes water. "Oh god, wine is so gross."

"You brought *wine*?" Mitchell laughs.

"We're being fancy, aren't we?"

They both crack up, but Mitchell's laugh falters when he looks over Kenji's shoulder and sees Logan.

"I thought he wasn't coming tonight," Mitchell says.

Kenji studies Mitchell. "Guess he changed his mind. You okay?"

I frown at the question.

"Why? Do you and Logan have beef or something?" I ask, popping a grape into my mouth. "Dad did just call him a 'slime,'" which I can't say without laughing.

Mitchell makes some noncommittal noise, a flush covering the back of his neck. Kenji looks between me and Mitchell, and his eyebrows float up.

"Does he still not—"

Mitchell swivels his head around. "My mom's staring at us, isn't she? I can feel it like the freaking eye of Sauron."

I look over and, sure enough, my dad and Julianne are watching us from their gourmet picnic spread with that beaming look they gave me at graduation. The same look they give Mitch at his wrestling matches.

Profound pride.

She says something, and Dad bursts out laughing. Despite his concern about me and Clara, he looks more relaxed than I've seen him in a long time.

And my injury, my academic probation, everything I'm keeping from him are the exact things that could ruin it. That could give him a literal fucking heart attack.

Kenji takes another sip, but Mitchell declines, since he's driving and going for Legacy. "And reminder, my mom's, like, *right there*," he mutters.

But he doesn't seem to be as concerned with our parents as he is with Logan, who he keeps stealing glances at. I wonder what that's about. Kenji notices, too, and drapes an arm around Mitchell's shoulders, probably to get him to relax. Though it seems to have the opposite effect, since Mitch goes quiet and flushed beside him.

I don't usually drink. It fucks with my training, and I learned quickly that I'm a lightweight. Plus, I do stupid shit like what happened with Delaney.

But right now, I like the idea of forgetting about everything.

I reach for the "water" bottle and take a long sip.

CHAPTER TWENTY-TWO

CLARA

NOW

THOUGH WE'RE OUTSIDE, THE stage lights start to flicker indicating the show will begin soon. I tuck my camera away, frustrated. None of the alumni theater Legacies had a bad word to say about Amaya.

What if I'm totally off base about her running the account?

Since she's onstage tonight, I'll have to wait until after the show to talk to her.

I look around, trying to decide where to sit. I had planned on avoiding Reid tonight. To keep away from him for both our sakes. But in the car he reminded me all over again why it's so hard to do that. So hard to stay angry. The fact that he found that shirt because he knew it would make me laugh; offered to help me with the doc even after I blocked him. The way he remembers everything about us.

I don't know if I'm ready to move past what happened with him and Delaney—or if I even should. But with nowhere else to sit, I find myself drifting toward the blanket with him, Mitchell, and Kenji.

As I do, I notice several people are looking at Reid and the other Legacies with odd expressions. Talking about them. The Legacy Lore posts are clearly starting to seep into town. We need to figure out who it is before things get out of hand. Before something irreparably damaging comes out.

When I get to the blanket, Kenji has his arm around Mitchell. I try to give Mitchell an *Oh my god* look, but he's watching Reid warily.

Reid is leaning back on his elbow, nonchalant and entirely too languid. A water bottle vertical against his lips. When he releases it, he coughs.

Kenji slams a hand across his shoulder blades, laughing. "Dude, slow down."

I sink down next to Mitchell, who immediately grabs my arm. "Guess who Logan's here with?"

My eyes fly wide as I follow his gaze. Nicole is leaning back against Logan's legs, seemingly poised to watch the show like that. Are they actually together? It seemed like when Reid and I caught them kissing last night it was more of a spontaneous thing. But Mitchell doesn't know about that.

"Kaywut'm I missing here?" Reid's voice comes out loud. Too loud.

"Oh, sweet summer child," Kenji says, patting his head, making Mitchell laugh a little.

I lean back and study him. "Was that even a sentence?"

"It was a *question*."

I watch Kenji take another sip from the water bottle and put it together as I turn back to Reid. "Are you . . . drunk?"

He swats at nothing in the air. "Hardly. I'm buzzed at bezzt."

I scoff. "'Bezzt' is definitely a word a sober person would say."

He shrugs. It's a slow movement that seems to take effort.

I don't like this. It would be one thing if he was having fun, letting off a little steam.

Instead, it seems like the reverse is happening. His eyelids are heavy, his stare vacant. A despair I know too well, a misery that I learned to recognize as a child, lines every feature of his handsome face. Like the alcohol is forcing his mask to slip.

"Here." I offer him an actual water bottle, and he takes a long swig.

The crowd around us starts applauding as the actors take to the stage.

"Shhh," he whispers. "It's *starting*."

It's not even ten minutes into the show before the sky shifts from a hazy twilight to a starlit black. A few minutes more, and Reid lowers himself horizontally and sags against me. I freeze, stunned as he props his head on my lap, wrapping his arm around my leg. Just like he used to. Just like the photo I have of him.

"What are you doing?" I whisper, discomfited.

His eyes stay closed when he whisper-slurs, "So tired. Juss a lil nap."

It's a jolt, having him close like this. Achingly familiar but also confusing. I could maneuver him off me. He's so out of it I'm not even sure he'd notice.

But as I feel the rise and fall of his rhythmic breathing against the tops of my thighs, I can't bring myself to do it. Despite everything, he still feels comfortable enough with me to relent like this. To finally rest. That's enough for me to stay as still as possible.

Which makes the next two hours a torturous practice in restraining myself from the incandescent urge to slide my fingers into his hair like I used to. Especially with him looking criminally cute in that shirt. But I focus on the show, digging my hands into the grass behind me, and somehow, improbably, resist.

When the final scene ends and the audience applauds around us, Reid doesn't so much as stir. After the curtain call, the crowd mills and Mitchell and Kenji get up to stretch. Mitchell shoots me a *look* when he sees his brother sprawled across me now. I guess it was so dark during the show that he didn't notice.

Furious heat climbs my face, and I shake Reid's shoulder harder. "Reid? Show's over."

His inhale is sharp, and he blinks several times against the dark. Up at me. The moment it registers, he springs back as if hit with a live wire.

"Whoa—" His voice is rough and sleepy. He drags a hand down his face. "How long was I out?"

"A little over two hours."

"Jesus. Sorry for"—he gestures awkwardly to my lap—"I didn't realize."

"It's okay." I stretch, arching my back and pointing my toes against all the tingling sensations as the blood finally rushes back to my limbs. "My legs are totally asleep, though."

"Why didn't you wake me?"

But I can't respond because my breath catches. His hands have moved to my leg closest to him, massaging it the way he used to after long runs or whenever I'd get a cramp. He doesn't seem to realize he's doing it, like he's still half asleep, running on autopilot.

"Um, you don't have to do that."

He follows my gaze, and his hands freeze around my calf. But he doesn't move them. Our eyes meet again, and we're locked staring at each other when Josh appears out of nowhere and throws his arms out wide. His cheeks are red and his eyes glassy as he stares at Reid's hands on my leg.

"Ohhhh, look at this!" he exclaims. There's a sardonic edge to his words that only means trouble. "Wow, are congratulations in order?" His booming voice gets the attention of everyone hovering nearby, including Nicole and Logan. "Guess you guys got over that whole video thing?"

Reid slowly pulls his hands back and balls them into fists.

That whole video thing.

"What are you doing?" Nicole hisses at Josh.

Josh shrugs. "Reminiscing." He shoots Reid a lazy grin that doesn't reach his eyes.

Logan starts to laugh, but it fades when his gaze collides with Mitchell's. But Josh keeps going. "God, that was all so . . . *high school.*"

Nicole tugs on his arm. "Josh, stop it—"

"I'm just saying! You get to college and none of that shit matters anymore, you know? Well, I guess Clara *doesn't* know—"

But before he can finish his sentence, Reid launches to his feet.

CHAPTER TWENTY-THREE

REID

NOW

@haikuforyou
Cover me with all
The vines that haunt your mind so
I can grow with you

I STEP TO JOSH sneering down at Clara, ready to knock him the fuck out. Only I'm groggy and my knee is stiff and sore from lying in that awkward position so long that I stumble.

Thankfully, Mitchell is right there and catches me around the arm before I eat shit in front of everyone.

Josh's eyes narrow to slits. "You *are* injured, aren't you? I knew it!"

"He's wasted," Mitchell shoots back. "He and Kenji pounded a Hydro Flask of wine. Look at him."

The whole group turns to watch Kenji, who has his hands over his head as he sways to the medieval music still pouring through the speakers by the stage, obviously toasted. I squeeze Mitchell's shoulder, and he squeezes back.

Josh makes a disgusted face. "What are you, my mom? Who drinks *wine*?"

With him properly distracted, I turn to Clara and notice she has her camera out, and it's focused on Josh.

"Let's talk about the 'video thing,' Josh."

His eyes widen as he stares at the camera.

"Unless you're scared to go on the record?" she goads.

I do my best to suppress my grin. Which is near impossible when he puffs up his chest and predictably says, "I don't have anything to hide."

Clara walks Josh down by the stage, close enough where I can still see them but too far to hear anything they're saying. She lifts her camera in a way that's determined. Even in my addled state, it's clear she's ready to follow through on her plan. Though after what he said earlier, I'm not sure he has anything to do with the posts.

But the only thing he's better at than me is lying. If anyone can get him to admit the truth, it's Clara.

I lower myself back onto the blanket, watching them intently. I can't believe I fell asleep on her like that. That she didn't just push me off her.

The fact that she's talking to me, maybe even willing to forgive me? I hoped for it but didn't expect it. Now I don't know what to do with it. Everything between us is entirely too breakable.

My brain feels like soup, so I wonder if I imagine when Logan says quietly to Mitchell, "You look good" before walking off. Mitchell stares after him, scrubbing a stressed hand across his eyes. Kenji pulls him into a hug, and they talk in low voices on the other side of the blanket. I'm unable to make sense of it before Nicole sinks down next to me.

"Somehow Josh has gotten even worse, hasn't he?" she asks, tossing her thick hair over her shoulder to look at me.

I snort. "I didn't know that was possible."

Her high-pitched laugh punctures straight through my skull.

Nicole maneuvers herself directly in my line of sight, cutting off my view of Clara and Josh. But not before I see Amaya walking from backstage, her fingers flying across the screen of her phone. I realize then that I haven't seen a phone out of her hand all weekend. Not even when we ran this morning.

"Are you okay?" Nicole's sympathetic voice cuts into my thoughts. "I mean, I saw the way people were looking at you tonight."

So it *wasn't* in my head. Great.

"I'm fine," I say automatically.

"This Legacy shit is so much."

Her sigh is weary, and I let out a concurring grunt.

"And now these posts? *Who* could be doing this?"

Despite the sluggish pace of my thinking, I manage to recall her conversation with Amaya about Legacy Lore this morning at the Fun Run. "The *only* thing I know is that it's not Clara."

Nicole nods slowly, chewing on the inside of her cheek like she doesn't quite believe me. "*Everyone* is talking about it. If I lose my scholarship, I lose school, my sorority, my team—everything." She shakes her head, her eyes getting teary. "We can't let that happen, Reid."

"We really can't," I agree, trying to keep up. Hoping she means "we" as in all of us Legacies.

She sighs and scoots a little closer. I lie all the way back, more exhausted than ever.

Her laugh is close to my ear when she says, "You have grass in your hair." I frown when I feel her fingers dragging through it but am too tired to say anything.

She keeps talking, and I vaguely note I should be paying better attention, but I can't quite hold on to what she's saying as sleep pulls me under again.

CHAPTER TWENTY-FOUR

CLARA

NOW

WHEN I ASKED REID to get under Josh's skin, I didn't think he'd try to fight him. It seems like he's begging for a reason to hit something. Someone. It's not like him.

But at least it worked.

Josh and I get settled in a well-lit area by the stage. Every interview requires a slightly different approach. I know Josh well enough to know that subtlety won't work with him. It's best to go full throttle and launch in before he can change his mind.

After I have him introduce himself and his Legacy position, I say, "Why don't we start at the beginning. Can you describe the video that was played during the assembly last year?"

"Really? I doubt my dad wants that in the banquet hype video."

My nostrils flare, but I have to stay calm. I don't want Josh alerting Principal West that I'm not making the type of video he expects. "I already have enough footage for that. This is for my own doc project while everyone is home. Are you okay with that? I figured since you have *nothing to hide . . .*" I trail off.

Josh crosses his arms and sighs. "Okay, fine."

"The video," I prompt.

"Right. Um, it was a recording of you and me in a, uh, compromising position."

In an effort to blaze past the awkward moment, I don't break eye contact or momentum when I fire the next question. "Did you take the recording?"

"Like I told everyone last year, *no*."

"Do you know who did?"

"Nope."

I bristle at his attitude but keep going. "What happened after?"

"Amaya dumped my ass, and you got disqualified from the program for using me."

My mouth drops open. "*Using* you? Really?"

His gaze hardens on mine behind the camera. "You'd literally never paid attention to me before that night and hated me after."

I'm stunned for a moment. Is that what he really thinks? It doesn't seem like an act, so I ask, "Is that what you told your dad?"

"More or less."

How much of that impacted Principal West's opinion of me? The selection committee? Obviously, the rumors held enough weight to get me disqualified. I've long suspected that Josh was the source of them to make himself look good. Especially since he's always trying to get his Dad's attention.

But I can't get worked up and scare him off right now. I decide to change course and grab on to the part about Amaya.

"That must've been hard when you and Amaya broke up. I know

you were together a long time," I say, reaching for sympathy even as I'm seething inside.

He frowns. "What does that have to do with anything?"

"Legacies are interesting. Legacy Lore seems to think so," I say. "You two were like a power couple."

I feel gross buttering him up like this, but I can tell it's working when he straightens his shoulders, the corner of his mouth hiking up. "True."

"Have you noticed the post about Amaya isn't that threatening, though? Not compared to yours. I mean, cheating is a pretty serious accusation."

His face doesn't move. Like he's purposely controlling his reaction. "It is."

"I would understand if you did it. Everyone is under so much pressure, you as the principal's son most of all. If you didn't do something to distinguish yourself like get valedictorian, that wouldn't be a good look for him or the program."

Josh tries to hide his surprise, but he doesn't do it well.

"Legacy Lore is grasping, I have nothing to hide," he repeats. But it sounds more hollow this time.

I zoom in a little. "Kind of seems like an angry ex-girlfriend move, doesn't it?"

Josh bursts out laughing, picking up on the implication. "No way. Amaya gets enough attention onstage, she wouldn't do something so pathetic."

I narrow my eyes as I study his face, trying to discern whether he's lying. Keeping the shot steady, I inch closer.

"I saw the texts she sent to the *Mean Girls* cast last year. It read like someone who rage texts a lot."

He rolls his eyes. "I told her not to send that. She hadn't slept in three days. But I've only ever seen her get that way about theater. She's literally living her dream life in New York, she couldn't care less about Woodhurst drama anymore."

He makes a good point. Which is *really* annoying. I haven't seen much of her this weekend besides when she was onstage tonight for the show. Like she has better things to do than get caught up in Legacy mess.

"Well, some people think you're behind the account," I try. Though I sound a little desperate, even to myself.

He shoves his hands in his pockets. "You mean *Rousseau* thinks I'm behind it. More people assume *you're* behind it since you have more against Legacies than anyone. Nicole got your scholarship, and your best friend and ex-boyfriend hooked up. You hate me—it all tracks."

It does track. Almost too well.

"It's not me," I say, thrown by how easily he flipped the accusation. It's only now that I'm remembering he did really well in debate. Because he's such an asshole, I forget he's actually smart.

"I've told everyone it doesn't make sense since you stalk us in plain sight."

I scowl at him, but he stares past me, as if something catches his attention.

"If anyone knows how to stir up petty shit for no reason, it's Nicole."

"Nicole?" I pause, frowning. "What does Nicole have against the other Legacies?"

"She's not the kind of person who needs a reason to cause trouble," Josh says ominously, gesturing behind me with a nod of his head. I turn and see Nicole and Reid lying side by side on the blanket. She's laughing and touching his arm. Leaning down and—*brushing her hands through his hair.*

Even though we're not together, even though I don't even know how he feels about me anymore—to actually *see* another girl touch him like that sends an anguished rush of possessiveness straight through my veins. I want nothing more than to sprint over there and smack her hand away.

Which is probably exactly what Josh wants me to do. He's using Nicole to distract me, since the two of them have always had it out for each other. But I still have more questions. Questions I've *needed* answers to since last year.

Taking a deep breath, I force myself to turn back around and refocus.

"When she saw that video at the assembly, she wouldn't let it go until Amaya dumped me." He shakes his head bitterly.

Now that he's brought up the video again, I can ask him for the real truth about that night.

"Did you ever stop to consider that what happened between us last year had nothing to do with Legacy and was just a drunken mistake?"

He looks up at the sky as his cheeks grow red. After a long pause he says, "Of course I did. It was for me, too."

I'm barely able to get the next question out through gritted teeth. "Then why didn't you say anything?"

"I dunno. It didn't seem like it mattered."

My heart thuds harder as I try and fail to swallow the sudden lump in my throat. Somehow, he was the one who had the power to fix this. The power of being believed.

And he didn't use it.

Because of that one rumor, that one mistake, my entire world got turned upside down. My voice shakes with unspent anger when I say, "Well, it did."

He's looking everywhere but at me. "Sorry," he mumbles. "I didn't think it would be that bad. I obviously didn't know you'd be disqualified. Then I knew it wouldn't make a difference to say anything after it was already decided."

"It would've made a difference to me."

There is more to ask him, more I should get out of this as a documentarian. But the camera is starting to shake the more furious I become. The footage will be useless if I don't calm down.

For as angry as I am, I refuse to do what the Legacy Lore account is doing. If I'm going to feature him in the story, it should be the whole picture. I manage to ask him a few more questions about the assembly, about becoming valedictorian, about what Legacy means to him. We're wrapping up when there's a long pause and he mutters, "I really am sorry."

"I don't want your apology," I spit out. "I want to know who took the video. Who sabotaged me."

"Why does it matter?" he asks over a sigh.

"Because I deserve to know who ruined my life," I say. "Whoever is making these posts is threatening to do the same thing to all of you. Don't you want to know the truth?"

When some of the color drains from his face, it seems to finally hit him that he's one rumor away from sharing my fate. His gaze is unwavering when he says, "I swear, Clara. I don't know who did it."

Shit. I believe him.

But I need to be thorough. "Your dad never got any leads?"

He scoffs. "You're smarter than that, Clare-bear. He never even looked into it."

I'm disappointed in myself for being surprised. I've known for a while that the Legacy Program isn't this motivating track to get us to strive for more. Maybe that's how it started, but it's become a biased, unfair competition that pushed all of us to the point of obsession. That favors the shiniest players.

But now I know for certain that I didn't fail it. It failed *me*.

Josh visibly winces as a tear slips down my nose that I swat away quickly. I'm about to put my camera away when his expression turns conflicted as he looks over my shoulder again. It seems like he's wrestling with whether to tell me something.

I wait him out. Whatever he sees on my face makes him decide to tell me what he's been holding back.

"Did you know Rousseau tried to give up his Legacy spot?"

I frown. No. There's no possible way . . .

Josh rolls his eyes like he thought it was a ridiculous thing to do and continues. "I overheard my dad talking on the phone about it right before graduation. He wanted to give his scholarship to you, but the committee wouldn't let him."

The hair on my arms stands up as a disbelieving, "*What?*" tumbles out of my mouth.

Even after I ended things, he still tried to do that?

"Why are you telling me this?" I choke out.

It's not like Josh to be nice out of nowhere. Especially when it comes to me and Reid.

He shoves his hands in his pockets and shifts uncomfortably again. "I guess because if it were me . . . I'd want to know."

Josh's first experience with empathy is a strange sight to behold.

A few of the lights shut off as they finish cleaning the stage and amphitheater for the night. Stunned, I walk off and approach the blanket, my head and heart stirring.

Thankfully, Nicole's gone. Mitchell and Kenji are deep in conversation, Reid beside them, looking half asleep. But he sits up when he sees me.

"That go okay?" he asks.

I nod, and he looks relieved. I can't say more yet. Not in front of the other guys. Not with my heart beating out of my chest.

Just as we're heading out, Delaney rushes over to us from backstage, an excited look on her face. Maybe she found out more than I did about the posts.

"Okay, I just caught Nicole and Amaya talking in the bathroom. I didn't hear much except Amaya being mad about some sort of hookup and Nicole sounding all panicked saying, 'What if she posts that? He *can't* find out.'"

Reid and I exchange a glance.

Delaney catches it immediately, a wild glint in her eye. "What was that? What do you know?"

"We kinda walked in on Nicole and Logan making out in the guest room last night at Kenji's," I say.

I cast an apologetic look to Mitchell, who's gone completely still. That face is the exact reason I didn't say anything.

"Ewww." Kenji shudders. "I have to burn all my sheets."

"But what was Nicole worried about posting?"

"I was filming. She had a fight with her boyfriend, so she probably doesn't want him to find out about it."

Nicole must really think I'm Legacy Lore if she's that worried I'd post the footage. Anxiety pools in the pit of my stomach. Unless I can prove otherwise, it's going to be all over town soon that I'm the one behind this.

I *have* to figure out who's doing this before more damage is done.

“Is Amaya still here?” I ask, hoping to get my interview with her now.

Delaney shakes her head. “She seemed pretty freaked out about what Nicole said and took off.”

Damn it. If she’s behind the account, it would make sense she’d tried to act like she was nervous about it.

As we all walk to the parking lot, I fill Delaney in on what Josh said about Amaya and Nicole.

What doesn’t make sense is why Nicole would be making out with Logan one night and flirting with Reid the next, all while worried about her boyfriend finding out. Sure, she’d been drinking, but she never struck me as the cheating type with how outraged she was by Josh’s behavior last year.

I huff an annoyed sigh that we’re no closer to finding out what happened last year or what’s going on now.

Delaney nods. “It’s been a *long* day. Let’s see what we can find out at the Legacy Brunch tomorrow. You’ll be there, right?”

I nod. Since Amaya’s gone and Reid is clearly not up for it now, the brunch will be my last chance to interview them both before tomorrow night’s banquet.

Mitchell and Kenji wrestle Reid into the back seat. Less than a minute on the road, we go over a bump, and he slides into me again, his breathing rhythmic. I watch him a moment. His face is slack, and it’s a stark contrast to the stress that’s been tightening his features since he got home.

I want to draw my fingertips across the purple hollows under his eyes. As if he can hear my thoughts, a slight frown appears between his eyebrows and he shifts, agitated.

On instinct, I apply light, soothing strokes to the tresses of his hair. It’s softer than I remember. Messier now that it’s grown out a little.

A tidal wave of regret hits me square in the chest as I watch his expression smooth with my touch.

The longer we drive in silence, the deeper Reid seems to sink into sleep. We pull up to the lone stoplight in town, and I clear my throat and say, "Reid's out again."

"Damn, I forgot what a lightweight he is," Kenji says, laughing.

Mitchell sighs. "Do you mind if I drop him home first?"

I shake my head. "Of course not."

It's a good thing, too, since once we get to their house, it takes the three of us to get him inside while Reid grumbles and stumbles. He's entirely uncooperative. Thankfully, his parents are already asleep. I know his dad doesn't like me. None of the adults who were at the assembly last year do.

Slowly the guys guide him to his room while I head to the kitchen to grab a glass of water and a few painkillers, only to quickly realize I have no idea where they are. I aimlessly open cabinet doors, lost in my thoughts. Overcome with the revelations of the night. If Reid really tried to give up his scholarship for me, it would be the most selfless, loving, *reckless* thing anyone has ever done for me.

When Mitchell pops into the kitchen a few minutes later, he has an exasperated look on his face. "He wouldn't even let me take off his shoes."

"Does he do nothing but lift now?" Kenji asks, rolling his shoulders like they're sore as he follows him in. "Remind me how heavy he is the next time I think it'd be fun to drink together."

"He hasn't been sleeping," I say defensively.

Mitchell opens the correct cabinet and hands me a tall glass. "How do you know?"

I avoid his side-eye while I fill it up. "He told me."

Their silence is indication enough that they're exchanging a *That's interesting* look behind my back. I pick up the water glass and pills. "I'm just going to leave these in his room."

"Take your time," Mitchell calls after me.

I can practically hear Kenji's jab to his ribs as they both chuckle.

My footsteps feel plodding and heavy as I walk down the familiar hall to his room. It's lined with several photos of their parents' wedding among the redwoods, their arms lovingly wrapped around Reid and Mitchell. Boys to be cherished.

I arrive at Reid's closed door and knock softly. When there's no answer, I gently push it open and find him asleep on his back, sprawled like a starfish. Still fully clothed on top of the gray comforter, though he did kick off his own shoes.

Stepping between piles of clothes, shoes, and a crate full of books, I make my way into the dark room, lit only by the small lamp beside his bed.

I set the water and pills on his nightstand, which has a few charging cords and is piled high with the *Glass Swords* paperbacks, the spines cracked and covers worn from multiple reads. Drawing my finger across the tattered edges, my heart squeezes.

Reid turns onto his stomach, grumbling something indecipherable against his pillow. His arm hangs over the edge, his jacket bunching at his shoulders and under his rib cage.

As I start to pull his sleeve low past his hand to try to get it off him, he groans, "Fuck *off*, Mitchell."

"Calm down, you'll sleep better if you're comfortable."

He lifts his head at the sound of my voice and looks over his shoulder. His brow furrowed and disbelieving. "Clara?"

I have to actively ignore the flip in my stomach at the sight of his hair so disheveled.

“I was trying to help you get your jacket off,” I say, my cheeks on fire.

He looks down himself, obviously confused, but nods slowly.

Together we make short work of it as he eases his arms out of the sleeves. I also hand him the pills, which he takes without protest, and he gulps down the entire glass of water.

“Why are you here?” he asks.

I can’t tell if he means here in his room or here for him. Either way the answer’s the same.

“I just want you to be okay,” I say quietly.

He sighs and lies back. “I haven’t been okay for a really long time.”

It’s the most honest thing he’s said all weekend, but I *hate* how resigned he sounds.

I’m sure he’s already passed out again by the time I stand and drop his jacket on the chair by his bed. I flip the light off and turn to slip out the door, but his warm hand closes around my wrist.

My pulse thunders as our eyes lock.

“Stay?” He bends his elbow and tugs—gently and just once. “Just for a minute?”

There’s a plea in his voice that strikes me deep.

I don’t know what it means that he asks, but I do know what it means that I want to. We’ve crossed somewhere that’s at once new and as well-worn as the books beside the bed. Keeping my eyes on his, I nod and sink onto the mattress beside him.

He hooks a strong arm around my waist and draws me close. I’m immediately overwhelmed—by the complete and total feel of him and the soft, warm sheets that smell like fresh laundry and his cologne.

He blinks slowly while his eyes roam my face, and it feels like even in the haze of sleep, he still sees me. *Really* sees me. A tiny gasp escapes my lips as he grazes a thumb across my jaw. Him touching me like this ignites every tender memory between us. I wrap my fingers gently around his wrist in response, hoping he knows I see him, too.

Neither of us says a word. Something settles inside me for the first time in months as our breathing syncs and his eyes flutter closed, my hand in his.

My heart still his.

CHAPTER TWENTY-FIVE

REID

THE DAY OF LEGACY BANQUET

@haikuforyou
The world is burning
But no hotter than I do
for each inch of you

I SURFACE SLOWLY, SHEETS tangled around my torso. Warmth all around me. My limbs are heavy, my mind, for once, is quiet.

It's still early, but . . . I feel *rested.*

I inhale deeply and catch my favorite floral scent as if I'm still in a dream. But it's too real, too present. My eyes slit open.

Weak predawn light nudges at the window, and it's just enough to be able to see an empty glass on my nightstand that wasn't there before, and the wild waves of dark hair splayed across the pillow next to me.

Clara's hair.

She's here. In my *bed.* I take in the rest in increments; her entire body curled around me like ivy, one leg tucked between mine, an arm on my chest. Our hands are linked together. Even in sleep.

That pries something in me already burning to open.

How did this happen? I squeeze my eyes tight, trying to remember. There are only pieces and flashes. We were at the show. I downed more wine than food or water or *air*. I tried to fight Josh? And I vaguely remember being jostled back home.

Clara standing by my bed. Asking her to stay.

But when she agreed and actually got in beside me, I was sure it was a dream.

A dull pain shoots up my other arm, which is trapped beneath her. With a wince, I do my best to free it smoothly, but I rustle her and an adorable, protesting little grumble sounds from the blankets.

When I peel the comforter back from her face, my breath gets stuck. I love that I get to see her like this. At least once. Her eye makeup is smudged and her lips a little swollen from sleep. For all that we've shared, we've never woken up together in the morning. We had a lot of firsts left.

She looks so peaceful that I try to extract myself without waking her. But just as I untangle our legs, she tightens her grip on my hand, and her eyes flutter open.

I wait for her to freeze or back away. But she doesn't.

A small smile curls her mouth as her eyes meet mine, and the deep hurt we share longs to slip away, forgotten. But without that hurt, that distance between us, I'm not sure I'll have the strength to leave for Stanford tomorrow.

"What time is it?" Her husky voice is raspier with sleep.

I check and it's not even seven.

"I should probably get home," she murmurs.

"Yeah, okay. I'll take you."

Only, instead of getting up, she hugs me closer. Wrapping both arms full around me until there's no space left, she nuzzles her face in the crook of my neck. There is no one on this planet who loves to cuddle as much as Clara Suarez. I thought I remembered how good it felt, but the reality is so much better.

What changed? I'm afraid to ask and risk ruining this moment.

I run my hand down the length of her back. "I forgot about Kolara," I say, amused.

Her voice vibrates against my chest when she groans. "That was the worst one."

"Oh, c'mon, it was clever. You cuddle like a koala, your name is Clara. Kolara. Perfect nickname."

She *tsks*, and I can picture her smiling eye roll.

I close my eyes, savoring the feel of her in my arms. "I stand by it."

"Okay, RiRi."

I laugh. It feels strange. And good. I don't know what territory we've crossed into now, or even how we did it, but there's an ease between us that hasn't been there since last year.

Despite how good this feels, my knee is stiff and sore. I apologetically maneuver myself and stretch my arms high over my head. Cool air hits my stomach where my shirt rides up. Clara eases off me, her cheeks pink, which fills me with a feeling dangerously close to smug.

"Be right back." She hops off the bed and uses the adjoining bathroom. Then I do, too. While I brush my teeth, I prepare myself for the inevitable. Clara will be sitting in the living room when I get out, ready to go. Ready to put distance between us again by pretending like this never even happened. Whatever it was.

But when I emerge, she's settled back on the bed, sitting upright. Waiting for me instead of hiding from me.

"How're you feeling? Did you sleep?" she asks.

I nod and perch beside her again, leaning back against the headboard.

Best sleep I've had in months, I think ruefully. "Pretty sure you saved me with that water. I'm never drinking again."

She tries to laugh, but it doesn't quite get there. When she turns toward me, the sleeve of her shirt slips down her shoulder. I quickly flick my gaze upward to stare at the ceiling. If I keep looking at her rumpled in my bed I won't be able to stop myself from crashing my lips to hers.

Which would be a *very* bad idea.

"I heard something last night I need to ask you about," she says, her tone turning the air serious.

Never good words in Woodhurst. "Okay . . ."

"Did you really try to give up your Legacy spot for me?"

My pulse picks up. It was never something I wanted her to know since it hadn't worked. Which made no fucking sense. But there's no point in lying to her about it now, so I nod.

Anyone else might hug me or cry. Instead, she smacks me, right in the chest.

"Ow."

A shocked laugh escapes as I rub the spot. There's the Clara I knew.

"How could you do that? I never wanted you to hold yourself back for me. Ever."

I don't like the way she says that. Like she's someone who isn't worth bending—even breaking—for.

"I also have my athletic scholarship; it would've been okay."

She frowns. "That only covers part of your tuition. You told me that having both was a big help to your family. You deserve them. Why would you do that?"

I meet her gaze. "Because you deserved it, too."

She's so close I can see the flecks of gold in her green eyes. Emotions I could never name pass through them.

I look away first.

"It won't matter much longer since I'm probably going to get kicked out anyway."

Her gasp is loud in the quiet room. "Because you're injured?"

"No," I sigh. "Because I'm failing. I just found out I'm on academic probation."

It's a weird relief to finally say it out loud. But she doesn't respond right away. In the silence, the sounds of the birds outside filter in as the mountain wakes up.

She shifts to lean back against the headboard beside me, her expression a bit stunned. "Then shouldn't they give you a tutor or extra credit or something? I mean, they can't just *kick you out.* You're the state champion—"

I scoff. "Yeah, me and every other guy on the team. But I'm the only one who can't seem to keep up with it all. If I lose my scholarships, that's it. We can't afford it otherwise."

"Is that what your dad said?"

I shrug, and understanding crosses her face. I don't have to respond for her to know.

"You haven't told him?"

"He'll freak."

"Yeah. And he'll *help,*" she says simply. "Reid, you can't keep this from him. You can't figure this out alone."

Frustration starts to claw at me. I do my best to keep it at bay. "What difference does it make?"

"Whether or not you finish college? A pretty big difference."

"It's just—" I stop myself.

She scoots closer, crossing her legs under her. "What?"

"I thought it would feel different—when I finally got to this level."

At her silence, I scrub a hand across my jaw, the stubble scratchy against my palm. "Like all the hard work would've meant something. But it's . . . hollow. I'm not sure it even matters to me." My voice catches, and I clear my throat. "I know that makes me sound like a prick."

She shoves me lightly. "Not possible."

I shrug like that isn't the point and stare at my hands, which are bunched around the sheets.

Her voice is quiet but firm when she says, "You give your jacket to anyone who looks cold, you made even the slowest person on the team feel like they mattered because you stayed until everyone crossed the finish line, you're honest in a way that makes people trust you, you believe in others more than they believe in themselves."

Her gaze snags on something behind me.

"And your favorite character from *Glass Swords* is Ziva." She leans across me to grab one of the dog-eared books from my nightstand and holds it up for emphasis. "*Ziva.* The sworn-shield with the heart of gold who everyone else in the fandom forgets about."

She's so close now—our shoulders pressed together, the lilac scent of her hair present with every breath—and all I can think to say is, "Because the kingdom would've collapsed without Ziva. He never surrendered."

Her expression is pained and understanding all at once. "It's okay to surrender sometimes."

I'm completely thrown by the care in her tone. I swallow, try to keep my bearings. I stare at the poster that sits on the wall opposite from us of the quote I told her about. The one that's motivated me throughout my entire journey as a runner:

To give anything less than your best is to sacrifice the gift.

"No." I set my jaw, ashamed of myself for even hinting at giving up. "I can't stop."

She reaches toward me and slowly threads our fingers together. I blink down at our hands, and how they just fit. We *always* fit. Touching in our sleep is one thing, but this . . . what is this? Pity? Guilt?

Or something else?

She squeezes, and my thumb brushes across the back of her hand in response.

"Look at me," she says.

It's a quiet but forceful command that raises the hair on my arms. The air becomes charged and alive between us as my gaze drags up slowly, following the path I wish my lips could. The bare skin of her shoulder, her long neck, the freckle on her cheekbone. It finally lands on her eyes, smudged and gorgeous—a soft jade in the light. My heart slams hard against my ribs as I stare into them.

Harder when she says, "You have so many gifts."

Jesus, I can't take it anymore.

Winding my hand around the nape of her neck, I draw her to me and finally do what I've been thinking about since I saw her on that deck at Kenji's. Clara used to ignite when I kissed her, but this kiss—it's soft, gentle. Almost painfully cautious. Did I misread this? Did I just ruin everything all over again?

Embarrassed, I try to back up. "Sorry—"

But her fist grips my shirt at the center of my chest, holding me in place. Her eyes are pleading, not a trace of humor or distance in them. I feel the shaking words against my lips as she whispers, "Please don't stop."

It unlocks me.

As I catch her mouth with mine again, every moment we've spent apart fuses us back together.

But I don't want to rush this. I kiss her slower. Deeper. She tastes better than I remember. My fingers tangle into the thick tresses of her hair, and she melts against me, bringing her mouth to mine again and again.

We fall back onto the bed, into each other. We've resolved almost nothing, but part of me—most of me—doesn't care right now. All I know is the more open she is with me, the more desperate I am to get closer. Especially when she breaks away and her words, "I missed you," come out as a tremulous murmur against my skin.

I drag my thumb across her bottom lip in pure awe that this is actually happening.

"Me too," I rasp. "So fucking much."

I press a kiss to the bare skin of her shoulder and continue the path up her neck. Her fingertips play with the hem of my ridiculous BOP TIL YOU DROP shirt I can't believe I'm still wearing, and I finally wrench the thing off. My pants are next, and hers, too. She slides her warm palms down my chest, my stomach. I tremble under her touch.

Our lips meet again, and this time, there's no shred of caution. Every part of me remembers what she likes, how else we fit.

The need between us grows, and I firm my grasp against the small of her back. Her responsive arch has me bunching the fabric of her shirt in my fist. I think of the ink I saw on her skin at the hot springs, hungry to see it.

My breathing goes ragged when she wraps her legs around me, leaving no space between us. I get a strong grip on her waist, drawing her hips flush under mine. Her hands travel and—*Jesus*—all thoughts cease when she touches me like that. I suck in a breath as she nips at my mouth.

I'm about to tug her shirt clean off when we both freeze at the sound of footsteps followed by a hard knock at my bedroom door.

"Reid? You up?" It's my dad. Of *course* it's my dad.

I press my forehead to Clara's and let out a slow exhale.

"Yeah," I say evenly, so he doesn't open the door to check. To find the girl he's convinced is a bad influence half naked beneath me.

At least I resist the urge to say, *I sure am*.

Like she can read my mind, Clara stifles a laugh with her hand. I widen my eyes at her playfully, my face on full fire.

"Good. We have the Legacy Brunch this morning, and I figure we should go for a real trail run before that. Coach Carr can't be happy about you taking so many days off."

Fuck.

"Um, yeah—okay." I slide off Clara. The humor drains in an instant, replaced by dread and a heaviness I can't name.

"Great! Ten minutes?"

"Yep."

I wait until his footsteps disappear down the hall, and my body has calmed down enough to stand.

The silence between me and Clara is awkward and unsure. Her bare legs are out of the covers, her dark hair is wild in a way that has me clenching my jaw, wishing we could've finished what we started.

But wanting each other was never the problem. It was this part. In the quiet spaces. It's where she's tenser. More guarded. And now I am, too.

I push my hands through my hair and start hunting for some running clothes.

"Are you seriously going to go run?" Clara asks. "On your knee like that? After everything you just told me?"

"I have to."

"You don't. Talk to him," she says.

I shake my head. It's not fair to put this kind of stress on him. The second I tell him about my injury, he'll pounce on it like it's a project.

Same with academic probation. He probably *would* hire a tutor with money we don't have or talk to my professors or get me on some sort of plan or schedule to catch up. He'd treat me like I'm a broken thing to be fixed. His problem to solve. The way I've always been.

I want to be something different, even if I don't know what that is yet.

Worst of all, it would be letting everyone down. I think of all the people staring at me at the show last night. The comments on the Legacy Lore posts.

My kids looked up to you!

I can't let that happen. I pull on a T-shirt and black running shorts.

"Is this really what you want?" she asks.

How can she understand me so well but not understand this? I'm going to a college that people would kill to get into and am on one of the top teams in the nation. It's not about what I *want*. It's about what's best. But she's not deterred by my silence.

"Don't you think your dad would do *anything* to help you if he knew how miserable you are?" she asks, zipping up her jeans.

I spin around to face her. "Like you know how miserable I am?"

But she doesn't flinch or back away at my tone. Her eyes narrow. "I do. Because I know you. And I have *hours* of footage of you doing exactly this. Pushing yourself too hard. Ignoring every warning sign from your body, your mind. This"—she says, gesturing to me—"is what you do when you're afraid you're not enough."

A headache is forming at my temples. In the ensuing silence, I pull on my watch and zip up a hoodie, avoiding her gaze the entire time.

Her voice is barely above a whisper when she says, "You're disappearing."

Good, I think.

She steps closer and hooks her hands in the front pockets of my hoodie to pull me closer. "I won't let you."

I stare deep into the dark green pools of her eyes that have always tugged too much truth out of me. They're full of determination. Certain she can fix this. Maybe even fix us.

I want to believe it's possible. But how can I when I don't know that she'd be there—really be there—for the fallout? Who's to say she wouldn't dump me out of nowhere or block me again?

"Clara, I don't know if I'll ever run well again. My grades are shit, I'm so *fucking* tired, everything I planned has hit this total dead end—"

"A detour," she interjects.

"What?"

"Maybe it's a detour," she repeats softly. "But it's not a dead end."

My breath shudders in response to the echo of the words I said to her once. The hypocrisy is almost too much to bear. She was so upset when her plans didn't work out that she broke my heart on the side of the road. But I'm supposed to feel *great* that everything I've worked for could be over if I don't get my shit together?

"So—what? Are you saying I should quit?" I challenge.

She inhales, like she's mustering some serious strength when she says, "I'm not saying that. But 'quitting' isn't a dirty word, Reid. It's always an option."

Anger rises in me, unbidden but unstoppable. "You would know."

"What's that supposed to mean?"

My reply comes out more forcefully than I expect. "You quit us without flinching."

The blow lands, and hurt flashes across her features. Hurt she doesn't try to disguise. That throws me off more than anything else has this morning.

"Is that really what you think?" she asks.

It doesn't sound defensive. It sounds . . . sad.

"What was I supposed to think?"

"It wasn't without flinching." She sits on the edge of the mattress, her voice thick with emotion. "It . . . destroyed me."

It's a dagger. No, a thousand daggers.

I squeeze my hands into fists, every thought and feeling from the past year clashing and crashing together until I feel like I might detonate. "Then why did you do it?"

The shadow of her lashes fans across her cheeks as she closes her eyes, thinking. "I was scared. You—*this*—wasn't in my plan. Then when my plan fell apart . . . I didn't want you to get stuck here. You were leaving. You had to go."

"You didn't even give us a chance when I *was* here," I say, my eyes digging into hers. "I did everything I could possibly think of to give you what you wanted."

"You did," she agrees quietly, looking down at her hands. "And I know it wasn't enough, but I gave you more than I ever thought I was capable of."

We stand there a moment as that settles between us. A part of me wants to drop all of this here and now and pull her into my arms. But too much of our history stops me. Never knowing if how I felt or what I said would drive her away. Like the thing that's lingered since her birthday last year.

"Did you ever read the card?" I ask. The birthday card with the poem I wrote her. That confessed everything I needed her to know. She never said a single thing about it and I never asked.

Her mouth opens, closes. "What card?"

I can't tell if she's playing it cool, lying, or just trying to let me down gently. Maybe she has no idea what I'm talking about. But a calm clarity settles over me as I realize it doesn't really make a difference. I've known all along she only wants me when it doesn't mean anything.

My voice is small, anguished. "We can't keep doing this."

Our eyes meet, and I know immediately it was a mistake to come back here. To be with her again. To remember how soft her skin is and how her breath skips when I touch her in a way she likes. To remember that our connection is still strong enough to scare the shit out of me.

It took me months to forget. But now, I know again. I *know.* And I'll have to carry that knowing through every torturous, lonely minute at school all over again.

Because the problem is the same as it ever was: She doesn't want anything real, and I don't know how to stop myself from loving her.

"I have to go," I say. "Can Mitchell drive you home?"

I lace up my shoes, avoiding her eyes the entire time. My knee feels fine. It'll be fine.

"Reid—"

I walk out the door.

None of us get what we want, anyway.

CHAPTER TWENTY-SIX

CLARA

NOW

BEFORE I CAN SAY anything else, Reid walks out of his bedroom without so much as a backward glance. I'm left standing there in the wreckage of what neither of us can seem to repair.

His touch was searing, his kisses almost bruising in their intensity. When he wrapped his body around mine, I never wanted to let go as my heart sighed, *Yes, this, finally.*

But the moment I brought up last year, he shut down. Maybe no matter what we want, what he *needs* is closure. The thought forms a breathless ache in the center of my chest.

I hear a door open across the hall, followed by tense, low voices. Reid telling Mitchell to get up about five hours earlier than he usually would. Then several fast footsteps and the firm closing of the front door.

Reid's in a darker place than I realized. If things are as bad as he says they are, it's almost as if he wants them to implode. And they will if he keeps running on an injured knee or avoiding what's going on at school.

I hate seeing him in pain like this. I wish I could *do* something.

Mitchell appears in the doorway, puffy and mussed from sleep.

He raises his eyebrows, and with every drawn-out syllable dripping with implication says, "Sleep well?"

I slump onto the edge of the bed and bury my face in my hands. "I don't want to talk about it."

He steps into the room. "Good. Literally always err on the side of sparing me the details of my brother's sex life."

"We didn't—"

But I stop. Because we *almost* and, god, I wish we had. I feel my cheeks heat at the thought.

"Ewww." Mitchell grimaces and playfully covers my face with his hand. I shove it off as I stand up.

"Where's Kenji?" I ask in an effort to change the subject.

The humor drains from him instantly. "He left last night when it was clear *you* weren't coming out."

I frown at his tone. "What does that mean?"

Mitchell turns. "It's too early for boy talk. C'mon."

When we get to my house, Mitchell not only invites himself in but also immediately helps himself to a massive bowl of ice cream. For breakfast.

I was hoping to crawl back into bed for a few more hours, or get ahead on editing footage before the brunch, but Mitchell flops on the couch with his giant bowl of feelings and I can tell—early or not—we need to talk about the boy.

"What happened?" I ask, perching on the couch across from him.

"It's nothing. Or it's Logan. I dunno. I'm fine," he grumbles, before shoving a large bite in his mouth.

I narrow my eyes. I'm so tired of these brothers and their "fine."

Through my interviews, I've noticed Mitchell responds better to a challenge than to direct questions. I nudge him with my foot. "What do you care? Logan was an asshole to you, but you have Kenji."

His spoon clatters loudly against the bowl as he eyes me like I wounded him. "Bite your tongue. I don't have Kenji. There is no *having* of Kenji."

"I was there when he put his arm around you," I say.

"And *I* was there when he told you that you looked hot."

My face screws up. "Mitchell, it's *Kenji.* He tells everyone they look hot. You can't seriously think he's into me."

Even saying the words makes me want to laugh. It's only Mitchell's serious expression that keeps it in.

"How would I know?" he asks. "He's such a fucking flirt I have no idea who he's into. He's off at college happily slutting it up and I'm here pining like a Bridgerton brother just desperate for him to look at me."

He aggressively shoves more rocky road into his mouth.

After the way Logan treated him, I don't blame him for feeling insecure. Even though I've caught more longing stares on my camera between Mitch and Kenji in the past twenty-four hours than I know what to do with, it still wouldn't be enough to convince Mitchell. Logan had watched him longingly, too, but always wanted to keep their relationship a secret. He said it was about securing Legacy, but he's only ever openly dated girls after they broke up, too. Mitchell has every right to be confused.

"Kenji isn't Logan," I say gently.

"True. Logan was terrified of standing out, whereas Kenji relishes it."

Mitchell polishes off the bowl, then pushes both his hands through his hair like he does when he's upset. The small huff of laughter that escapes him is humorless. "God, that guy messed with my head."

I swallow at his choice of words. The same words Reid said to me when we broke up.

You do nothing but mess with my head.

"Reid said I did the same thing," I say quietly.

Mitchell's eyebrows rise in surprise.

I don't ever talk to him about Reid, which he clearly prefers. But the situation is eerily similar, and my feelings about Reid are becoming so gnarled, I'll never be able to make sense of them in time if I don't start untangling them.

"I thought by keeping things low-key that I was protecting both of us from getting hurt," I say quietly. "Maybe Logan was doing the same thing."

Mitchell rears back a little. "Are you seriously being a Logan apologist right now?"

I grimace. "Not on purpose. Am I?"

He holds up his forefinger and thumb an inch apart. "Little bit."

I put my hands up. "Sorry—I know he broke your heart."

Mitchell winces at that, but I keep going.

"I'd just hate for you to miss out on something good because you think the way he acted was about *you*. It wasn't. You should talk to Kenji. Tell him how you feel."

Mitchell bursts into a laugh that takes over his whole body.

"What? Why is that so funny?"

It takes him a few seconds to answer. "It's not—it's good advice. I just wish *you* would take it, since you're obviously in love with Reid." He says it like a joke, but as our gazes meet, whatever he sees in my eyes makes his go round with surprise. "Holy shit. You are. You're in love with him, aren't you?"

I stare down at my hands, my face instantly flaming. "Don't tell him," I say in a rush.

"What?"

"He's got enough going on right now—"

"No way." Mitchell leaps to his feet, suddenly agitated. "You can't do this to him again. Clara, what you did? That shit *broke* him last year."

My pulse begins racing so hard I feel it in my fingertips.

It's been an unspoken rule that Mitchell and I don't talk about Reid for *this* reason. He's spared sharing the things that would burrow deep.

But now that we've torn open the subject, Mitchell no longer holds back what he's clearly kept in all year. "What happened at the assembly was so fucked up. I know that. My skin crawls any time I think about it. But it wasn't Reid's fault."

"That's not why . . . I wasn't about to ruin his time at college, Mitchell. A long-distance relationship would've made him unfocused, and he would've ended up hating me for holding him back. I had to let him—" My voice breaks and I stop.

Mitchell's eyes widen, and he puts a hand over his heart like he's touched. "Oh my god, you *White Fang*ed him. Or, like, the butterfly thing. Loving so much you let him go."

I nod. "He even tried to give me his Legacy spot, did you know that?"

Mitchell goes still. "Yeah, I did know that."

"And you didn't tell me?"

"He told me not to."

"See? This is *exactly* why I had to break things off. It makes no sense that he would give up something like that for me."

Mitchell frowns. "Actually it makes perfect sense. He *believes in you*. It wasn't because of his feelings for you. I mean, okay, it wasn't *just* because of that. You got cheated out of a chance you deserved, and he was just trying to make it right. He was trying to"—his shoulders sag—"he was *trying*, Clara."

Tears heat the backs of my eyes.

Reid always tries so hard. Too hard. It's what's breaking him now and what was always difficult to keep up with then. But hearing Mitchell say it like this, I'm starting to wonder if Reid tried that hard for me because . . . I didn't try enough.

"Did I give up too easily?" I ask.

Mitchell shrugs. "That's probably being too hard on yourself. But you did pivot to tree person, and that was a dark timeline for you, I'm not gonna lie."

I kick him, and he laughs.

But he's also not wrong.

When that video played at the assembly, it silenced something in me. No matter my love for Reid, I couldn't stand the idea of him being with *that* girl. The one who was messy and broken and stuck.

But he didn't see me like that.

It wouldn't stop you. Nothing can stop you.

I lost almost everything that mattered to me last year. I thought that those losses defined me. But I'm still here. Still trying. Still fighting for what matters to me.

Maybe that's what defines me.

Looking at Mitchell now—who's so afraid to get hurt again he refuses to acknowledge what's real even when it's speaking ridiculous Shakespearean English in his ear—I'm starting to see that pushing Reid away time and again didn't protect either of us from pain. It actually invited so much more in.

When Mitchell goes to refill his bowl, I pick up my phone to check my favorite poetry account the way I have all year when I miss him. It *still* hasn't updated. But I can't linger on that long when in the next moment, both our phones chime. We share a quick glance. That can only mean a text on the group chat.

Sure enough, Kenji sent an update from the Legacy Lore account with the text, Another reason we hate Josh!!! He's why I had to retake that AP Calc final!!!

> **@LEGACY_LORE:** A former Woodhurst student entrepreneur who relocated to a different school midyear has revealed his number one customer. Anyone recognize a certain Legacy? More soon . . . ♥

The post includes several screenshots of text messages between Anderson Beck, who got expelled last year for selling answer keys to tests, and Josh negotiating where to meet and the price for both the midterm and the final.

Mitchell lets out a low laugh. "Oh, this is bad."

As I read through the texts I think of Josh's response when I asked him about the cheating accusation. *I have nothing to hide.* He said that about what happened between us last year, too. He's a good liar.

Still, this isn't exactly hard proof.

"I mean, there's no way to know for sure it's actually Josh and Anderson sending these."

Mitchell shakes his head. "You know nobody cares about proof. The damage is done."

The comments prove Mitchell's point. They're scathing. Of Josh and the school. Starting to call into question the Legacy Program.

As someone also trying to tell that story, I should be excited that its faults are starting to show. But I'm not.

Whoever is behind this account isn't trying to right wrongs or bring the truth to light, they're trying to ruin reputations. They seem hell-bent on forcing out anything that could threaten the Legacies' scholarships. Their very futures. Everything Reid has worked for.

I *refuse* to let that happen to him.

Which is exactly why I'm making the doc.

If Reid is still willing to talk to me after what happened between us this morning, I can finally get his interview at the brunch with just enough time to finish putting the video together for the banquet tonight. To show the *complete* story.

Hopefully before any more rumors get around.

CHAPTER TWENTY-SEVEN

REID

NOW

DAY OF LEGACY BANQUET

@haikuforyou
Larkspur survives frost
Fighting against a cold fate
We could be like that

I THINK I FINALLY pushed too far. The run with my dad was manageable until the final hill. I pretended my shoelace came untied and told my dad to run ahead. I ended up having to walk the rest of the way home, and even that was a lot on my knee.

After I shower and dress in jeans and a hoodie for the Legacy Brunch, I hobble to the kitchen for some ice and ibuprofen. For the first time since I got home, I'm not sure I can keep acting like it's okay.

I don't move from the couch until the front door explodes open announcing Mitchell's arrival home. Everything he does is loud—it's why living with him is fucking exhausting.

Jesus, was he with Clara this whole time?

I assumed he was going to go straight back to bed once we left based on the deluge of curse words he threw at me this morning when I woke him up to take her home. Keys clang into the bowl by the door. His shoes hit the wall as he kicks them off. The cacophony of Mitchell.

A large shadow looms over me, but I barely glance up.

"Aren't you supposed to be at the Legacy Brunch?" Mitchell asks.

"I'm waiting for Dad," I say. My words jumble together, smushed against the cushion.

"What happened?"

"Go away."

"You go. If you want to wallow so bad, you have a whole-ass room you can do that in." He flops next to me. "You obviously want to talk."

He's got a point because I don't leave.

"So talk," he says.

I sigh. Turn so my face is less consumed by the pillow.

"Letting Clara sleep over was a mistake."

The memory of her twined around me drags a miserable sound from my throat.

"Why?" he asks.

"We shouldn't have gone there. We're not together."

"Technically you never were."

My nostrils flare. "Thanks for that."

He shrugs. "Just saying, what's different now?"

"Nothing," I snap. "That's the problem. She still doesn't want me."

All I hear then is a loud, long *laugh*. Okay, that pisses me off. I sit up.

"Dude, it's not funny," I near shout. I feel my face heating, the angry vein in my temple throbbing.

Mitchell keeps laughing and rakes his hands through his hair like he wants to pull it out. "You two are trying to kill me."

And before I know what's happening, I throw myself across the couch to get him to shut up, headbutting him in the process. We fall to the ground in a shattering crash, Julianne's potpourri bowl flying as we knock against the coffee table.

"Get off!" he yells.

But every pent-up, twisted feeling urges me on. Because I can't have her. Because without him, I'm terrified I'd have no one.

He gets a grip around me and throws me back, then in a spastic spray of limbs, he swoops a leg around, pinning me. He's got me locked on the ground, his legs squeezing me in a vise. I try to escape, but he pins me harder. I can't move.

Brilliant idea to sucker punch a wrestler.

He's panting, too, swipes the back of his hand under his nose, leaving a faint trail of blood across it. He pinches the bridge of his nose but still manages to glare at me.

"Let me up," I say.

"That would be a fuck no." His nose sounds stuffy and all of a sudden, I realize what a complete asshole I'm being.

I thump my head against the carpet, giving in.

When he accepts my defeat, he smacks me against the face, *hard,* then releases me. I scramble up.

"Better?" he asks.

Not exactly. It felt as though I could've kept punching faster and harder and it never would've been enough. But that's not about Mitchell. My chest rises quickly as I rub a palm across my stinging cheek. "Sorta. I've been wanting to do that since you sent that photo and I thought you and Clara were hooking up."

He rolls his eyes. Scrubs a hand down his face. "God, I really should've told you a long time ago that I like Kenji."

There's a significance to his tone that makes my eyes widen. "Wait—like, you *like* him?"

He nods. "I'm bi."

"You are?"

"C'mon," he says, goading. Like I should know.

I slowly stretch my leg out and lean back against the couch. Trying to catch up with something I've long wondered but figured was none of my business. Memories shudder through my mind, so many things clicking into place.

"Oh my god, your *Spider-Man* thing?"

He lets out a low laugh. "Was more of a Tom Holland thing, yeah."

"You made me watch that movie a hundred times."

"Like you cared when you had your Zendaya thing."

I shove him lightly, and we both laugh.

We sit in silence a few minutes, only the distant sound of my dad's electric razor from his back bathroom cutting through it.

"Do our parents know?" I ask.

He nods. "And Clara . . . and Kenji . . . and Logan."

My eyes widen. "Damn. Okay." I shake my head slowly as that settles in.

"You're not freaked out?" he asks, looking more unsure than I've ever seen him.

I get why he might be afraid I'd be weird about it since not everyone is accepting or understands. Especially in a town like ours. But I hope he doesn't seriously think I'd ever feel that way.

I frown and elbow him. "Of course not. That would be like you freaking out that I'm straight."

"That does freak me out."

We both laugh.

After another moment I say, "Hold up, why *Logan*?"

His sigh is heavy. "You weren't the only one who got dumped last year."

Wow. I hate that I had no idea any of this was going on for him. He's been a rock of support for me while going through it all on his own.

"Shit. I'm sorry. Thanks for telling me," I say seriously.

"I know I should have sooner." He sighs and looks down at his hands plucking up fibers from the carpet. "I've wanted to for a while, but . . . I care what you think. Maybe the most. And I was worried it might change things or something."

"I hope it does."

He studies me and smiles as he gets my meaning. I want him to feel like he can be himself around me. Always.

"Don't go through shit like that alone next time."

He nods. "I won't. But for the record, I didn't. Clara helped a lot."

My heart picks up that this is what they've been hiding. She was supporting him in a way I didn't even know he needed. That, more than anything, reminds me why I fell for her in the first place.

"We don't need to hug or any—"

I draw him into a hug then. It's quick, him smacking me hard against the back, making me cough. But when we pull apart, his eyes are glassy.

"Anyway," he sniffs. "You're a dumbass."

I snort. He's not wrong.

Each piece of potpourri clinks against the glass bowl that we thankfully didn't break as I clean up.

"Talk to Clara," Mitchell urges.

When he stands, he helps me up, too, just as my dad emerges ready to go to the brunch. As we follow him out the door, I turn to Mitchell. "For what it's worth, I think Kenji likes you, too."

He flushes and I climb into the car with a grin.

By the time we arrive at Woodhurst High, the Legacy Brunch is packed. Is the entire town here? The overhead music booms in a way that rattles my very cells, making me already wish I could leave. A giant, glittery banner is strung over the stage that reads, *Welcome, Legacies!*, and there are dozens of round tables covered in navy and white tablecloths, the school colors. The enticing scent of buttery pancakes and bacon hangs in the air.

Principal West rushes me and reminds me about giving a quick speech once everyone is done eating, to thank them for coming and for all their generous donations. I'm starting to count the hours until I've completed my guest of honor duties and can be done with all this.

Though that will mean it's time to go back to school, which is a less-than-comforting thought.

There's a long buffet line, and everyone's conversations and laughter around me add to the noise. Add to my growing agitation. I pile my plate high with food and cross through the room to a table far from the town crowd so I can eat in peace. But then my dad soon joins me.

"They taking care of you over there at that fancy school? Your fall last month seems to have slowed you down a bit."

My pulse picks up. "I just didn't feel like pushing."

"Since when is a five-miler pushing?"

I swipe the thin paper napkin across my lips. "No—it wasn't. Just—forget it."

But I've already said too much because he's eyeing me closer than before. He leans forward, dropping his voice low. "You'd tell me if something serious was going on with you, right?"

All I can do is nod.

"You sure?"

"*Yes*. I'm just a little hungover and didn't want to tell you, okay?"

When I look at him, his mouth has flattened in disappointment, but at least the half-truth works. He reaches for his water glass and plunks it in front of me. "Hydrate."

I drink it down while he proceeds to lecture me.

"A little indulgence is to be expected at your age, but it's not like you to drink. Was this with Clara?"

The empty glass strikes the table hard as my anger spikes. "*Jesus*, Dad. No. She had nothing to do with it."

"I know she stayed over."

My neck gets hot. I notice her over his shoulder then, interviewing Amaya, who's swiping tears off her cheeks.

"You're an adult now, but . . ." He sighs and rubs his forehead. "Well, what am I supposed to think here? As far as you're telling me, you've been fine all year, but the minute you see her again you're drinking, staying up late, your times are off. For all I know, she could be buttering you up, trying to get your scholarship money again."

I stare at him, too stunned to even speak for a second.

"It's a slippery slope, Reid, and you have put in too much time and work to get sidetracked from your goals. She's a distraction."

I almost laugh at the irony as I hear Clara's voice from this morning, urging me to talk to him. To tell him everything even if I don't understand it all myself.

Now I know he couldn't possibly understand, either.

My voice is a furious calm when I say, "You couldn't be more wrong about her."

After a long stretch of silence where I'm convincing myself slugging my own father would be the exact wrong look for the Legacy guest of honor, he says, "Okay—but I need to know your head is in the game. That Olympic coach, Coach Andrews, reached out again because he's traveling nearby for one of his athletes. You've been dodging his calls, so I invited him to the banquet tonight."

"What?"

"I don't know why you look so shocked, this was always our plan."

"*Your* plan."

He frowns. "Meaning?"

Before I can answer, someone calls his name and he says, "That's one of the benefactors. We'll continue this later."

As soon as he walks off, I bury my face in my hands. My breath is too short, my entire body covered in a nervous sweat. I've let this go too far. What am I going to do?

I just might puke.

But I can't wallow long because moments later Clara slips into the chair beside me like she'd been waiting. She has on pink lip gloss and a dark sweater and jeans. Her hair is pulled back in its usual high ponytail, highlighting the sharp slant of her cheekbones.

"Hi." Her smile is timid, and I instantly feel both anchored with her beside me and like absolute shit for walking out on her this morning. For letting myself get sucked into my own self-pity instead of hearing her out.

"Hi."

There is so much to say, neither of us seems to know where to start.

"Ready for your interview?" she asks.

I don't know what I was expecting, but it wasn't that.

"Now?" We probably talked about this last night and I just don't remember. I'm wearing old jeans and a gray hoodie that's torn at the neck, and my hair is a mess as usual. I should probably get it cut soon.

Her eyes flit to it at the same time and light up with amusement. Great.

"I have to edit the video for the banquet tonight, and I managed to get Amaya's interview by catching her off guard about the latest posts."

My eyebrows rise in interest, but her sigh is frustrated as she turns her phone toward me. The one about Josh cheating is pretty damning, and as Delaney predicted, the screenshots of Amaya's texts to her cast were just posted.

"She cried—like sobbed. Maybe I was wrong about her being behind the account."

"Maybe." I nod slowly. "But don't forget that she's a good actress."

"Yeah . . . I just feel like we're missing something crucial." Clara tucks her phone away and studies me. "Yours is the last interview I need for the video, though. It's now or never."

She always told me she wanted to make films that matter. The glimpse I got of the doc she made last year filled me with all the confidence I needed for her to tell my story then. To trust her.

But I have too much I need to hold back. Too much I don't want her to show.

Principal West gestures to me that it's time for my speech. "I gotta do this," I say, instead of giving her a straight answer.

Her sigh is heavy as I get up gingerly, favoring my knee as much as possible, and follow Principal West to the side of the stage where the other Legacies are huddled together, waiting to be introduced and paraded around all over again. Amaya and Josh are deep in conversation with Delaney hovering, trying to make it seem like she's not listening to them.

"I'm going to annihilate whoever is trying to get me to lose my scholarship," he says to Amaya.

When he catches us all looking at him he grimaces.

"It's not fucking true," Josh says so defensively it seems like it probably is. "And if my dad or anyone on the board hears about this account, we're all fucked."

Delaney and I exchange a glance. We haven't really spoken since she and Clara cleared the air yesterday, but we have bigger issues. Josh is right. We've been lucky so far that no one official has found these posts.

I twist my watch around my wrist, trying to puzzle out who could be behind it all over again. Everyone seems likely in their own way. It doesn't make sense that it would be a Legacy doing this and risking their scholarship along with the rest of ours, but at the same time, the people going for Legacy are cutthroat for their own reasons.

I watch Amaya closely, more convinced that Clara's theory about her is right even if she didn't reveal anything outright in her interview. She's on her phone all the time, even now, saying she's talking to her friends back in New York. But all weekend she's hung back, acted nervous—almost as if anticipating something.

I'm pulled from my thoughts when Logan hands me a mic and instructs me on the timing for my impending speech.

"They got you working this weekend, too?" I ask, surprised.

Logan shrugs, his tone bland. "Plight of being the go-to AV guy. Hank is useless. They have me running the banquet tonight, too. But I'm used to it since I never got to sit in the audience for any event in high school, either."

It's the way he says it that something clicks. He's the *go-to* AV guy. For *every* Woodhurst event. Every show, every performance.

Every *assembly*.

"Not once?" I prod. "Not even the Legacy assembly?"

He seems distracted, trying to untangle the mic cords. "Nope, worked that one, too. At least it meant I didn't have to see my parents' faces when my name wasn't called."

If he worked the projector at the assembly, that means he had something to do with showing the video.

As if he can read my mind he says, "Before you even ask, I had no idea that video of Clara was on the flash drive Josh gave me. I just hit Play."

I go cold all over.

"*Josh* gave you?"

"He brought it to me right before the assembly started and said that it had the video on it that I was supposed to play."

That lying *motherfucker*.

The feedback from the mic shrieks through the speakers the moment it hits the ground. Ignoring the pain in my knee, the voice in my head, the terms of Legacy, I charge over to Josh and slap his shoulder to spin him around.

"What the fu—"

With as much force as I dare, I crunch my fist against his nose.

CHAPTER TWENTY-EIGHT

REID

NOW

@haikuforyou
Given the chance to
Remind them of who we are
I would show them all

THE FIGHT IS UTTER chaos.

For the first few seconds I have the advantage and whale on Josh, holding nothing back. Every time I ever wanted to hit him comes surging through my fists. When he tripped me at state, when he talked down to Clara, every time he opens his fucking mouth.

"Reid! Stop it!"

I know it's Clara, but that only urges me on. Along with adrenaline and the satisfying crunch of bone and muscle as I try to hurt him as much as he hurt her. Knowing he kissed her, touched her, only adds to the fury.

But despite the blood pouring down his nose, he recovers much quicker than I expect and throws himself at me with a savage force. A folding chair breaks our fall, and we land in a crash against the hardwood floor of the auditorium. But I barely register the hard ground or the shocked, horrified screams of the crowd.

Josh hovers over me, a wild look in his eye as he hits me so hard my head snaps back. Pain explodes through my head for a second. In the next moment, massive arms encircle him from behind, which allows me to scramble out of the way of Josh's next blow. Mitchell holds him with one arm and shoves me back with another.

Even with my brother in the way, I lunge for Josh again, thinking of all the ways he lied, all the times he ruined everything. He struggles against Mitchell's hold, too, but Mitchell's a lot stronger than him. It takes Kenji, my dad, and Principal West getting between us before it's over.

I'm panting and sweating, and my eye is already swelling, but I have never felt more satisfied in my life than knocking that smug look off Josh West's face.

Principal West's voice is gruff; the words come out through gritted teeth. "Both of you outside. *Now*."

But my knee is screaming, and I don't trust myself to walk. Not in front of all these people. Instead, I sink into a chair pretending like I need to catch my breath. Like I'm hurt worse than I am. Josh slumps in one, too, wiping the blood off his swollen nose. West seems to decide that the next best thing to do is end the brunch.

The crowd dissipates reluctantly. None of the Legacies or my friends leave.

Clara rushes over to me, her eyes wide and terrified. I feel her shaking fingertips featherlight across my face. "Are you okay?"

"Get your camera," I say over a grunt.

"What?"

I grab her hand against my cheek and squeeze it gently. "Just do it."

Though she looks exasperated, she does. She steps off to the side, pointing it at the surrounding group. Poised to capture everything.

Good. Let her get Josh's confession on the record once and for all.

My dad sprints to grab the first aid kit from his office and several packs of ice. When he returns, a queasy feeling takes over seeing the stress and worry in his eyes. But I can't see much more once he slaps an ice pack on my face.

He checks me and Josh both for serious injuries. Once he's determined they're nothing more than swelling and cuts, Principal West takes over. His arms folded tightly across his chest.

Anger makes his words quake. "A fight between my own son and the guest of honor. In all my years as principal, I have *never* been so disappointed. What could possess you to pull this in a room full of the wealthiest, most influential benefactors this school has ever had?"

I think Josh narrows his eyes, but I can't quite tell from the swelling. "Ask *him*."

West turns to me. "Well?"

"Josh took the video of Clara and played it at the assembly."

There's a collective gasp. Clara looking the most stunned out of everyone.

But Josh scoffs. "What the fuck?"

"*Language*, Joshua."

Josh grimaces, then immediately winces at the motion. "I already told you *on camera* that I had nothing to do with it."

I gesture for Logan to step forward. He does so reluctantly.

He's pale, clearly freaked out that his off-the-cuff comment resulted in all this. "Sorry, man, but you know you gave me that flash drive when I was working the projector."

Josh opens his mouth to answer then closes it. He shakes his head slowly. “Yeah, I gave you the flash drive my dad told me to give you. I didn’t know what was on it. I was just the freaking messenger.”

I spin to face Principal West, and the motion makes my eye throb. I press the ice pack harder to it.

West holds up his hands to calm the murmuring of the group. “Clara submitted a flash drive with her documentary sample as part of her Legacy application. I assure you, and the selection committee can attest, there was no such video on it at the time we reviewed it.”

I study him. He’s a jerk for a lot of reasons, but it doesn’t seem like he’s lying. He seems freaked out that it was tampered with on his watch.

If they’re telling the truth, then Josh really had nothing to do with it. Which means as good as it felt, I just *really* fucked up. The Legacy terms include a zero-tolerance policy for physical assault. For all the ways I’ve tried to keep it together, I just let it all go in one impulsive moment.

Clara meets my eyes over her camera, clearly putting the same pieces together.

“Unfortunately, I’m going to have to take this incident to the board for review of your statuses and ban you both from the banquet tonight,” West says.

Josh glowers at me. “Happy? She seriously worth all this?”

I have to control my breathing as he reminds me that even if I punched him for the wrong reason *this* time, I was still right to do it.

“Can I speak to you a moment?” Dad asks Principal West.

Dad pulls West aside, and they have a conversation in low, tense tones. When they’re done, West looks notably perkier.

“Well,”—he claps his hands once—“Reid, I understand and can even appreciate how . . . passionate you are about this issue. It’s natural for young men to work through their conflicts this way.”

Clara's and Delaney's identical scoffs are the only sound in the room.

"Considering the *caliber* of guests coming tonight, we can't very well make any rash decisions today. I do believe I can convince the board we should review it at a later date."

The "caliber of guests" meaning the Olympic coach Dad convinced to come here. To meet with the athlete I'm not sure I even am anymore. My lungs feel tight knowing I'm trapped, as a mix of relief and disgust flow through me in equal measure. I can hit the shit out of the principal's own son and still keep my Legacy spot and scholarship, but Clara did nothing wrong and lost hers. I want to punch something all over again.

I would if my knuckles didn't hurt so badly.

The crowd continues to disperse, but I don't move. I'm not sure I can. My dad is about to approach me, a furious look on his face, and I catch Mitchell's eye, silently pleading with him to intervene. He nods and slings his arm around my dad, talking a mile a minute. Somehow convincing him to give me some space right now.

Amaya is tearful as she helps Josh up. "You poor thing," she murmurs, before shooting me a glare. He wraps his arm around her, and she nestles closer against him as they walk slowly away from the group.

"I thought you were over all that," Nicole says to me. She gnaws on her thumbnail, a panicked look in her eye. A look I don't quite understand but that tugs on the murky memory of our talk after the play last night.

I just stare at her, trying to remember what she said. But I don't before Amaya calls her over.

Which leaves me with Clara.

She puts the camera down on the table beside us and lowers herself to my eyeline.

"Your beautiful face," she scolds.

I snort at the playfully forlorn tone in her voice and regret it immediately when pain sweeps through my nose.

As she takes in the various states of my injuries, I watch her expression shift from concern to relief, landing somewhere in between. When she's seemingly satisfied I'll live, she leans back on her heels.

"You finally punched Josh West," she says, her eyes shining. "How did it feel?"

I sigh. "It would've been better if he had actually done it."

She shrugs one shoulder up. "It's okay. Thanks to you, I think I know who did."

I sit up straighter, which causes my ribs to ache. "You do?"

"I *knew* Logan was the one who ran the projection booth, but when Delaney and I asked around about it last year, Amaya said he was sitting with her during the assembly. It wasn't until you called him out just now that I realized she was lying."

My stomach sinks. "Why would Amaya lie about that? To cover for him?"

"Not him. Think about it," she urges me. "We know Amaya didn't take the video because she was in New York. We now know Logan *played* the video at the assembly . . . and we know that he and Nicole hooked up the other night and have been acting like a couple all weekend out of nowhere. Maybe that was something going on all last year and we didn't even know."

"Okay . . ." My head hurts.

"Who else would Amaya protect?" she asks.

Protect.

That's when the drunken memory hits me. The last thing Nicole said to me before I passed out last night.

You can trust me, she breathed in my ear. *If it hadn't been for me, Amaya wouldn't know what kind of guy Josh is, and you wouldn't know what kind of girl Clara is. I'll do anything to protect my friends, Reid.*

"Amaya lied about him sitting with her not to cover for Logan . . ."

My voice is barely above a whisper. "To cover for Nicole."

The corner of her mouth curls up, and she nods.

"*Nicole* took the video."

CHAPTER TWENTY-NINE

CLARA

NOW

"WHERE IS SHE?" REID grinds out. He springs up quickly—too quickly—and he nearly topples over. But I'm right there, gripping his arms to steady him.

"Is it your knee?" I ask.

A muscle jumps in his jaw. "Yes, but I'm fine."

I glare at him. "Bullshit."

Though I keep my grip firm on his forearms, he guides me away from him. He tries to take a step, and the lack of expression on his face betrays just how much pain he's in. I blink around the room and notice that several people are watching us. Watching him.

Looking at him with greedy eyes, delighted in their shock that the Golden Boy finally snapped. Considering just how hard to push him off the pedestal they put him on. Panic flares, hot and fast. I may be irritated with the way he keeps avoiding this, but that doesn't mean I want any of his secrets to come out under anything but his own terms.

"Lean on me," I say quickly.

"I don't need—"

I crowd his space and get the line of my shoulders under his arm. "Shut up and lean on me. Like Josh did with Amaya, act like it's from the fight."

Contempt curls his lip, clearly unhappy at the prospect of giving Josh that satisfaction. But he must see there's no other choice because the stubborn champion finally relents. He hunches onto me and grips his rib cage. I notice Josh smirking across the auditorium, and everyone still hovering around starts talking again in hushed whispers.

A pained grunt escapes Reid.

Biting my tongue, I slowly lead him out behind the school, where we used to run practice drills. I'm carrying a lot of his weight, and it takes longer than I expect to make it to the media room where I edited all my footage for the yearbook. Thankfully it's unlocked.

When we finally get inside and I close the door, he slumps in a chair, sweat beading his brow.

"What do you need?" I ask.

He scrubs a hand across his good eye, battling some internal war before he finally says, "Ice."

I nod and run back to the gym to get him a pack left on the table. When I return, he has his leg propped up and he lays the ice across it.

I study him a long moment. A black eye, swollen and bruised knuckles, and an injury he refuses to let heal. It takes everything in me not to tell him to talk to his dad again. He didn't want that from me this morning. But it hurts to see him like this. Battered and exhausted. Angry in a way that no amount of fighting will fix.

"Why, Reid?" I start. "Why won't you just ask for some *help*?"

"I—" He shakes his head, his chest rising and falling more rapidly.

But when he looks in my eyes, instead of more excuses or denials, the truth finally slips out. "I don't know how."

His face flames with the admission.

My voice goes soft, and I can't keep the words from shaking. "Can I help you figure it out?"

He looks around the room at the camera equipment, understanding my meaning. I'm asking him to trust me enough to share his story. To see that maybe by doing so, it might make a difference, even if neither of us knows how yet.

He nods slowly. "Okay."

I smile a little.

"But before we do this, we need a plan to confront Nicole," Reid says.

My smile immediately falls. I stand up and busy myself with attaching the camera to one of the tripods and checking the lighting and sound without responding.

The realization was thrilling at first, but now it's settling in. Nicole hated me that much. Walked into the room that I thought was private and decided instead of confronting me then or even after, to film it. And not only that, but to play it for the entire school and half the town and take what was rightfully mine right out of my grasp.

It's such a gross violation, a shiver runs across my skin.

"Clara."

I almost knock over the camera as I spin to face him. "And do what? Humiliate her like she did to me? Like Legacy Lore is doing to all of you?"

His tone is icy. "To start."

I entertain the fantasy a moment. I imagine unveiling her confession at the banquet. Hearing the town's shocked gasps and maybe even laughter at her. Turning the tide away from me, only to pull her under.

It makes my stomach ache.

"That's not who I am, Reid. I just wanted to know. And now that I do, I can move on."

"Bullshit."

I glare at him. But his gaze, bruised and swollen as it is, is unflinching.

It's the same thing I just said to him knowing he's hiding behind "fine," and I hear his callout in a new way. My bad habit is to pretend, too. To let my features smooth and my emotions still. But I don't want to do that with him anymore. I don't want to do that with him *ever* again.

"You can't let her get away with this, Clara. She wasn't chosen. *You* were. She stole Legacy from you."

My heart races at the seriousness of his tone. The protectiveness in it. He's right. She did. And I don't even quite understand why. But I don't want to be the messy, lost girl anymore. What I have here for my documentary about Legacy is something real. An investment in my future. If I come for Nicole without hard proof, I look petty and trapped in the past.

I say as much and he drops his hands, frustration plain on his face. "I get that. I do. But what if we get proof?"

"How would we do that? She's not going to tell me anything."

His good eye narrows and he sits up straighter. "True. But maybe she would tell me."

"You?"

He swallows and won't meet my eyes again when he says, "She likes me."

The pink of his cheeks is too sweet to tease him about. But I can't keep the irritation out of my voice when I say, "Oh, I know." Because I've known that for a long time.

"We could do it at the banquet tonight," he says significantly. "We can get her to confess it on camera, and all we do is hand it over to

Principal West. Nothing public. Just evidence that she was the one who did this. It wouldn't be doing anything other than telling the truth."

I nod. I don't like it, the idea of setting her up. But I don't know if there are any appealing alternatives. I could confront her, but she could just lie. There's no way she's going to share it without prompting, knowing she could lose her scholarship for unsportsmanlike behavior.

But it also might come out another way. Now that Amaya's screenshots have been revealed, that leaves Nicole and Reid as the final intro posts that Legacy Lore hasn't followed up on.

"What exactly did the post say about Nicole again?"

We look it up quickly.

> **@LEGACY_LORE**: Meet Nicole Kelly: This scholar and athlete is determined to win at all costs. That cutthroat ambition will get you far . . . or get you caught. More soon ♥

My pulse is pumping knowing what this means now. "Whoever is running Legacy Lore knows she took the video, too. I bet that's the evidence they're going to drop."

He nods, the idea clearly taking hold. "This would be a hell of a thing to get caught for. Nicole humiliated Amaya, too. She has to be behind Legacy Lore."

It makes sense, but something still feels off. Partially because Amaya seemed genuinely upset about all of this during her interview. But if it's not her, I have no idea who it could be. Which would mean I have no way of stopping them.

"What Nicole did is obviously going to come out anyway, Clara." Reid leans forward, forearms resting on his knees. "*You* should be the one to tell this story. Not anyone else."

There's a hint of the competitor returning to his voice that infuses a confidence in me, too.

My head is spinning, and Reid's eye is getting more purple by the minute. I'm aware I'm running out of time to get his interview. Running out of time to edit before the banquet tonight. Running out of time to set this right before everyone leaves tomorrow.

My anger started as a slow simmer, but it's beginning to boil.

This is truly my last chance to settle this.

"Tonight," I agree finally. "We can do it at the banquet tonight."

He grins. It's lopsided from the swelling, but I have to admit, the black eye works for him in a rugged, brooding way.

I adjust the camera's focus and pull out my notebook, opening it to a page covered with questions.

"Can we get started now?"

CHAPTER THIRTY

REID

@haikuforyou
Lost in the thicket
Of your laugh, your hair, your lips
Never to return

AFTER I INTRODUCE MYSELF, the interview starts with Clara asking me what my favorite part about running is. That's easy enough to answer.

"I like that you only need to focus on what's right in front of you. Once you pass someone or hit a mile mark or whatever, it's behind you and it doesn't matter anymore. Looking back is a waste of energy. There's only forward."

There's a slight glint in her eye when she says, "Well, *my* favorite part is when it's over."

That pulls a laugh out of me, and she grins. I feel my shoulders loosen, and we move on to talking about what it was like to move to Woodhurst and start running for the team as a senior.

"It was intimidating, honestly," I say.

Her expression is surprised. "But you were on track for state."

"Exactly. Expectations come with a lot of pressure." I rub my palms up and down my thighs. "The whole town is rooting for you when you're a Legacy. To have that kind of support at your back means something. I don't want to let anyone down."

Her expression softens a little. "How would you let anyone down?"

I wish I could wrap a hand around my throbbing knee, but I fold my hands in my lap and squeeze them instead. "I guess . . . not achieving all my goals. I might not ever be a champion again."

"Do you think anyone ever achieves *all* their goals?"

"I doubt it."

"Then why do you have to?"

I stare at her, and she stares right back. "Aren't we supposed to be talking about the Legacy Program?"

"We are. But I can rephrase the question if you want."

If I wasn't so focused on keeping up, I'd be amazed at how good she is at this. She tucks a loose strand of hair behind her ear and keeps going.

"As a Legacy, do you find that you get the benefits and opportunities promised by the program?"

I nod. "Definitely. So long as we don't step a toe out of line."

She raises an intrigued eyebrow, seemingly surprised at my candor. It's the fuel I need to keep going because with everything that's been happening this weekend, Nicole sabotaging Clara for a spot, and Legacy Lore on a deranged power trip—I'm not about to sit here and pretend like this program is perfect anymore.

"It *is* an incredible opportunity, and I'm grateful for it. But . . . the cost is really high. The standards for keeping the Legacy status and scholarship are almost impossible when you consider that a rumor, or video, or picture out of context could take it all away." I shake my head, getting worked up. "What kind of program allows that? Like in your case, they were more concerned about their public image than your *actual* life."

Clara doesn't say anything, but her eyes are glued to me, absorbed. Giving me time to consider my next words carefully.

I rub the back of my neck. "I get that being a role model is an important responsibility. But what about this program's responsibility to take care of us? To allow us to, I don't know—fuck up?"

Her grin is sly, her tone playfully obtuse. "The Golden Boy fucks up?"

A derisive laugh escapes me, and I fold my arms across my chest. "Probably more than anyone."

"Some people say the program is motivating."

"Which is really weird," I blurt.

She leans forward. "How so?"

"Don't get me wrong, I think for some people this program is what makes them dream big. But . . . it just seems like it rewards peaking in high school."

Clara laughs.

I'm relaxed now, making it easier to open up. "Think about it. You were disqualified, right?"

Her face grows serious, but I hold her gaze.

"But it doesn't mean you won't go on to do amazing things. I'm sure lots of other alumni have even when they weren't Legacies. There are infinite possibilities, and to expect us to have everything already figured out by the time we graduate high school seems . . ."

"Unfair," she finishes my sentence, her eyes never leaving mine.

I think we're talking about two things at once when I nod. "Yeah. Really unfair."

She swallows and breaks the moment to look at her notes. She seems flustered as she turns the page once, twice, then back to the first one again. "Um— What have you gotten out of the Legacy Program?"

I frown, thinking. Other than the money, it's hard to come up with any other positives of the program. After a small stretch of silence I say, "A lot of the Legacies work really hard, and I find that inspiring. I'm a competitive guy, so that part of it is fun for me." The image of Josh's petulant face flashes through my mind. Clara returns my smile like she knows exactly what I'm thinking.

"Is there anything that you regret?"

My pulse picks up as her eyes blaze into mine. As I realize that this is my chance to finally say what I need to say to Clara. What else do I have to lose at this point?

I let my Channel Nine smile fall. "I messed up last year. With you."

A slight crinkle forms between her eyebrows. "I didn't mean personally—"

"I know."

I think of all the poems I've squirreled away and posted anonymously over the past several months, the only place I've let myself be really honest. Not just about her but about myself. She wasn't the only one who held back last year. I let us go on without telling her how I felt or what I wanted for way too long. Then I let it all out in that card and never even asked her about it before today because I got so embarrassed.

I don't know that I'll ever get another chance to own my shit.

"You told me *a lot* that you weren't ready for something serious. And I pushed it. A *lot*. I've been trained hard to keep going, to never give up, but . . . that was unfair to you. To us. I'm sorry if I pushed too much."

Our eyes catch, and a soft flush spreads across her cheekbones.

"Don't be." She blinks rapidly, her lips pursing like she's trying not to cry. Her voice is thick when she says, "You were so good to me, and the way you never gave up on me made me feel like I really mattered to you."

"You did."

She bites her lip, her nose going a little pink. "You did to me, too."

My knee protests, but I get up from the official interview chair and reach for her hand. She takes it, and I pull her to me. We stand there wrapped in an embrace that feels . . . final. Sad and sorry. Heavy and hopeful. I don't know if what we're doing here is healing the past or trying to have a future.

Once we get settled back in our chairs, she asks a few more questions about the year, about Stanford—all things we've covered off camera that she wants to be sure are included here.

"Last question," she assures me when I rub a hand across my knee. "Was it all worth it?"

Her focus on me is intense, and it feels like we've veered again. Like she's asking me something deeper than about being a Legacy.

Though my heart is aching for her, and she's being softer and more open with me, I don't know what to say.

Because I still don't know if we want the same things.

CHAPTER THIRTY-ONE

CLARA

NOW

I STUDY REID INTENTLY as he grapples with the last question I've asked at the end of all my interviews.

Was it all worth it?

There's something that flickers across his features—an uncertainty of some sort before finally, he says, "Too soon to tell."

I know he's talking about Legacy. But there's a part of me that knows—after this conversation, after what happened between us this morning—he's talking about us, too.

When the official part of the interview is over, he removes his mic and I take down the equipment. We talk through the plan for tonight, which includes him picking me up later for the banquet so we can arrive together and find Nicole.

Just before he leaves, he hovers in the doorway. We share a long, wordless look that's painful in its understanding—that this might really be it. The closure we needed.

I bite the inside of my cheek, refusing to cry. Not because I don't want him to know how I feel, but because once I start, I don't think I'll be able to stop.

Just after he leaves, Logan passes through the door, his arms full of mic wires. "Hey, sorry—just need to put these away."

Since he's here, I ask him to look over my sound settings in my editing software. He sets his keys and phone down beside the computer and peruses it, making minor adjustments here and there. His phone buzzes constantly against the desk. I take a subtle peek and catch a guy's name on the screen.

"That should do it," Logan announces, and I whip my gaze away.

When his phone buzzes again I say, "Someone's popular."

"Hardly." He laughs. "My mom heard about the fight." He shoves it into his pocket, avoiding my gaze, and I can't help but feel sad that he feels the need to lie about texting with a guy.

Once he's gone, I immediately get to work. The media room is the perfect place to edit, and I want to get as much done on this initial video as I can.

I think back to what West said to me last year when he yanked my dreams out from under me. *You want to make documentary films? It's worth your time to* impress *people who have money, not deter them.*

It was a harsh insult then, but now it's my fuel. Because he's gone on and on about the new donors and benefactors. The exact people coming to the banquet tonight.

I plan to impress them.

I start by going back over Reid's interview. As I watch and splice the footage, I'm moved by his answers all over again. By his honesty about the program. About us. He didn't have to open up like that. He could've kept things surface-level and impersonal. But it seemed like he didn't want to pretend anymore, either.

The only thing Reid didn't divulge outright is his injury or the true impacts Legacy has had on his time at college.

But I have the footage I need for that. Because I don't want Reid to live under the threat of accounts like Legacy Lore spreading rumors about him, contorting the truth. This is my chance to protect him from that.

I review my notes, making sure I've tracked everything from his interview, before I move on when I see a note to myself that I forgot to ask him about.

Did you ever read the card?

I had no idea what Reid was talking about this morning when he asked me that. But I know someone who might.

I send a text to Mitchell. Do you know anything about a card Reid gave me last year?

When he doesn't text back right away, I keep working.

As the hours pass and light shifts outside from a bright white to a golden hue, I barely move from the editing chair. Splicing and cutting as fast as humanly possible, grateful I did so much of the work last year. I intercut between all the footage I already had with all the interviews I've gotten this weekend.

When it's as close to done as I'm going to get it before the banquet, I lean back.

My eyes are burning. A bit from staring at the computer all day, but also with pride. For the first time ever, I *know* that this is good.

When I have time to fully complete it, this is a doc that could get me back into CAFA.

Only . . . what was true last year is still true this year: It's *highly* personal. Incredibly raw. It highlights pieces of my friends' and former teammates' lives in a way that I'm not sure I can show without upsetting them. Or revealing all they've been hiding. All the program hides.

And it shows Reid completely unguarded.

I'm taking a big risk including everything. Though I think this is what he needs, uncertainty lodges in my stomach and festers as I race home to get ready.

An hour later, Reid appears on my doorstep looking like suits were invented just for him. The one he's wearing is dark, and the crisp white dress shirt is open at his throat. His hair is perfectly mussed, and I can smell his clean shaving cream and woodsy cologne from here. Even with a purple eye and a bruised jaw, this boy makes my brain stop.

"Damn," I blurt appreciatively.

His grin is modest but confident. It falters slightly as his gaze rakes up and down me in a way that shoots fire across my skin.

I smooth my hands across the skirt of the dress Aunt Xi gave me. Made out of a soft emerald-green satin, it's got a vintage vibe—thin straps, a fitted bodice, and an A-line skirt that flares out and hits me a little above my knees.

"Ready for some subterfuge?" he finally asks, a glint in his eye.

A fresh burst of nerves tumbles through me. "Ready" isn't the word I'd use. Terrified we've got it all wrong. Worried about what else Legacy Lore might do tonight. Hopeful our plan for Nicole is the right one.

One of the straps slides down my shoulder as I shrug. His gaze follows the slip of fabric as I readjust it and say, "As I'll ever be."

Just as Reid is taking my camera bag to his truck, my phone buzzes with Mitchell's response. You mean the one for your birthday?

I frown. Reid didn't give me anything for my birthday. I had found it unlike him at the time, but I wasn't about to ask. Then we broke up and that was it.

Mitchell sends another message. Didn't he put it in your backpack for you to find? God, he's so dramatic.

My backpack? I haven't used it since school got out. With a quick shout at Reid letting him know I forgot a jacket, I sprint to my room, tearing open the closet. Pushing clothes and shoes and boxes aside, I finally see the dark green canvas tucked in a heap under some sweaters. Turning it over, I shake out the contents on the floor.

I spread all the papers out and *there*—among them, crumpled and dirty, is a small, purple envelope that apparently has been sitting here for six long months.

I open it, smooth it, and read it in dawning disbelief. Blood thrumming so hard it's all I hear.

To my favorite light-chaser,

You asked to see them so many times, I finally had to give you one. To be honest, my pen hasn't stopped moving since I met you. Ink spilling with your laugh, your touch, the continuous torturous prospect of your mouth on mine. Every word looking for you. Every page another freeze-frame in our story.

I don't want to scare you, Clara. I just want to love you.

Happy birthday.

Love, Reid

If love means chasing
fading light, I'll run, chest burning
into your night

I run my fingertips across the words, my eyes filling and my heart squeezing with every single one. A shocked laugh caught in my throat at the total impossibility of this.

He wrote me a poem.

This poem.

The exact same one I have tattooed on my skin.

CHAPTER THIRTY-TWO

CLARA

THEN

WHEN I COULDN'T BRING myself to pick up the next *Glass Swords* book after graduation, I started reading poetry. A lot of books that Reid had recommended. He loved short-form poems—haikus and brief sonnets. Fast and powerful, like the way he ran. The more I read, the more I sought out. I started following accounts online that I liked, one in particular that Reid would've loved called Haiku for You. The first post stopped me in my tracks in part because of the self-deprecating caption (*when you make a haiku account but the poem doesn't want to cooperate*):

> If love means chasing
> fading light, I'll run, chest burning
> into your night

I liked that it wasn't a perfect haiku. Something about that made sense. An acknowledgment that sometimes the rules work against you.

I tried to scroll through the profile, but it was the first and only post on it so far.

I read the poem over and over. Those few sparse words reminded me of the darkness that had consumed my life, my home, my future. The black hole that I tried to hide from everyone.

Until Reid.

He was too shy to ever share his poetry with me, but I wished I could send this one to him. Tell him it reminded me of him and the way he ran toward me, instead of away from me. Tell him that it felt like the love between us—active and alive—that I could never say in words. That I never let him speak aloud.

But I knew he didn't want to hear from me, so I never did.

Over the following months, as I sank deeper and deeper, I held on to the memory of Reid telling me that a setback wouldn't stop me, held on to the poem, reading it day after day. Grateful to whoever wrote it for giving me hope that there was something on the other side of this pain.

I checked the profile occasionally. They posted other poems. Full of heartbreak and longing. Somehow reflecting everything I was feeling that summer, too.

But the first was my favorite.

Eventually, I knew that I wanted those beautiful words on me forever. As a reminder of what I finally knew to be true. Even if we never spoke again, Reid would always matter to me.

He cracked something open in me I never wanted to close again.

When I told Mitchell about getting the tattoo, his face screwed up in concern. "Are you sure about this? This is some random poem off the internet, I feel like you should know who wrote it . . ."

I shook my head. "I don't need to know."

For whatever reason, the poem felt like it belonged to me. I wanted to keep it that way.

The buzz of Aunt Lisette's needle kicked on and became background noise as it lanced and vibrated against my skin. Every stroke an agonizing bolt.

Throughout the whole process, slow tears slipped down my nose. But not because of the physical pain. Because for the first time, it felt as though I was claiming a different path for myself. A promise to let love in.

Even in darkness, to never stop chasing light.

CHAPTER THIRTY-THREE

REID

NOW

THE LEGACY BANQUET

@haikuforyou
There are secrets here
In the infinite abyss
Between words and breath

CLARA IS SILENT THE entire drive, fully immersed in thoughts that don't seem wise to disturb.

She slows to a stop just before we make it to the entrance of the Lodge and checks that the lapel mic she gave me is secured to the inside of my suit jacket.

It hits me that this is it. Our last night before goodbye. I stare at her. The golden lights that line the walkway to the Lodge peek through the tall pines and create a soft glow across her face. Her dress hugs her torso and flares out over her hips into a skirt that looks almost liquid. I can hardly stand to look at her she's so beautiful.

When she exhales in a whoosh, I realize she's nervous.

I wait. The only sounds are the distant slam of car doors and the lazy swish of Crescent Lake lapping at the shore behind us.

Finally she says, "Are you sure about this?"

The corner of my mouth lifts as I try to focus on the tasks ahead instead of the rapid rate of my pulse.

"Absolutely. Chin up, Suarez." I put a finger under her chin to raise her bowed head until our eyes meet. "We're finally going to make this right."

She nods.

As soon as we get inside, my dad walks up to us, accompanied by Principal West, Josh with a small Band-Aid across the cut on his nose, Mayor Harper, and Coach Andrews, the Olympic coach I met last spring. Dad side-eyes Clara, but he has his congenial expression on. They're all dressed in suits of various shades of charcoal, and my dad isn't wearing his baseball hat for once.

"This is quite an event," Coach Andrews says. He's a tall man, with a weather-beaten tan and dark stubble.

He gestures to the decorated lodge, which looks like Woodhurst High exploded over it with all the blue and white decor. A balloon arch by the door, big bouquets of flowers in the center of the intricately decorated tables, and a photo booth with a massive flower wall and neon sign that displays *Legacy* atop it. There's a slideshow going on behind him with rotating photos of me and all the Legacy alumni throughout the years.

"Reid, it's great to see you again," Coach Andrews says, holding out his hand to shake.

Though my stomach is doing somersaults as I think about my injury, I give him my best guest of honor grin. "I appreciate you coming all the way here."

"Wow, that's a shiner."

Principal West laughs. "Our boys tend to lock horns from time to time." He slaps a hand on Josh's back, making him wince. "We've got real competitors here in Woodhurst."

I don't think I hide my disgust well enough because Dad glowers at me. Straightening my spine, I enact the first part of the plan. Well, my plan, anyway. "I'd like to apologize to you about that," I say to both Josh and Principal West.

Josh frowns, not believing me for a moment.

But I don't care, I just need Principal West to bite. I go on, "I'm sorry for starting a fight—that's not the kind of Legacy I am or want to be."

Dad nods approvingly.

I keep going. "I never got to give my speech, but I'd still like to if at all possible. I'd like to make it right."

I feel Clara's eyes on me, her confusion, but I keep my gaze trained on a beaming Principal West.

"Thank you for that. You know we'd love nothing more than to hear from you this evening."

As the conversation goes on, I try to keep my guest of honor mask on, but I'm distracted by the odd glances I'm getting from people as they walk past us. While it might be to do with the state of my and Josh's faces, and whatever rumors they heard about the fight, it seems more significant than that.

"Reid?" Clara nudges me with her elbow.

"Huh?"

Dad says, "He asked how your training is going for regionals?"

I blink. "Oh. Um, fine."

Coach Andrews frowns a bit but nods through it. "Okay."

I see a flash of red hair in the crowd. Perfect timing. I excuse myself and grab Clara's hand. We walk as quickly as I dare over to where Nicole is laughing as if she hasn't orchestrated the downfall of Clara's life.

Or maybe that's exactly why she's laughing.

"Ready?" I ask Clara in a low voice.

She nods and straightens her shoulders. "I can't believe you're still mad about that," she exclaims loudly, causing several people hovering around the photo booth to face us. Including Nicole.

"Whoever posted that video did me a favor," I snap.

Even though it's what we'd agreed to say, Clara flinches. I wonder if I laid it on too thick, but we're in it now, so I storm off as best I can and hope that this has the effect I expect.

I walk to the refreshment table and grab a water cup for something to do with my hands. A moment later I hear the distinct clacks of high-heeled footsteps approaching me.

"Reid? Are you okay?" Nicole asks.

I twist my features trying to look upset, which isn't too hard these days. "It was always a bad idea, me and Clara."

Nicole sighs. "I could've told you that. But I hate being right about stuff like that."

Her barely contained glee would suggest otherwise. I squeeze the cup tighter.

"Yeah, well, you're a good friend," I manage.

Nicole steps closer, her eyes flashing. God, I hope we're not wrong about this.

"You're not still mad about the video even though you beat the crap out of Josh this morning?"

I let out a humorless laugh. "Nah. Any excuse to punch Josh."

She laughs, too, and though I now *despise* this person, I shoot her the smile that always makes Clara blush. It has the same effect on Nicole. It feels wrong on every level, but I remind myself that this is *for* Clara.

"I was mad at first," I admit, "but I get why someone would do it. Josh was awful to Amaya."

"*Exactly*," Nicole rushes to say.

"And she deserved to know the truth." I square my shoulders and swallow down my own disgust when I say, "I did, too. About Clara. I should've listened."

I hold Nicole's eyes as long as I can stand, and she steps closer to me, drawing her hand down my arm. "When I saw them together at that party, I knew I had to do something to protect my friends."

I try to sound impressed and shocked. "It was you?"

She looks around before nodding, a coy, smug smile on her lips. "I mean, I wasn't the one straddling a guy with a girlfriend. I just caught it on camera."

The plastic cup collapses in my grip, spilling water onto my jacket cuff. I let out a long exhale, fully aware that there are dozens of people pressed around us trying to listen. I do my best to keep the fury out of my voice. "If you wanted her to break up with Josh, why didn't you just show the video to Amaya? Why play it at the assembly?"

Nicole frowns, and I wonder if the question was too insistent. Too obvious. I force myself into my competitive mindset. The way I get before every race, no matter how unimportant. How much I want to win when I'm on that course. I step closer to her and nudge her with my elbow.

"I mean, I get it," I say. "*Anything* for Legacy, right?"

She looks at me closely, a flash of camaraderie in her eyes before lowering her voice. "Josh saw the Legacy list before it went out, and

Amaya told me that neither me nor Logan were on it. When Logan managed to snag the flash drive from Josh, I knew what I had to do."

I almost laugh. Of course Josh was never as innocent as he was claiming. Satisfaction pours through me all over again knowing his entire face hurts right now. But the fact that they *all* played a part is truly nauseating.

My heart is hammering against my chest as she continues. "Logan said everyone else breaks the rules, why should we have to play by them? And he was right. All I did was show them the truth."

I give her a tight smile. "Sounds familiar."

I look over my shoulder and catch eyes with Clara through the crowd, camera pointed directly at us. The Bluetooth mic on my jacket poised to pick up everything we're saying. Clara nods like she got it all, her face a furious pink.

Nicole follows my gaze, and she pales as she puts it together. "What is this?" She steps backward. "You set me up?"

Clara approaches, green eyes blazing. "I wasn't the one who sabotaged a friend. I just caught it on camera."

Red splotches instantly appear across Nicole's neck. "Legacy Lore was right; betrayal really doesn't come from your enemies."

"I could say the same thing about you."

Tears spring to her eyes, but if she's trying to make me feel bad it isn't working.

"What are you going to do with that?" Nicole barks at Clara.

"I'm not sure." Clara lowers the camera to her side. "But I'll tell you what I'm *not* going to do. I'm not going to show it in front of the entire town. I'm not going to intentionally humiliate you and ruin your life. I'm not going to do what you did to me."

Clara walks off, and when I turn to follow, Nicole calls after me, as if

I owe her anything. I ignore her and walk closely behind Clara. I can feel her breaths shake as I press my chest to her back.

"I can't believe they all knew," she whispers through gritted teeth over her shoulder to me.

I give her waist a small, reassuring squeeze. At least we made it through the first part.

Our walk through the crowded room is cut short when my dad catches me by the arm, directing me to the table for dinner. Kenji and Mitchell are seated beside me and our parents, and though they're cracking jokes—and for the love of god wearing Hawaiian-print shirts—it still isn't enough to get me to fully relax knowing what's coming.

Clara sits at the table beside us with her mom and Mayor Harper, her hand protectively on her bag the entire time. We're only halfway through the meal when Delaney rushes over, carrying her phone. Clara frowns, blinking rapidly while they have an urgent, whispered conversation. Something about her expression has me leaning across the small space between our tables.

"What is it?"

Instead of answering, she grabs my arm and gets the attention of our friends to follow as she weaves me through the circular tables. Delaney, Kenji, and Mitchell walk with us past the coffee bar and into a quiet break room off the bustling kitchen. Since Clara works here, nobody stops her. She closes the door behind us and rifles through her bag.

"What are we doing?" Mitchell asks.

"Connor," Clara bursts out.

Kenji's face screws up in confusion. "No, I'm *Kenji*."

She cuts him a look and wordlessly pulls out her laptop. She turns the screen toward us and opens what looks like an editing program.

After a moment hunting through a cascade of multicolored video files that make my head spin, she lands on the one she's looking for.

Clara drags the progress bar to a point, then in a breathless voice says, "Here. Watch this."

We do.

It's the video clip of Kenji's guest room from the party the other night when we accidentally walked in on Nicole and Logan making out. Them springing apart and Clara lowering the camera so it's facing the floor. But we can still hear what they're saying. She turns up the volume.

It's a scramble of movement and Clara's high-pitched promise to delete it. We exchange a glance now, and she flushes since she clearly *didn't*. Then Logan's voice filters in. "West mentioned you're working on the new video. I'm doing sound for the banquet, so let me know if you need anything."

Then comes the sound of his footsteps as he got close to Nicole and said something to her in a low voice before leaving. I was so distracted by seeing Clara, I hadn't clocked any of this.

But it's crystal clear on the audio: "I won't tell Connor if you won't."

She slaps the space bar to stop playback.

The silence hangs until Mitchell's words come out slow like he's approaching a wounded animal. "While I get you're trying to help, I'm already over him, Clara."

"That's not—" Clara's sigh is heavy as she closes her eyes and gestures to Delaney. "Tell them the other thing."

"I've been messaging with a few of Reid's teammates," she says.

My pulse starts to pound at her tone, making my injuries throb.

"I just heard back from Connor, the same guy who kept giving us shots that night."

We both shudder at the memory and she continues.

"Well, I guess he's also Nicole's ex or boyfriend, I dunno—they hook up at meets or something. Anyway, he's been following Legacy Lore from the beginning, and he told me he's been texting with the person running it."

"And I saw Logan's phone earlier," Clara says. "He was texting someone named Connor."

Oh, shit.

I have to sit down. But Mitchell looks more confused than ever. "So they're dating?"

Clara gives him a long look. "God, Mitchell, I have no idea! Focus. Logan's texting with someone who was there when Delaney visited Reid. And Logan and Nicole are—whatever they are. He was on the cast text thread with Amaya."

Mitchell's eyes widen as he finally catches on. "And he worked with Anderson Beck at the tennis club."

Nicole's words slam into focus—

Logan said everyone else breaks the rules, why should we have to play by them?

Our eyes lock and Clara nods. "What if *Logan* is Legacy Lore?"

CHAPTER THIRTY-FOUR

CLARA

"LOGAN," MITCHELL REPEATS FOR the third time, shaking his head in disgust.

"I can't believe I didn't put it together sooner," I say. "His whole family were Legacies. In his interview he made it clear how embarrassed and bummed he was that he didn't get selected. But because I related, I didn't think that meant he had a whole revenge-plot side hustle."

"Well, you are making a whole movie about it, too." Kenji puts his hands out as if weighing scales.

"It's different," I say flatly.

"I should've seen this coming, too, this is *so* him," Mitchell says. "He talked about nothing else last year. It's why he didn't want us to be public—thinking it would affect his chances." He says it like he's swallowing glass.

I reach out to put a comforting hand on his arm, but Kenji beats me to it. "Couldn't it be a different Connor?" Kenji asks.

I start pacing, the swish of my dress the only sound in the room for a moment. "It's possible . . ."

Delaney's eyes pop wide. "Wait. Wasn't Logan also the one who started the rumor about a girl using Josh for Legacy?"

I nod vigorously. "Yes, during truth or dare. I forgot about that!"

"He lives for drama. He's seen, like, every reality show," Mitchell says.

"Well, if it really is him, we need to do something before he does any more damage," Kenji says.

Just then, Delaney's phone chimes. She pulls it out of the pocket of her cerulean dress, and my stomach drops at the look on her face.

"Too late," she breathes, and turns the phone toward all of us.

@LEGACY_LORE: An Olympic coach is actually here in Woodhurst, but according to a current teammate and our own cross-country Legacy, the Golden Boy won't be going for gold anytime soon . . . ♥

Nicole: Did he tell you what the dr said? Is it serious?

Connor: It's a tear. Doesn't need surgery but the trainer said he could be out for the season—maybe longer.

Nicole: Omg that suuuucks. Poor Reid

Connor: I tore my knee junior year. I haven't been the same since. At least now I have a chance at beating him.

No. *No*. Fucking *Connor*.

Reid has gone white. "I had no idea he knew those details. Why would they do this?"

"Especially *Nicole*," Delaney exclaims. "She's, like, in love with you."

My stomach sours knowing that's probably exactly why she did this. To get Reid back for the way he confronted her. I didn't think she had any other ammo against us, or I never would've done it that way.

"I bet she *just* sent in these screenshots to whoever runs Legacy Lore, not realizing it was Logan," I say to Reid. "This way, all the drama would be focused on the post and not on her."

"Why?" Delaney asks, trying to keep up. "Why would the focus be on her?"

I take the moment to explain as succinctly as I can how we figured out she was behind the video last year and the confession we just got from her.

"Damn, you two have been busy. I thought you were just making out this whole time," Kenji jokes.

When Reid doesn't so much as crack a smile, Mitchell and I exchange a concerned look.

"Sorry about the tear, man," Kenji says seriously, and pats Reid on the shoulder. "I didn't know it was that bad."

Reid stares at his hands. "No one did."

I hate the heartbreak in his voice. A swell of anxiety goes through me all over again at what I put in the doc. He really didn't want anyone to know this. *Any* of this.

Maybe I am no better than Logan. I wonder if there's time to change it. If I could just make some quick tweaks—

Principal West's voice filters through speakers introducing the Legacy video. *My* video.

Guess not.

My mind is racing while he talks, and an idea starts to form. Watching everyone for so long through my lens, I've learned a lot about how their minds work.

"I think I know what to do."

I tell them as quickly as I can, even though it's a wild, long shot. But if it works, it would be worth the risk.

We race back out to the event.

CHAPTER THIRTY-FIVE

REID

@haikuforyou
They have never seen
the other side of the moon
But I have in you

I RETURN TO THE Lodge banquet room with a hollow feeling in my chest. Sure, now when anyone looks at me, all they see is a failure. A liar.

I can't catch my breath.

Clara beelines to the AV area, where she and Logan quickly hook her laptop up to the projector.

Principal West is giving his annual "For the pride of Woodhurst High" speech, and I barely hear it. Not until he says, "Without further ado, it's time to watch the new video celebrating the Legacy Program's twentieth year and all our special alumni."

This whole thing feels like a warped mirror of what happened last year. Everyone—the Legacy committee, half the town, our families—all here to see her work. But the difference is Clara hovers beside the AV table, guarding it with her life. No surprises tonight.

Well, except our own.

She's leaning against the wall, emerald eyes already fixed on me. I can see the nerves in the way her fingers twist.

The lights in the Lodge dim, and the conversation quiets to murmurs before stopping entirely as the doc begins.

The scene opens the same way it did last year. With Delaney twirling and stopping, twirling and stopping. With close-ups of her pinching her body, holding her head in her palms in frustration. Then it cuts to Delaney a few days ago, looking drawn in comparison, sitting in what looks like her bedroom.

Delaney's smile is timid. "I'm Delaney Whitlock, and I'm a dance Legacy."

It's a similar opener for everyone. All of us who are supposed to be remarkable but have done nothing but lie and betray each other for this program.

Amaya's voice cracking through pneumonia last year, and her sitting down on the stage for her interview this year, her under-eye circles darker. Josh (his complexion ruddier), Nicole (unsmiling). After their introductions and explanations of what it is to be a Legacy, it cuts to me.

"Hi, I'm Reid Rousseau, cross-country Legacy."

Off-camera Clara's voice: "And state champion."

"Oh, yeah, that," on-screen me says with a shrug. The crowd around us laughs.

But I can't tell if they're laughing with me or at me. Sweat forms on my hairline, and I can't get comfortable in this chair.

Only after my opening scene from last year where I'm repeating drills and say "It's about what you do when you're tired," instead of cutting to rock music like it did, it fades to a shot of me right after the Fun Run yesterday.

My voice filters as a voice-over. "The whole town is rooting for you when you're a Legacy. To have that kind of support at your back means something." It plays over a slow-motion shot of the cheering crowds and kids wearing *Future Legacy* shirts.

"I don't want to let anyone down."

Then a focused shot of my bleached knuckles gripping my knee.

Anxiety funnels through me faster, and I dart my eyes around. Anyone who's seen the post would know what this means. That Clara chose to show the very thing I've tried to hide all weekend.

It transitions into a montage of me talking to people all weekend—smiling, laughing, nodding, and listening. Kids, parents, my teammates. Before intercutting it with another shot of me leaning against a pillar in a stolen moment before the Shakespeare show where my head is leaned back, my eyes closed, trying to calm my racing pulse.

It's totally exposing.

The entire doc is like this. Not just of me, but everyone. The way Josh mocked and messed with me last year, then spliced with a distant shot of Principal West lecturing him this year. The way his face fell after as West walked off. Only then to turn to a sneer during his interviews.

Questioning the value of the program the entire time. The impact it's had. The narrower her attention on each of us gets, the clearer it becomes that the program has infused the school and town culture with something darker than anyone wants to admit.

Punctuated by my interview: "It just seems like it rewards peaking in high school."

My heart is beating out of my chest at the shot of my face, the barely hidden pain there as I grimace and limp when I think no one else is looking.

"To expect us to have everything already figured out by the time we graduate high school seems . . ."

"Unfair," she finishes off camera.

I nod. "Yeah. Really unfair."

Then it shifts to covering Clara's disqualification, summarizing it from interviews. Making the point of just how desperate this program makes people. My hands ball into fists when I look over at Logan, whose face is totally impassive as he watches.

I'm pretty disgusted when Nicole says, "Legacy is competitive. You have to be willing to endure whatever comes at you. No one is entitled to it."

Josh's response follows. "When everyone started talking about you, it took the heat off me, okay? I was under a lot of pressure last year with Legacy and running and securing valedictorian—I just needed one thing to go right."

That selfish asshole. I glare at the back of his head and even with the lights low, I can see his ears are bright red.

Clara asks if he knows how she could have been sabotaged. When he says he doesn't know, off camera she asks, "Your dad never got any leads?"

Josh scoffs. "You're smarter than that, Clare-bear. He never even looked into it."

A collective gasp travels around the crowd.

The story expands to include interviews with older alumni, and former Legacies, some who used the program to launch their lives and others who felt held back by it and the expectations of the town.

But it doesn't stay on that point too long, either. It includes moments of camaraderie and bonding that Legacies experience. The way it motivates some of us and brings the town together every year. She includes

Principal West's perspective, and as he sticks to the same motivating messages he's always used, it seems more unhinged as it contrasts with all of our actual experiences.

It's a more complete picture than the one I saw last year. But it's just as revealing. Highlighting how grueling and competitive the program is, while also not taking away how positive it can be, too.

The doc comes to a close with a song playing over a series of silent shots of each of us from the weekend. Clara asks off camera, "Was it worth it?"

There's a quick flash to each interviewee's answer. Josh rears back a little, surprised by the question. "Of course."

Delaney goes still and thoughtful. "I don't think so."

Amaya laughs. "I have no idea."

Nicole nods once. "Absolutely."

Finally, it ends with a shot of me looking out over the horizon at the overlook. The exhaustion and stress on my face this year compared to last is stark. Haunting. My voice filters over it with the last line from my interview, "Too soon to tell."

It fades, and I can hardly breathe. Because now I know what I have to do.

CHAPTER THIRTY-SIX

CLARA

I IMMEDIATELY SECOND-GUESS EVERYTHING I put in the doc when Reid's eyes land on mine across the room. Did I reveal too much about him? Everyone?

I had convinced myself even if it upset some people, even if it upset him, this was the right move. Stories that rattle are the ones that matter most. They're the ones I want to tell.

But they all have real futures on the line. Their families, colleges, fancy coaches. And given the stress of the weekend and everything Reid's going through, I might have gone too far. I might have been too shortsighted.

The doc ends and, to my shock, the applause is loud, and some grins are wide. Especially from my friends and their families. Sure, there are several people who look aggrieved. Principal West looks like his bright red head is going to combust. That's to be expected. Yet the overwhelming consensus is positive.

Though, in the sea of varied expressions turned toward me, Reid's remains indecipherable. I wish I could pull him away where we could be alone. To explain.

But a profusely sweating West gets up on the stage.

The feedback from the mic screeches through the speakers, enhancing the awkward, lingering silence while West adjusts his necktie and looks out at the crowd. "Well, I'm a bit lost for words." His glare lands squarely on me, and my returning smile is false as my stomach churns.

A chair scrapes across the hardwood floor as Reid stands and stares at West. He doesn't speak but several people look to him.

"I'm not sure we have time for your speech now, Mr. Rousseau," West says grimly. Clearly upset with how honest Reid was in his interview.

But Reid isn't deterred. He starts to walk to the stage, his steps slow and careful. The applause that follows is confused, scattered. Everyone unsure what to think about their Golden Boy now.

He walks up the steps, and, having forced his hand, West gives the mic to Reid.

Reid turns toward the crowd, his black eye and bruises muted by the soft light in the room. He doesn't smile. Doesn't charm. He puts a hand in his pocket, and stares ahead bearing a thoughtful expression. But when he starts speaking, we can't hear him.

Which is exactly how we planned it.

There's a rumbling through the crowd and someone shouts, "Mic's not working!"

Logan huffs out a frustrated sigh and jumps to his feet. He charges toward the stage as I hoped he would to adjust it, and I grab his phone quickly from the table. My heart is pounding hard at the remote look on Reid's face. At the seconds I have to use the passcode I saw Logan put in and get the proof we need.

I do.

With a prepped draft no less. Nothing like a little intel from his ex-boyfriend to know that Logan was meticulous about preparing his social media posts. A sickening wave of disgust goes through me seeing them all.

Seeing that he really is Legacy Lore.

But I can't linger. I hit publish on the draft that includes a screenshot of a text conversation between Logan and Nicole about the video of me and Josh; all identifying information about himself is blacked out.

I have mere seconds, but I can't help but scroll through the DMs. My heart pounding harder at the dozens of messages. Mostly from current Woodhurst students sharing gossip from this year's Legacy hopefuls.

He's going to keep doing this even after this weekend?

Then this better work.

I tap on the necessary settings and after I unplug my laptop from the projector, I gently return the phone and nod at Reid. Logan's checking wires when Reid turns the mic back on.

"Oh, there we go," he says, his deep voice amplified through the space. "Guess it wasn't on."

Logan throws his hands up, rolling his eyes.

Reid turns toward the crowd again. "Hi, everyone. I'll keep this brief since I know you may not want to hear from me after what you saw in that video. You had a perception of me, of all of us Legacies, and I can guess that this video might have changed that."

He pauses. I try to swallow the knot in my throat as he looks at me, holding my gaze a beat. The crowd hangs on his silence as much as his words. Because as shy as he is, as low as he feels, and as hard on himself as he may be, he's dazzling. He always has been.

"All of us work hard to be exemplary. To represent Woodhurst well and do you proud. But what you just saw is the ugly truth. Legacy has driven us—all of us—to the point of breaking."

He lets the stunned silence sit a moment before he continues.

I look over at Principal West and several alumni, who are all members of the selection committee, talking heatedly. They keep looking between Reid on the stage and me, as if trying to decide what to do.

I remind myself I'm no longer their student. West already paid me for the work. I made the doc I wanted to make for me, for Woodhurst and my friends. For Reid.

Whose eyes lock with mine at that exact moment, color high on his cheeks. I can see there's a flood of words he wants to say, but based on his stony expression I can't tell if they're good or bad. I get my answer when he goes rogue a second later.

"I'd like you all to pull out your phones and search for a social media account called Legacy Lore."

My entire body tenses. *What?*

What is he doing?

This wasn't the plan. But he nods to the crowd, and in the next moment, everyone in the room has their phones out. The hum of shocked, whispered conversation rises as they read through the posts.

Though I do note there are several people who don't look scandalized. They're probably the ones who have been commenting on the posts and saying things they never would to our faces.

But all I can truly focus on is Reid.

The entire town now knows about his injury, his grades—everything. But he doesn't return my imploring look. Instead he says to the crowd, "*This* is what the program has become. Threats. Backstabbing. Humiliation. Betrayal. Using what we're going through against each other. All for your approval. And I'm no exception." He shakes his head. "This program could be what it claims to be, but this is what it *really* is."

Our eyes meet again, and though my astonishment shifts to pride as I watch him claim everything he's tried to hide, I'm still not sure if he's angry with me or not.

I played a part in forcing his truth out. And he could, and maybe even should, resent me for that.

He looks away and faces the larger crowd again. "Before you donate or move here or submit an application to be a Legacy yourself, please think about whether this program is something you want to be part of, or something you'd like to change."

Just as Reid hops off the stage, a high-pitched exclamation pierces from the center of the room. *"What?"*

Every eye goes to Nicole as she stands up, turns on her heel, and comes charging toward the AV table.

Here we go.

"I *knew* it was you," she accuses. "*You're* Legacy Lore."

Both Logan's and my head whip to her at the exact same time.

But Nicole is staring at *me*. Just like I knew she would.

"What are you talking about?"

She waves her phone in my face. "This one that just went up about me proves it."

Logan's brow furrows, and he discreetly pulls out his own phone, blinking down at the screen. A small group forms around us including my friends, Reid, Josh, Amaya, Coach Rousseau, and my mom.

Principal West storms over seething. "Can we not have *one* event go smoothly this weekend?"

But Nicole doesn't seem to notice or care about the disruption she's causing. She looks around at the group and straightens her shoulders. "All that stuff you said about not humiliating me was total crap."

"We all know you're the one behind the posts, Clara, just admit it," Amaya says, backing Nicole. "You're bitter about what happened at the assembly even though you deserved it, and you're always following us around with your camera."

Even though I saw her rage texts and I had suspected her of being capable of the Legacy Lore posts all weekend, my mouth still drops open in genuine shock. In all my interviews with Amaya, every time we talked, she was kind to me. I didn't realize her being a good actress meant she was being so fake to my face.

Delaney and I exchange a look when she briefly glances up from her phone.

"You literally just saw why I follow you all around with a camera," I shoot back.

Principal West is rubbing his temples as Nicole appeals to him. "She's lying. Clara is the one doing this." She gestures around the room to everyone holding their phones. "Trying to get us to lose our scholarships and ruin *everything*."

Logan's eyes widen a touch. But I see something else, too. Irritation. He doesn't like that I'm getting the credit.

"Why would she do that?" West asks, exasperated.

"Isn't it obvious?" I goad.

"Revenge," Nicole spits out first. She stares at the camera slung over my shoulder, thinking I have proof of her confession, in addition to the Legacy Lore post everyone has now read. Backed into a corner, she says, "I knew you'd try to get me back for showing that video at last year's assembly."

Nicole's accusation—and admission—carries across the entire lodge.

Reid reaches for my hand and squeezes. I stare at it a beat, wondering if it's friendly, protective, or means what I want more than anything in the world for it to mean.

My mom turns to Principal West, speaking for the first time. "She'll be disqualified, right?"

West holds up his hands as if telling her to slow down.

"Don't try to placate me, Ryan. It's only fair," Mom insists. "Nicole just admitted to sabotaging Clara, and based on the terms and standards we *all* have had to accept over the years, it's only right that she should lose her spot as a Legacy, too."

"If I lose my scholarship so should Reid, since they filmed me talking about it without me knowing. It's the exact same thing," Nicole says with a triumphant jut of her chin.

I slide her a cold gaze. "But I wasn't recording."

Nicole blinks. "What?" She looks at Reid. "No, but you said—"

"Did we?" he asks, shoving his other hand in his pocket. "I don't remember saying that."

"Not my style," I say honestly. "You brought this all on yourself."

A long *ooooooooo* ripples through the group as Nicole's mouth opens, then closes. Even Coach Rousseau looks like he wishes he had popcorn.

Reid and I exchange a glance. I wasn't about to compromise his scholarship with this plan, but I quickly realized that she only needed to *think* I was going to reveal all of this for her to tell on herself.

Seeing her shock now knowing I bested her is how I imagine Reid felt when he slugged Josh earlier today. The deepest satisfaction.

Principal West looks around, catching eyes with several

disgruntled-looking members of the committee. “Ms. Kelly, I’m afraid we’ll have to review this. I’m incredibly disappointed in you willfully taking an opportunity away from another student.”

“No! That’s not fair!” she cries. “I wasn’t *trying* to sabotage Clara, okay? I honestly thought Josh would take the heat. I still can’t believe he didn’t!”

Neither Josh nor Principal West will look her in the eye at that.

“And the whole thing was Logan’s idea!” Nicole exclaims.

“I think we’re losing sight of things here—” Coach Rousseau tries to interject.

But the group turns to look at Logan, and he shrugs, the picture of nonchalance. “It opened up a spot. Not that it made a difference for me, but I would’ve done anything to get one.”

Reid visibly bristles, and I squeeze his hand harder so he doesn’t do something rash like lunge for Logan.

“Like start a gossip account?” Mitchell asks, shaking his head in disgust.

Logan’s ears turn pink the longer Mitchell looks at him. “I don’t know what you’re talking about.”

“Really?” Kenji steps forward. “Then why are you logged in to the Legacy Lore account right now?”

Logan’s expression becomes even more baffled when Delaney stage-whispers, “Turn around.”

Anchored only by Reid’s warm hand in mine, I’m not sure I breathe while Logan and the rest of the crowd all turn to see that his phone screen is being cast through the projector onto the giant screen onstage. It’s still open on the Legacy Lore account.

A text comes through from Mitchell that crosses both the phone in Logan’s hand and the giant screen in real time.

Hi Logan!!!!

All of the color drains from his face.

"*Logan*," Mayor Harper exclaims from across the room. She slams a palm against her chest and takes a long sip of white wine.

"Well, shit." Logan smirks like he's impressed. "You got me."

There's a collective gasp from the group at him confirming it. Josh looks murderous, his injuries adding to the effect.

"But c'mon," Logan says directly to Mitchell. "You have to admit it's kind of awesome."

Mitchell scoffs. "You thought I'd enjoy you tearing down my friends? My *brother*?"

Logan pushes a hand through his sandy hair. "You follow all those celebrity gossip sites, what's the difference? I thought you'd understand. Both of our brothers are these pillars of Woodhurst. This program fucked Noah over, and it's obviously doing the same to Reid. To all of you."

There's a long, ringing silence.

"But why would you spread rumors about them if you were trying to help?" I ask. "That's not the way—"

"Oh, please, don't feed me that sanctimonious crap. You can do it your way, I've done it mine." He shrugs and looks at Principal West. "I was proving the point that *no one* meets the standards of Legacy. That's how messed-up the program is."

"How noble," Mitchell deadpans. His usually playful air is gone, replaced by a tone so cold it makes Logan blink. "So you still would've done this if you had been chosen as a Legacy? You would've revealed your own secrets for your 'cause'?"

The look between them is loaded.

When Logan says nothing, Mitchell nods slowly. "You're better than this, Logan. At least you used to be."

Kenji rubs a comforting hand across Mitchell's back, and for the first time, Logan's nonchalant bravado slips off his face.

He really thought Mitchell would understand. Maybe even admire him for it. I wonder if deep down that's even why he did it.

West huffs out an impatient noise, squeezing his eyes shut. "You all are supposed to be the best. The brightest. The leaders in this town. The scholarships are for you to better yourselves—to *be* better. Your squabbling and infighting and attempts at discrediting this program is a profound disappointment. How did it come to this?"

"Didn't you watch Clara's video?" Kenji responds over a humorless laugh.

Principal West draws up to his full height and looks at me with barely disguised contempt. "I sure did. And, young lady, it was *not* what we discussed."

I suppress my eye roll at "young lady" and say, "You asked me to make a video about the Legacy Program, and I did." My voice is clear and strong, not even a hint of a shake despite the increase of my pulse.

He reddens. "It was supposed to be exciting. *Positive*. Look what it's done to all of you. This was—heavily skewed."

"I thought it was really well-balanced," Reid says.

"Me too. I loved it," Delaney says, linking her arm with mine. "It's like what Reid said, it showed it how it is, not how we all *act* like it is."

"That's all well and good, Ms. Whitlock, but she made our program look—" Principal West adjusts his tie, his gaze darting between Reid and Coach Rousseau. "Well, it wasn't flattering."

"To say the least," Reid's dad agrees.

"You know what?" Reid scoffs. "You have *no* idea how flattering it was."

He lifts his chin and appeals to his dad, ignoring West. "Clara could've revealed so much more about me; that despite my knee being fucked, I keep training anyway. That I'm not just failing a few classes, I'm on academic probation. She probably could've shown that I haven't slept in *months*. I have no doubt she has footage to support all that."

I swallow. He's right.

"But she did none of those things. She was protecting me while still telling the truth. It was flattering as hell."

Both Principal West and Coach are shocked silent, and the people around us are all looking at one another like they can't wait to talk about this later.

Everyone except my mom and our friends, who are looking at Reid with various shades of concern and worry. Especially Mitchell.

Which is exactly why I didn't reveal any of those things in such black-and-white terms in the doc. Not the way Logan tried to with his account. Everyone's story is more complex than that.

West shakes his head quickly. "But competition is healthy. This program keeps the students motivated. So many of you would be adrift without a solid trajectory," he insists. "It—it—"

"It sucks, Dad," Josh says.

"Joshua."

"After everything you've heard tonight—you're either not listening or are in denial." Josh shoves his hands in his pockets and holds his dad's eyes, a silent conversation occurring between them before Josh says, "Just look around."

West does. I'm not sure what he sees, but he grows quiet. Starts to fumble with the keys in his pocket, the tie around his neck again.

"Well. Let's put this away for now. I have benefactors to face and a committee to update. I think it's time we call it a night."

He and Josh walk to the other side of the Lodge speaking in low voices. Logan tries to slink off, but Nicole and Amaya bound after him, their faces furious. They're obviously not going to let him get away that easily, and I'm glad of it. We may not like one another, but their anger is more than justified.

The focused interest drains from the larger group, and the awkward energy drives the rest of the crowd to gather their things, including Coach Andrews as he pulls on his coat to leave. Reid's dad follows him out, talking rapidly.

My mom lingers and wraps her arms around me.

"Thanks, Mom," I say into her shoulder.

"What a night, huh? I've wanted to tell Ryan West off since ninth grade." She giggles.

I relax in her arms, under the awning of her laugh, and let myself absorb the love she pours into me when she can.

"And believe me, your movie was beautiful," she says. "I know it's going to be incredible when you finish it."

I smile and squeeze her harder. Finally having done something she can be proud of.

"I'm sorry for the way this program treated you and ruined your plan," I say.

Mom's eyebrows meet, her expression thoughtful. "I know it's hard to imagine at your age, but my plan wasn't perfect. You're all well aware by now that Legacy and this town make it seem like there's only one right way to do things." She pauses and looks at me, warmth in her eyes. "But how could my own way be wrong when it gave me you?"

My whole heart swells.

We both notice that Reid is hovering just out of earshot, hands shoved in his pockets, waiting. She's never liked that I got involved with him, and I'm afraid of what she's going to say.

"I love him," I blurt, cutting her off before she can. Pleading for her to understand. I can't believe how easy that is to say after reading his card, knowing the words on my skin are *his*.

Mom's expression softens with surprise.

"I'm still making my own path," I reassure her. "But . . . I want him beside me while I do it."

If he'll have me.

She glances over at him again, then turns to me and says seriously, "Sweetie, there is such a narrow window for happiness in this life. If you found yourself some, don't let it go too easily."

I nod and clutch my rib cage where my tattoo lives.

No matter what it takes, I will never make that mistake again.

CHAPTER THIRTY-SEVEN

REID

@haikuforyou
If love means chasing
fading light, I'll run, chest burning
into your night

WHEN CLARA'S DONE TALKING to her mom, I waste no time. I wrap my hand around hers, desperate to get her alone.

"Can we—"

A stern voice cuts me off. "Reid."

Damn it. It's my dad. Impeccable timing as always.

"We can talk after," Clara says with a reassuring squeeze of my hand. But I don't let her pull away.

"Come with me?"

She looks at my dad over my shoulder, uncertain. "You sure?"

I nod. It's the only thing I am sure about.

Watching her documentary confirmed what I've long known. That despite so many people judging her and accusing her of being a bad influence on me, she is actually the one person who makes me want to be better.

We walk across the Lodge, the event clearly over. Most people have left, and the tables are scattered with discarded napkins, wineglasses, and utensils.

I lead her to the table where my dad and stepmom are sitting. Coach Andrews is gone, and Dad looks more stressed than ever, a wounded expression on his face as we get seated across from them. "How could you not tell us about all this, Reid? How—" He clears his throat. "How could you not tell *me*?"

I look down at the table. "I'm sorry. I didn't know how," I admit. "And with the bills and everything, I didn't want to worry you."

Dad's eyes go wide. "Kiddo, believe me, I've already been worried."

That hits me square in the chest and I snap my gaze up, breathing out a light laugh. "You haven't called me 'kiddo' since I was little."

"Probably because that's how it's feeling right now. You aren't sleeping again?" His eyes are red and full of dismay.

I swallow and shake my head.

"You've been in pain," Dad states.

I straighten. "I've been icing it and—"

Dad shakes his head vigorously. "No." He presses a splayed palm against his own chest. "In *pain*."

I go still. Silent. The muscle in my jaw is taut against the swell of emotion clogging my throat. Clara squeezes my hand, her touch strong and reassuring.

After a long stretch of silence, I finally manage a quiet "Yeah."

Dad stands and comes around the table. He pulls me up and practically swallows me in a hug. The kind I've needed from him for years. I bury my head into his shoulder, and I realize I'm crying. By the way his breath comes out uneven, I know he is, too.

We stand in a long embrace, and when we pull apart, both Clara and Julianne swipe their eyes, too.

"I hate that you haven't let me be here for you," Dad says.

I shove my hands in my pockets and shuffle awkwardly. "It's because you always—" I stop.

Dad frowns and urges me to keep going.

"You always try to fix everything *for* me. You had this plan that just doesn't make sense to me anymore. And I think I wanted—needed—to figure this out for myself this time."

We settle back into our chairs and Dad studies me closely.

"You do have a habit of that," Julianne says, nudging him.

I shoot her a grateful look when Dad nods. "Fair enough. So . . . what have you come up with? Tutors? Trainers? Some time off?"

Hope leaps through me. "Something like that." I glance at Clara just before shocking the table silent when I say, "I don't want to go back to Stanford."

Dad looks like he might pass out. "Wait— Hold on—"

But I cut him off. "I *do* want to finish college. I want to run again. But it isn't a good place for me. I never see my coach, the guys on the team are toxic as fuck." My mind is still reeling with the fact that my own teammate revealed all that stuff about me online. "I'm failing because I'm so tired. I can't focus and I need . . ." I trail off and look at Clara, gathering my strength. "I need *help*. I haven't felt like myself for a long time, but I didn't even realize it until I came home."

I wait in silence for my dad to say something. He's raking his hand back and forth across his forehead, the lines of his weathered skin smoothing and pulling. "I know college is a tough transition . . ." He trails off and sighs. "This is a big decision."

Clara's entire doc showed me what I needed to know in no uncertain terms. Not only did she capture what it takes to become a Legacy, but she showed what being a Legacy *took*. From me and all of us. As deft and nuanced as it was, it was still a stark awakening. Reminding me who I was before all this. The whole of me. I summon the strength to say it even as my voice shakes. "It's not the transition. I'm not okay, Dad."

Silence descends over the table while my dad's eyes fill. I hate it, putting this on him, but keeping the stress and pain from him is crushing me. I need him to see that if I have to do this alone any longer, I'll fall completely apart.

"I hear you, kiddo." Dad drags a hand across his mouth. "I knew it as soon as I saw Clara's video." He fixes his gaze on her, gratitude and newfound respect in his eyes. "Thank you."

She seems too overwhelmed to do anything but nod. I don't want to push the subject now, so I tell Dad we'll really talk it through tomorrow before I have to go back.

Once they leave, I feel as though a boulder has been lifted from my chest. I grab a hold of Clara's hand again.

"Come with me." My voice is gruff.

She frowns as I lead her away from the Lodge, away from the lights and anyone else still around. The air is fragrant with the heavy scent of the surrounding pines. We get to the enclosed solarium that overlooks the lake. It's an extra guest area beside the Lodge with plush couches and large windows. Most important, it's private.

"I'm really proud of you for talking to your dad," she says as I close the door behind us. "I'm so sorry if I ruined your chances with that coach, or if I forced your hand about school in some way. I was just trying to help—"

I cut her off as I crush my mouth to hers. Her surprised whimper is enough to set me on fire. She has nothing to be sorry for. I know that video was her love letter to her friends, to Woodhurst.

To me.

I break away to look at her. Cup her jaw with my hand and just take her in. Her flushed cheeks and bright eyes. Holding her in this moment, knowing in my marrow that she is going to change the fucking world.

She pulls back and raises an eyebrow. "Big fan of documentaries, huh?"

"Yours, yes. I'm so proud of you."

She turns my favorite shade of pink, her smile radiant. "Then you're not mad that I included all that stuff?"

I shake my head. "The opposite. It helped me realize . . . I need to face this. Only . . ." I trail off.

"What?" she prods.

Our breaths are heavy and loud in the quiet space, our lips so close. But something holds me back from brushing them together again. It's hard to believe this broken-down version of myself is really the one that she could possibly want.

"I'm obviously not the same as I used to be. What if—" My voice catches unexpectedly, and I have to wait several breaths before I can speak again. "What if I can't be who you need now? I don't ever want to hold you back."

"Reid." She grazes her lips across mine. "You're the only reason I'm still pushing myself forward."

A satisfied noise sounds from the back of my throat as I catch her mouth with mine again. I wrap both hands gently around the side of her neck, tracing my thumbs down the column of her throat, down farther around her shoulders, her torso, her waist, every part of me ablaze.

I kiss her harder, touch her softer. Urging her mouth open with my tongue as I press her against the wall, my body flush with hers. She pushes her hands under my jacket around to my back, yanking my shirt up until her fingers find skin. Clutching at me. Moving against me. Dragging her nails across my back so fiercely they're sure to leave marks.

One of her dress straps slips down, and I pepper kisses across her bare shoulder. Her head falls back, and she threads her fingers into my hair as I reach around her, grasping for the zipper.

But it catches halfway down her back. I grip it tighter and try to loosen it—pulling it up again, then down the other direction. But it doesn't budge. It's completely jammed.

I huff a laugh against her collarbone. "Sorry—it's stuck."

Her exhale comes out in shaky streams across my neck. "Of course it is. Here."

She spins around so I can get a better look at it. My knuckles graze the notch of her spine, and goose bumps cascade across her soft, bare back in response. I see where it's caught, and after working it a moment, the zipper relents and glides all the way down.

I graze my fingertips across her skin, gently nudging the fabric open to finally reveal her tattoo. My heart completely stops.

The plant is larkspur. A flower that's all over the mountain and one that survives through the heaviest of winter snowfalls. It frames the words of a short poem that I underline now with the lightest of touches, barely comprehending what I'm seeing.

"This is . . ." I trail off.

She nods.

"From the card?" I ask.

"From your account."

I freeze. *That's— What?*

She turns to face me, rushing to explain. "I found it over the summer and connected with the poems in every way. I didn't *know* they were yours—but they felt like you. They *always* felt like you."

My breath stutters.

She goes on. "And when you mentioned the card this morning—I didn't know what you were talking about. It's been buried in my backpack, untouched, since last year. But I found it today and"—she exhales in disbelief—"I couldn't believe it was the same one. I still can't."

I clutch her rib cage, holding her in place with my palm. The odds of this are so close to impossible I can't wrap my head around it.

"So, you did this because it reminded you of me?" My thumb swipes across the spot for emphasis, sending a soft shudder through her.

"Yes."

I meet her eyes again and ask softly, "But . . . why?"

The word has cracks. As much as I can believe that things between us are different now, I don't understand how she could've done this *then.*

She lifts her eyes to mine. "Because I love you. I've *always* loved you."

A part of me wished. Even knew. But I've never been more stunned to finally hear her say it.

That she loved me.

That she *loves* me.

She curls her fingers around the lapels of my jacket, and my voice is unsteady, reacting to her touch.

"This is— I'm overwhelmed—"

Clara sank my words permanently into her skin. The poem I wrote in the dark of night in my bed, unable to sleep, thinking of her. Craving her.

The first poem I ever posted to an account I've told no one about. It isn't technically a haiku, but I couldn't alter it any further. It was exactly what I wanted to say. Exactly how I felt about us.

The love I've felt for her is a burning, blazing kind that has never—not once—dimmed.

She takes a step back. "I didn't do this expecting anything. If this whole weekend has been about closure—I understand. I really wouldn't blame you if you hate me."

I huff out a laugh. "*Hate* you?"

"Last year . . ." She trails off. "I messed up. I'd wanted only one thing my entire life, and I didn't know how to handle wanting you just as much."

Jesus, she's trying to kill me.

But this is nothing like last year. She's not hiding from me or pretending with me. Because we're talking more openly, it no longer feels like she's about to slip through my fingers any moment or like I'm pushing to make something work.

We sink to the couch that's pressed up against a wall. I brush her hair off her shoulders, and when I cradle her face in my hand, she leans into my touch. I just want to look at her all the time.

"I tried to let you go," I admit. I kiss her again, softly, then pull back and finally—*finally*—tell her what my feelings have been building to since she dared me to jump into that lake full of eels. "But I love you too much."

I feel her smile again across my lips and we get lost in each other. She climbs onto me, her dress riding up to her hips. She gasps when I open the back of it just enough to look again.

There it is. I drag my lips across the inky words, press kisses into each of them, causing her to bare her throat and cling to me by the time I'm done.

Her name falls from my lips more than once. Her sighs and moans drugging. I'm so delirious, so gone for her, nothing exists but this. No one exists but us.

She may not be engraved on my skin, but she's under it in a way that's just as permanent.

What was I thinking pushing her away? I know now that I never could.

CHAPTER THIRTY-EIGHT

CLARA

REID KISSES ME LIKE he has no intention of stopping.

All my senses flood with him. The slight scratch of stubble on his chin and the strong weight of his legs around mine and the soft, grumbly sound he makes against my lips when I wrench him closer. Urge him on.

I surrender completely. Somehow, we found our way back to each other. Somehow, we both showed the worst of ourselves and still believed in this enough to try again. I can't bring myself to rush.

I thread my fingers through his hair and tug. He rumbles a hungry sound across my sternum in response and in one swift motion he flips me, so we're lying on the couch, him hovering over me. I draw my fingertips across his face—his cheekbones and jaw and lips. The bruises and cuts. Our eyes meet, and we pause, absorbing each other.

"I never stopped loving you, Clara." His voice is rough, barely above a whisper, and the words feel as igniting as a caress.

My heart is a hurricane, heat burning my cheeks as I stare up at him, amazed that we're here—that he still loves me, too. That he's as much mine as I'm his. It took us awhile, but it's clear to me why now.

A love this big needed time to grow and settle into.

He captures my shaking hands, his unwavering gaze darkening as he draws his lips across my fingertips with a kind of reverence. The slow savoring between us picks up to a clutching, furious need. His hands are everywhere. Mine are, too. We never stop kissing—even as we shed our clothes, even as we laugh and fumble through the awkward bits.

He's adoring and consumed. I follow his every move, melting against him, biting my lip hard to keep quiet. Reveling in the feeling of his strong hands squeezing my thighs, the short breaks he takes from my lips to whisper things across my throat and the shell of my ear.

"I love you," I gasp over and over. An apology. A devotion. I'll never be able to say it enough.

Afterward, we collapse in a heap, his head resting on my chest, both our bodies slick with sweat. I've never felt so happy. So right.

There's a loud bang outside the solarium that forces me to remember that despite the privacy of this space, we are at the lake and probably shouldn't linger.

"What was that?" I murmur.

"I don't care," he answers sleepily.

But there's another crash outside and two low voices laughing. We exchange a confused look, and he reluctantly climbs off of me. Once we're dressed, Reid looks deliciously disheveled, and I do my best to help him get himself together as he tucks his shirt back in.

My fingers linger in the tangles of his hair when he turns and kisses my wrist.

"Did I tell you enough how beautiful you are?" he asks softly.

Heat blooms across my skin. "Yes. That's one of the *many* things you do very well."

"Good," he says, pleased.

We hover, looking at each other a long moment.

"Are you really okay with leaving Stanford?" I ask.

I want so badly to tell him that I think taking time off is exactly what he needs, but I don't because I'm not sure the feeling is entirely selfless. The thought of him coming home makes me giddy. For him, yes.

But also for us.

"It's . . . uncomfortable. But I know it's the right move for me," he says with unwavering conviction.

It makes me smile. I love seeing his confidence returning.

When we get outside to investigate the noise, the culprits are wrapped in a kiss so intense I immediately spin on my heels to look away.

Reid's eyes fly wide. "Oh god."

They separate long enough to notice us, which seems to be a feat in and of itself.

"Heeeeey," Kenji says through a lopsided grin. He puts an awkward hand on his hip. "We were, uh, looking for you."

Mitchell's eyes are half-lidded, a dark flush covering his entire face.

"Quite the effective search party," Reid deadpans through a smirk.

"We found you, didn't we?" Mitchell says, his voice having taken on a dreamlike quality.

He looks between me and Reid, while I look between him and Kenji, then our gazes collide again as we both smile wide with understanding.

"Except *we* found *you*," Reid points out. "Though I really wish we hadn't." He scrubs at his eyes.

"We were literally doing the same thing," I remind him in a low voice.

He slings an arm around my shoulders and presses a kiss to my temple. "Yeah, well, I liked *that*."

I elbow him as I flush all over again.

"Now you know what it was like to go literally *anywhere* in Woodhurst last year," Kenji says.

"Seriously," Mitchell agrees. "Need we remind you two of the hot springs?"

My cheeks flame hotter, and I throw both my hands up. "Okay, let's just drop it."

Though instead of being embarrassed or bothered, Reid shrugs, smug as hell. Crunching footsteps have us all turn to find Delaney bounding over to us, her expression thrilled with what has to be fresh gossip.

"Having a party without me?" she asks.

"It's never a party without you, DL," Kenji says.

She grins beatifically. "That's true. Okay, two things. One, Amaya and Nicole actually used their bullying powers for good and got Logan to delete Legacy Lore. It's *gone*."

All of our eyes widen. "*No*."

She nods, jumping up and down unable to contain herself and shows us on her phone to prove it.

"Wow . . ." I say, looking at the empty profile.

It *worked*.

"Oh my god, are we all basically spies?" Mitchell asks.

Kenji puts a hand over his mouth. "I think we are. Should we plan a heist?" Mitchell laughs, but it falters when Kenji threads their fingers together. He stares at this public declaration and a slow-rising smile takes over his whole face.

"What was the second thing?" Reid asks Delaney, before they completely divert us.

She brightens. "Oh, right! One of the donors left this for Clara." She reaches into the pocket of her skirt and hands me a business card.

"She said to give you this and to have you message her. She's on the board for the California Young Filmmakers' Contest," Delaney says, bouncing on her toes.

I stare at the small, thick card in my hand. It shakes a little. Overhead the sky is alight with stars, and inhaling the fragrant mountain air brings everything into focus.

Despite having spent so many years desperate to get out of Woodhurst, I hadn't quite considered what it would be like to actually leave the mountain. My family. Everything I've known.

"You can always come back," Reid says, reading my mind. Knowing I've jumped ahead about a thousand steps already.

I nod.

"But"—his voice turns as gentle and serious as he is—"you have other lives to live first."

I look up at him, and the crushing sadness that's been weighing me down all year melts away.

The five of us fall into step toward the parking lot. Reid is beaming the entire slow walk, his arm wrapped around my shoulders in a way that radiates pride. His fingertips skimming the part of my ribs with his poem.

If everything had gone to my perfect plan last year, none of this would have happened. I couldn't have made *this* documentary. I couldn't have helped my friends see just how broken the program has become. I would have lived in constant fear of maintaining a path that closed off the possibility of other ones.

It's like my mom said, there is no one right way.

It always bothered me that people in my family and around town talk about Mom's brilliance and potential like it's a thing of the past. Like her life ended when she was nineteen just because it took an unexpected turn. Because it didn't.

And I realize now that mine hasn't, either. I'd rather do something worth talking about, than be the one doing the talking.

Even if my doc doesn't do much for Woodhurst or the Legacy Program—even if it doesn't get me into a film festival or CAFA—it was absolutely worth it.

Because it brought each of us back to ourselves.

It brought Reid back to me.

CHAPTER THIRTY-NINE

REID

SPRING

@haikuforyou
Foundations still hold
In a dry and cracked desert
We are made to mend

I REALIZE CLARA'S FALLEN too far behind me, and I double back toward her on the trail. She's hunched over, her breath rushing out hard.

"Could you not sprint for three miles straight? *Uphill,*" she emphasizes.

I grin at her. "I'm still two full minutes behind my PR."

"I cannot wait for you to be around actual runners again," she says. "Am I wheezing? I sound like I'm wheezing."

Ever the dramatic, my girlfriend. "You want to stop?"

She looks longingly at the trail that would take us back down toward the parking lot. "I very much do. But they said it's good for your conditioning, so . . ." She picks up her feet and sprints ahead, trying to outrun me.

Laughing, I catch up to her easily.

My dad was obviously upset about me leaving Stanford, but he allowed it in the end. Clara's film was the convincing he needed—the support I needed. It scared off the Olympic coach, but I'm surprisingly okay with it. That was never my plan. And who knows, that doesn't mean it won't be in the future.

Of course, moving back home came with a list of conditions. Dad and Julianne insisted that I continue my academics at Woodhurst Community College, and that I rehab my knee correctly. He also got me to see a psychiatrist, and the antidepressants have helped me . . . a *lot*. I'm sleeping again and setting my own schedule.

It's been a shockingly good few months. Even more so with Clara.

When we reach the peak, I throw my head back. The afternoon sun beats down on my face. I gasp, grateful there's a cool breeze up this high. As we catch our breath, she leans back against me, and we stare at the landscape around us. The snowcapped mountains across the canyon, never quite melting even in summer. The explosive greens and bursts of yellow wildflowers at our feet.

Once her breath returns, she says, "I thought that was supposed to be a casual run to prove to our lazy friends that we're better than them?"

I think of Delaney's, Kenji's, and Mitchell's comments in the group chat about how gross we are for either being so in love or running together every morning.

I grin again and pull her into a sweaty hug. "C'mon, Clara, we already know Mitchell and Kenji are better than us."

She laughs against me. "That's true."

They are monstrously cute together. Once Mitchell graduates and Kenji and Delaney come back home at the end of their semesters, I just know we're going to have an epic summer together. Even if some drama is promised with everyone else returning, too.

Her phone pings, and we both go still.

"Is that it?" I ask.

Clara's face is anguished as she stares at the notification.

"Open it."

We shift to sit on the bench at the overlook, and I wait for her to tap on the icon, but her thumb hovers. She looks at me, her green eyes wide. "I can't do it."

No matter that she entered *LEGACY* into that Young Filmmakers' Contest and *won*—earning her a massive scholarship in the process—she still thinks it's possible that she didn't get in again to CAFA.

Whereas I'm convinced she could teach at the school at this point, but what do I know?

I look at her intently. "Yes, you can."

She lets out a pathetic little whine. "What if they reject me this time?"

"Then you go to one of the five other schools that already accepted you and fold in an eloquent fuck-you to them in your Oscar speech."

She laughs, and I smile into her shoulder.

"Okay." She lets out a nervy breath.

I'm sure she's about to open it, but at the last second, she lowers her arm again. I squeeze my eyes shut while she tries to convince herself that she doesn't want what she wants. Classic Clara. "There are a lot of other good film schools."

"Which is why you applied to other places this year."

She looks over her shoulder at me. A tendril of her dark hair falls across her face from her ponytail, and I gently push it back.

"And I've heard they're pretty snobby there."

The corner of my mouth lifts. "So, you'd fit right in, Attenborough."

She elbows me in the ribs, and we both laugh.

"I just . . . don't know if I'd survive it."

It's amazing that she forgets just how strong she is. This entire year she's done nothing but prove over and over that she'd never give up. That despite disappointments and setbacks—and half the town shunning her for a while—she knows exactly what she's doing.

But I'm always happy to remind her. "Of course you would. You already have."

Though I can feel the rapid rate of her pulse against my chest, I give her a reassuring squeeze and put a finger under her chin to lift it. "C'mon, champ, quit stalling. Let's go."

With a shaky breath, she raises the phone and together we watch as she taps on the icon. The email opens wide, and I only get as far as *Congratulations* before she screams and throws her arms around me.

I take her home immediately, and as soon as she bursts through the front door, she's yelling for her mom. Their thrilled screams reach all the way out to the driveway.

Within the hour, her entire family descends. My parents and Mitchell are on their way, too. There's food and cousins running everywhere. Her Aunt Xi brings all the ingredients to make enchiladas. Clara volunteers to help her with that while I assist her Uncle Marco with rearranging the furniture so there's enough space for everyone.

"So, how does it feel? You're about to go out there on your own," I hear her Aunt Xi ask her in the kitchen over the scrunching of aluminum foil around a pan.

"Scary," she answers. "But exciting."

"You've had to grow up earlier than most kids your age," her Aunt Xi says quietly.

My stomach twists, but I can practically hear Clara shrug. "I wouldn't know the difference."

"Your mom is so proud of you. We're all so proud of you. I just hope you know we've got her, even when you go your own way. Okay?"

Clara's quiet a moment, then her voice is a little thick when she responds, "I could never go if you didn't."

After a moment of sniffling, I shift to help with the chairs outside but freeze when Aunt Xi's voice goes arch. "*So*. Tell me how things are going with the boyfriend."

I cough, and they both descend into giggles.

"Oh girl, you are one hot blush."

Over the course of the evening, she beams answering question after question about CAFA and documentaries and what she wants to work on next. Her phone never stops lighting up with notifications—many from Kenji insisting we're all famous now, but also from alumni and former Legacies, responding to her post. I watch her with the widest grin on my face, and something stirs in me, too.

I know I've needed this time off. I've needed these months of rest and rehab and writing enough bad poetry to fill two full notebooks and dozens of posts.

Maybe I'm ready to do more than just make it through the day.

After dinner, Clara and I walk outside to watch the sunset. We take in the explosive colors in the sky, and she sighs against my neck.

"I'm going to miss this."

I pull her closer, feeling the same way.

My head is calmer. I'm still unsure about a lot, but I do know that I'm more okay now than I've ever been. I'm excited to get back out there in a real way. Not for Woodhurst or my dad or my legacy. But for me.

And now, as Clara squeals and plans and has absolutely *zero* chill about this next huge phase, I know I'm ready to meet her at every single turn.

I'll run with her whichever way she goes.

We link our hands and share a smile as we walk the trail back home.

Even though we both know that, together, we're already there.

ACKNOWLEDGMENTS

THIS STORY AND I have been on an arduous journey together. One that forced me to grow in about a hundred different ways. A super intense, deeply painful, and ultimately beautiful experience. I'm immensely proud to share it with you and so happy to officially thank the *many* people who helped me navigate the layers of this process.

Starting with endless gratitude for my agent, Chelsea Eberly. Not only are you an incredible champion of my work, but your story mind is truly unmatched. I will never get over the way you helped me unlock this one.

Thank you to my amazing editors, Brian Geffen and Carina Licon, for your steadfast support and for helping me dig deeper as a storyteller so that I could make this story what it was always trying to be.

My eternal gratitude to the enthusiastic and supportive team at Henry Holt, including Jean Feiwel, Ann Marie Wong, Gabriella Salpeter, Tatiana Merced-Zarou, Lelia Mander, Allene Cassagnol, and Alexei Esikoff. And a very special thank-you to Abby Granata for the gorgeous cover.

A special thank-you to Huyen Vu at Greenhouse Literary for all that you do!

Immense appreciation to all the folks at Rights People who tirelessly champion my books around the world!

Thank you so much to the authors generous enough to read and blurb this book including Becky Albertalli, Kristin Dwyer, Samantha Markum, and Jenna Evans Welch.

Without Tierney Anderson I never would've started this story. You got that first shaky draft out of me (and pretty much every draft since) with your tireless enthusiasm. Thank you for your constant support on this wild journey. I couldn't do it without you.

I don't know what I did to deserve Katryn Bury and Kara Trella, but it must have been pretty good because you two have gone above and beyond for me with this book. Kate, thank you for every plot walk, talking me off every ledge, and helping me level up my mystery writing. Kara, thank you for sharing your incisive editorial mind and incredible wisdom with me. Love you both!

To my brilliant 911 crew, Alexa Lach, Kristin Dwyer, and Jenna Evans Welch, who refused to let this sink me by offering so much invaluable support, advice, and unflinching faith. THANK YOU FOREVER I LOVE YOU.

If it weren't for the beloved Vault chat, I don't know how I would've stayed sane this year. Caitlin, Nirmaliz, DeAnna, Alexa, Kristin, and Joss, thank you for sharing your friendship, support, jokes, and genius with me every day.

To Helen, Chelsea, and Maggie, nothing is more soul-filling than twenty-plus years talking about art, music, gossip, and more with you. I'm so grateful for all your support and that, even from afar, we get to do this life together. Love each of you so fiercely.

Yes, I'm thanking my therapist here. I truly do not know how I'd have gotten through the whole "book two thing" without you. THANK YOU.

The deepest gratitude forever to the Writing with the Soul community.

Biggest hugs of appreciation to all my friends and family supporting me and my books!!

I wrote this book during the most difficult season of my life. If not for Justin, loml and real-life romance hero, I wouldn't have finished it. Thank you for keeping me afloat (and fed) and believing in and supporting me and our family with such fervor. What a gift it is to love you.

To my boys, the lights of my life, thank you for keeping me grounded, laughing, and inspired. Love you more than words.

After the storms we've weathered throughout my writing this story, I would not be upright without my sisters (or my bros-in-law, Chris, Jared, and Kyle, who held it *down* for us). Nora, Carmen, and Dolores, thank you for your unflinching understanding, your deep wisdom, your unabashed humor, and so much more. I love you, Sauvy Bs.

Dad and Mary, thank you for always listening and for sending me so much encouragement through every draft and phase of this book.

Mame, thank you for sharing your love of literature with me always, and *especially* this year.

Jim, I wish you were here to share this book with (and laugh about Reid's poems together). Miss you.

Mom, to whom this book is dedicated, the gratitude I feel that we made it through this season is soul-deep. The world would heal if everyone had a mom like you. I love you.

Finally, thank you to my readers. I write to not only find the light but to create something of it through love stories. It's my hope that my books are a place you feel welcome to tuck into, even on your darkest days.

ABOUT THE AUTHOR

EVA DES LAURIERS became a die-hard romantic when she married her best friend, the boy she sat next to in eleventh-grade calculus. She now holds both an MSW and BA in psychology. As a clinical social worker, she had the privilege of working with the vibrant and complicated teens for whom she now writes. When she isn't writing, you can find her wandering through the redwoods, staring at the sea, or pretending she's in a music video. She lives in Northern California with her husband, their two children, and her collection of kissing books. She is also the author of *I Wish You Would*. Visit her at **evadeslauriers.com**.